Scar

Ryan Frawley

ISBN: 098690130X
ISBN-13: 978-0986901300

	A	B	C	D	E	F	G	H	I	J	K	L	M	N	O	P	Q	R	S	T	U	V	W	X	Y	Z
A	A	B	C	D	E	F	G	H	I	J	K	L	M	N	O	P	Q	R	S	T	U	V	W	X	Y	Z
B	B	C	D	E	F	G	H	I	J	K	L	M	N	O	P	Q	R	S	T	U	V	W	X	Y	Z	A
C	C	D	E	F	G	H	I	J	K	L	M	N	O	P	Q	R	S	T	U	V	W	X	Y	Z	A	B
D	D	E	F	G	H	I	J	K	L	M	N	O	P	Q	R	S	T	U	V	W	X	Y	Z	A	B	C
E	E	F	G	H	I	J	K	L	M	N	O	P	Q	R	S	T	U	V	W	X	Y	Z	A	B	C	D
F	F	G	H	I	J	K	L	M	N	O	P	Q	R	S	T	U	V	W	X	Y	Z	A	B	C	D	E
G	G	H	I	J	K	L	M	N	O	P	Q	R	S	T	U	V	W	X	Y	Z	A	B	C	D	E	F
H	H	I	J	K	L	M	N	O	P	Q	R	S	T	U	V	W	X	Y	Z	A	B	C	D	E	F	G
I	I	J	K	L	M	N	O	P	Q	R	S	T	U	V	W	X	Y	Z	A	B	C	D	E	F	G	H
J	J	K	L	M	N	O	P	Q	R	S	T	U	V	W	X	Y	Z	A	B	C	D	E	F	G	H	I
K	K	L	M	N	O	P	Q	R	S	T	U	V	W	X	Y	Z	A	B	C	D	E	F	G	H	I	J
L	L	M	N	O	P	Q	R	S	T	U	V	W	X	Y	Z	A	B	C	D	E	F	G	H	I	J	K
M	M	N	O	P	Q	R	S	T	U	V	W	X	Y	Z	A	B	C	D	E	F	G	H	I	J	K	L
N	N	O	P	Q	R	S	T	U	V	W	X	Y	Z	A	B	C	D	E	F	G	H	I	J	K	L	M
O	O	P	Q	R	S	T	U	V	W	X	Y	Z	A	B	C	D	E	F	G	H	I	J	K	L	M	N
P	P	Q	R	S	T	U	V	W	X	Y	Z	A	B	C	D	E	F	G	H	I	J	K	L	M	N	O
Q	Q	R	S	T	U	V	W	X	Y	Z	A	B	C	D	E	F	G	H	I	J	K	L	M	N	O	P
R	R	S	T	U	V	W	X	Y	Z	A	B	C	D	E	F	G	H	I	J	K	L	M	N	O	P	Q
S	S	T	U	V	W	X	Y	Z	A	B	C	D	E	F	G	H	I	J	K	L	M	N	O	P	Q	R
T	T	U	V	W	X	Y	Z	A	B	C	D	E	F	G	H	I	J	K	L	M	N	O	P	Q	R	S
U	U	V	W	X	Y	Z	A	B	C	D	E	F	G	H	I	J	K	L	M	N	O	P	Q	R	S	T
V	V	W	X	Y	Z	A	B	C	D	E	F	G	H	I	J	K	L	M	N	O	P	Q	R	S	T	U
W	W	X	Y	Z	A	B	C	D	E	F	G	H	I	J	K	L	M	N	O	P	Q	R	S	T	U	V
X	X	Y	Z	A	B	C	D	E	F	G	H	I	J	K	L	M	N	O	P	Q	R	S	T	U	V	W
Y	Y	Z	A	B	C	D	E	F	G	H	I	J	K	L	M	N	O	P	Q	R	S	T	U	V	W	X
Z	Z	A	B	C	D	E	F	G	H	I	J	K	L	M	N	O	P	Q	R	S	T	U	V	W	X	Y

Scar: 1. *n.* A mark left after the healing of a wound or sore; a blemish resulting from damage or wear.

2. *n.* A protruding or isolated rock; a precipitous crag; a rocky part of a hillside.

Scar: *Irish. vt.vi.* diverge, part, separate.

Foreword

Ours is a fractured time. In a world of shrinking possibilities and growing fears, the future has become an enemy. It seems each advancement of our scientific knowledge brings our species only new worries, new fears, new problems that cry out for solutions which will, if found, present newer, more intractable problems of their own. Scarcely a week goes by without the announcement of some new wonder drug that promises to free us from the grip of disease; barely a week goes by without grim news of some new epidemic, as though a hydra of illness thrives on our attempts to subdue it. In this context, it would be meaningless to call schizophrenia an epidemic, even in such a place where one can see its symptoms displayed on the nearest street corner. Those of us who work in the field of mental health soon come to know the withdrawn, hunted look, the disordered thoughts, the bizarre language and delusions of the sufferers of this cruel disease. Around the world, studies show that one in every hundred people is afflicted; here in Canada, schizophrenic patients occupy more hospital beds than sufferers of any other disease. Clearly, this is a condition of severe economic, not to say social and moral importance. And yet, though continual advances in treatment are trumpeted by the very drug companies that profit so handsomely from the prevalence of this and many other diseases, we are no nearer to finding a cause, let alone a cure, than we have been at any time since the illness was first described. As our technical knowledge increases, our understanding shrinks, until the psychiatrist is reduced to the role of a pusher, blindly issuing panaceas to a conveyer belt of zoned-out, disenfranchised 'consumers'.

My intention, however, is not to suggest that drugs have no place in the treatment of schizophrenia and other psychoses; nor is it to prescribe the recovery of the patient described in this particular case as the methodology for all the millions who suffer like him. The first course of action in the treatment of schizophrenic individuals remains, and should remain, the administration of antipsychotics. Even in Dermot's singular case, while pharmacology seemed to do little to treat his positive or negative symptoms, it is doubtful that he would have survived long enough to recover in his own way had he been left to do so unaided.

Dermot was involuntarily admitted to Riverview Psychiatric Hospital in March 2008, following the recommendation of Vancouver General Hospital staff psychiatrist, Dr. Evan Taylor. He had been brought to the hospital by the police, who arrested him along with two other men with whom he had been engaged in a brawl in a downtown alley. It quickly became clear to the arresting officers that Dermot was suffering from severe mental illness, and their decision to take him to hospital was supported by a young woman who was also at the scene of the fight and claimed to be his girlfriend.

Piecing together the details of Dermot's past proved to be a challenge. In this, I was greatly assisted by his partner, Grace. Much of what we know about his history, medical and otherwise, comes from things he said to her in the past regarding his childhood, upbringing, earlier psychotic episodes and so on. Of the period prior to Dermot's immigration to British Columbia in 1998, we know nothing for sure. It has proved impossible to contact any members of his family; Grace has never met or spoken with any relative of his, and Dermot was particularly reticent on this matter, consistently refusing to give any kind of contact information. That he experienced, some time in adolescence, a profound psychological breakdown cannot be doubted. If he was treated in any way at this time, we cannot know. In Grace's opinion, he was not; it was at her urging that he began to see a therapist, Dr. Ian McCullough, in 2005. When Grace met Dermot, she maintains, he was a fully functional individual, and there is little reason to doubt her sincerity. However, as the relationship progressed, cracks began to appear in Dermot's psyche, cracks severe enough for Grace to insist on his seeing a therapist, despite his inherent mistrust of psychology – a mistrust I don't think he ever lost. His animosity towards therapists in general, his reluctance to take prescribed treatments, despite clearly understanding the dangers of relapse, and his seeming familiarity with the processes of psychological counselling may suggest that Dermot had received some form of therapy prior to his relationship with Grace; but this is speculation. Many people mistrust doctors in general, and psychiatrists in particular, without having any prior reason to do so.

This story, however, is a story of hope. Dermot's story, told here in his own words, is the very model of a purposive psychosis: an illness brought on by a need to understand one's place in the universe, a psychological breakdown that may almost be seen as a sickness of the soul. This story is a monument to the human capacity for regeneration, as well as a testament to the folly of relying too heavily on chemistry to treat what I have come to see, in many cases, as a spiritual crisis.

A note on the text: On my suggestion, Dermot was supplied with a journal and writing materials. He was a voracious reader, and after our preliminary counseling sessions, I suggested he might find it easier to express himself in writing. As a rule, schizophrenia does not lend itself to sustained writing; the disordered thoughts and random associations caused by the condition make coherent communication, especially of the kind displayed here, almost impossible. But in this, as in many other things, Dermot was exceptional. Why he chose to write about himself predominantly in the third person, and allowed himself an author's license to occasionally witness events he could not possibly have been physically present at is unknown. However, from observation of schizophrenic patients, it seems to me not altogether surprising. Many schizophrenics, and many other sufferers from various neuroses, construct fantasies around themselves. Some have been known to create a supernatural helper, invisible to all but themselves – the adult equivalent of the common childhood 'imaginary friend'. Some go further; by identifying themselves with this 'other', they achieve, if not control, at least some distance from their own inner turmoil, becoming a detached observer of their own lives. The peculiar lack of empathy common in schizophrenics may be a symptom of this external identification.

As a result, what follows may be viewed as part memoir, part fiction, part re-telling of traditional folk tales, part metaphysical treatise; but it adds up to a kind of collage, a composite portrait of a man experiencing something quite profound. Dermot did not date any of his writing, and so I have tried as far as possible to present it in a linear fashion; however, given the varying sources for his writing, including his father's notes and letters Dermot wrote but never sent to Grace, it has not always been clear which events followed which in sequence, or what is truth and what is fantasy.

In compiling this study, I have endeavoured as far as possible to let Dermot speak for himself. To this end, I have tried to refrain from editing or otherwise interfering with his written text. Where such intrusions are necessary, for example to give context to a particular passage, I have endeavoured to keep footnotes and other obstructions to a minimum. The picture that emerges is a remarkable one: a man suffering from a schizophrenic crisis so severe as to be life-threatening, and yet able to convey the turmoil of his inner world, for the most part, in lucid, coherent writing – this is a rare and valuable thing. How much of the story he tells is actually true, in the common sense of the word, is up to the individual reader to decide for his or her self. What I do not doubt, what no one should doubt, however, is its naked emotional truth. The fear, the terrors, the feral joys of the nightmare world Dermot experienced have their echoes in each of our own lives. We, too, have demons to face. We, too, are surrounded by heroes and saints. We, too, are guided by

6

the past, our own and that of our species, as we journey through a life none of us understands any better than Dermot did. His peaks may be higher and his troughs deeper than our own, for that is the nature of his sickness; but the pattern remains. All in all, if I may venture a personal opinion, it seems to me that this poor man, in his fractured, cut-off state, managed to claw his way towards something like wisdom. I feel privileged, as a doctor and as a human being, to have been able to witness this man's return from the outer edges of human experience. It has been my privilege to call him my patient, and my friend.

Dr Thomas Kinsella
Riverview Psychiatric Hospital
December 2008

The wind whipped across the bare back of the ridge.

Bending the short grass as it went, hissing through the flailing trees, shivering the torches in the cold wild air, it swept on past the procession, howling over the hills and the mounds and vanishing into the wide, trackless lands beyond the horizon.

The torches came up the hill.

Like their brother, the wind, the mourners moaned and cried as they came, a steady, ceaseless sound, the breath of the gods in the bottomless night. Like their parents, the bright hard stars above, they clustered together, their torches a tight constellation against a field of featureless black. Like their sisters, the trees, they clung to the watchful sky, buffeted by the wind, groaning and swaying but standing firm.

The torches came up the hill.

Up on the ridge, the barrow waited.

From the barrow, it could all be seen. The hill, the stones, the village, the river, the forest – the whole of the valley. The whole of the world. What lay beyond sight of the barrow was void, an unknown wasteland filled with dangers from the dungeons of fevered dreams. Giants stalked the land;

monsters lurked in gloomy lightless woods; cruel gods played games with dead men's bones. But the valley was safe beneath the eye of the sleepers in the barrow, the ancestors who watched over their people from the heights, awaiting their second birth.

The barrow dominated the valley. Sullenly it sulked under heavy skies, grey with menace. It blazed like a beacon in the sun, a white flame on the ridge, both promise and warning. Beneath the moon it shone a pale answer back at the sky, the ancestors and the gods reflecting one another in the night.

Its dull white walls were blank in the light of the torches.

This was a holy place. This was where the wind was born. From this ridge, this tomb, came the power that kept the people of the valley safe. It was ancient. When the elders of the village had been raucous brats, the barrow had been here. There had never been a time when there had been no barrow. Sky and valley and ridge and barrow, they had always been and would always remain. It was here that the villagers buried their dead.

He had been a great man. As a youth, no one could stand against him. It was said that he had walked far, beyond the valley, beyond sight of the ridge. There he had great adventures, if tales were true, and met many curious things. The gods spoke to him, as they had to his father, and his father's father. He was of the line of kings, high in the favour of both sun and moon, and even in great age had been both strong and swift of thought. And he had died. And his people, led by his sons, had prepared his body and brought him here, to dwell with the kings of men until his second birth. He would do in death as he had done in life; he would protect and guide his people in the valley and intercede for them with the gods.

The tomb gaped open, the womb of the earth. The stone walls of the passage sweated water in the torchlight; dark doorways opened on every side. Only a few were permitted to enter here; the power of the ancestors was very great. The visitors clustered together, fearful even to touch the damp walls of this holy place, the house of the dead and the source of life. The flames of the torches licked the low ceiling, hissing like wild cats.

The narrow passage opened out into a round chamber, walled and roofed with rock, as though giants had fashioned it in the birth of the world. This seemed to be the limit of the tomb; but it was not so. In the back, low down in the wall of rock, there was a gap, too small for any but a child or a ghost to pass through. Through there, some said, lay another, greater burial chamber, the eternal home of the first and most ancient of the ancestors. Others maintained that it was the entrance to the underworld, where the spirits of the dead would depart once their bodies had been interred. Beyond it lay another dark passage, as anyone could see from outside the barrow; it went on twice as long as the passage the mourners took before sinking into the earth, beyond the knowledge of the living. And when the wind blew hard and cold around the homes of the villagers, when it moaned and wailed on wild winter's nights, they knew where it blew from: that small black hole in the back of the tomb.

But no one living had ever passed through, and that was not why they had come tonight. They laid their king in the burial chamber, taking care not to disturb the older bones that lay scattered all around. Adorned with feathers and copper and red paint, curled like an infant in the belly of his mother the earth, he awaited the next life. Singing, the mourners retreated, and the ancient dark came creeping back out of the dripping walls.

The torches filed down the hill.

The wind whipped across the bare back of the ridge.[1]

---

[1] This appears to be the oldest of Dermot's notes, and so I have included it at the beginning of this study. It is significant in that its authorship is unclear; that is, the handwriting is Dermot's, but it seems he attempted to use more than one style of cursive. Nor is the paper the same as that which I supplied to him. There are several passages among his notes that are written in this style, and all deal with a similar theme – they are either ancient mythological tales, or musings written from the point of view of Dermot's father. This leads me to believe that these are copies that Dermot made of his father's notes – see note 20 in the main text.

1

The wind rustled the grass in Cloonashee.[2] He sat on the ridge, perched on a sun-warmed knuckle of rock that burst there through the shallow soil, gazing out over the western ocean, eyes straining for a glimpse of that mythical land beyond the sea his ancestors had so desperately believed in. His father's ghost rattled the leaves of the trees greening behind him, burbled in the liquid voice of the river, cried with the birds against the injustice of flesh.

The sea looked like aluminium foil, crumpled by wind and waves into an impossible distant dreariness, washing unseen the flinty shore of this blood-soaked land. Hidden by the monstrous curve of the earth, Grace lay huddled in the arms of last night, a splinter of rosewood sunk in tender flesh. By the time he got to where she was, she'd be long gone, spinning through the lifeless distance of empty space on a lump of insensate rock like the stones in his father's garden, crawling underneath with pestiferous life in a dark hollow of decay. Worlds seen and unseen crowded around him. If there was any secret to learn, anything in the darkness other than the reflection of his own face at the bottom of a stagnant well, it was here, in this land of murmuring

---

[2] Cloonashee does not appear on any map of Western Ireland that I have been able to locate. I have found Clonshee, Clonashee and Cloonshee, but not Dermot's ancestral home. However, given the apparent size of the place, it is quite possible that it does indeed exist. My geographical resources are somewhat limited here.

ghosts. He is part of everything now, I know that.[3] I learned my lesson well. Energy cannot be created or destroyed; that's just physics. Basic physics, intermediate metaphysics; everything that was, is; everything that will be, therefore, is; there is no past or future, and the moment alone encompasses everything that was, is, or shall ever be, world without end. I know that. But what use is that, when I need him here, now? When my personality is crumbling into nothing like a sea-washed cliff in the place my father was born, and I need his common sense, his uncommon strength? I feel him all around me, all the time, like the breath of God, but when I reach out my hands, there's nothing there. When I call for help, all I hear is an echo.

Birds chattered in the hedgerows, each day a threat, a challenge to be overcome; or else be destroyed. He watched a sparrow flit into the branches of a low tree sprouting on the near bank of the river. There is special providence in such things as this. He willed it to reappear, to move on from that tree to another. Five seconds. Ok, ten. Twenty. Nothing. Anything, Father, anything to believe that the agglomeration of genetics, experience and individual inspiration that made you still exists somewhere, in the song of the birds or the path of some wandering star. Nothing. No breeze blew. No leaf fell. Adrift in an insensate void, the land slick with blood as meat liquefies under the grass, eyes on the rocky ground before him, he followed the wind down the hill.

---

[3] The shift from third to first person narration is jarring for the reader, but characteristic of Dermot's style, and so I have opted not to correct it. Besides, these rapid shifts in perception resemble the disordered thoughts of the schizophrenic patient; perhaps a little of Dermot's state of mind may be better understood by this somewhat unconventional device.

2

This was unbearable. Surely Alex couldn't be far away now? The airport wasn't that far. He was much better at this. And of course, he'd have Dermot with him.[4] The rock star. These vultures would have a whole new audience for their endless questions.

"More tea there, Owen?" Owen's sudden smile didn't reach his eyes.

"No thank you, I'm fine."

A greying woman sat down in the armchair opposite. It was impossible in this barrage of forgotten family to pick out the relationships between these people. Owen was pretty sure this woman was his second cousin - he seemed to remember a younger version of that face looming over him on some barely-remembered childhood trip to Ireland - but he had no idea what her name was.

"So your brother's coming out from Canada, then?" she asked, for at least the second time. Owen was starting to wonder if she even knew where or what Canada was.

"Vancouver, yeah" he grimaced. "Long way out."

"That must be an awful flight?" she went on. "Hours and hours, I suppose."

"I think it's about ten" said Owen.

---

[4] As mentioned in the introductory note, Dermot here allows himself license to imagine a scene at which he was not present. I have seen him do something similar in conversation; he would describe events taking place as though he had been there when I knew he had not. It is almost as though his sense of himself had eroded to the point where he no longer distinguished between himself and those around him.

"Have ye been out there yerself?"

"Vancouver? No. I keep meaning to, but you know, finding the time..."

"It must be lovely out there. Is it in the mountains at all?"

"Yeah, I think so."

"I suppose they have bears and wolves and all type of things like that still?"

"I suppose so. Not so much in the city itself, but outside of it, yeah."

"Your father spent some time out there, didn't he?"

"He did, yeah. On and off. It's one of the things we used to hear about growing up, you know. Canada was always this amazing land out over the sea where anything was possible. Ireland, too, in a way."

"Well, this is home, y'know. My Mickey's travelled a lot, all over the place. Sure, he was just in Africa last year. Africa, can ye imagine?" Owen nodded unenthusiastically. "But he always says, wherever he goes, that Ireland is home. And yer father was the same way. He always loved this place."

God knows why. Owen hadn't been here for at least fifteen years, and it was just as primitive as he remembered. This house, the 'new house', and the old cottage just across the river. That was it. Nothing else for miles around but wide green fields, some dotted with dull, lazy cows; most simply empty. It was hard to believe that this was the twenty-first century, in what was allegedly a first world country: it was like stepping back in time. A fire for warmth, bare slate flagstones on the floor. They were burning chunks of mud in the fireplace, for God's sake! It was depressing. This wasn't home. This was the place where he had been subjected to endless family holidays in the rain, with nothing to do and nothing to eat and a bunch of people he didn't know asking him questions he didn't want to answer. And it seemed that nothing had changed. Dad must have been playing some sick joke when he decided that he wanted to be buried here.

"Do ye hear from your mother at all?" She was talking in a hushed voice now, as though that might make an indiscreet question somehow easier to answer.

"Not lately" Owen replied cheerfully. "She died a few years back."

"Ah, it's terrible" she sighed, as though she meant it.

"Yeah, well, we didn't hear too much from her for most of our lives anyway. It wasn't that big a deal, really. We hardly knew her. She was just this stranger who would call up drunk once every couple of years."

"D'ye think that was what got her in the end? The drinking, I mean?" Owen had to lean forward now to catch the old ghoul's words.

"Probably. I'm not too sure of the details." There was an uncomfortable silence. The fire hissed and popped. Owen heard laughter around the kitchen table, where the rest of the family was sitting. And here he was, one of 'the English'[5], keeping apart in the corner by the fire. If only they'd leave him in peace .

"I met your mother, y'know" the unknown cousin went on. "A few times. Years back, when you were just children, of course. I always got on well with her. Mary was a lovely woman. Lovely. Beautiful, too. Of course, she was hardly more than a girl herself back then. And she made your father very happy."

Owen said nothing. He had no recollection of the beautiful girl this woman remembered. His memories of his mother were tiny and vague, dwarfed by the vast shadow of the pain she had caused his father. If his mother had truly ever made him happy, it must have been long, long ago. And it was the last time anyone ever did, that was for sure.

The mystery cousin seemed to finally realise that she might have said too much.

"Will ye have a bite to eat, Owen?" she suggested brightly.

"No, I'm fine, thanks." Owen was feeling hungry, but the kitchen didn't look too clean. If all he could have was their awful boiled food, he'd rather starve.

"Are ye sure? I'm just gettin' up meself, it'd be no trouble" she urged.

---

[5] Dermot and his brothers are the English-born sons of Irish parents; a common enough subgroup in their generation, and the one preceding it. The diasporas of various cultural and ethnic groups throughout history have continually resulted in this kind of identity crisis in the children of immigrants; a phenomenon that seems only to become more widespread in a globalising world.

"No, honestly, I'm fine" replied Owen. Laboriously, she got up from the chair and waddled over to the merry folk at the table. Not a moment too soon. But Owen wasn't alone for long.

"Don't enjoy yourself too much" said Sarah, slipping into the warm chair. Owen's smile was more genuine this time; with Alex's wife, he could be himself, or at least a more realistic version of himself.

"Who are these people?" he asked in a low voice.

"You're asking me?" said Sarah quizzically. "They're your relatives."

"I swear, half of them I've never seen before in my life. And the ones I have met, it was so long ago that I barely remember anyway. I have nothing in common with these people. So what if we have the same name or the same nose? I have nothing to say to them." Sarah smiled.

"Well, that woman who was just here is called Agnes. The one with the glasses at the table is Bridgid, and her husband Patrick is next to her. This is their house." Owen turned towards the table as she spoke, the fire suddenly warm on his cheek. "Across the table, we have Paddy – that's the old gent in the cap – and that big bloke is Tim, of course – your uncle, right?"

"How do you know all this? You only just met them." Sarah shrugged.

"I'm good with names" she answered. "Couldn't exactly say I know any of these people though."

"Well, that makes two of us" Owen said quietly.

Gravel crunched outside, and an engine groaned into silence.

"That'll be the lads" said one of the men at the table. Seconds later, Owen heard a knock at the door. Bridgid put down her wine glass and moved into the hallway. The room fell silent behind her, awaiting the new arrival.

Thank God, Owen mouthed to Sarah. She smiled into her drink.

Dermot followed Alex into the room. It was just as he remembered from so many years ago; the solid wooden table, the slate floor, the peat fire with its unforgettable, instantly familiar smell. Only everything was smaller

As he walked in, everyone seemed to begin speaking at once. Women he half-remembered embraced him; men he didn't know shook his hand.

"How was the flight?"

17

"Dermot, is it? Well, look at ye now!"

"How's that Canada treatin' ye?"

"Did ye find us alright? That road can be murder."

It was all he could do to keep his feet, to smile and shake hands and pretend he knew these people. Over in the corner, he saw Owen standing up. Sarah stayed in her seat, though she raised her glass towards him.

"Hi, hello, nice to see you again" he managed.

"Ye must be tired. D'ye have a hotel booked? Or will ye stay here with us? We've plenty of room. The bed's all made up ready for ye." This, he knew, was Bridgid, and this was her house. If he remembered correctly, she was married to Patrick, who was one of his father's nephews. She was older and greyer, but she still had the same no-nonsense manner he remembered from his childhood, that peculiar aggressive form of hospitality the women here cultivated.

"Uh, no, I didn't have a place booked...but I don't want to be any trouble..."

"Ah, go on with ye. Sure, 'tis no trouble at all, is it, Pat?" She went on without waiting for an answer from her mumbling husband. "Ye can share with your brother. There's plenty of room. Will ye have a bite to eat?"

"Oh, no thanks" said Dermot. "I ate on the plane."

"Sure that's not a meal. Will you not have a bite? Just a sandwich or something?"

"No, honestly, I'm fine" said Dermot.

"Will ye have a drop, Dermot?" offered Patrick, heading to the fridge. "We've beer and stout, and there's whiskey on the table."

"Or wine" Bridgid cut in again. "We've wine, if you'd rather."

"A beer'd be great, thanks" Dermot said, hoping that accepting something at least would quiet the storm of questions and offers that surrounded him. Patrick slipped a cold bottle into his hand.

"Ah, jaysis, Pat, will ye get him a glass? D'ye want a glass, Dermot?"

"No, I'm fine like this" Dermot tried, but it was useless.

"Get a glass out, will ye? You'd think we had no manners at all, drinking out of the bottle all the time like a bunch of drunkards." Dermot couldn't help smiling at Bridgid's ferocity and her husband's weary compliance. It was as though they didn't feel their guests felt welcome unless they, the hosts, were working hard. Thanking Patrick for the glass, Dermot finally saw his chance to head over towards the fire, and his brother, while Alex, joking with the old men, began loading up his second plate of dinner. For that alone, Dermot knew, they'd like him here. They were always suspicious of a man without a ferocious appetite.

"Nice flight?" Owen asked. Dermot groaned.

"Don't ask. I swear, next time I'll take the boat. Or walk; it'd be less painful."

"I'll be sure to give you six months notice when I'm about to kick the bucket, then."

"Don't bother. I've got no intention of showing up at your funeral anyway."

"Fair enough. I wouldn't want you there. The only reason I'd go to yours is to have first crack at that girlfriend of yours."

"Why wait 'til I'm dead? She doesn't" Dermot grinned, and Owen laughed.

"And how are you, Sarah?" Dermot asked, turning to Alex's wife.

"Oh, I'm fine" she replied with a smile.

"You feeling overwhelmed by all these crazy micks?"

"No. Well, maybe a bit. But everyone's so nice. And they love Clare."

"Where is Clare?"

"She's in the other room with the rest of the kids. I'll bring her out here if you like."

"Oh, no need. I'll go say hello later. She's probably met enough new people for one day anyway."

"So how long are you over for?" asked Owen.

"I took three weeks off work. It hardly seems worth coming over for any less than that."

"They don't mind you taking that much time off?"

"No. They owed me some vacation. Besides, under the circumstances, they didn't really have much choice."

"Are you coming back with us after the funeral?"

"I thought I might just stay here, actually. You know, it's been so long since I was last here, and I was actually thinking about coming over even before…all this." Owen snorted.

"Can't think why. This place is a hellhole. I've got nothing to say to these people, and we'll always be second-class citizens here. We're always the English, even to our relatives. As for the rest of the population, they hate us. It's the IRA heartland down here."

"Still? I thought things had got a lot better over the past few years."

"I haven't had any problems" added Sarah, "and I'm more English than any of you."

"You haven't tried to get served in a shop yet" said Owen. "That's what you get for bringing civilisation and the rule of law to a country."

"So Alex tells me the funeral's next week?" Dermot deftly changed the subject. The history of the Troubles was not an argument he wanted to have with Owen, particularly in this time and place. Owen nodded.

"Wednesday. I'd have it sooner if I could and get the hell out of here, but it turns out there's a lot of paperwork involved in transporting a corpse."

"So it's not going to be an open casket?" Owen shook his head, and Sarah sighed softly.

"No" said Owen. "That was a bit of an issue. It's the Irish thing, apparently, to have an open coffin, to have a wake around the body, all that. But you can't transport an open coffin between countries. It has to be closed and sealed. I swear they all think we did it on purpose, just to spite them. They keep saying, over and over, ' Ah, 'tis terrible, dough, terrible altogedder, that we can't say goodboi to himself to be sher', like we had any choice in the matter. Besides, it's too late. At this point we wouldn't want an open coffin even if it were possible. It's a week since he died."

"But you got him a place in the old churchyard?"

"He bought it himself, nearly thirty years ago" said Owen. "In fact he bought two, one for himself and the other for mum, I assume. I guess he forgot to change it after the divorce. After Wednesday, that space reserved for her will be the only grave left in the churchyard."

"Well that's lucky" said Sarah. "That he got the last two spaces, I mean." Owen snorted.

"It's not luck" he said. "That graveyard is hundreds of years old. It's been full this last century, at least. But half the stones in there have our surname on them, and you can't read most of the rest. Dad cut a deal with Father Doolin; they're just going to bury him on top of someone else."

"That's awful!" gasped Sarah. "And illegal, surely?"

"Who's to say?" Owen shrugged. "It's one of the older graves. The headstone was worn away to nothing. The grave was easily two hundred years old, and the records from back then aren't that accurate as to who is buried where."

"And after all that time" Dermot added, "it's basically an empty grave anyway. Especially in peaty, acidic soil like the stuff around here, even bones won't last long. After two hundred years, there's probably nothing left but a kind of rusty stain." Sarah looked at him in astonishment. "I studied archaeology[6]" Dermot smiled by way of explanation.

"Do you think we can maybe change the subject?" Sarah shuddered in disgust.

---

[6] As far as I can tell, Dermot never received his degree, though it seems he did briefly attend university. He has never answered my questions on this subject, and I did not press for answers; such details, in the end, are probably irrelevant.

3

"Dad? It's me, Owen. Can you hear me, Dad?"[7]

The oxygen hissed in the plastic coils that kept his father connected to the world. The minute he came to the hospital, saw his father's bed empty, followed a nurse to this small room with its beeping monitors and whispering gas tanks, Owen knew that there was no other way for this to end. His father was going to die, today, right now. Owen could feel the faint strength failing in the leathery hand he held at the bedside. They had known this, of course they had; the minute he had gone into hospital, eighty-two years old and utterly demented, the unspoken truth was that he would never come back. But now it was happening, and he was all alone.

Owen watched his father's shallow breathing, the frail ribcage rising and falling feebly, each breath one closer to the end. Say something, Owen. Anything. Pierce this silence, or else you're just standing there, watching a man die.

"It was raining earlier. But it's stopped now." He could see the sky bulging in the raindrops that clung to the hospital window, each a prismatic prison for an entire world. "When I was coming here there was that smell, you know, when it hasn't rained for a long time and then it does and the roads give off that kind of sweet smell – do you remember that, Dad?"

---

[7] Dermot was not present at his father's death, and the effort he clearly put into writing this rather moving passage makes one wonder if he felt guilty about not being there; he imagines the scene in great detail, as though attempting to inject himself psychically into the past.

His father's eyelids fluttered, a shimmer of watery blue appearing for a moment in the hollows of the old man's gaunt face.

"The council workers were cutting the grass yesterday. Do you remember, Dad, the smell of cut grass? And when it rains on the grass, and the smell is even stronger, and you just want to roll around in the stuff? It always makes me think of childhood whenever I smell cut grass. It reminds me of you, Dad, mowing the lawn in your shirtsleeves while we played outside. Do you remember that? It's funny how your childhood's so short, really, but it's such a big piece of memory. Do you remember your childhood, Dad? Growing up on the farm in Ireland, with Joe and Tim and Padraig and Seamus and Mary and all the rest of them – do you remember that, Dad? Your brothers and sisters?"

His father's eyelids fluttered again. There was no way to know if the old man could hear him, walking alone on the pristine paths of eternity; but Owen couldn't stop. He was watching his father die, and there was nothing he could do to prevent it, but he would not let him die alone. If there was any part of him left that could still hear or understand, Owen wanted him to know that he would be missed, that there was someone there with him right at the end, that he was not forgotten. And though he knew his words could not help his father now, that there was no way he could follow their trail back to light and life, he had to keep talking about the world his father was leaving. He had to give him a little of its light so he could see his way to wherever he was going.

"It's a beautiful world, Dad. The sound of the streams in the mountains, rushing towards the sea. Or the sun coming up in a haze, with the beams of light trailing behind it like wings. Or the sea, Dad – you must remember the sea. You grew up by the sea, didn't you? It must have been beautiful, with the sun setting on the horizon and the water turning all golden. Or when the wind whipped up a storm and the waves crashed against the cliffs and threw spray hundreds of feet into the air – do you remember it?"

Every day there was less of him. Every day Owen came down to the hospital, and most days his father hardly knew him. Now and again there was a faint trace of recognition – not that of a father for his son, maybe; but he at least knew that this was the man who came to visit him every day. But there was less of that each time.

"Or the sky – the sky. When did you last see the sky, Dad? It's – it's grey today, you know. Lots of clouds. But some are higher than others – there's these sort of bands of cloud. Up high it's just one solid

23

gray mass, and then down below, there's these smaller, darker clouds – I guess they must be rainclouds – and they're all torn to shreds and flying across the sky. There's no wind that we can feel, but I suppose there must be up there, cos the rainclouds are just flying, Dad. And you can see out west, where the sun is setting, even the high clouds have parted, and the light comes through, all pale and orange. It's – it might be a nice day tomorrow." He gulped.

Yesterday, though; he came down to the hospital and sat by his father's bedside, as usual. There was no question now of a conversation; the old man hadn't said a word in days. So Owen sat, and talked, of any trivia he could think of, until visiting hours were over, and he felt the shame of relief that he could go home. But as he stood up to leave and say goodbye, his father reached out to him. He shook his hand, Owen's hand engulfed in his father's huge hard paw. Then he punched his son on the chest, and winked. Owen smiled, and his father smiled back, a measure of human contact across the grey gulf of madness.

"Don't be afraid, Dad. It's a beautiful world, but you've got to leave it sooner or later, right? I bet it's got nothing on the place you're going to. Just – I don't know. We'll miss you, Dad. But you've got to go. And we know that. You won't be forgotten, not ever. But you've got to go."

The old man's chest heaved, the blind organism struggling against the eternal while the mind walks free in the gardens of paradise.

"Go on now, Dad. We're all sick of the sight of you anyway" Owen said, almost choking on the weak joke. His father's chest was still forever; his hand would have dropped if Owen had let go of it. He squeezed it tight.

"Goodbye, Dad" he whispered.

His father's chest rose, the tortured lungs filling with pre-packaged air – and then he was gone. Something indefinable left the room, as though his father's body instantly darkened and shrank, and you could see the moment it left.

The monitor beeped. Owen watched dully as though from a great distance, still holding his father's hand. A nurse came in, checked the monitor, checked the old man's pulse, sighed. She turned to Owen.

"He's gone" she said softly. Owen nodded, gazing out of the window at the lightening sky. The nurse switched off the monitor, and then the oxygen.

The air felt heavy. Carefully, he laid his father's hand down on his motionless chest, and, without knowing why, Owen crossed the room and threw open the window. Outside, a siren howled from the street. The curtains twitched in a damp breeze. A dog barked. He watched the cars like bugs manoeuvring around one another in the car park below, oblivious to the lives blooming and fading around them each day.

Owen checked his watch.

7:47.

Time to go home.

4

"He'll be a happy corpse, then." The men around the table murmured their agreement.

Owen turned to Tim, dressed in his best funeral suit, a few stray wisps of white hair sticking out around the sides of his cloth cap.

"What?" said Owen.

"The rain" Tim explained. "It means a happy corpse, they say." The men murmured and nodded again. Owen shook his head. He was beginning to think these people were fucking with him. Tim, especially.

The night before the funeral, the warm weather had broken, and threatening thunderheads had risen from the sea to shadow the valley. Around four, Dermot had woken from deep sleep; the sky right above the house was torn apart, and the roof trembled beneath the shattering blows of hailstones. The sun rose on a liquid world, gloomy and dank. The river bubbled happily between fields, its grey surface rippled with a million tiny explosions of rain. The stones in the graveyard dripped slate-coloured water onto the sodden earth.

"Twas a lovely speech Dermot" said Bridgid. "Lovely. Wasn't it lovely, Mary?"

"What was lovely?" Mary, Dermot's first cousin, asked in surprise.

"Dermot's speech. Wasn't it lovely?"

"Oh yes. Twas lovely, Dermot."

"Lovely. Ye did him proud, ye did. If he could only have heard it himself." Dermot smiled in thanks. Over in the corner, Sarah was supervising Clare as she ran around the pub, under tables and chairs, harassing Bridgid and Patrick's youngest, Michael, who at eleven was above such childish games. The old men clustered at the bar, talking in low unintelligible voices. What could they possibly find to talk to each other about, day after day, sharing such a narrow life in this narrow valley? Alex was at the buffet with an assortment of cousins, cheerfully answering their questions between mouthfuls of food. Owen stood aloof between the buffet and the bar, his paper plate empty but for a sausage roll with a single bite taken from one end. He had been here a week, and already Dermot seemed to notice that he had lost weight. Alex was gaining, if anything, filling himself with whatever was put in front of him. At home, he had confided to Dermot, Sarah kept him on a diet, but on holiday, he was his own master.

"It was a good turnout" he remarked to Bridgid. "I mean, considering Dad hadn't lived here for so long."

"Your father was well liked around these parts" Bridgid answered. "No matter where he travelled, he never forgot that this was where he came from." Dermot wondered if this was perhaps a sleight aimed at himself and his brothers.

"And, of course," Bridgid went on, "the name alone means something to the people around here. There were people at church who probably never met your father, but they knew his father, or his brothers and sisters. We've lived in these parts for so long, tis small wonder." Dermot smiled, though the thought twitched in his mind that Bridgid had married into this family, and to include herself in that 'we' was perhaps a little presumptuous.

'The Rocky Road to Dublin[8]' played quietly in the background. For a moment, staring out of the streaming window onto the dim road outside, Dermot allowed his thoughts to wander. This song always reminded him of his father, and what his life must have been when he first walked the well-trodden path from his home to hated England, driven by want and desperation into the arms of his enemies. All the battles he must have fought that his sons would never know. A strange, familiar feeling was flexing its wings in an old part of himself.

"He was an educated man, your father" Bridgid was going on as Dermot refocused himself on her chatter. "He never went to school past the age of fourteen, but the first time I met him, I remember thinking, now here's a man who knows a thing or two. Though you'd never think it, would you? Growing up here all those years ago, without even electricity, and the poverty back then, and just that tiny schoolhouse over the hill with only the priest to teach them. But your father was a clever fella, just like his brothers."

---

[8] A popular Irish folk tune. See note 100; clearly a favorite of Dermot's.

"Yeah, he was" Dermot agreed. "He was always reading. When we were kids, he always insisted we had to read. That was how he taught himself."

"Well, of course, they're all great readers, the lot of them. The Fallons always have their noses in a book."

"Ah, Bridgid, will you leave the poor fella alone? You'll have the ears talked off of him."

"Fiona!" Bridgid warmly embraced her interrupter. "We're so glad you and Sean could make it! Dermot, have you met Fiona?"[9]

"Nice to meet you" she said, and he echoed a beat behind.

"So you're the firstborn son? The errant Canadian?"

Dermot smiled.

"You could say that, yeah" he said.

"Fiona is my Sean's wife" Bridgid beamed proudly. Fiona rolled her eyes as Dermot raised his eyebrows in surprise.

"Now, Bridgid," Fiona remonstrated in a tone that suggested they had both gone over this territory before, "we're not married yet. We haven't even set a date yet." Bridgid tutted loudly.

"Young people these days" she complained to Dermot. "How long do people have to be engaged before they marry? My Sean's got nothing but air between his ears to keep a girl like her waiting. He needs a good kick up the arse, that one. And I should know of all people." Fiona laughed loudly.

"It's not like that" she said to Dermot, almost apologetically. "It's a mutual decision."

---

[9] It is interesting to note Dermot's near-total lack of physical description of people in his otherwise carefully written narrative. However, it is perhaps not so surprising; despite his occasional imaginative forays, Dermot was not writing a novel. He did not invent these people. He already knew what they looked like; why bother to describe them? But for the sake of the reader, I will venture this much: Dermot was 30 years old at the time of his father's death. His cousin, Sean, was around the same age, and so we may confidently put Fiona somewhere in that 25-30 age group too. Bridgid is Dermot's first cousin, but she is Sean's mother, and so mid-fifties seems like a reasonable assumption.

"Ah, go on with you" Bridgid replied dismissively. "Sure he must be mad not to have the ring on your finger already. Isn't that right, Dermot?"

"Oh, Bridgid, please" Fiona protested. "You're embarrassing him."

"Rubbish. You're a man, Dermot; wouldn't you run to the altar for a fine figure of a girl like this one?" Dermot smiled politely, and a sudden cry pierced the heavy air; Clare, absorbed in some game of her own devising, had run head-first into a chair. The guests turned, the women tutting sympathetically; Bridgid's question disappeared into the general murmur.

5

Untangle for me the roots of this blasted treeζ, Father, where apes hang gibbering from the lower branches, and find me sleeping in a cold cavern of earth, an acorn-husk clutched to my chest. I have been made weak with visions before,[10] so I know what to do. I'll close my eyes, my ears, my mouth, and trap it all inside this tomb of flesh. It's trying to share with people that brought me to this place; never again.

Take me back, Father, back to where my hopeless hope was conceived and miscarried. Take me back to Cloonashee, in the hollow of the hills that march in a barren plateau to the celebrated cliffs overhanging the wild Atlantic. Let me see the sea, from the top of the Top Field, a rippling curtain flecked with sunbright gold between green-brown earth and glowing white sky. Through the haze of distance, we might glimpse the Aran Islands as dim grey shapes like whales in the dazzling waves, appearing and disappearing like the land of the gods.

Come with me now over the shoulder of the hill, protected from the winds of the sea where the dead rise, Spanish sailors and Gaelic heroes, the wasted children of the Famine in their tattered rags, to where the parish of Cloonashee sleeps. On the south side of the river, cut into a bank at the very top of the hill, the old house squats, its whitewashed walls three feet thick, thatch on the roof like something straight off a postcard. Ould Oireland. Home to our family for the last four hundred years, only Tim now lives there, well into his seventies, still living in the house he was born in with eleven siblings. Come with me across the potholed road with a rogue strip of grass running rebelliously down its cracked center; at the height of the family's wealth, you could stand up at the top of Top Field and look

---

[10] A fairly clear reference to Dermot's troubled psychological past.

east, and you'd hardly be able to see a blade of grass that wasn't owned by Tim or his brothers.

But the brothers are gone, across the sea or under the ground. Padraig lies now in an Australian graveyard, and Owen in an American one. David and Sean are both still alive, one in a New York hospital, the other in a San Francisco nursing home. Anthony died in the Korean War, for the promise of American citizenship. Joe sleeps beneath the land he had worked with Tim all his life, the last but one to be buried in the ancient Cloonashee graveyard, where half the headstones had the name Fallon, and half of the rest were too old to read. The girls, Mary and Susan, both still live: Susan somewhere in Australia, whereas Mary made it only as far as Galway. Maire and Eamon never made it even that far, dying before their teens. And Michael, now, swept to hated England by the riptide of history, has come home to the Cloonashee graveyard, the last grave now filled, the gates padlocked shut. The old bloodline rusts in the rain from the sea.

The halls here are gravestone gray;[11] every time it rains I think of home. I stand in the storm until my features blur and the fire in my heart boils the rain off my face. The endless rain and her bottomless absence, a wedding in black. I'd give anything I'll ever have, heart or blood or bone, to see her once more turn and walk away from me.

---

[11] Eggshell white, in fact. For whatever reason, it seems to have appealed to Dermot's sense of drama to paint our facility with a darker palette than is absolutely necessary. While any form of involuntary treatment carries with it inevitable stresses for the patient, the grim Dickensian asylum described in these pages is almost completely a construction of Dermot's own.

6

It starts with fear.

Fear comes leeching from the darkness, crawling head-first down the walls, writhing like grey snakes along the empty hallways towards you. The shadows hide terrors; the light betrays you[12]. You know it's all in your mind. You know that. You made it all up, these half-formed creatures that haunt your steps, threaten your life, poison your sleep. You know that.

But it doesn't help. You still fear them. Every time you turn a corner, you put a demon behind it, following you, and almost break your neck fighting the urge to turn around. You stumble in through the front door, just a little out of breath, your heart beating just a little faster than it should. And you'd like to laugh, but it's not funny. You know there's nothing there, of course. No monsters, no angels, no devils. You're playing tricks on yourself again. But that's what scares you. Not the threat of being found torn apart in the hallway of your downtown apartment building, your blood crusted on the rented carpet, every cycloptic door closed fast against your final gurgling screams – not that. It's the fear itself that scares you, this rootless, vaporous fear that climbs your spine like a rising violin howl, and the certain knowledge that now, right now, something nameless is working its way towards you, and only you. The fear of losing yourself in the dark paths of insanity, when the monsters you know you invented become more real than the faces of the ones you love, when the hell your mind creates becomes your reality. The certain knowledge that what your life was, with all its compromises and comfortable half-

---

[12] Just to further muddy the waters, it seems Dermot is now talking about himself in the second person.

truths, is about to be swept away like an army in rout.[13] And what comes after?

"So, what, do you have split personalities or something?"

"No, it's not that at all. I - sometimes my brain gets confused by all the information coming at it at once. Like – like filters, that's how I always imagined it. It's like a normal person's brain has these filters that help you to ignore a lot of what's going on around you and concentrate on what you really need to know. Like in a crowded pub, let's say. There's people all around you, all talking at once, and music playing, all that, but you block it all out and concentrate on what the people with you are saying or doing. I have trouble doing that, even when there's not that much going on around me. Like now, for instance. I'm talking to you, but I have to really, *really* concentrate, because if I don't, I'll get distracted by that cloud in the sky that's shaped like a face, or the green of the fields, all the different shades of it, and the way you can see each blade of grass, and really that's all the field is, a million blades of grass all separate from each other, but they all form one single thing so huge they're not even aware of it[14] – you see what I mean?"

Fiona nodded her head.

"I think I'm starting to" she said slowly. And Dermot wondered to himself, his thoughts in his head muffled as though he was speaking underwater, why, on a beautiful day in such lovely surroundings with this incredible woman, he was even talking about this in the first place.

"And then, what seems to happen is that, because you can't tell what you need to hear and what you don't, you start hearing things. It used to be if I was somewhere crowded, with lots of people talking. When I was in school, let's say, and all the kids in the class were all messing around while the teacher was elsewhere, and I'd start to hear my name coming out of all the chopped-up sounds."[15] It was no use. Almost anything else would be a better subject to talk about, but it was

---

[13] A vivid description of the inner life of the schizophrenic. Fiona's response is sadly typical.

[14] In light of later revelations, this offhand comment assumes a deeper meaning.

[15] Indicates onset of symptoms in adolescence; in England, where Dermot grew up, compulsory schooling ends at sixteen. Again, this is typical of schizophrenia in males.

no use. He was in the grip of one of those masochistic confessional manias he sometimes got, or used to get, when he wanted someone to like him.

"Later, you start hearing it when there is no background noise. Just my name, at first. Then other noises. Voices, but not like in the movies, not telling me to kill people or anything – nothing that ridiculous. They were creepy because they were so vague. They never talked to me, as far as I remember – I could just hear things going on independently of me, like when you have a radio half-tuned and you pick up snatches of different stations among the static."

"After that, I started seeing things. Just movement, at first, in the corner of my eye, and when you turn to see what it is, it's gone. I mean, I think everyone gets that sometimes. I got it a lot. Then – it's weird – you start to imagine what they are, men or monsters, whatever, and then that's what you see. You know it's at least partly your own imagination, but you can't stop it, and once you've put a face to this faceless thing, that's what it is, and always was, and no amount of logic will stop you from seeing it."

That wasn't all. That wasn't even the main thing. Dermot talked more about the visions, the wildness, the depression, because it was far easier for her to understand these things. What he could not quite convey was the unforgettable clamour inside his head, all the time, a mingled roar of ecstasy and despair. His crazy juvenile dance on a knife-edge of euphoria and horror. Everything mattered, and nothing did. The great mystery of life, the real and pure light, was in there somewhere, among the howling madness. All those years ago, he had felt it, so close all around, but he had never quite pierced the veil. And he was scared to his soul that now, he never would.

He stopped, finally, the wound having bled itself out for now. Fiona said nothing. She didn't even look at him.

"That's what it is, mostly" he said with an effort. "It's an inability to sort through what's necessary for you to know and what's not. I have to try really hard not to get lost in my own head. If I don't, then I end up staring at a single leaf for hours at a time, watching the way light moves across its surface as though it contains all the mysteries of the universe."

They walked slowly across the field, towards the dark line of trees that marked the banks of the stream. He could hear it before he could see it, chattering wildly in a hundred voices, the happy ghosts of an ancient land. The tree line was too dark, cutting his vision like a knife, a void in his sight that he couldn't help but peer into as it sucked the colour and life from the green fields all around, now so bright that he found it hard not to close his eyes.

"But there must be something you can do about it?" Fiona said, frowning at the grass.[16] something you can do about it?

"What?" Dermot asked. Her words seemed to float in his skull, and he knew there was a question in them that he had to answer a certain way, but they writhed like snakes under his hands and slipped away.

"Your...problems, I mean. You could get some help with them, surely?"

"Oh. Oh, yeah. No, I do. I'm on medication. It works pretty well, usually, but I left the pills at home. I left in a hurry, and didn't think of it."

"Well, that's understandable, given the circumstances" Fiona mumbled.

"Yeah. Anyway, I didn't think it would matter. I've gone this long without them before, [17]and I was fine. And they say you need the medication less as you get older, anyway. I guess I'm not there yet, though."

"Well, you're not that old."

"No, but...sometimes I feel it. I was thinking the other day, I'm only a year younger than my father was when I was born. Everyone's settling down and starting families – look at Alex. He's been a dad for five years, married for six, and he's my little brother. I know that's not for me, I know that, but...I don't know what *is* for me, that's the problem."

---

[16] Dermot was supplied with as much paper as he needed for his writing, but he persisted in writing one text over another. Whether this was for some effect he wished to create, or whether they were later corrections is not clear. However, it seems to me that this over-writing occurs more frequently at moments of greater psychological stress, and so perhaps Dermot is attempting to convey something of his disordered thoughts through this literary device.

[17] See introduction re: Dermot's non compliance with prescribed medication.

"Well," Fiona said consolingly, "it was different in your father's time. My mother was barely into her twenties when I was born, while I'm closing in on thirty and still not settled down."

"You're getting married, though" Dermot said, his eyes on the approaching darkness of the trees.

"Well, yeah, but...all I'm saying is, everyone's different, right? Your brother's happy enough with his family, and more power to him. But that doesn't mean everyone has to be like that, or should want to be like that. The world's not like that anymore, much as my mother seems to think it is. Sean's mother, too, for that matter. I mean, I love Bridgid, but..." Dermot laughed.

"I know what you mean" he smiled. "She can be a little...eager, let's say." Fiona smiled too.

"Yeah, that's one way to put it. If she had her way, the wedding would be tomorrow. I try to tell her that it doesn't work that way anymore, that there's a lot of planning that has to go into it, and...and maybe we're just not there yet, anyway. We will get married, eventually, but there's a lot we both still want to accomplish before that happens."

"Ah sure, what's to accomplish? Go on with ye now. Ye young folk these days, ye'd think ye had all the time in the worrild". Dermot attempted a creaking imitation of his cousin. Fiona laughed.

"Your accent's terrible," she smiled, "but you've the gist of it, yeah."

The stream was louder now, the darkness of the trees stretching out towards them. Dermot studied the ground. He had just imagined looking up into the dark branches and seeing menacing faces there, bitter and twisted with age-old evil, and now he knew that he would. The light faded around as the noise of the water grew, as though he were descending into some river-carved tunnel far below the surface of the bright daylight world.

Slipping into the cool shadows, they stopped on a shady bank where the rolling grass of the fields came to an abrupt stop, overhanging the river that cut its way through the brown clay. Dermot watched the sleek hump of the water as it rolled over a large round rock in the middle of the stream, bunching like a flexed muscle. Fiona sighed and kicked off her shoes, paddling her feet in the cold water. After a moment, Dermot did the same.

"Isn't it lovely here?" she breathed.

36

"It is" Dermot agreed. "It's weird being here, though. Maybe because I haven't been here for so long, but I still kind of know my way around. Maybe that's why there's this strange familiarity about this place, or maybe it's something deeper than that. I mean, Ireland was always this backdrop to our childhood, even though we didn't really know it that well. All the different places my father travelled, but this was always his home. The music, and...I don't know. You just get this strange sense of a country when you live outside of it, this feeling that even though you don't know the place, maybe that's where you should be, where you belong." He stopped, and smiled.

"Sorry. I don't mean to wax so philosophical. I think I've talked enough today about my random thoughts. You must think I'm crazy."

"Not at all" she said. "I don't exactly know what it is, but I think you're right: there is something about this place. It's... ancient, and mysterious, and... almost like another world. The first time I came down here, I felt it."

Abruptly she stood up.

"Come on" she said, holding out a hand to him. "Put your shoes on."

"Where are we going?" Dermot grinned, struggling to his feet. Her hand was soft and remarkably warm, pulsing with the warm life of summer.

"I'm going to show you where you are" she said. "I'm going to show you your father's country."

Still hand in hand, she led him along the bank of the river, under the cool bridge where their voices rang with the noise of the water and out into the sun again on the other side. Keeping to the riverbank, occasionally wading where barbed wire fences marched right to the water's edge, she led him through lush green pastures where cows grazed contentedly and the thick grass rippled in the breeze from the sea.

As they walked, the river grew louder, its waters swelling and surging, the far bank retreating further and further from them as the river widened and deepened. Pools of sweat began to gather under Dermot's arms and spread down his sides, but the noise of the river at least made him feel cooler.

They came to a place where the river slowed its flow, pooling for a while in a deep cutting before chattering on into shallower and narrower regions. In the middle of the swirling water rose a hump of green earth, barely bigger than a large car. Its summit was ringed with trailing bushes and clusters of dripping ferns, crowned by two stunted trees that hissed in the wind.

"Wow" said Dermot, childlike in the presence of all this nature. "Let's climb up there."

"No" Fiona said, clasping his hand.

"Why not? It's not that high."

"You can't go there" Fiona replied. "That's Morwenna's island."

"Who's that?"

Fiona regarded him coolly, blue eyes shining beneath half-lowered lids.

"Morwenna is one of the local mythic characters" Fiona began, smiling slightly. "Some kind of malicious spirit or witch. The island is hers, and she won't allow any mortal to set foot there.

'The story goes that a young man named Colum wanted to marry a beautiful maiden named Nuala. Nuala's father was a wealthy landowner in these parts, and he wasn't going to give away his only daughter, as well as her impressive dowry, to just anyone. So before he would permit Colum to marry his daughter, he insisted that the lad bring to him a flower of unparalleled beauty in exchange for his beautiful daughter – a flower that only grew on Morwenna's island, where no man had ever set foot.

But Colum was brave and in love, and he feared no fairies or ghosts. He set off for Morwenna's lair, promising Nuala he'd be back the next day with a bouquet as big as his arms could carry. But Colum didn't come back the next day, or the next, or the next.

'And so time passed. Spring bloomed into summer, and summer greyed to autumn, and Colum never returned.

'The trees fell. The grass grew.
The trees fell. The grass grew."
Fiona stopped. A cloud seemed to have passed across Dermot's face.[18]

"Are you alright, Dermot?"

"What? Oh. Yeah. No, I'm fine. It was just – what you said – the grass and the trees. It reminded me of something. But I don't know what. It's nothing. You know when you half-remember a dream when you first wake up, but you can't quite catch it and put it in words, and it slips away? Kind of like that. Forget it. What happened to Colum?"

---

[18] More on the inserted pieces of text: in this context, the inserted text might almost represent an auditory hallucination, which would be consistent with the progress of Dermot's relapse.

"Well," Fiona restarted, "time passed, and he never returned, and people said good riddance. Those who make light of the fairy folk deserve to come to a bad end, they muttered. But Nuala never stopped hoping and waiting for her lost love. Until one day, a great wind blew across the valley. And on that wind, Nuala heard Colum's voice, calling her. Then, forgetting her father and her position, she followed the river, just as we did today, and came to Morwenna's island. A single tree grew on it then, and when the wind whipped through the branches, the tree called her name in the voice of her beloved.

Bravely, Nuala stepped into the flood and waded across, driven by Colum's voice. But the moment she set foot on the island, she too was transformed into a tree. And there they are now, the two of them, reaching out their fingers to each other. And when a storm wind blows, they sing to each other to drive away the fear and the sorrow of their lonely immortality."

"That's quite a story" Dermot said. "Where did you learn that?"

"Sean, actually" she smiled guiltily. "When I first came down here to meet the family, he took me around and told me the few old stories he remembered, knowing I'm interested in that kind of thing. If I wanted to hear more, he told me, I should talk to Tim. He's the one. The whole mythic history of the valley carried round in the head of an old farmer who left school at thirteen. That's folk wisdom for you."

"It's beautiful" Dermot said. "Beautiful and sad. But has no one really ever set foot on the island? I mean, a story's one thing, but you don't actually believe it, do you?" Fiona smiled back at him.

"Well, it's easy to put to the test, isn't it?" she goaded. "If you know better than the backwards folk round here, go ahead and climb up there. See what happens to you."

"Fine" said Dermot defiantly.

"Fine" Fiona echoed.

The wind hissed softly in the twisted branches of the two trees.

"You know, it is kind of high" Dermot grinned. "Maybe it's not all that safe..."

Fiona laughed loudly.

"Fair enough" she said. "Safety first, right?"

"Can't be too careful" Dermot smiled.

They walked on upstream, the river cutting deeper between the banks. The noise of it filled Dermot's ears now, outsinging the birds as it rushed and foamed over smooth stones on its way to the sea. He felt like he could sit and listen for hours and never get tired of its infinitely modulating song.

"Nearly there" Fiona called up ahead, raising her voice now to be heard over the chattering river. Up ahead, the stream swept boldly around a bend, licking the high bank as it turned and ran towards them. Dermot followed Fiona around the bend, and the roar of water filled his ears. In front of them, the water leapt from a stony height and thundered into a dark pool right at their feet. The banks around the pool were thick with ferns that hung out over the water, flecked with the spray from the waterfall, as though trying to bathe themselves in the bright curtain of water. The falling stream cut a dark channel through the wet plants, and the light of the sun sparkled on the water and glowed green in the branches of tall trees that shed their leaves into the foaming pool. Everything in that place was green and young and vibrant; the air smelled damp and earthy, but fresh, heavy with the clean water of the falls.

"There now," said Fiona proudly, "look at this place and tell me you don't believe in fairy tales. Isn't it beautiful?"

"Oh yeah, it's stunning" he agreed. "Wish I had my camera."

Fiona turned towards him.

"Wh – what are you doing?" she cried, turning away quickly.

"Going for a swim" Dermot grinned. "Care to join me?"

"No, I don't think so, Dermot."

"Ah, come on. Doesn't that water look nice and cool? Just think how good it's going to feel after all that walking in the hot sun."

"I'm sure it will. You can tell me all about it."

"Where's your sense of adventure?"

"I must have left it at home with my swimming costume."

"Are all married people this boring?"

"First of all, we're not married yet; and second, I'm not boring, I just don't – "

With a loud whoop Dermot leapt from the bank into the water. Fiona stepped back from the splash.

"What're you like, Dermot?" she shook her head.

"Come on in" he panted, his voice ringing in the narrow space. "It's very - refreshing."

"No thanks" she laughed. "I'm fine where I am."

"Suit yourself" Dermot called as he paddled towards the falling water. "Your loss."

"Yeah, right" she smiled. She heard Dermot coughing beneath the waterfall, his naked body lost in a storm of water. Boring? She'd see about that.

Slowly, Dermot came wading out of the water and struggled back up to the bank.

"Where are my clothes?" he said, puzzled. Fiona smiled beatifically.

"Cold in there, was it?"

"Extremely. What have you done with my clothes?"

"Nothing. What would I want with your stinking rags?"

"Don't test me, Fiona. I'll throw you in there, I swear."

"Yeah, right. You couldn't if you tried." Amused and a little irritated at the same time, Dermot peered half-heartedly behind a few bushes.

"Come on, where are they?" he insisted. Fiona just laughed.

"Fine. You think I won't walk home naked? I don't care."

"You wouldn't" she smiled.

"You sure? Let's go. It's hot out; I'll dry on the way. Off we go, come on."

"Jesus, Dermot. Stop."

"What's that husband of yours going to say when he sees the two of us walking back home and I don't have a stitch on? I'll let you explain, shall I?"

"Alright, alright, you win. Here's your clothes." Fiona reached around a moss-covered rock behind her and held out the bundle. Dermot stretched nonchalantly, his arms straight out above his head.

"I'm not sure I want them now" he pondered. "What with it being so warm out and all."

"Come on now, take them."

"No. No, I think I'll go as I am. Thanks anyway."

"Well, I'm not carrying this stuff. So you either get dressed or it's going in the river."

Finally, Dermot reached for his clothes.

"Get a good look, did you?" he smiled as he pulled his pants on.

"Can't say there was much good about it" Fiona shot back.

41

7

The dark wooden desk squatted silently in the corner of the room. Owen approached nervously, almost with a sense of fear, as though he were still a child and his father might come up the stairs any moment and tell him off for snooping around in his desk. But he was no longer a child, and his father would never tell him off again.

The top of the desk was bare but for a crucifix and a framed photo of Clare, taken two years earlier. Almost ashamed, Owen pulled at the top drawer of the desk. It didn't budge. He pulled harder. Nothing. There was no lock that he could see. As Owen searched around the closed drawer for the source of the obstruction, he saw three large nail heads in the wood at the side of the drawer. Who would nail a drawer shut? And why? It was more than curiosity now; it was a challenge. Looking around the room for some kind of tool, he picked up the brass crucifix.[19]

---

[19] Remarkable. Given that this passage describes an event that Dermot could not possibly have been present at, we may assume that these details are invented; in which case, a crucifix makes an extraordinary thing to use as a pry bar. Few symbols are quite so loaded with meaning, so open to a range of possible interpretations, as the millennia-old figure of a chastised and dying divinity. But what Dermot is trying to say with this potent symbol is unclear. If he is presenting Catholic iconography as a means with which to pry into the secrets of the human psyche, for instance, it is odd that he does so only here, and nowhere else. If the mysteries of his own past are better understood through the imagery of his seemingly abandoned religious upbringing, it is strange that he resorts most often to the images of paganism, the prehistoric

"Sorry, Jesus" he said, jamming the end of the cross into the gap between the drawer and the wood of the desk. It sank in up to the nailed feet. Jesus gazed up at Owen, his face a mask of pity and pain.

Placing his palm over the face of Christ, Owen pushed on the top of the crucifix, trying to prise the drawer loose. The thorn-crowned head dug into his skin. He felt something begin to give, and pushed harder. Abruptly, Jesus sank towards the top of the desk. The metal of the cross had begun to bend. There was a tearing noise, and a sliver of wood flew from the drawer and bounced off Owen's leg. With a clatter, the warped crucifix fell onto the desk. The wood was cracked; the top of the drawer had broken off; but it was still shut.

Owen slid the crucifix towards the back of the desk. He still had enough Catholic guilt to feel bad for what he'd done. But he couldn't stop now. On top of the fridge downstairs, he knew, there was a key to his father's shed.

A few moments later, Owen returned, with a hammer, a crowbar, and a chisel. Sticking the end of the crowbar into the hole he had made with Jesus' help, he forced the other end down towards the top of the desk. He could hear the wood creaking as he leant all his weight on the lever. Still the nails held. Owen pushed harder.

With a crack, the drawer front gave way, and the crowbar broke through the wood, its pointed end striking him high in the thigh.

"Ow! Fuck!" he cried, pulling the crowbar from the mangled drawer. Enough was enough. Seizing the crowbar by its straight end this time, he swung its heavy hook down at the top of the smashed drawer. Again, and again, he struck the stricken wood, the pronged metal hook gouging deep into the timber. With a grunt, he pulled it free, and most of the wood came with it.

Carefully, wary of splinters, Owen reached in through the shattered drawer front and extracted a sheaf of papers in his father's handwriting. And, in the midst of them, a red notebook.[20]

---

mythology of the Celts, to interpret his neuroses. What, if anything, Dermot makes of this sacrilegious act is never made clear.

[20] Regrettably, if this notebook still exists, or ever did, it is not in Dermot's possession, or mine. It would seem that all that remains are the translations Dermot made from it, which I have attempted to demarcate by using a different font; see introductory note on the text.

8

On Tuesday, it rained. Grey sheets swept in off the sea, hiding the mountains, misting the windows into blank white blocks, as though the world outside had been washed away. The whole world can be contained in a drop of water – wisdom is found in the unlikeliest of places. Conan-Doyle believed in fairies[21].

Everything is the same, electrons in an atom and planets in the cosmos. Cleave a piece of wood, and I am there.[22] Once you realise this, then you become part of everything, everywhere and all at once. Like a dead man. Our recycled carbon spins endlessly through space even as our memory calcifies into anecdote in the minds of those we leave behind, and the immortal atoms of our body dance forever through all matter. In death, as in life, we remain a part of all things.

It's raining in the graveyard at Cloonashee, too. I hang from the edge of a leaf in the hedge, its inverted green image reflected in my watery skin where the sky becomes an ocean beneath me, and gravestones hang from a green sky like bats.[23]

---

[21] Arthur Conan-Doyle, best known as the author of the Sherlock Holmes stories. He was a noted spiritualist with a deep-seated belief in the supernatural, although why Dermot mentions him here is unclear.

[22] From the apocryphal Gospel of Thomas.

[23] It is not unusual for the schizoid patient to project their psyche outwards from themselves, even into inanimate objects. I had a patient once who used to claim to watch his physical body sleep while his consciousness took on the form of the sprinkler pipe above his bed.

The paint was peeling on the warped wood of Tim's door; it flaked away from Dermot's knuckle as he knocked. From inside he heard the muffled sound of the old man getting out of his chair and slowly coming to the door. Light pooled on the threshold. The sweet smell of peat burning rolled smokily around Dermot.

"Why, Dermot, tis yerself." Without another word, Tim turned and shuffled back into the cottage. Dermot followed, closing the door behind him.

Tim settled back into his straight-backed chair by the fire's side. He exhaled noisily, the chair creaking beneath his still massive frame. Over seventy years old, he was well over six feet tall and heavily built. Dermot had heard stories as a child of Tim's legendary strength, and size: of how, when the ass had broken his hip with a kick, the small rural ambulance had not been able to fit him inside; of how they had used the cart they used to take cows to the market to take him to town; how the bonesetter had worked the whole day on him with nothing more than a drop of whiskey to dull the pain, and he made no word of complaint. Just looking at his hands, huge and thick and worn by years of hard labour, Dermot knew that this man must have been a force of nature in the days of his youth, implacable and unstoppable. It was sad to think that time would soon conquer a man of such strength.

"How are you doing, Tim?" Dermot said, cheerfully and a little loudly.

"Oh, fine" Tim said, and Dermot smiled. His father would have replied in exactly the same way, even while cancer was ripping his body apart.

Bricks of turf popped and whined on the fire. Startled by sudden movement, Dermot's eye lit on a black beetle that scurried across the flagstone floor. Its thin legs a blur, it vanished into the shadow beneath the wooden table[24].

The two men watched the fire in silence, Tim's craggy face an unreadable chart of shifting orange light and deep black shadow.

"So the funeral went well, then" Dermot tried.

"Oh, yeah, twas grand."

---

[24] Old farmhouses are filled with such pestiferous life. Though we wonder whether there was, in this case, any such insect. This is how the hallucinations often start; vague shadows and blurs of movement in one's peripheral vision.

Tim's chair creaked slightly.

Dermot scratched his neck.

With a popping sound, the fire found a pocket of air in the dry turf. The thick silence closed around them once more. In the dim warmth of the small room, Dermot began to feel drowsy.

"It's just...you know, while I was writing his eulogy, I realised how much I didn't know about my father. I mean, I knew him, but only as a father, as a family man. I hardly know anything about his life before I was born. I only know what kind of father he was, not what kind of man he was." His words faded back into the warm silence. In the firelight, Dermot saw Tim's head shift slightly towards him. The red glow from the fire gleamed in his eyes.

"I was just about to go for a stroll" Tim said. "Will ye join me, Dermot?"

"Yeah, alright" said Dermot, standing up from the bench at the side of the room he had only just sat down on. There was something in the way Tim was looking at him that made him suspect that this 'stroll' might mean more than it seemed to on the surface.

Dermot led the way outside. Tim picked up a smooth wooden stick from the stand by the door, which he swung closed behind him without locking it. Cold stars glinted in the dark sky above like fistfuls of gems; more stars than Dermot had ever seen. The sky was full of them, and the longer he looked, gazing upwards in quiet awe, the more he saw. Tiny points of light appeared out of darkness like the lights of a great city shining out against the twilight.

With a grunt, Tim started up the slope at the back of the house to the road. Dermot followed behind, slowly; Tim walked with his left leg held stiffly out to the side, leaning heavily on his stick. He turned right on the road, not even looking for traffic. Dermot fell into step beside him. Neither of them said a word. There was no sign of life, on the road or off it. Even at this early hour, the fields all around seemed barren and deserted, falling into slumber with the failing of the sun.

The two men reached the crest of the hill a few yards south of the cottage, and the potholed road began to sink before them into another shadowy valley. At the bottom of the hill, the white walls of the church seemed to glow faintly, the rays of the sun absorbed all day and now slowly released into the gathering night. Still there was no noise of an engine, no voices, no human sound of any kind. Not even an animal could be heard in the deep grey twilight; only the breathing and the crunching footsteps of the two men that seemed by contrast impossibly loud.

Without a word, halfway down the hill, Tim turned to his right. Dermot followed uncertainly; the rusty iron gate of the cemetery loomed up before them. Why were they here? It was not yet a week since they had buried his father; what could have changed since then?

The gates were shut with a heavy padlocked chain. Dermot saw Tim fumble something from out of his pocket, and the chain rattled in his heavy hand. With a squeal that seemed deafening, he pulled one of the gates open.

Inside, the thick hedges cut off the last grey daylight that lingered behind the hills. There were no streetlights out here. But the night was clear, and the stars so bright and numerous now that they seemed to cast a pale shadowless light on the leaning tombstones and the uneven grass.

Dermot followed Tim down the slope of the graveyard. Away to the right, he could just make out a small mound of earth piled beside what he knew was his father's grave. Always more coming out than going back in. His body in earth, the measure of a man in the mud he displaces.

Picking his way between gravestones, Tim moved towards the bottom corner of the cemetery. Dermot followed carefully. Almost hidden under the wild ancient hedge, he saw a dark square shape, too sharp-edged and hard to be natural. Tim stooped awkwardly over it. As Dermot came up behind him, he saw that the old man was lifting a wooden cover from a square formed by four low walls of the grey stone so abundant in these parts. Inside, he saw only darkness.

"It rained on Friday" Tim said in a low voice. He seemed to be waiting for something.

"Yes" said Dermot hoarsely, and cleared his throat. "Yes, it did" he said, more clearly this time.

"Come closer, lad" said Tim. Dermot kneeled beside him on the cold grass. Even leaning over the wall, he could see nothing; just a dark pit in the earth whose end lay beyond sight.

"When it rains" Tim said beside his ear, "the water flows down the hill, through the earth, and ends up here. Do ye understand, Dermot?

The water in this well has flowed through all the graves of your ancestors, including your father, now. Do ye understand?"[25]

It was too dark now even to see Tim's face; but Dermot could hear the intensity in his voice, something he had never before in his life heard from his taciturn uncle.

"Yes," he managed, "I think I do." Unseen water splashed and trickled, and Dermot felt something damp and cold in his hand.

"Drink" said Tim.

"But – isn't it..."

"This is what we do" Tim interrupted. "This is how our ancestors live on in us. My father showed us this well when his father died, and we all drank. We drank again when my father died – your father included. Why do ye think he wanted so much to be buried here? It was his place to show ye, but since he never did, I'm showing ye now. Drink."

Dermot hesitated a moment before raising the cup. The water was icy cold, but it tasted clean. He felt a thin stream trickle down his chin as he drained the cup.[26]

"Good lad" said Tim, reaching for his walking stick. "Give us a hand up, will ye?"

---

[25] Here we see for the first time the well, the archetypal representation of the hidden depths of the subconscious. For a fuller treatment of this subject, the reader is referred to *Headwaters: The symbolism of water in world mythology*, Fergus McIntire, 1987.

[26] We may see in this odd behaviour a form of ritual cannibalism, a practice that has occurred in cultures across the world from the most ancient times to the present day. And we needn't turn up our noses at what we perceive as savagery; what is the Christian Eucharist but the eating of the flesh and drinking of the blood of the sacrificed deity? Catholics in particular profess a belief in transubstantiation; that is, the communion wafer quite literally becomes, through the ritual of the Mass, the actual body of Christ. And though we might sneer at the unscientific nature of such a claim, we would do well to remember that Catholicism remains one of the world's most popular religions; 17% of the world's population currently follow this belief system.

9

Airport lighting, void of shadow and depth, made wraiths of the family hunched around the plastic table of the coffee shop. Bedraggled armies of shuffling ghosts filed past, red-eyed and grey-skinned, mouths listlessly opening and closing like the gasps of suffocating fish. The ceiling mounted speakers chimed and mumbled, barely heard through the dull drone of travelling zombies. This is the dead time the expat knows well; drinking overpriced coffee and making conversation of almost supernatural banality while waiting for someone to leave. You can dress an airport up as much as you like, and turn it into some kind of parallel-universe shopping mall; even throw in an utterly fake MDF-panelled pub, if you like, but it will never feel like a place that anyone chooses to be.

Owen is averaging one glance at his watch every four minutes; Sean is not far behind. Alex is a little more relaxed, only checking the time every seven minutes or so. Clare, lacking the adult's social skills, is panting with boredom, eyes rolling and tongue lolling like a beaten horse. Sarah keeps making furtive motions and cooing sounds at her daughter, trying to convince the child they'll be getting on the plane soon without reminding the adults of the impending separation none of them have forgotten for a moment.

"I think this coffee cost more than the flight" Alex mutters, frowning at the shallow white cup.

"Wouldn't be surprised" Sean woefully agrees.

"So what are you going to do here by yourself?" Owen asks his brother, darting a quick glance at Sean as he speaks.

"Dunno. Explore. Re-acquaint myself with the family. Get to know the ancestral homeland, that kind of thing" Dermot replies, deliberately avoiding looking in Sean's direction. "It'll be nice to take a holiday."

"You think you might come over and pay us a visit in the near future?" Sarah asks, ignoring for a moment Clare's plaintive whining.

"Yeah, probably" Dermot answers. "Not sure when, though. It's been a while, I know; I'll have to go back soon or I'll lose my accent." Sarah smiled slightly, already turning to Clare again.

"Yes, we'll be on the plane soon" she says. "You can wave goodbye to uncle Dermot from the window."

"Will we see him?" Clare asks.

"Maybe, but he'll be very tiny, like an ant" Sarah replies. "We'll have to look really hard."

"Oh, I almost forgot to give you this" says Owen suddenly, rustling around in his carry-on luggage. Dermot prepares to launch into a half-hearted protest against his brother's parting gift, when Owen places a tattered red-covered notebook onto the table between them. Dermot's brow furrows.

"What's this?" he asks without moving.

"It was Dad's" Owen replies. "I found it when we went through his things."[27]

Dermot peels back the front cover; like sudden pressure on a tender area of bruised flesh, he is jolted by the sight of his father's handwriting, unseen for years, but never forgotten. But –

"What- what is this?"

"No clue" Owen replies.

"We couldn't figure it out" Alex adds. "It looks like some foreign language, or shorthand, or something."

Dermot rifles through the pages, scanning quickly for anything recognisable as a word he knows; nothing.

"That is – weird" he says.

"I know. The book's almost full, too; whatever it is, it must have taken a while to write. But none of us can read it."

"Did your dad speak any other languages?" Sarah asks. The brothers shake their heads as one man.

---

[27] This, it would appear, is the putative source of the notes Dermot attempted to write in a different handwriting; his father's notes on ancient mythology, etc. See introduction.

"Well, Gaelic" Dermot shrugs. He turns the open book towards his cousin. Sean shakes his head.

"It's not Irish" he says. "Nothing that I could make head or tail of."

"We thought, since you're staying here, maybe you might figure something out" Alex goes on. "I mean, if it's not Irish, then maybe not; but maybe you could ask around. Apart from us, the people Dad was closest to are all here – "

"The ones who are still alive" Owen cuts in.

"I mean, maybe Tim knows something. Maybe it's something from their childhood. Something they were taught in school, or something."

"Well, yeah" Dermot says slowly. "I mean, I'll give it a try, for sure. I'll have the time to work on it, anyway. And – it's nice to have it. Thanks, Owen."

Owen looks at the table.

An uneasy silence descends.

Someone's spoon clinks against the rim of a cup.

Sean shifts in his seat.

Clare hums contentedly for now, her small fist wrapped around one of Sarah's unused packets of substitute sugar.

"Well," Alex begins, and they all recoil from the table as though it had suddenly become hot to the touch, each of them recognising the moment once it arrived.

"Best be off" Owen says pointlessly, reaching for his bag. Dermot scoops up the notebook from the table. Sarah begins fussing with Clare, Alex hovering over them as Sean rises from his seat, his hand stretching out towards his departing cousins.

"Nice seeing you again, Dermot! Don't be a stranger!" says Sarah, wrapping her arms around him. She smells like shampoo and tea and some other scent Dermot can't identify; the ephemeral scent of motherhood charging back out of the recesses of the past. Clearly, it's going to be that kind of day.

Alex shakes his hand; theirs is not a family that hugs.

"Take care of yourself, mate" he smiles, suddenly becoming emotional. "Good to see you again."

"Yeah" says Owen, taking his turn to pump Dermot's hand a couple of times. "Have fun."

"Alright, Owen. Take care" Dermot replies. Sean shakes Alex's hand while Owen waits awkwardly nearby and Sarah leads Clare towards the gate. Separately, both Alex and Owen turn back briefly, waving shyly at the older brother they know will only ever be a background figure in their lives from this point. Years of separation beget more years; the place of exile becomes your true home. Every year Dermot lives in Canada makes it less likely he'll ever live in England again. Two weeks a year, and a phone call every couple of months. Dermot raises a hand.

They are lost in the crowd. Dermot sighs quietly. Sean says nothing.

"Well," says Dermot, "I guess we should head home."

"Ah, what's the hurry?" Sean says, a light in his eye.

"What did you have in mind?" Dermot asks. His cousin shrugs.

"Sure, I dunno. Pub?"

10

In this hellhole, every conversation becomes an exercise in futility. Questions, questions, questions; they can't stop asking me fucking questions. Not just the doctors, not just the nurses; the other patients won't leave me alone. It's like an old folk's home, like God's waiting room – like any institution, I suppose, packed to the rafters with the chronically bored. I swear, some of the maniacs here think they're the doctors. One wretch with thin dark hair and bulging eyes keeps accosting me in the cafeteria, asking me about my progress, using obscure medical terms as though he knows what he's talking about. Vile toad. [28]

I saw the doctor today, Grace, and he thinks I'm doing better. His praise makes me vomit acid all over the starched bedclothes. I don't want to do better, if better means what I know it does: a fading, a falling, an autumn of the mind, the light and life and beauty of revelation grading into forgetfulness, mundanity, fear. What they call madness is life; what they call hallucination is a spiritual experience, an encounter with the divine that most people spend their whole lives searching for. My nights may be riven by sorrow, pierced by spears of shame and regret, torn to pieces by anger and loss and desire and

---

[28] No such patient exists, nor ever did. Why Dermot chose to make his time at our facility seem so bleak is unknown, though the phenomenon is not uncommon. Given that his letters are addressed to Grace, the woman who put him in here to begin with, we may surmise that this is the victim's revenge.

despair –but very few people come as close to God as I do, every night. This is what the mystics waited for; hiding in caves from the desert sun and the poisonous world of other men; dragged out on sledges in the absolutely black and freezing arctic night; howling at the sky in the lightless forests of prehistory. They waited for the voices, the voices of the animals, the spirits, the gods, the ancestors, the same things I hear, each and every night, and they tell me it's madness. They treat it with drugs that slow me down, pull me back to earth like a gold chain around the neck of a swan,[29] keeping me tethered in an orbit of loss that we all feel, every day, because this is not what life is, and we all fucking know it. This is not what we were born to, an empire of things that swallows every genuine human emotion, until people download child porn in between yoga sessions because the only feeling they have left is the vague sense of self-disgust.

     I don't mean to scare you, Grace, but I know I will. You want me to get better, and I love you for that, truly I do. But I am better, better than I ever was, a better man than you ever met, because what they call my condition, after all the voices and the visions, after all the fear and horror and rage, comes down to love. Love for a world in which there is no duality, no good and evil, no right and wrong;[30] love for a world in which there is no division, no separateness between me and you, between me and the doctor, between me and that psychopath who won't leave me alone. Every cell in my body is made up of the exact same elements that make up every other cell in existence. That's a scientific fact, but science calls an experience of

---

[29] From an old Irish myth; I don't have the reference to hand.

[30] Dermot talks of love here, a kind of Buddhist belief in non-discrimination, where all the world is cosmically present in all things at all times; but this jars with the previous paragraph, in which he rails against what he sees as a world devoid of beauty and populated by self-loathing people downloading child porn. This disjuncture is not easily explained except to say that Dermot, like many schizophrenics, would often oscillate wildly between opposing viewpoints, spinning like the needle of a compass between two magnets, unable to determine which pole pulls him more strongly.

that truth a delusion, a symptom of madness. We can know the truth, but we aren't permitted to feel it.

11

"What's this old shite now?" Sean cast his eyes around the near-empty pub, glaring at the dark walls as though they had insulted him.

"What?" asked Dermot, the tip of his tongue clearing his upper lip of a trace of fragrant foam.

"This pop shite" Sean scowled. "What sort of a fucking tune is this? Roy! Roy, will ye get out here!"

The landlord sauntered in from the kitchen, thick-fingered, heavy-shouldered, a few obscene curls of white hair blooming above the top button of his straining shirt.

"Another one, is it, lads?" he asked, reaching for the tap.

"Grand. And get some real music on the stereo, will ye? I can't listen to this bollocks anymore!"

"Tis Sinead's idea" Roy said levelly. "Thought it might be an idea to attract some of the younger crowd, you know."

"Well, Dermot and meself *are* younger, and we think it's a load of balls, so give it a rest, will ye?"

Roy set two fresh pints on the bar in front of the cousins.

"The pair of ye are not as young as my Sinead" he smiled.

"Well, we're a fuck sight younger than ye, and we're younger than anyone else in this shithole" Sean shot back.

"Alright, alright" Roy said. "I'll see if I've an old CD in the back His Lordship might find agreeable."

"Fair play, Roy" Sean called after the landlord's retreating back. Turning to Dermot, he hunched his shoulders conspiratorially.

"Between you and me, that Sinead of his is some fucking weapon. Face on it like a melted wheelie bin."

"You know this guy, then?" Dermot asked.

"Who, Roy? Oh, yeah. Known him for years now."

"It's just – well, it's not exactly the local, is it?"

"It's local to the airport. I stop in if I'm after travelling usually."

"You travel a lot?"

"Not so much now. Used to go abroad for the rugby games sometimes. France, Italy, Scotland; you can go for pennies with Ryanair. Get a bunch of lads, hop on the plane, see the game, get plastered in Rome and be back home for Sunday dinner. Fucking magic."

"I went to Rome once. I love it there; it's beautiful. And the sense of history..."

"Dirty streets. And all those eejits on those fucking scooters. You take your life in your hands crossing the road. Ah – now *that's* a fucking tune!" Sean pointed directly above his head, as though the music was falling from the yellowed cracks in the ceiling. A spaghetti western opening, rattlesnakes and deserts and the setting sun; but then the whistle, and the drums, and that drunken-sounding voice; on the first day of March, it was raining.

"Good song" Dermot agreed. "Shane MacGowan's a genius."

"D'ye like The Pogues? Good man! What a fucking wreck your man is, though. I saw him in Dublin one time; came out on stage in a fucking wheelchair, he did. Bottle of vodka in the one hand, bottle of whiskey in the other. Keeled over after the third song, the fucking piss artist."

"Little bit fond of the smack, too, from what I hear."

"Wouldn't doubt it. Fucking junkie."

They reached for their beer simultaneously, as though they had trained for this; with perfect precision, they sipped for an unpremeditated but exactly equal length of time, and set the glasses down on the bar as one man.

"Still, he wrote some good fucking songs. Good on ye, Roy!" Sean yelled at the barman, who waved without looking over from the far side of the bar, where he was helping a bedraggled old man count out enough change for another drink.

"Are you going to be alright to drive home?" Dermot asked, the alcohol allowing him to say what he'd been thinking for the last couple of pints.

"I'll be grand" said Sean. "It's just the one road, and I could drive it with me eyes closed. Driven it asleep, more than once, and always made it in one piece." Dermot, unsure of how to respond, chose to take another swig instead.

The boys from the County Hell. This is not the song you listen to while sipping a cool glass of wine, or doing the laundry. Dermot felt a loosening inside himself; his immediate family were gone, their plane already landed back in England. Everyone here knew him only as a child, Michael's son; they had no idea what kind of a man he was. There is no feeling like that of being alone among strangers; Dermot's blood wakened at the thought, the possibilities of reinvention, the boundless freedom of being in a place where the only past he had was vague memories of the child he had once been, and the long slow history of his blood; as a man, an individual, he was unknown. He drank again, and Sean followed his lead.

"Tis always funny, coming home" Sean said quietly. "I mean, it's grand and all. But – you know."

"It's weird, isn't it? Dermot smiled. "You have your life, your job, whatever. And your family don't really know anything about your life, except what you tell them. You make your own way in the world. Then you go home, and you feel like a kid again. Except – different. You feel different, like you're spying on your own childhood. Nothing's changed, and everything has. All the battles you've fought, that your parents will never know. They used to know everything, when you were a kid, but then you grow up, and you realise, they didn't know shit."

Sean leaned his elbows on the bar, his broad hands held, fingers spread, in front of his face.

"These hands" he said slowly. "This is me. This is how I've taken care of meself. These two hands. Since I was fourteen years of age. Everything I have now, it's because of these two hands."

"Me too" Dermot replied. "I mean, I've done my share of shit jobs. More than my share. Mixing concrete on sites, digging fucking ditches. I worked for my dad for one summer; he had me breaking rocks. I mean, breaking rocks, like a fucking chain gang! There I was, in the height of summer, thirty degrees in the baking sun, and I'm swinging a sledge and breaking fucking rocks! The man was a slave driver!"

"I never had anyone taking care of me" Sean mused. "I mean, you know, respect to me parents, and all that. But, you know, I was the oldest. I always had to look out for the young ones. It's like – I see how me ma is now, with Michael. She was never like that with me. Never. I was the first born; he's the miracle baby. She was told she'd never have another, after Siobhan; but then along came Michael. When I was the age he is now, I was out working on the farm. Driving the cows, cutting the turf. Ma would never let Michael work like that now."

"But you're a better man for it, right?" Dermot ventured. "That's how I see it. If they hadn't raised you the way they did, you wouldn't be the man you are now."

Sean nodded slowly.

"S'right" he said. "Right enough."

"I mean, I went to Vancouver with nothing, basically" Dermot went on. "I didn't know anyone there, I didn't have a job lined up, and I didn't have anyone helping me. No one. I just did it, myself, and I did alright. Now, I have a decent job, a nice place – I mean, I'm a long way from being rich, that's for sure. But everything I have, I earned for myself, without help from anyone. It's mine, completely, because no one helped me get it. Just me."

"That's it" Sean nodded. "These two hands. Everything I have – the company, everything – I built that all from scratch, with these fucking hands. Didn't need anyone's help. I mean, you take Fiona – don't get me wrong. But I say to her all the time, everything you want, you have to earn it, you know? She's at university, you know, all that, which is fine, but it's – I just think she needs to decide what it is she wants, you know? Because, I mean, I fucking *love* that girl. I fucking love her to death, right? I mean, that's it. Fucking love her. But it's like, what do ye want? I mean, I'm doing pretty well now, with the company and that, and I just think maybe we should start thinking about a family, and all that. I mean, that's the whole point, isn't it? That's why people get married in the first place. And I know I'd be a good father, and I know she'd be a good mother, so it's like – what's the problem? I'm fucking ready, right now. But she wants to study this, and study that, and fuck knows what else, and that's grand, but – where's it all going? What's she going to do with all these degrees? Getting an education's fine and all, but what's the point if ye can't make any fucking money out of it?"

"Over-intellectualisation," Dermot's mouth twisted awkwardly around the word, "that's what it is. I mean, I went to uni for a bit, but....fuck that. What's the point? Every cunt on the street's got a degree now anyway. You just end up in debt, with no job, and fuck all to show for it after four years."

"This is it" Sean said grimly. "I'll support her in whatever she wants, because that's what you do, right? But it doesn't make sense to me. If your education can't get you any work, then what was the point of it all?"

"Exactly" Dermot agreed. "That's how I see it. You know, the funny thing is, when my old man gave me those horrible fucking jobs on his sites – that was when I dropped out of uni. I hated that shit, but – I suppose he was doing me a favour, getting me paid to do shit that didn't need doing. He'd never give me anything for nothing, that just isn't his nature. Or mine; I wouldn't take anything he'd offered, if he'd offered anything. But now I think about it, I suppose he was helping me, in his own way."

"I never really knew your dad" Sean offered. "I mean, I remember him, a bit, from when you lot would come back for a holiday, and that. But everyone speaks highly of him around here. You know, any brother of Tim's – we're family, after all."

"Family" echoed Dermot. The two men drank again, the glasses floating light in their hands now.

"Roy!" Dermot bellowed, his heart shooting sparks in the cave of his chest, "couple more pints over here!"

12

Ua wm mopisls la ssxp ltqg comdioe?

Page after page, it went on, seemingly meaningless letters strung together in his father's bold, deliberate hand. There had to be some trick to it, he knew; it didn't look like any language spoken by any people on earth. It was a code. But his father was dead.

"What're ye lookin at?"

Dermot looked up from the red notebook in his lap. Michael stood unselfconsciously in front of him, peering at him from behind his round glasses.

"A book." Dermot had never been entirely comfortable around children.

"What kind of a book is it?" asked Michael.

"I don't know" Dermot replied honestly. "My father wrote it, but I can't read it."

"Why not?" Michael persisted. "Why can't you read it?"

"It's not in English" Dermot replied. "I think it's written in a secret code."

"Can I have a look?"

"I don't know" Dermot tried valiantly as the boy reached a hand – his father's short fingered, broad bladed hand, as yet unvarnished by weather or work – for the blushing book, "it's pretty complicated. Maybe it can't be solved, maybe only my father knew how to read it."

Michael sucked his lower lip, a sliver of white tooth gleaming in the summer light that lit the kitchen window with diffused glory and cut a sharp hot rectangle on the slate floor.

"It doesn't make any sense" he said to Dermot, peering at the thin red-skinned book.

"I know" said Dermot. "I've been asking people if they could help me, like your uncle Tim. He grew up with my father, so I hoped he might know something, but he couldn't make any sense of it. I'm starting to think I'll never be able to read it. It's probably nothing anyway."

"I bet I could crack that code" said Michael defiantly.

"Really?" said Dermot doubtfully. "And just how would you do that? You never met my father."

"I'm really good at puzzles. Just ask me ma." Dermot smiled.

"I'm sure you are," he said, "but this is tricky. Maybe there is no answer."

"I bet there is" said Michael. "And I bet I could find it. All ciphers have an answer if you know how to look."

"Ciphers? Where did you learn a word like that?" Michael rolled his eyes, as though he were dealing with an idiot.

"I told you, I'm good at puzzles. Look, I'll show you."

Half amused, half embarrassed, Dermot got up and followed the boy away from the fire. In the dark bedroom, a computer whirred into life. Within a few seconds, Michael was industriously clicking away.

"See? Look at this." Dermot stooped behind Michael, peering at the bright screen. "This website is all about cracking ciphers. It teaches you how to do it. We just need to find out what kind of a cipher it is."

"And how do we do that?"

"I dunno. I guess we have to try all the different ways there are of cracking them, and see which one works." Dermot frowned in the dark.

"How long will that take?"

"I dunno" repeated Michael. "Could take ages. Depends what kind of cipher it is. Looks like a polyalphabetic substitution. Those are the hardest to beat." Despite his scepticism, Dermot was impressed. Would he have been able to use a word like polyalphabetic at eleven? Maybe the kid really did know what he was talking about.

"Well," he said, sitting down heavily on the narrow bed, "it's not like I have anything better to do."

- and then the blood was pounding war drums in his ears as he hunched over the book, tracing his finger along the table, switching one letter for another as he pieced together his father's words, hoping against all reason that the last sentence, the last letter, the last word might give him something to cling to so that his life could go on as it had been before.

The fire drew grotesque shapes on the ceiling and floor, more shadow than light. Dermot slumped back in the chair, alone in the deserted kitchen in the dark watches of the night. He drew his hands over his face, covering his eyes, too late.

It's not proper to think these things about your own wife. But when the baby she now carries is born, will I really see my own flesh and blood? Or will a stranger laugh at me from the back of the child's eyes?

13

The wind whipped across the bare back of the ridge.

For five thousand years, it bent the short grass and shook the vanishing trees. The torches dwindled, and went out. Sheep grazed on the ridge, even on the tomb itself. Slowly, they too disappeared. The tomb sat silent and dark, its entrance sealed by earth and stone that cracked in the cold nights. No one came.

The grass grew. The trees fell. The people lived still in the valley, but the ancestors were lost to them. They forgot the other world, they forgot where the wind blew from. The tomb was a threat to them, brooding high on its lonely ridge, a place of ghosts and devils.

The grass grew. The trees fell. For the first time in centuries, a procession came up the hill. In the grey light of day, unsinging, unmourning, men with shovels slung across their broad shoulders struggled in single file against the wind. Towards the tomb.

Peeling back the turf like skin, they dug into the bare chalk of the walls. Shovel by shovel, the tomb slowly shrank, until the waiting darkness of thousands of years opened right at the workmen's feet, and the sun descended into the underworld.

The bones of the ancestors were examined and removed, without honour, without song. Their weapons, their charms and treasures were taken from them, their long sleep in the earth's cold womb cut short by the shovel blades.

The tomb, once emptied, was rebuilt, its walls and roof carelessly backfilled. A new entrance was cut behind the massive scored stone that once sealed the door shut. The mystery was anyone's now.

The grass grew. The trees fell.

"Hello? Helloooo? You see, there's no one around. No auld skeletons or goblins of any kind. Sure who'd be about on a night like this but ourselves?"

"God almighty, I can't see a thing."

"Watch yerself there, there's a puddle."

"Do ye not have a light at all?"

A blue spark echoed in the impenetrable darkness. The storm howled outside, the rain driven diagonally into the soft ground. She put out an invisible hand; felt the wet chill of an invisible stone wall; invisibly recoiled.

The blue spark flashed again. One more flash, and it found the lighter's gas, a tiny orange flame bobbing uncertainly in his thick hand. The halo of light crept out to the walls, reflected dully by the slick, sweating stones. She could see his face, glowing orange and deeply shadowed against a background of concentrated black, the eternal subterranean night. He was peering around at the darkness, a boyish smile on his boyish face, his blue eyes shining with excitement. Two tiny orange flames flickered in his pupils.

"What is this place? It's hardly drier than outside."

"Come in out of the door, then. It'll be drier at the back."

The light held in front, he moved slowly into the darkness. She had no choice but to follow the weak glow.

"That's enough now, Tom. It's as dry here as it'll get."

"Do ye not want to know how far this passage goes?"

"No, I do not. I don't care what this place is or who built it, or why, I just want to get out of here as soon as the rain lets up a bit. What are ye doin?"

"Takin a look around, of course. Where's your sense of adventure?"

"Oh, Tom, don't. There's sure to be all sorts of auld bones and things lyin around. Don't disturb them."

"Sure what harm can they do to us now? Besides, there's nothing here. The bones are all in museums, behind glass cases. And a few auld ghosts won't grudge us a bit of shelter on a night like this."

"There's a terrible draught" she said, pulling her damp coat tight under her chin.

"Come in out of the wind, then. There's a door just here, and a little room we can sit in. Come on now, it's as snug as ye could want."

He spread his own coat on the large flat stone that almost filled the small side chamber. Rummaging in the shapeless brown bag he brought, he produced a couple of candles. They sputtered in the damp air before the wicks caught, and the pointed flames swelled upwards. The dim light grew a little, enclosing them both in its warm halo, illuminating the stone walls and roof of the chamber.

"Candles? If I didn't think ye incapable of it, I'd've thought ye planned this all along."

Sucking the tip of his thumb where he had burned himself on the candle flame, he sat down heavily beside her.

"There now, isn't that better? Cosy, isn't it?" He put his arm around her, and she leaned against his shoulder.

"How old do ye think this place is?" she said softly, her eyes half closed.

"Oh, thousands of years, I should think" he said airily. "Funny, isn't it, to think of the people who built this place, all that time ago. And all the people who've come and gone since then, with their own troubles, their own stories, that we'll never know. And now there's the two of us here, one more story added to this place; our own little story that no one'll ever know." He bent his neck to kiss her hair. She smiled and pressed against him a little more.

"Doesn't sound like that storm's about to stop any time soon" he said, looking up at the low stone ceiling as if he could see through the earth to the streaming sky outside. "We might be here a while." An idea, never far from his thoughts, had floated back into view.

"I guess it's not such a bad auld place after all" she sighed.

"D'ye think, Mary" he began, a roguish smile lighting his features from within even as they glowed in the candlelight from without, "d'ye think –"

"Oh, I can guess what's on your mind alright, ye auld goat" she snapped. "Me mother was right about you, Tom. Ye've an incurably filthy mind." But her smile belied her.

"Come on now, Mary. Isn't this romantic?"

"An auld tomb from pagan days?"

"The candles, the storm..."

"Mouldy bones, cold rocks..."

"You, and me, keeping each other warm..."

"I'll catch me death of cold..."

"No one around for miles. We could be the last two people on earth, with the sky howling with rain outside, and us all safe and warm."

"If we'd the whole world to choose from, we'd not be in here, I'll tell ye that."

"Ye've no poetry in your soul" he mumbled in her ear, his hand slipping deftly inside her blouse.

"Ye've no brains in your head" she smiled, but she didn't stop him from kissing her neck.

"You're beautiful, Mary" he whispered, running his hand down her body inside her clothes.

"Oh, is that right?" she smiled, her pupils widening with the onset of pleasure. He nodded against her bare shoulder, shifting his weight against her, pushing her down onto the flat rock. Closing her eyes, she surrendered to the moment.

The grass grew. The trees fell.

The wind whipped across the bare back of the ridge.

Maybe that's really how it was. Probably not. But this is the cross I build for myself, night after night when my love is far away and the wolves circle the house. This crown of horns. It's not proper to think these things about your own wife. But when the baby she now carries is born, will I really see my own flesh and blood? Or will a stranger laugh at me from the back of the child's eyes?

See? There's something going on here – do you see? As though the ghost of my father were peering over my shoulder, scrawling notes in my blood. Work it out on your fingers. It doesn't quite add up. I'm hardly the most reliable witness, but believe me; I know what actually happened and what didn't. You can always tell the unreal from the real; the imagination never quite gets the lighting right. Think of the ambient sunless glow of dreams. Like those theologians who argue the historical fact of the Resurrection by pointing out that if it was a lie, they would never have claimed it was first seen only by women, because they were not considered reliable witnesses. The visions don't prove the falsehood of my story; my story proves the truth of the visions.

I'll fight. I'll go down fighting. And I will go down. That's what we do. We fight, even when fighting can only make things worse. I'd rather lose than win their way, be left lobotomized, sanitised, empty and drained and smelling of disinfectant, like school after the kids have all gone home.

They've got nothing on me; that's what they don't realise. They can't fucking touch me, because they don't understand who I am. They have no idea of what I've become, the razor flash of savage joy, the knives of blood in my veins, the desperate howl at the back of my eyes. I watch the world burn every day beneath the pitiless sun. I am the Son, my Father's Son. No one comes to my Father except through me.[31]

My fists turn to steel and scrape sparks down the wall. They can give me all the drugs they want, it won't make any difference. Drugs treat sickness, and I'm not sick. I am uniquely, horribly healthy, boiling over with life and with understanding.[32]

A metal wheel is turning inside my head, the agony of near-enlightenment. This is the price, Grace, and I've known it since I was fifteen.[33] Your first pain, if it hurts enough, will teach you that there is a

---

[31] John 14:6. Dermot falls back here on the imagery of his Catholic upbringing, and it is interesting to see himself identifying with Christ, the Son of the Father; Christ is resurrected through intense suffering, and presumably Dermot hopes for something similar himself. It is also interesting to note that when Jesus hung in agony on the cross, his father was nowhere to be seen.

[32] Dermot's psychosis is clearly apparent here as he rails against invisible, unnamed persecutors who wish to cure him of a condition he refuses to acknowledge as a sickness. Even so might the rabid dog speak to those who come to euthanize it.

[33] Presumably this refers to Dermot's first psychotic episode; this is well within the median age range of the onset of schizophrenia. It is also typically the age in which individuals in primary cultures may undergo the 'shamanic experience'; a profound schizophrenic crisis which enables the chosen individual to communicate with the

world out there known only to madmen and saints. Strait is the gate. They tell me that this, too, is a symptom of my 'condition'; delusions of grandeur, a messianic complex. What's Latin for bullshit?

There's courage here that they miss, and maybe that's not surprising. We live in a world that celebrates self-preservation, where bravery is a symptom of madness. But this is my desperate bravery, my feral courage: to bear this agony upon myself, the agony of the ape sprouting wings for the first time, exposed to the hatred and scorn of his peers. I'm bringing messages from the mountain. Blood never comes out.

---

powers of the unseen world that underlies the world we see each day. This is universal, experienced in primitive cultures throughout the world, and in it we may see the raw beginnings of religion and human spirituality. However, in such cultures, the aim is not to 'cure' the sufferer of his symptoms. The task of the older shaman is to help the youth to adapt to what is seen as his destiny, his sacred calling. The shaman is one who journeys in the other world and brings back gifts of insight and healing to his tribe, his culture; his psychological crisis becomes the means by which he is able to provide guidance and spiritual protection to the members of his society. The shaman's position in society is one of honour and respect; often, his psychological breakdown is seen as a kind of death, from which, however, he returns with a deeper understanding of the mystical. Clearly, Dermot often thought of his own madness in much the same way, for all the suffering it brought him. And while the modern methods of analysis and pharmaceutical treatment did little to re-orient him as a productive member of his own society, the obscure signposts of ancient myths did seem to offer him some sense of direction in the twilit Otherworld he had fallen into. Perhaps there is a wisdom there that our technocratic age needs to relearn.

14

"Are you sure?"

A handful of grass spun dizzily in the river's silver flood.

"I'm not sure of anything" Dermot replied, the fluid music echoing his voice, its eddies and waves readily becoming sound, as though he could, with practice, learn a hidden language from this water and this land, another code to be broken that might reveal even worse secrets. Innocence never feels like innocence until it's lost, a gigantic hieroglyph scratched into the dirt of a windswept plain that can only be seen from a distance unattainable to the long-dead artists themselves.

"Maybe you got the translation wrong" Fiona offered. Dermot shook his head.

"There's no way" he said solemnly, his eyes unfocusing slowly as he stared into the rock-spiked bed of the river. "Without getting too technical, it – it just couldn't happen. If I translated the code wrong, it would be gibberish. It would never come out as actual words that made sense, but were different to the original. It's impossible.[34]"

"But maybe – like you said, maybe it's just a novel. A story."

All the birds were singing, the trees and the hedgerows alive with them. If singing is really the right word. It's just the noise they make, the voices they're born with. Translate that code, and all you'll hear is desperate pleas for sex, howls of pain, screams of rage and hunger. It's a wonder ornithologists can get out of bed each morning.

"Maybe it is. But – I really hope it is. But it doesn't read that way. At the start, all the business with the tomb, yeah, he's telling a

---

[34] The nature of the code supports this claim. But I stop short of endorsing the more supernatural aspects of Dermot's story.

story, even if it's true. But the whole – I mean, why use my mum's real name? Who would do that?"

"Maybe it was just convenient?" she suggested. Dermot scowled at the grass.

"I read *Lolita*[35] too" he said. "That didn't wash there, and it doesn't here."

Everything looked harsh in this light. He hardly dared look at Fiona; with the world around them burning in this blinding yellow glow, her pale skin and golden hair would be an unendurable nimbus[36] of light, too bright for human eyes to bear.[37]

"I just have to know" he murmured. "I have to find out. And I'm hoping that as I translate more of the book, it will all be explained, and it will all be a joke, and everything will be back the way it was. But however it turns out, I have to know."

"So how did you crack the code? You still haven't told me." The closest thing Fiona dared to a change of subject.

Dermot tugged again at the springy grass.

"Oh, Michael did most of the work. He's really good at it. I was never that precocious as a kid. Or I don't think so. It's hard to remember that far back." He smiled self-deprecatingly – a pale, ghostly thing. But it was a start.

"So how did the code work? I love a good mystery" Fiona persisted.

"Well, it's...never mind. It's gonna sound weird."

"Oh, come on!" she protested. "You can't say something like that and then not share it! Come on, out with it."

"You won't laugh, or think I'm crazy?"

---

[35] Novel by Vladimir Nabokov. Those familiar with this masterpiece will recall the episode Dermot refers to here, in which a pervert attempts to pass off the discovered chronicle of his monstrous lust as 'notes for a novel I'm writing'. The excuse is a flimsy one.

[36] Defined in my dog-eared dictionary as "the halo or cloud of light that surrounds the heads of divinities, saints and sovereigns"; the reader may decide which is applicable here.

[37] This kind of sensory overload is a common experience among schizophrenic patients, especially at the beginning of a psychotic episode.

"That depends on what you say. I promise nothing."

"OK, fine. The code works by swapping each letter for another, but what letter you replace it with is determined by a keyword. With the keyword, cracking the code is simple, though time-consuming.[38] Without it, it's almost impossible. Michael tells me there are ways to find out the keyword, but he's too young to really understand them, and I'm too stupid. The thing is, I guessed the keyword."

"How?" Fiona prompted, drawn in by his dramatic pause.

"It came to me in a dream" he stared at the grass, and then at her. "My father told it to me."

"Your father? You mean -?"

"Yeah" Dermot said quietly, his eyes sinking from her face again.

"I can't believe this, Grace. I can't believe you'd do this to me." Grace shrugged her slender shoulders.

"Come on, lighten up" she smiled. "It's not that big a deal if you don't make it one."

"Not a big deal? Maybe not to you. But Owen's in love with you, you know that?" Grace smiled, and shrugged again.

The floor felt sticky under Dermot's feet, as though the linoleum was melting and pooling around his bare toes. He walked into his father's kitchen, but the ceiling towered above him like a cathedral, huge arched windows glowing with a grey light along one wall. His

---

[38] The Viginere cipher makes use of a table containing the letters A-Z along the top. The next line down starts at B and goes through to A. The third starts at C and ends with B, and so on, until there are twenty-six lines containing all the letters of the alphabet, with both the top horizontal and the vertical axes reading from A through to Z. The text to be encrypted is transcribed one letter at a time according to a predetermined keyword; for instance, if one wishes to encrypt the letter J using the letter M as the key, one would simply find the letter J along the top axis, find M on the vertical axis, and find the letter where a horizontal line from M would meet a vertical one from J – in this case, V. This is indeed very time-consuming, even where the key is known.

father leaned on the counter, his arms folded, talking with Mr Wallace, Dermot's old English teacher.

"Dad," Dermot said, but his father didn't seem to hear him. He went on chatting with Mr Wallace, who gave Dermot only a cursory glance.

"Dad," Dermot tried again, more urgently, "Grace slept with Owen, and now he's in love with her. But she doesn't care about him, or me."

Mr Wallace grinned broadly as he turned to Dermot.

"Well, as long as she's getting a good hard cock to suck each day, why would she care whose it is?"

Dermot swung his whole weight behind the punch he landed on Mr Wallace's cheek, but the teacher just laughed louder. Dermot punched him again, and again, and slowly Mr Wallace's knees buckled, and slowly he sank to the ground with Dermot on top of him, punching for all he was worth, but the laughter went on filling his ears.

The light changed. Dermot was outside now, and it was grey and gloomy, though he didn't feel cold. There was grass beneath his feet now. He was in the graveyard, the ancient resting place of his family.

"Why are we here?" Dermot asked his father. Something about the place that he couldn't put his finger on made him feel uneasy. "Dad, we shouldn't be here."

Without a word, his father pointed to a clean, blank headstone. One name, or word, was carved in huge letters across its sheer surface: MIOTAS.

"Miotas? Who's that? What does it mean?" Dermot asked, but his father gave no answer. Somehow, though, Dermot knew that he was terribly sad about something.

Like icy water injected into his veins, Dermot remembered why being in the graveyard felt so wrong.

"Dad?" he said. "You're dead, Dad."[39]

---

[39] I have elected to use a lighter coloured font to represent another of Dermot's idiosyncratic tricks. The reader will have noticed his tendency to refer to his visual hallucinations as 'visions'; Dermot always wrote this word in a bold, jagged sort of handwriting, as though he had gone over the text multiple times with his pen. The above dream passage, along with several others, was written in the same way. The effect is striking; these passages describe those

The sound of his own voice woke him up.[40]

"Miotas" Dermot repeated. "That was the keyword. No idea who or what it is, but–"

"Myth. It means myth" Fiona said.

"Myth? Really?"

"Yes, really" Fiona gently mocked. "It's Irish."

"Myth?" Dermot mused. "But why?"

"Isn't it obvious?" Fiona smiled excitedly. "It's not true, Dermot. Your father was your father, and this book is just that; just a story, just a myth."

"Do you think so?" he asked.

"Yes. Of course. Don't you?"

Dermot thought for a moment. Another handful of grass span in the water at his feet.

"If it's not true" he said finally, "why write it? And in code, too. All this effort to hide something that's not true just seems a bit ...pointless. Like Alex said, what's the point of writing a novel in code? And – myth? A myth's not quite the same as a lie, is it?"[41]

---

things which Dermot himself seems to doubt the reality of. If it is written in this way, Dermot seems to be saying, it isn't real.

[40] I have never found dream analysis to be a particularly helpful method in the treatment of schizophrenia. Besides, a dream this direct needs no explanation. Far be it from me to accuse my subject of lying; but this seems to me rather too narrative, too linear, too cinematic to really be a faithful recounting of the actual images experienced in the schizophrenic brain. My own dreams are rarely this cohesive.

[41] Far from it. Myths, according to Joseph Campbell, the great mythologist of the twentieth century, are "the interface between what is known and what is never to be discovered, because it's a mystery transcendent of all human research. The source of life. What is it? No one knows." As a student of Celtic history, much of which comes to us cloaked in the trappings of legend and myth, Fiona ought to have known better than to equate myths with lies. Some lies are truer than most so-called truths.

"No, not quite" Fiona conceded. "But a myth isn't a literal story of what happened, either. Even primitive cultures often understand that their own myths are just symbols."

"Symbols? But if this is a symbol, what's it a symbol of?"

He abruptly turned his head to the darkness of the trees. Fiona followed his gaze.

"What's wrong?" she asked. Dermot blinked.

"Oh. Nothing' he said. "Just thought I saw something."[42]

"It all leads to here" Dermot went on after a while. "My father grew up here, and he was buried here, and even though most of his life was spent abroad, it's this place he came back to. And brought me back to. And if he really does want me to figure this all out, if he really is out there somewhere watching over me, then this is where he wants me to be. But why?" Abruptly he smiled.

"Sorry" he said. "I'm not superstitious usually. I don't even believe in ghosts – I don't think I do, anyway. I'm sure there's probably some psychological explanation for that dream. Maybe I heard that word when I was a kid, and it lodged in my subconscious somewhere, and[43] – "

"You really don't know where you are, do you?" Fiona smiled, clasping her knees to her chest. "This land is full of ghosts. Can't you hear them?"

She tilted her head to one side, as though she really were listening for the watery echoes of history. Dermot said nothing. He didn't want to listen. He knew if he did, he'd hear more than a few impotent ghosts.

---

[42] Visual hallucinations now. Dermot's illness is worsening.

[43] Spare us the pitiful grasping of the amateur psychologist. Psychology, I sometimes think, is rather like dancing; many people think they do it well, but very few have any real aptitude for it. A few episodes of *The Sopranos* and a Cole's notes on Freud does not a psychiatrist make.

The stars riot in the torn battlefield of the sky, light upon light.

"Do you love her?"

A million tiny candles burning in a field of absolute black.

"I don't know. That's hard. What does that mean? I don't necessarily believe that we are put on this earth to be with someone. You meet someone, you like them; maybe you fall out later. I don't know."

The longer you look, the more you see, dim light appearing right in front of your eyes where before there was only the freezing void.

"Do you love my cousin?"

"I'm marrying him."

Movement in his peripheral vision; a streak of light from a falling star, so fast he hardly believes it happened.

"That's not an answer."

Each light a star, each star a sun, a billion potential worlds out there, distances so vast that anything becomes possible.

And yet the faint blue light is strangely sterile.

"I can't leave Sean. I..."

The light from our own sun is eight minutes old
by the time it reaches us. Those dim stars just at
the edge of vision, hundreds of light years away –
when was their light born? Who walked the hills and
forests of this land when this light, this one, here, was
born in the heart of a nuclear furnace?

"I mean – this is what it is. I – we… I don't regret
what just happened."

This is why the tombs were built, up on the
hills in the frosty dawn of history; the earthly
echo of the remote universe up above, home
of the gods and the dead.

"Nor do I."

"But this isn't, real, you know? It's just
something in a story, a dream that we'll wake
up from some day and go back to the real world."

How many of the stars he sees, here,
tonight, still exist?
How many of them are ghosts?

"OK. I understand, Fiona. I'll
take whatever I can get of you.
I'd never do anything to hurt you."

The infinite refractions of solitude; the impossible
vastness of the
darkness between worlds.

"It's nice, here, though, isn't it? Under the stars.
All those potential worlds out there. Maybe, in
some other time or place or universe, we might
have met first, and been very happy. D'you think?"

But the distance leaves him cold. Stars
exist only insofar as they are looked at.
His own stars lost in her night-hidden eyes.

15

Understand, Grace, that I never would have chosen this. I know we never promised each other anything, we never spoke about forever – but come on. We're both too proud to admit what we mean to each other, but I was happy with you. I was. I knew you were unfaithful[44], but I didn't care – that's not true. I told you I didn't mind because I know it's not your choice, any more than this madness is mine. It's a compulsion, a curve of the brain, a tiny black bubble in each of our hearts. And I put up with it because I'd rather share you than have nothing at all.

Understand, Grace, that I'm not mad. Really, I'm not. I understand. This war is mine, and I never asked you to fight in it. I never wanted you to. I took those pills to protect you from it, as well as myself. But you can't run forever. I wasn't myself on those pills. I was happy, but it wasn't me being happy. I was hiding for a while, hiding from the heavy debt of history, the sufferings my ancestors endured just to bequeath me this eternal war. This is who I am, not the dull mannequin you saw leaving for work every morning, coming home every evening. This is the real me, dancing on the needlepoint between genius and madness. This is me, in this cell, drunk with rage and loss, trapped in this concrete circus tent where men howl like frightened animals as their souls fry in the electric light. This is the real me, an ape

---

[44] Another thing Dermot never spoke about. Of course, I met Grace several times during the course of Dermot's treatment. A beautiful young woman, by any standard; but the care and attention she showed him in that time was truly moving. Dermot was not always as easy to be around as his writing would suggest.

with angel wings, mining the hollows of Hell for the secrets demons guard.

Understand, Grace, that it's nothing to do with you. When you came to visit me yesterday, and I didn't say anything the whole time you were here[45] – please understand, it's not because I'm angry at you, or because I don't want to see you. But sometimes I'll be like that, the days when I'm losing the battle, and it takes everything I've got to stay afloat, not to drown in the blood-black ocean in my head. There were days, weeks, like that, before the pills, before I met you[46] – that's what I was running from, but that time is over. The pills make life possible, but I'd rather lose this fight than continue to avoid it. This is what I was born for, and I can't run from it any longer. If I have to die to be who I am, then that's what I'll do.

Understand one thing, Grace, if nothing else, because this is important. This is not an illness, it's a journey. For all the horror of the visions, for all the misery and pain, there are moments of glory so powerful and pure that they make the miserable ninety-nine per cent a price i'm willing to pay. There are moments when the walls drop away, the earth stops spinning, the whole Copernican universe slows down and stops like an old watch someone forgot to wind, and I dance in the space between atoms, a part of all things, and all things a part of me, the inner and outer worlds reconciled and inverted, and there is no more time. Understand this, Grace, please understand this, because this is the secret I bring back from the Otherworld, the leprechaun's gold, the fire of Prometheus – I am everything. Pick up a stone and I am there. I am in every trembling leaf, and in the wind that makes them shiver. I move in you and through you as you do through me. Understand this, because I may not make it back. It's one thing to find the treasure in the depths; it's another to make it back to the surface alive.[47]

---

[45] See?

[46] Those glimpses of his past again, like trying to piece together Irish history from the legends of Cuchulainn or the Fenians – but let's not get ahead of ourselves. Dermot is more than a little guilty of his own obstructive myth-making.

[47] This from a letter written to Grace, but never sent.

16

"So are ye making any headway with your father's book at all?" Bridgid, leaning across the table to heap mashed potatoes from a huge white bowl onto Michael's plate, turned brightly to Dermot. His mouth full of half-chewed bacon, it took Dermot a moment to answer.

"Getting there" he said, and swallowed. "It's slow work, having to translate each letter one at a time. But it's like anything else; the more you do it, the faster you get at it."

"So what's it all about?" asked Patrick from across the table. "Was he writing a story, or what?"

"I don't really understand it myself" Dermot replied, stretching out a hand towards a bowl full of peas. "Some parts of it are about him, his own life, like a diary, and then sometimes it's about ancient tombs, and archaeology, and things like that. I'm not sure he had any clear intention in writing all this stuff himself. I haven't got all that far into it yet, so maybe it all makes sense further on, I don't know." He felt he was babbling a little, hiding in plain sight.[48] Fiona had stood up to go to the bathroom, and his eyes followed her around the table, past Sean, who reached out to her as she went by, trailing an arm along her waist. As though his cousin's hand was his own, synaptic reflexes meshed by the mystery of blood, he could feel the rough fabric of her jeans, the sudden ridge of a pocket, the jealous scar of a seam clinging to the soft flesh beneath. With every mouthful of food he could taste her; with the lunatic clarity of recent memory, he could see her splayed out before him, the graceful arch of her legs guiding him as he moved triumphantly through her; her honey-coloured hair pooling messily around her head as she thrashed, senseless, in her own private hollow of bliss. The tiny whimper in her throat that he had just

---

[48] I can vouch for Dermot's skill at this.

learned; the flush in her cheeks that only he noticed when he sent her back to play the good little wife-in-training to his cornuted cousin. On such things as this does man's ego feed.[49]

"And it was young Michael who figured it out?" said Patrick around a mouthful of vegetables, his broad face grinning with pride.

"That's right" said Dermot, looking over at his young cousin. Michael picked at his peas as though unaware he was the topic of conversation. "I think I wouldn't even have tried to decode my father's book if it wasn't for him. I didn't even know it was a code, let alone how to crack it, until he showed me."

"Ah, he's a grand one for stuff like that" Bridgid beamed. "Aren't you, Michael?" The boy shrugged without looking up, humiliated by excessive praise. "From the age of five he always had an answer for you. Smart as a whip, that boy."

"Didn't he fix the hoover for you that time, Bridgid? What was he then, six?" Patrick asked rhetorically, rehashing the family legends for Dermot's benefit.

"That's right, he did" Bridgid nodded. "Took the whole thing apart, and had it back together and running like a song an hour later. Sure, I still don't know how he did it."

"Ma," Sean cut in, chuckling in anticipation, "do you remember the time when he fell off the fence and cut his leg? Didn't he start into telling you about gangrene and tetanus and what have you, and himself barely nine years old?" Sean always spoke cheerfully; it was what he was good at. Sadness didn't suit him. At the funeral, Dermot remembered, Sean's pious expression had fitted him even worse than his cheap suit. This was his kingdom, the world he was born into; the eldest son fearless at his father's table, the prince of all he surveyed.

Patrick and Bridgid had almost the same laugh in a different key, Dermot thought; does marriage make two people one flesh so much that they start to become identical? Or is it that people look for in their spouse what they most like in themselves?[50]

"That's right" Bridgid giggled. "A rare old lecture he gave me, the little professor with his knees all torn and bleeding. That's where

---

[49] It is not for the therapist to make moral judgments; I leave that to the audience.

[50] Given his family history, we may forgive Dermot a little cynicism regarding the institution of marriage.

you got that scar on your knee, love, d'ye remember?" Michael nodded emphatically, glancing briefly at his mother before returning his attention to his plate.

The light in the room seemed to dim, great wings blocking the sun. Dermot sawed mechanically at a piece of bacon, staring from under lowered brows as Fiona re-entered the room, light and distance seeming to stretch before her as she advanced, like celluloid blackening and curling away from a naked flame. He watched her hips circling the table, her pelvis an easily-imagined golden bowl beneath her jeans, coming towards him, towards him, towards the invisible straining fibres of his lust-racked body. She sat beside him again, and he felt the weight of her on his lap, the angle of her descent in the pit of his stomach; he almost sobbed at the agonising little wiggle she made as she adjusted herself in her seat. At this distance, he could watch her with his eyes closed, the billion cells of his bright blood absorbing every twitch, every tremor, every breath of her body as though he had created her himself.[51]

"And then there's that other one, that scar on your shoulder, isn't there?" Bridgid went on. "D'ye remember how you got that one?" Michael looked up, shaking his head, finally seeming interested in the conversation. "That was from when ye were about three years old, and ye went for a ride on the donkey up at Tim's, and ye fell off onto the road. Ye scraped your shoulder so badly, but we were just glad ye didn't land on your head. As a matter of fact, ye did bump your head; there's a scar there too, just a little one, but ye can't see it through the hair." Bridgid fell silent, gazing at her son, lost in the bittersweet orbit of a mother's memories.

Dermot glanced over at Fiona. Something in the way she didn't look at him told him she knew he was watching. Her cheeks coloured. He suddenly felt cold, and far from home. No one knows me like that, he realised. No one on earth knows things about me that I don't. The parts of my life that I don't remember are gone as though they never existed, as though I was born five years old at the moment of my earliest memory. There's no one to sing the story of my scars. No one, not even the most fervent and greedy lover, will ever know me like that.

Patrick cleared his throat.

"Dermot, will ye pass me the peas?"

---

51 ǀ

17

The wind ruffled the grass on the banks of the river. It swept along the shallow valley, rippling grey water and green grass. It howled like a hound around the palisade, a thorny crown on the summit of the hill.

Finn slitted his eyes against the wind, his golden hair around his head like a sun in storm. The dogs whined and strained at their chains. Night was coming on.

"You know we've been here nine nights now?" Donn's eyes dark under dark brows. Finn let the wind answer.

"Isn't it true that you are bound not to stay here for ten nights?" Donn pressed. Finn turned to him.

"You know that it is" he answered. One of the dogs yawned and scratched himself in the dying light. Another licked his lips noisily. "But where would you have us go?"

"I know a place" and Donn's dark features brightened, "The house of Angus, son of the Dagda. My son is being raised there." Finn sucked his teeth. Angus, the Son of the Young. He was no stranger to Angus, or to his eerie palace. Angus had tried to cheat him once before in a sporting contest, a hunt, and his own son lay dead as a result, killed by Finn's warriors. But night was coming on.

"Fair enough" he said. "Take us there, Donn." Donn smiled his assent. As his back turned to his leader, Finn loosened his sword.

The wind whipped across the bare back of the ridge. Dogs and men climbed wearily up the hill, the night thick around them, a black wall pressing against the halo of light from the torches they carried. Donn went in front, torch held aloft to light the ground before him, his favourite dog straining at its leash as it sniffed some faint scent in the short grass. Finn came behind.

Up on the ridge, the mound of the sidhe waited.

The sidhe dominated the valley. Sullenly it sulked under heavy skies, grey with menace. It blazed like a beacon in the sun, a white flame on the ridge, both promise and warning. Beneath the moon it shone a pale answer back at the sky, the ancestors and the gods reflecting one another in the night.

Its dull white walls went blank in the light of the torches.

Donn stopped, his dog cringing now at his feet. Finn drew level with him. The vast white mound sat like a tomb before them, dead as the stars above.

"Where is everyone?" Donn wondered aloud.

"Welcome, Donn son of Duibhne" came a voice from the darkness. "You keep exalted company." Finn turned, his hand already on his sword. Angus stepped forward into the small ring of red light. A head taller even than the tall men of Finn's household, he towered over the small company, his eyes shining brightly in his fair, beardless face. A supercilious smile played on his thin lips.

"The great Finn mac Coul" he said, inclining his head slightly in acknowledgement.

"Angus mac Oc" Finn replied.

"A pleasure to meet you once again" Angus beamed. "Please, you will join me in my humble abode for a feast?" As he spoke, Angus stretched out a long arm, towards a dark entrance in the wall of white stone that no one, not even the dogs, had noticed a moment before. Torches burned in brackets on either side of the doorway; shadows flickered on the triskelia carved on the massive stone lintel; but no light seemed able to penetrate the forbidding darkness of that silent doorway.

The dogs whined, the hairs bristling along their spines. A low murmur rose from some of Finn's companions. Only Donn seemed unperturbed.

"I've never been known to refuse the offer of a feast yet, Angus" Finn replied. His host's smile deepened as Finn, without even a torch, disappeared into the primordial darkness of the mound, dragging his reluctant dogs behind him. He was lost to the view of his men almost instantly.

Clutching torches and swords and dogs, the others followed their leader into the mound.

"Welcome" Angus said again, arms flung out to encompass the hall they found themselves in, "welcome to Brugh na Boinne." To those who had never entered the sidhe before, the contrast was intoxicating. From the menace of the haunted mound outside, a dark monolith glowering in the ancient night, they found themselves, once inside, in a huge hall, big enough for any king at Tara. Torchlight flickered on the walls; warm fires burned in wide hearths on either side of the great oak table, large enough to seat a hundred men at once. Angus stood at the head of the table, Finn at his right side, the steward of his hall at his left. The steward was a thin man, past the prime of his years, his hair grey and thinning above his angular face, though he stood tall beside his tall master. There was music in the hall, and women furnishing the table with all kinds of meat and ale for the tired warriors. Their confusion quickly changing to joy and laughter, Finn's men set to the meal with hardly less ferocity than their dogs.

From the raised dais at the head of the table, Finn looked out across the hall. Two young boys played together among the feasting men and women, one fair, the other dark. The women fussed over them whenever they passed, first one then the other, so that all took them to be brothers.

"Tell me, Angus," said Finn, "who are those children who play together as brothers in your hall, though they do not look alike?"

Angus smiled deeply.

"Those boys, O Finn," he replied, "are my foster sons, and the pride of my household. The handsome dark-haired boy is Diarmuid, son of Donn, warrior of the Fianna. The other is the son of Roc Diocain, the steward of this hall."

"This is your son, Donn?" Finn asked of his companion.

"Indeed it is," grinned Donn, "and have you ever seen a finer boy than him?"

"'Tis a shame, though" one of Finn's men mumbled from across the table. Donn started in his seat.

"A shame? What shame?" he cried.

"Why, that the son of yourself, a leader of the Fianna, should be rolling around on the floor with the whelp of a commoner."

A ripple of laughter rose from the men at the table. Finn watched Donn's face redden as the blood rushed to the roots of his dark hair. But he said nothing.

Pipes and fiddles blazed; men sang and laughed; the fires leapt in the hearths. The more the men ate, the more the women of Angus' household brought to the table, until there was hardly a warrior who had not taken more than his fill, and still the table was full.

Finn's dogs growled beneath the table. Full himself, he idly took a shank of meat from the table and threw it to the floor. A great barking and growling broke out as two of Finn's prize hounds began to fight over the morsel. Snapping and howling, they tore through the hall, scattering the children and the serving maids, while the men leapt out of their chairs to pull the dogs off one another.

But no sooner were the dogs separated and restrained then another great howl, this time all too human, was heard from the far end of the hall. Roc Diocain, Angus' steward, crouched at the side of the table, his face wet with tears and his arms dripping with blood, the mangled remains of his son in his arms.

"My son!" he cried, "my son! He is dead! He is dead, and it was the hounds of Finn that slew him!" The men of the Fianna stood around the table like so many trees. Hunting, fighting, feasting; this was what they knew. A father's inconsolable grief was beyond their field of experience.

"How am I to be satisfied?" wept the steward. "He was my only son." Finn looked over to the two panting dogs, chained and held apart by two of his huntsmen, their fur torn and their muzzles bloody.

"Find the mark of tooth or claw on your son," said Finn, "and I will answer for my hounds. I will give you what satisfaction is in my power."

A buzz rose around the table at his words. Women of Angus' household came forward, and gently, irresistibly, took the body of the child from the distraught steward. Poring over the body, probing the bloody mess of the child while the entire hall held its breath, finally, one of them rose, looked at Finn, and shook her head.

"You see?" Finn spoke to the steward. "It is not my hounds that are guilty of the child's death."

"Then who is?" cried the steward. "Who did this thing to me? They say, Finn, that you have the power of divination. Tell me, then, who visited this woe upon me?"

Finn stared into the eyes of the steward, and saw only terror and desolation in them. So he called for a chessboard and a gold basin full of water to be brought to him. Angus nodded his assent, and the serving women hurried to attend to him.

Finn sat down with the chessboard and the basin. He could feel them watching him, the eyes of Angus and his servants and those of his own men fixed on him, waiting for judgement. He felt especially the wild, red-rimmed eyes of the steward upon him. But he put them out of his mind, retreated to the place behind his eyes where there was calm, and true judgement. Washing his hands in the basin, he traced droplets of water with his finger on the orderly squares of the chessboard, letting his hand move of its own accord, trying not to think about what he was doing. Silver lines seemed to glow between the droplets of water his hand left on the neat pattern of squares, linking them together in a sequence of events.

He saw Donn's dark eyes beneath dark brows.

He heard the laughter of the men of the Fianna.

He saw the two children fly from the fury of his own hounds.

He saw the fair-haired boy, the steward's son, run in terror under the table, hiding between a warrior's thick legs.

He saw Donn's dark eyes.

He saw Donn bring his knees together, the child between them.

He saw Donn grit his teeth, place his hands on his thighs to apply more pressure.

He heard the child scream as his bones began to crack.

He saw Donn's dark eyes.

The pattern faded.

"Who, Finn? Who killed my boy?"

Finn looked up from the board. He met the steward's frenzied gaze.

"Your son is dead, and no vengeance will return him to you" he said. "I myself will pay a blood-fine for your loss." Roc Diocain shook his head.

"No" he said, "no, no, no. No fine could be half as heavy as the loss I have suffered tonight. All the riches of kings would not repay me for the death of my only son. Finn, you know who did this thing. Tell me. That is the fine I demand of you; the knowledge of my son's murderer."

Finn sighed.

"Donn, son of Duibhne of the Fianna" he said finally. "Donn killed your son."

The steward laughed madly.

"Donn?" he cried. "But how perfect! I could not be so easily revenged on any man as I may be on Donn. Here is his son, Diarmuid, childhood friend of my own dead child. Put him under my knife, and if I allow him to live, you will know that I forgive my son's death."

Angus sprang up from his seat. "Foul traitor!" he cried. "Serpent! I loved your son like my own, and your loss is no more grievous than mine. Now you would threaten the life of my other foster-son, Diarmuid. This is how my love is rewarded!"

Meanwhile, Donn sprang up from his seat and leapt over the table towards the steward, his hand on his sword. But before he could

90

reach the steward, Finn leapt before him and seized his arm, and others of his men sprang forward to restrain Donn.

The steward picked up his son's body once more, and wept. Softly now he spoke, to the broken body of the boy.

"I put you under bonds to bring Diarmuid O'Duidhne to his death; you shall not die before him, nor shall your life be longer than his." The company fell silent at the whispered malice in his incantation. From the body of the boy, it seemed to some nearby, a shadow rose, and charged like a wild boar to the door of the hall, and out into the darkness of the night.

18

The view from this ruthlessly clean hospital window is sometimes quite spectacular. For instance, I can see, from here, that there were certain consolations to our fugitive affair, the delicious torments of illicit love.

It was the weekend. Sean was home from work, and the day was glorious, the fields burning green under a sky so blue it was as though there were no such thing as clouds or night. The sun burned as though it could never go out. [52]

Dermot sat in a shady corner of Bridgid's kitchen, reading the Clare Champion[53], pretending to care about the hurling[54]. You understand the sports you grow up with, and that's it, he thinks, and then a flare goes up in his veins, every hair of his body and cell of his skin straining towards the door, because Fiona just walked into the room, and the sun dimmed as though ashamed.

---

[52] Another of Dermot's bizarre shifts in narrative perspective. It is possible, in fact, that he came to feel himself a different person when he was hospitalized; that the Dermot who wandered the fields in Ireland was not the same man who occupied a bed in our facility. This is schizophrenia writ large, of course; but we may ourselves have had a similar feeling. Time changes us all, and trauma changes us even faster; how many of us have never felt that the person we were a decade ago is an utterly different individual to the one who stares out from the mirror today?

[53] A local newspaper. Sometimes the most offhand details yield rich clues to the patient researcher.

[54] See note 122.

She and Sean were heading out to the beach. She was wearing sandals, a green tank top and denim miniskirt over her bikini. Sean was still in their bedroom; Fiona and Dermot were the only ones in the room.

He didn't precisely look at her; she didn't exactly look at him. You might almost have thought they were strangers, but for the wild charge that entered the room with her, the feedback of two people devouring each other's presence through every sense *but* sight.

Her long legs even longer under that short skirt, she stalked towards the couch, hardly bending her knees as she walked, her hips rolling from side to side like a ship in a gale. Smoothing her skirt behind her, she sat on the sofa, facing Dermot.

The paper rustled in his hands.

She crossed her legs.

Every shredded nerve in his body took in the long muscle of her thigh as it swelled out from under the skirt that slid towards her pelvis. He could feel his tongue in the groove between muscles, could taste the slight sheen of sweat that sprang out on her skin in the fierce sunlight that transfigured her porcelaneous complexion.

She pretended not to notice.

He moved the paper fractionally lower, his eyes drawn desperately over the top of the quivering page.

She was wearing sunglasses, looking up at the sky through the window, looking anywhere but at him.

She stretched like a cat in the sun, and her breasts strained against her top, the outline of her bathing suit clearly visible under the thin fabric. The air hummed.

Sean walked in, and the spell was broken. They left, a happy, smiling young couple in the warm bosom of summer, and Dermot was left alone with a photographic memory and a sterile bathroom. Torture, oh, torture! The heat would have been too great, the strain too much for an already fragile mind to bear, were it not for the certain knowledge that soon, maybe that very night, his trembling hands and eager tongue would roam just as ardently as his eyes had done over the immaculate topography of her body.

19

My breath stinks from refusing food.[55]
Here I sit, Grace, a thinning silhouette in the spears of moonlight,
gazing from a gloomy window out at a broken silver world.
They're coming for me, with buckets of drugs to suck the thoughts
from my head, leave my brain crumbling like leaf mould in a rainless
autumn.
They're coming for me with plates of food, steaming dollops of death
and gristle on plastic trays, stinking up the hallways as they come.
They're coming for me with starched white breasts and quivering
nurse-quims, nubile girl-things in squeaky flat shoes.

---

[55] The course of Dermot's illness was typical in this one regard: it
was not a simple progression from illness to health. From the
fearful near-mute I admitted to the hospital under police escort,
Dermot progressed to become something like he must once have
been: thoughtful, intelligent, even humorous on occasion. But there
were many setbacks along the way; the road to healing is often a
convoluted one, with many pitfalls and stumbling blocks. Dermot
battled continually with depression. At one point, he did indeed
start refusing food. Although this may have been a rather half-
hearted suicide attempt, I believe there may have been some other,
rather more obscure motivation behind it – perhaps a wish to
transcend the mundane physicality of the mortal body. In our
sessions together, he had hinted at something like this, the fasting
of various mystics and shamans in order to produce a visionary
state from which one can survey the next world. As mentioned, he
read voraciously.

They're coming for me with diagnoses and prognoses and neuroses and psychoses, waiting for me to slip, to tempt me back to a world where nothing means anything, where everything has a price.
It's just this, Grace, just this: there is no one in this sphere of being, not one person on this rag of filth, who wouldn't sell me to my enemies for a bottle of cheap wine and a few glass trinkets.

20

"How much for the lager there?" Sean pointed a stubby finger towards a rectangular box on a low shelf behind the cashier.

"22 Euro" the man behind the counter said.

"22 Euro? Jaysus, are the cans made of gold?"

The cashier stared blankly at Sean. Dermot smiled; he was getting used to Sean's bluntness.

"Tell you what," Sean went on, "I'll give you twenty for it."

The cashier shook his head uncertainly.

"The sticker says twenty-two..." he mumbled.

"And I say twenty, and if you want more than that, the fucking sticker can buy it. Look, we've cash on us, right now. Do ye want to sell the thing or not?"

The cashier shrugged.

"Fair enough" he sighed, and heaved the case onto the counter.

Outside, Dermot lifted the beer into the trunk of Sean's car.

"I can't believe he went for that" he grinned.

"Ah, fuck it" said Sean, lighting a cigarette. "If ye don't ask, ye don't get, right? Robbin' bastard was charging way over the odds anyway; he's lucky I gave him twenty for it."

"That would never work in England" said Dermot, slamming the trunk shut. "Or Canada, for that matter."

Sean started the car, and Dermot swung himself into the passenger seat.

"So what's the plan?" he asked.

"Well now" said Sean between drags, " we've the crate in the back, so I say we go drink these in a hedge somewhere, then take a wander down into the town and see what kind of trouble we can get ourselves into."

"Sounds good" said Dermot. "Where will we leave the car?"

"Wherever" Sean shrugged. "We'll just park it up in a field somewhere, and we can come back for it tomorrow."

Dermot shook his head at the novelty of it all. No traffic regulations, no tickets, no thieves, none of the things that he had to think about in the city when he planned a night out; just fields and cows and people you'd known your whole life.

"Alright" he said, still smiling, "let's do it."

The wind whistled in the leaves of the few trees around them, but the shoulder of the hill protected the two men from the cold air from the sea. The grey shapes of gulls dotted the sky beyond, almost hovering in the swirling currents of air above the rocky bay that lay just out of sight on the other side of the empty fields. They perched on the hood of the car, a growing pile of empty and half-crushed cans at their feet. The cackling gremlins of intoxication were just beginning to gather in the corners of Dermot's drink-dulled mind.

"Tis not a bad ould place, when you look at it" Sean said, and drank from the can he held.

"There's a lot worse out there, that's for sure" said Dermot, and drank from the can he held.

"I mean, Dublin's fine and all, but do ye really want to spend the rest of your life in a place like that? The crime, the pollution; the price of a fucking house – god, you wouldn't believe it! I could buy thirty acres, with a house, down here for what a fucking one bedroom flat costs up there."

"Tell me about it" Dermot sniffed. "I mean, I'm a city boy, always have been. But – there's a lot I envy about people who live out here. I mean – like this, here. We can just park up in a field, get plastered, and no one's going to bother us. We can leave the car all night, and nothing'll happen to it. In the city, you can't do shit without someone giving you grief, or wanting some money off you, or something." He drank.

"Tis a better way of life out here" Sean said, staring out over the hill. "That's what it is. When I was a kid, you know, Michael's age, or a bit older, I couldn't fucking wait to get out of here and see the world. But then you get out, and see what's out there, and you realise there's nothing out there better than this. Just more chaos, more people getting in each other's way, more crooks looking to rob you blind. What's the point living in a city where you could drop dead tomorrow and no one would ever know it?" He drank.

"So are you thinking of moving back here permanently, then?" Dermot asked, his voice devoid of any kind of feeling. He drank.

"Dunno" Sean shrugged, and drank. "Maybe. It seems like the right time for it; I've got a bit of business going on down here now that might turn out to be worth a bit." He drank.

"Oh yeah?" Dermot asked, and drank. Sean nodded.

"Putting in a quote to do the landscaping on the big golf course there" he said. "We're down to the last three companies in the running. If we get it, it's going to double the size of the company in one go. Then we'll be getting somewhere. I can move operations down here, buy a place, really get things going." He drank.

"Nice" Dermot said. "Sounds great." He drank.

"Well, we'll see" Sean said. "Lot of things have to happen between now and then." He drank.

Dermot crushed his can and dropped it among the others.

"Another one?" he said as he made his way to the trunk. Sean crushed the can he was holding.

"Ah sure go on then" he said.

"So how does Fiona feel about moving here?" Dermot asked, handing his cousin a can before taking his seat on the front of the car. Sean smiled bitterly.

"Wish I knew" he said over the crack and hiss of the beer being opened. "She likes it, as a bit of a break, but she likes Dublin too. You know, she talks about going back to uni and getting another degree – another one." He drank.

"She's more of a city girl?" Dermot asked, and drank.

"She grew up in the country, same as me" Sean replied. "Well, maybe not exactly the same. In Offaly, in a town with about 2000 people in it. So it's the country, but not as much as out here. Anyway, she didn't much care for it. Hates going home, when she has to. Still, that's women, isn't it? Never met one who liked the place she came from." He drank.

Dermot thought about Grace, who never talked about her past, her childhood. He didn't know the name of the place she came from; up the coast somewhere, he was pretty sure. It didn't matter; the little she said, and the volumes she didn't say, were enough. In three years he had never seen her call her parents – her adoptive parents, that is. As for her biological parents – he didn't think she even knew them[56]. His demons were a matter of public knowledge, but she kept him away from hers.

"Yeah" he said, and drank.

"So these two lads go out golfing" Sean said abruptly. "And they decide to have a pint at every hole, so after they play eighteen holes, they're pretty tight, right? So then they decide to go to the brothel and get some girls, you know? So they go down there, and the woman there – the one who runs the brothel, the madam, is it?"

"Madam, yeah" said Dermot, and drank.

"Right, the madam. So your wan sees them coming, and she says to the other girls, 'Look how fucking wasted they are. We'll give them a couple of blow-up dolls; sure they won't know the difference.' So that's what they do. So the lads go into the rooms, you know, and ride the arse off these dolls, and have a grand old time. Then, the next day, the one lad says to the other, 'So how was the ride last night?' And he says, 'Ah, it was shite. I was pounding away there, and she just lay still, not moving, not saying a thing. What about yours?' And the first lad says, 'I think I had a witch.' Second lad says, 'Fuck do you mean, a witch?' First lad says, 'Well, we were getting down to it, you know, and I bit her on the arse, and she farted and flew out of the window.'" Sean drank as Dermot broke out laughing.

"I like that" he said, and drank.

"Tried that one out on the owner of that golf course" Sean said, and drank.

"Did you? How did that go over?" Dermot asked, and drank.

"Well, there he is, with his Bentley and his fucking staff and all the rest of it, right? And I can't be bothered with all that shite. Everyone calling him 'sir' and all the rest of it. So I just went up to him, shook his hand, looked him straight in the eye and told him that one. Thought he was going to piss himself, the silly old fart. Think that joke's

---

[56] Interesting. How I would have loved to have a good long talk with Grace. I'm sure a conversation with her would have shed much light on Dermot's personality, as well as her being a fascinating character in her own right. Alas, I never got the chance. Although I met her on several occasions, she never seemed entirely at ease around me.

the reason I'm in the last three. If we get the contract, I'll have to have that tattooed on me arse or something."

They drank.

"Ye know they had a race along these cliffs a few weeks ago? Oh yeah. Blindfold race, it was" Sean said.

"A blindfold race?" Dermot said incredulously. "You mean the runners were blindfolded?" He drank.

"'Sright, yeah" Sean replied, and drank. "All along the cliffs out there."

"Isn't that a bit dangerous?" asked Dermot, and drank.

"Ah no, sure they were careful enough, like" said Sean, and drank. "They each had a guide with them."

Dermot drank, and said nothing.

They drank.

21

As she walked into the flag-stoned room, leaving faint moist prints of her progress as she came, she saw Dermot stretched out on the couch near the fire, an arm slung across his face, his breathing slow and regular. She turned, heading back towards the TV room she had just left, when she heard him shift on the couch.

"Hi" he breathed.

"Hello. I thought you were taking a nap" Fiona smiled, padding back towards him.

"No" he sighed, dragging himself into a sitting position. He looked bad. Unshaven, wearing a ragged white t shirt and torn jeans, his eyes bloodshot and heavy.

"What's wrong?" she asked, denting the seat beside him and stretching a warm hand towards his forehead. "Are you sick or something?"

"No" he mumbled. "Just...depressed, that's all."

"About what?"

Sometimes it gets like this[57]. His body a waste, a useless vessel half filled with cold water, reflecting in its still surface the winter outline of a skeletal tree against a low grey sky. His mind drifting like a cloud weighed down with rain, aimless, floating on the shoulders of buffeting winds high above a barren landscape. No thoughts, no fears, no hopes; just this dull ache like a gulf in his senses, like walking into a

---

[57] The vast majority of schizophrenics suffer at least one bout of depression in the course of their illness; it is this depression, in part, that makes the disease so deadly. Dermot seems very familiar here with the mechanisms of his own melancholy. Suicide is a sad fact of life for sufferers from this cruel illness.

totally dark room and knowing simply by a change in the spatial quality of the black void around you that a chasm has opened up in front of your feet.

"Nothing." And he laughed, a dry sound like a twig snapping. "Everything. I don't know. There's things I could pin it on. My father just died. Then I find out he maybe wasn't my father. So now I'm here, and I can't go home, and I don't know what I'm doing ...you know." That laugh again; a sound that made something wild in her want to run. "But that's not it. Or maybe it is. But all these things were true last week, too, and I didn't feel like this. That's the nature of depression, I suppose."

"Do you suffer from depression?" she asked.

"I don't know. Doesn't everyone?"

"I mean clinically, though. I know you were on medication for – the other thing; I just wondered if you were on antidepressants too."

"I've tried them.[58] They don't seem to make any difference. Nothing does." He sighed again. "I'm sorry. I don't mean to bring you down. Really, it's not that bad. It happens sometimes, that's all. I've been through a lot worse."

Fiona sniffed as she stood and walked to the window.

"Well, you picked a good day for it, anyway" she said, her breath misting slightly on the cool glass. Outside, the sky poured, hanging damp and heavy above the roof of the farmhouse. Grey mist huddled in the fields, an impenetrable blank curtain between them and the river that, on a clear day, sparkled just outside the kitchen window. Everything is sealed off from everything else in this murk. On a summer's day, anyone can see anything, the horizon wide and clear; but as soon as the rain starts to fall, we[59] are all alone again.

Fiona turned back to face him.

"So what's the story? Have you learned anything more from your father's notes?" He could see her gaze fall across the red notebook he had left on the floor by the couch, along with the untidy mass of his own scrawled translations.

---

[58] Dr McCullough confirms that Dermot was briefly prescribed Zoloft along with his antipsychotics, but that the response was poor, and the treatment was quickly discontinued.

[59] Another characteristic shift in narrative perspective. The 'we' Dermot refers to here is vague; the whole of humanity, perhaps?

"Nothing" he said. "He hasn't mentioned anything since, about himself or my mother or...anything. It's just some story about a man killing another man's son because he didn't like people treating him the same as his own son" and his voice slowed as he spoke, because it was only when he summarized the story for someone else that he realised exactly what had happened in the sidhe at Brugh na Boinne, and there was still no answer, no explanation, but there was at least something that looked like a clue.

"Really?" Fiona gave no sign of having seen what he saw, a faint sheen as of something metallic in an otherwise lightless room. "Do you think he was just writing a story? Like a novel?"

"No" Dermot answered, trying not to look at the window yet hardly able to look anywhere else, like trying not to laugh at a funeral. "We talked about this before. Why would he write it in code? And the bit at the start, that's about my mother, no question. But now it's like he's completely dropped the subject, to go off on this tangent about – I don't know what. I just hope this isn't the whole thing. I don't even know if I'll learn anything more when I translate the whole book. Maybe I'll be right back where I started."

"Maybe" she said, sitting down beside him again. "Maybe you'll never learn anything more than you already know. But you're not going to give up trying to find out, are you?"

He could feel her looking at him, the way on a summer's day you can tell where the sun is with your eyes closed. He didn't want to look at her. He knew that if he did, the conversation would become something else, something between them, and therefore about Them, instead of his, alone.

He looked at the floor.

He looked at the notebook.

He looked at the fire.

He looked at her bare foot on the slate floor, her toenails pink with old varnish.

He looked at her.

Her blue eyes, the sun on the sea somewhere out west beyond Ireland's perpetual rain clouds, in her pale face with that perfect, perfect skin, soft and smooth and freakishly free of any sign of flaws or faults, and her hair like liquid gold even in this gloom, a light just behind –

She swung her leg over his and, straddling him, sat in his lap, fiddling with his shirt.

"So you know that Sean's out working, right?" she said, her eyes on his chest now, not on his.

He nodded dumbly.

"And you know that Bridgid's out in the town, and she took Michael with her, and the two of them won't be back for at least a couple of hours?"

He nodded again.

"So you know that we've the house to ourselves, for the first time, and for all we know, the last time we ever will?"

He nodded once more; this game has its rules.

"Now. I'm going to ask you something, and I want you to think carefully before you answer, right?"

An obscure smile lifted the corners of her mouth.

Her jeans stretched tight around her, straining where they bifurcated, an excruciating inch above him.

Her warm weight in his lap, pressing down softly, irresistibly, the rising desire burning a bright hot hole in the gloom that surrounded him -

"Is there anything I can do to cheer you up?"

The night was clearer, stars peeking out like flecks of white gold in the bed of a stream, tattered clouds rolling quickly by like great grey fish in the silent pool. Bridgid and Patrick slept, this night another in an innumerable haze of duty and habit. Michael slept, his head burning with the vivid dreams of children that he wouldn't remember to miss five years from now. Presumably, Fiona slept soundly in her fiancé's arms.

Dermot paced the cold stone floor.

Across the river, through the dark trees, he could see something. Something he knew was there. Up at Tim's cottage, there was a dull red light. And the biggest grey cloud in the sky curled above it like a question mark.

Fumbling for his shoes, Dermot opened the door to the damp wind, and headed for the road.

He stumbled slightly on the cattle grid at the top of Patrick and Bridgid's driveway, as he always did. The road was as silent and dark as it always was, a strip of very dark grey, once your eyes adjusted to the gloom, between the absolute pitch of the hedgerows on either side.

Dermot walked quickly up the hill.

He crossed the bridge, and he knew, there was no cloud, there was no light, only smoke and fire, coming from Tim's cottage. The damp asphalt slipped under his feet. He started to run.

The blood was pounding in his ears by the time he reached the top of the hill and turned down the pitch-black pathway behind the cottage. The white walls glowed dully in the dark. He could hear his own breathing, impossibly loud in a silence that had only the crackling noise of burning to underline it.

He skidded around the corner, and the heat of the fire rolled around him, and a huge black shape stood between him and it.

"Tim?" he panted.

"Dermot" his uncle replied.

The windows of the cottage flickered like cat's eyes in the firelight. There were no lights on that he could see. Tim stood like a rock before the bonfire that raged next to the stone wall in front of the house.

"Wha – what's going on? What are you burning?" Dermot gasped.

"Rubbish." Tim spat into the swirling depths of the fire.

"But it's after midnight! Why are you burning it now?"

Tim said nothing for a while. The fire moaned.

"'Tis the law" he finally said. "European regulations[60]. Can't burn a thing now; all has to be recycled. They've planes up in the air to catch ye doing it. They can see ye from miles away."

Dermot sat on the wall and paused to catch his breath. He was sure his uncle knew his business, this business he had been born into. But a learned Anglo-Saxon sense of logic refused to shut up.

"You don't think," he said finally, "that a raging bonfire would be easier to spot at night? I saw it from Bridgid's place."

Finally Tim turned to him. His face in the firelight was red wrinkles on one side, darkness on the other. His eyes were deep pools of shadow. He said nothing.

Dermot waited.

Abruptly, the wrinkles rose and split and formed new crevasses. Dermot realised the old man was smiling.

"Ah," Tim said, "sure what government man would still be working at this hour?"

---

[60] I have no way of ascertaining if this is true or not.

22

I wear my body like armour in this tomb of lost souls, stalking the halls like the ghost of a god. There is no salvation for me in these endless talks with the doctor; they only leave him more confused, sending him back to the textbooks, scratching his head. The drugs don't work[61]. I can't sleep, I don't eat, I shit three times a day, and nothing they give me can help. I see dark shapes scuttling down the corridors in the half-light, faces peering in at the windows, every keyhole calling my name. Yesterday, in the cafeteria, it was all skeletons. Everyone I looked at, it was as though I had x-ray vision; all I could see was bones. Skeletons forming an orderly line for their food, being dished out by a skeleton in an apron; those huge, empty sockets staring blandly at me as I recoiled in horror. The demons, the monsters; these are not hallucinations, these are the truth of a different world. "Delusions are simply... ideas believed by the patient but not by other people in his/her culture"[62] – I live in a sick society, but when I disagree with its motives and aims, it decides I am the one who is sick, and I am stripped of my rights and sent here. Sorry, Grace; I'm not mad at you. You did the right thing.

The drugs do nothing. The therapy does nothing. The other patients actively hinder me, bothering me with their blank stares, their empty eyes, their meaningless questions and endless small talk. If I get

---

[61] Easily said. Certainly, Dermot's illness resisted pharmaceutical treatment. But without the drugs, perhaps he might have suffered even greater agonies. Let's not get bogged down with hypothetica.

[62] From *Surviving Schizophrenia*, E. Fuller Torrey, 1983. As previously stated, Dermot was quite well read, and was clearly familiar with at least some of the literature on his condition.

anything at all out of this not-entirely-voluntary stay in the laughing academy, it is this: time. I need time – that's all I need. Something is growing within me, putting down roots, absorbing pieces of me the way a tree absorbs what it needs from the soil it finds itself in, nourished by the rot of the past. I just need time to bring it forth, time and silence, and I'll grow in the dark. If I had been born two thousand years ago, with my visions, I would have been a shaman, a druid, a holy man. My 'illness' would have been a gift, to my people if not to myself. To them, the things I see would have been real: invisible to those not chosen, perhaps, but very real. I would be one who walks half in the next world, instead of a source of shame and a burden on society. Assuming, of course, that I would have this condition at all, if I lived in a society ordered along more rational lines than this prison of tangled steel we find ourselves in, crushed by numbers and wealth[63].

Sorry, Grace. I know you don't want to hear this shit; I know it's just madness to you. But I'm on the edge of something, I know I am; I can't pretend that I'm getting better, if by better you mean further from revelation. I don't want to get better. I'd rather die in this terrifying, beautiful place, home of demons and angels, where beauty and pain run together in the ecstatic harmony of all being, than live in a world where you're just a number, and the number's never enough.

---

[63] Sometimes, Dermot seems to have a rather romanticized view of the pre-industrial era. The history of schizophrenia is littered with the corpses of its abused and misunderstood victims.

23

"Tim doesn't mind at all. And to be honest, I think he could maybe use my help around the place. You know, for as long as I'm here."

"Well if that's what ye want. Y'know, Dermot, we just thought you might be comfortable here, with the family and all."

"Of course, Bridgid. It's been great staying here. But with Sean and Fiona here now, and the kids[64] coming back from school, you could use the room. I'll be here every day anyway. It's just up the road."

"Young Michael's taken quite the shine to ye."

"He's a great kid. But I'll see him all the time. And he can always come up to see me at his great uncle's house."

"Well, if you're set on it. Fair enough, I suppose. But will ye at least come down for your dinner of an evening? I'll set a place for ye, same as before."

"Alright. Yeah, I'd like that."

"But that's not all there is to it?"

Dermot sniffed, his nostrils stung by salt air.

"No, it's not. There's just too much noise in that house – I mean, normally it would be alright, but lately – well, I've talked enough about

---

[64] Bridgid and Patrick's other children. Curiously, they are rarely mentioned, except here. I have not been able to find out how many there were, or their ages. But given that Sean is close in age to Dermot himself, perhaps late twenties, and Michael is only eleven, we may surmise that there could be quite a few other cousins that do not enter into this tale. Dermot seems to have preferred atmosphere to details.

my psychological problems. I don't think I'm going to have a relapse, but I'm starting to feel like I need some quiet, some space around me."

Fiona nodded, one hand near her face, unsuccessfully trying to restrain her streaming hair. She was the only person he could really talk to, but he couldn't tell her everything, either. Yes, the clamour of Bridgid's house played on his nerves. Yes, the scrutiny, the questioning glances, the unspoken accusations oppressed him. Yes, the cosy family dynamic he felt himself outside of made him feel more alone than he could ever be by himself. But that wasn't all. Watching her play house with his cousin while she still smelled of illicit sex sent creepers of envy, guilt, and demon lust stretching along the length of his veins, reaching blackly to choke his heart.

"I love the sea" Fiona said, her golden hair flailing in the foam-flecked wind that drove inland from the ocean.

"Me too" Dermot replied. "It's one of the reasons I chose to live in Vancouver, to be near the sea. Just watching it for a while – it's soothing, you know? It is over there, anyway[65]. It's not so wild as it is here." He looked out to the faint blue horizon, over the heaving shoulders of water crowned with white foam, roaring towards the shore and crashing upon the grey sand. The family dog, Seamus, sniffed along the ocean's edge, the red fur of his belly and legs dripping with sea water. A boy stood in the surf to their left, flinging handfuls of mud at the water in a pantomime of futility. A few hundred yards further along the beach, a man and boy, presumably father and son, were engaged in flying a red kite that whirled and twisted in the buffeting airs, whipping this way and that as though trying to break free of its terrestrial tether and soar unchecked among the wild winds of the world. They walked on, the rocky grey sand barely shifting under their feet.

"It must be beautiful out there" Fiona sighed.

"Yeah, it is. I've lived there long enough that you'd think I'd be used to it, but thank God, it hasn't happened yet. I mean, I guess the newness has worn off – I don't go out to the park every week, the way I did when I first got there. But still, I'll be going about my business, you know, just sort of caught up in day-to-day life, and then you remember that there's all this beauty, all around, and it's enough to make your

---

[65] Sheltered by the large land mass of Vancouver Island, the ocean at the edge of the city is indeed very calm. But the Director of a busy hospital does not have much time for the beach any more.

heart hurt. I'll be going home at sunset on a clear day in summer, and the mountains start to glow, and all the trees on the slopes look like tiny towers of gold, and the lights on the peak start to shine out like stars as the light fades and the mountains gradually turn purple and fade into the night. It's a spectacular sight, it really is."

"It sounds wonderful" Fiona breathed. "You must miss it."

"I guess" Dermot said. "But it's like anywhere, really. It has its problems. Living in the city wears you down. It makes you hard and cold. There's too many people, too many faces, and everyone you meet you know you'll probably never see again, so it's hard to care about anyone else. I like city life, but it has its drawbacks. It's nice to come to a place like this for a change of pace. Where everyone knows you, and your father, and all your family."

"It's nice for a change, I suppose" Fiona said. "But it's claustrophobic. Sean's family are all great, but – that's all there is here. And even when you go into town, there's just a few old farmers sitting around in the bar talking about the weather. Everyone knows your business. And they talk. I grew up in a small town myself, and the gossip – you wouldn't believe it. There's nothing else to do, so the old women sit around drinking 'tay' and making up stories that they come to believe. Before you know it, the town's turned against someone, just because of boredom and a few meddling busybodies."

"Maybe" said Dermot. "But for all that, this is a beautiful place too. In a very different way to the way Vancouver is. Over there, it's all wild and epic, mountains and ocean and all that space, a city carved out of nowhere within living memory. Here, it's wild too, in its way. But it's more ordered, more – I don't know. Vancouver is wild because it's still so new, and untouched. Here, the fields are empty and bare, but it's from abandonment. This place has such history to it, and you can feel it all around you, but the people are all gone. It's weird."

Fiona smiled.

"You see? The ghosts – I told you! This land is full of them. They come rising out of the sea, out of the lakes and rivers and bogs. The ancient Gaels thought of bodies of water as sacred, paths to the Otherworld. In this place, it's not hard to see why."

"No, it's not" Dermot agreed, his gaze cast out across the shifting immensity of the ocean.

"Your girlfriend must be missing you."

Dermot smiled.

"Yeah, she does" he replied. "She thinks I'm wasting my time here, that I'll never know for certain whether there's anything to my dad's notes, and I should just forget it. Maybe she's right, but I can't do that. I guess that's where she and I differ. I mean, she was adopted anyway[66]. She's never had a feeling of belonging, so she doesn't know what this all means to me, and how it feels to be here. The way it feels like home, but unfamiliar, too. And what it means to think that maybe I don't belong here after all, that maybe my father isn't really my father, and these people aren't really my family."

They walked in silence a while across the sand, Seamus trotting reluctantly behind them.

"What about you?" Dermot asked. "Can you see yourself living here permanently?"

"I don't know" Fiona sighed. "I do like it here, for a change, like you say. But I don't know if I could handle living here all the time. I know that's what Sean wants. He's been out in the world, but I think he's seen enough. Now he wants to come back to his little piece of heaven here and start a family just like the one he grew up in."

"And that's not what you want?" Dermot asked.

"I don't know" Fiona said. "It's a nice place to raise kids, I can see that. And it would be good to have the family around to help out – I'm a great believer in that. But – there's still a lot I want to do with my life, you know? There's a whole world out there I haven't seen, and I'm still young. I don't think I could be like Bridgid. I couldn't live just for my kids in the middle of nowhere. Not yet. Maybe not ever."

"Have you said any of this to Sean?"

Fiona smiled ruefully.

"It hasn't really come up. I know what he wants, and I wish I wanted it too, I really do. He's hoping I'll fall in love with the place while I'm here. Every time we see a house up for sale, he starts talking about prices and mortgages and how much his father's land is worth. Like I say, he's seen as much of the world as he wants to, and now he's ready to settle down. He wouldn't understand that I'm not in the same position, and maybe never will be."

---

[66] Oh, for an hour or two with Grace on the couch! This ghost-woman, this troubled, hyper-sexualized mythic figure – what a study she might have made, had there been time!

The dull roar of the ocean washed away the silence that fell again between them. The sunlight broke like waves around them, the endless sky and the infinite ocean mirrors of each other, the eternal reflection of immortality in the midst of which they walked together, two dark points against the light like full stops..

24

Shadows climbed the thick walls of the cottage, writhing in the light of twisting flames. Stare long enough into the fire and you'll see anything, as though the ancient turf in the long slow life of the bog has stored its story within itself, only to be released by flame. Dermot thought of the rings in trees, the varves[67] in glaciers, the layers in ancient bogs he had studied years before in class, piecing together events from the faint echoes still remembered by the inanimate objects that witnessed them. Old men huddle in damp cottages, burning Irish history to keep warm.

Nothing moved in the cottage. There was no sound. Tim had no TV, no radio. He sat beside the fire, breathing slowly, the shadows of his face making it impossible to tell whether his eyes were open or closed. Dermot sat on a hard wooden chair drawn up before the fire, watching the flames. There was nothing else to look at, except the moving shadows. But he knew not to stare too long at those. Like the fire they sprang from, they too in time would start to form patterns and tell their own story. But it was not a story Dermot wanted to hear. At least the fire was warm.

"Ye look like yer father, ye know" said Tim suddenly. "I didn't really see it when ye first came here. But I do now. Though he was never as thin as yerself."

Dermot smiled. He knew he was a long way from fat, but no one in Vancouver would ever have described him, at this point in his life, as thin. It was different here. Men were supposed to be like Tim himself must have been, silent giants with hands like shovels and shoulders wider than a doorway. We live in a steadily diminishing

---

[67] A geological and archaeological term. Scraps of his education float to the surface from time to time.

world, dwarfs in a long line of giants, and those that come after us will not believe the stories we tell of the strength of our ancestors. These are years of wasting, the dotage of the West.

"It might be a strange thing to say, Tim, but I feel closer to him now than I have in years." The old man simply nodded, the sweet peat smoke from the fire softening his features where he sat by the hearth. There was no other light in the small room. The whiskey on the table and in Dermot's glass blazed orange, half fire itself, warming the insides as the flames warmed the outside.

Tim drank his whiskey from a heavy brown mug.

"The dead aren't gone" he said quietly. "We pour our blood and the sweat of our brow into this land. We give our lives to it. When we die, it takes us in like a lover, and gives back all we put into it. It's a cycle. Everything is.[68]"

---

[68] Perhaps so. Illness and health are simply words, two points along the continuum of what it means to be human. We are born, we grow, we get old, we die; in the interim, some of us go crazy, and others try to help. What is this life, this endless pantomime to an indifferent audience? From time to time, we might envy the simple life of an old farmer who has always known his place in the world. His stars are fixed, and guide him through a life not unlike that of his parents and grandparents; but for us, swept up in the tide of modernity, there is nothing to tell us how to live. The old belief systems are crumbling. This, in a nutshell, is Dermot's problem; but it is more profoundly the problem of his age. The old rituals and myths that told people how to live together in society are gone, and nothing has replaced them yet. And by getting bogged down in the metaphor, instead of focusing on that to which the metaphor refers, the 'great' religions have made themselves irrelevant. They no longer serve the functions of a healthy mythology: to guide members of a society through every stage of their life in a manner that is compatible with the aims and social mores of that society. Nor do they serve to direct people's thoughts beyond the temporal, towards the great transcendent mystery of living that has been called God, to reconcile the transient with the

Dermot sipped from his glass, feeling the eager liquid spread in his chest like the roots of a tree. The whiskey, the fire, the dark windows giving on to a blackness so absolute it could be the frigid end of the world, with all existence beyond the light of the flames fading into an endless nothing – anything was possible in such a world.

"When you took me to the graveyard that night," Dermot began, and watched a black beetle scurry across the stone floor[69], losing itself in the gloom near the wall, "when I drank from the well, I had a dream. About my father."

Tim didn't move. Dermot took another sip from his glass.

"He showed me – a codeword. He – did you know he was writing a book?"

Tim shook his head.

"Well, he was, but it was written in code. You remember that notebook I showed you, the one that looked like it was written in a foreign language? The one Owen found among some of Dad's things after he died? That's what it was. I was getting nowhere with it, but then I had the dream, and Dad gave me the codeword." He stopped, waiting on a reaction from Tim. He almost wanted disbelief, laughter, something to bring some sceptical daylight into the dark, smoky room. But Tim didn't laugh.

"What kind of a book is it?" he asked at last, as though making conversation, as though there was nothing strange in the story he had just heard.

"I don't know" replied Dermot. "It's all over the place. It starts off being about an ancient tomb, then there's this scene where this modern couple go there... but the woman has my mother's name, and then at the end there's this bit in the first person, where he wonders whether his wife was cheating on him, and whether the child she's pregnant with is even his. I mean, that's me, isn't it? But then it doesn't mention it again, as far as I can see. It takes another turn and starts telling another story, about old times again, feasts and men with swords and warriors murdering each other's sons."

---

eternal. Dermot finds more truth in the folklore of ancient Ireland than in the theology of the day; some of us are less fortunate, and have yet to find anything to believe in.

[69] See note 24.

Tim leaned forward in his creaking chair, the dim light catching his blue eyes beneath pure white eyebrows like water under ice in the depths of winter.

"D'ye remember the names of the warriors in the story at all?" he asked. Dermot's brow furrowed. Was the old man even listening to him?

"There was Angus, and Donn," Dermot began, looking into the golden depths of his drink. After the laborious, letter by letter transcription of the passage, he had read the story twice over, looking for some hidden meaning that he still hadn't found. Most of the characters were still fresh in his memory. "There was Finn – he was the leader of the warriors. There was the steward, Roc something. His son didn't have a name, I don't think, but the other boy was called Diarmud, or something."

"Dermot" said Tim.

"What?"

"No, the name. Tis the Irish spelling of your name, near enough. It's Deer-mwid, but you can pronounce it Dermot. Some do, anyway."

"Really?" Dermot sat forward, his chin in his hand, feeling the heat of the fire in his face. "I'm Diarmuid? I don't understand."

"It's an old story." Tim leaned back in his chair. "A thousand years old, or more. Finn and the Fenians.[70] Even as a boy, your father loved those stories. We all did."

"So it's not a novel" Dermot mumbled at the fire. "He wasn't making that part up. It's a myth. That was the codeword" he said

---

[70] Finn McCool and his band of warriors, the Fenians, are in many ways the Gaelic counterparts of King Arthur and the Knights of the Round Table. The stories surrounding them are legion, incorporating the remnants of Ireland's prehistoric belief system as well as the usual folk-tales and legends concerning place names; there is not a county in Ireland without some local landmark associated with Finn and his warriors. To what extent there was ever such a historical personage as Finn has kept scholars of antiquity in debate for many years. See Charles Squire, *Mythology of the Celtic People*, 1912; D. O'Hogain, *The Encyclopaedia of Irish Folklore, Legend, and Romance*, 1991.

suddenly, looking up at his uncle, "miotas. Fiona told me that means myth."

"It does, yes" Tim nodded.

"But what do you think, Tim? Is it – is it possible? My father giving me the code for his notes from beyond the grave?"

He heard the old man exhale heavily. A swell of smoke rose from the burning pile of turf and drifted lazily towards the chimney, blackened by centuries of use on thousands of firelit nights just like this one.

"When your father and meself were boys," he said slowly, "there was a farmer in the parish, away up the road there. He was rich, you know, compared to us anyway. Big shiny tractor he had, all to himself, that he used to rent out to the rest of us when we needed it. This was back in the thirties, mind you, when we barely saw a car on the road from one month to the next. That tractor was the envy of the parish.

'But the farmer had a son, who was a bit of an eejit, to tell the truth. One day he was driving the tractor, and he probably had a bit of drink on him too, because he put the thing in the ditch at the side of the field and rolled it over a wall. He was lucky he wasn't too far gone to jump clear in time, or the thing would have rolled over him, too.

'Well, his father was fit to be tied, with the tractor ruined and the wall smashed to boot. He had to repair the wall, and the gate that the son had destroyed, and he needed stone. Now, there's stone in these parts, you know, for those who'll work for it. But he wanted it quick, and he wanted it easy. So he went up on one of the hills round about, and he took a great big stone from an old ruin. The times were different back then, with no cars, no electricity, no radio. We all knew the old stories, about the Fenians, and the Tuatha.[71] They used to say those ruins up on the hills were the work of the little people in ancient times, and it wasn't wise to anger them. But he was a stubborn man, and a modern man, with his tractor and all. 'Whist your noise about Little People' he said, 'ye might scare children with your auld nonsense, but I'll take notice of fairies when I see one meself.' So he

---

[71] The Tuatha De Danaan, the pre-Christian deities of Ireland, dwindling in later tales to heroes or demons or fairies; the best known of these being the whimsical figure of the Irish Leprechaun, far removed in time and dignity from his original status.

took a great big stone from an auld tomb, and set it up in his field to hang a gate from it.

'Well, it was all fine til he came to drive the cattle through the gate from one field to the next. No matter what he did, he couldn't get a single cow to pass through that gate. The dogs nipped at their heels, and he beat them with a stick til the blood ran down their sides, but they wouldn't go through that gate. Twas a pity to see them there with their eyes all wide and sweating as though they stood before the gates of hell itself, not moving as the farmer cursed them and beat them every which way."

"So what did he do?" asked Dermot.

"What could he do? There was no moving the cattle past that stone, so he dug it up again and put it on the wagon and took it back up to where he got it from, up on the hill there, and he left a couple of coins there too, by way of an apology. Then he went and paid for some other stone, from a quarry, and set that up as a gatepost, and the cattle were fine after that."[72]

Tim leaned forward again, a half-halo from the fire glowing in his thin hair.

"What I'm saying to ye is, there's things that go on in the world that school won't teach ye about, and they won't talk about it on the television, but they go on all the same. I saw those cattle with my own eyes. Don't be too quick to say, this can happen, this can't happen, because there's not a man alive who's seen half of all there is in the world."

---

[72] Rural Ireland, and rural anywhere, for that matter, abounds in stories of this nature, or did so in the very recent past. What future such folk-fancies may have in a globalised world is uncertain.

25

"Are you serious?"

"I'm sorry, Grace."

"Sorry? Then why are you doing this?"

"It's…just what I feel I have to do."

"Bullshit. What are you going to do? Stay there forever?"

"I don't know. Just…I can't leave, not now. This is where I have to be right now."

"So you get what you want, and I get to go fuck myself?"

"This isn't what I want."

"That's a fucking lie. If you don't want to do this, then don't."

"It's not that simple."

"Yes it is, it always is. Did you meet someone over there?"

"No, of course not. That's…that's not what this is. I have to deal with this, here and now. I've been hiding for so long, hiding from who I really am, but I can't hide anymore."

"You're still hiding."

"What do you mean?"

"You're hiding behind phrases and bullshit psychobabble so you don't have to tell me why you want to leave me."

"That's not it at all.

Grace…ok. I don't want to
be taking pills the rest of
my life, waiting for the next
breakdown. I don't want to
live like an animal in a lab,
medicated to the point where
nothing means anything anymore,
and you just grind out the days as
you wait for your own destruction. I
want my life to mean something. I
want to know who I am, who I
really am, not the name on my
credit card statement or the
number on my tax return.
This is the only way I have a
shot at something more."

"That's what life was with me? Grinding
out the days?"

"No, Grace, I mean
…it's not you – "

"Don't fucking say it! Don't say it!"

"I just mean, it's not your
fault. I'm happy – I was
happy with you. There's
nothing else you could
have done."

"You think I'm stupid? I know it's not
my fault. Why would I think that it was?"

"You – you wouldn't.
You shouldn't. Just,
in case you did, I just
wanted to say…"

"It's your fault."

"What?"

"You're leaving me. You want out, and
you're such a coward, you tell me from five
thousand miles away. It's your fault."

"I understand that
you're mad – "

"Take your fucking understanding and choke
on it! You don't understand anything, you
self-obsessed asshole! If you understood anything,
you'd know that you need me now, if you're
really going through this profound thing you
say you are. If you understood the first thing about
me, you'd know that I'd be there till the bitter
fucking end, and the worse things got, the more
I'd want to stay."

                              "I don't doubt that. But
                               no one can help me
                          with this. The hallucinations
                           are coming back, and I'm
                             glad. I'm on the edge of a
                              cliff that I can't see the
                          bottom of, and I don't want
                           to take you down with me."

"Such an altruist."

                                         "Grace..."

"What?"

                                      "............."

"Three years, Dermot. Three fucking
years of my life I wasted on you, to have you
leave the country and never come back. No
explanation, nothing I can understand, just
fucking metaphors. This is how you come
to terms with who you are? By abandoning
the people who care about you?"

                "Look, Grace, I can't come back until this is over. That's
                    just the truth. And I don't know when that will be.
                Maybe next week, maybe never. But I know that when
                it is over, I won't be the person I was before. That's the
                    one thing I can be sure of. I can't ask you to wait,
                forever, for a guy that I know for a fact, whatever
                              happens, isn't coming back."

"..................-"

                                         "Grace?"

121

"... I loved that guy."

"He loved you too. What's left of him still does. Really, Grace, I wish I could have been a better man for you."

"Will I ever see you again? Or is this it?"

"I don't know. I don't know what to do. Everything's just so...fucked up, and I don't know where any of this is going to lead me."

"What about all your stuff?"

"I don't care. It's yours. Sell it, burn it, whatever. I'm just – tired of all this uncertainty. If I'm going to go crazy, I wish I could just get it over with."

"Listen, why don't you call me? Like next week sometime? I don't know what we'll have to say to each other, but when I think that this might be the last time we talk, I...I can't just switch it off. I'm gonna worry about you if I don't know what's happened to you."

"Ok. I'll call. I'm sorry, Grace."

"Don't."

"What?"

"Don't apologise. You'll make me cry again." [73]

---

[73] I have showed this passage to Grace, and she confirms that such a telephone conversation did take place between her and Dermot. While this is not a word for word transcription, it seems his memory for the details of this encounter was quite accurate.

26

The night hulked around the cottage, a thousand-eyed beast no door could keep out. It poured through windows, keyholes, cracks in the walls, pooling like ink on the doorstep. It padded silently across the flagstone floor, its breath unheard in the chimney above the cold ashes. It slipped into Tim's room, coiling around the old farmer where he slept on a narrow bed, his breathing slow and even in the place he had spent thirty thousand such nights. It crossed the living room, turned the corner, paused to blacken the primitive bathroom, and crept in to where Dermot lay awake listening to the scratching of rats in the attic, the darkness curling heavily on his chest like a cat.

The silence was stifling. He wanted to scream. He wanted to get up, run into the darkness, race around the cottage, anything to shake off this sense of impersonal gloom [74] that made him feel as though he were turning into stone in this ancient valley of stones. The faint breeze that ruffled the grass outside played in his hair. He could feel the frost nipping at his fingers and toes as it silvered the fields. The cold crack of the stones found its echo in his bones, and he shuddered with the land as it slipped into winter's grip,[75] the blood icing over in his veins while –

"Dermot!"

"Dermot!"

There was something there; he could see it with something more than sight, at the edge of the bed

The night has hands, fingers, teeth

it needs to feed

blood warming the soil it stains

"Dermot!"

---

[74] Classic schizoid neurosis.

[75] It is difficult to ascertain how factual this winter is, and how metaphorical. Grace is unaware how long Dermot had been in Vancouver before they found one another by chance; Dermot was unable or unwilling to give such details. Having no powers to check official immigration records, I can only say that Dermot left for Ireland on June 28th 2007, and was back in Vancouver by the start of March at the latest. It is therefore entirely possible that he spent

A tap at the single-paned window shattered the night into a thousand pieces.

His breath misted on the air and hung before him like a crystal curtain, mingling with hers as he swung back the door, letting the faint light of the stars into the wombic dark of the house.

For safety's sake, neither of them said a word. Their lips brushed blindly on the freezing doorstep, and he closed the door behind her.

Her hands were cold, raising a ridge of goosebumps along his bare back, but her body was warm inside her coat, and he pressed his hands to her sides where her ribs fluttered like the wings of a bird.

The bed groaned beneath them.

His mouth followed the hot paths of her burning blood, the veins of fire that pulsed against his searching lips, leading him on into warmer and warmer regions. He chased her heat, searching for the parts of her the night and the cold couldn't share. Her indrawn breath turned the night into fire, and the darkness became glass and melted like the long unraveling of years beyond count.

"So what was this, one last fuck to get it out of your system before you drop this bomb on me?"

"Jesus, Dermot, what did you think this was?" The hateful past tense. "This had to end."

"But why?" and he scowled invisibly at himself, the petulant child loud in his voice. She actually laughed, a little.

"I'm marrying your cousin, for God's sake! I should never have let things go so far, but now I'm putting an end to it."

"Let things get so far? You came up here tonight. I still smell of your sweat, and you want to tell me you *let* this happen? You *made* it happen!"

"Maybe." Her composure made him want to pull her hair out. He wished he could see her face. "We're both adults. No one pushed anyone into this. But I can't go on, creeping around like this. Someone's bound to find out; we've been lucky so far."

"Lucky." The word tasted like bile.

"It's got to stop."

---

fall and winter in Cloonashee; but there is no way to know for certain.

"Oh, now it has to stop. You weren't saying 'stop' five minutes ago when I was on top of you, but now it has to stop, now you've got what you want. You used me, Fiona."

"Don't say that."

"Then what would you call it?"

She said nothing, and he drew a long breath.

"And you tell me here, at night, so I can't see you, and Tim's in the next room, so I can't even raise my voice" he hissed. He felt her weight shift on the bed.

"How else was I supposed to tell you?" she whispered. "How much time alone could we spend together before someone figured it out? The night is the only time we can really talk[76]."

He sighed.

"I just didn't think you were that kind of girl."

"What does that mean?" she bristled.

"I thought you were better than that, that's all."

"Oh, for Christ's sake" she moaned. "When will you get it through that head of yours, I'm just a person? I'm not some mythic personification of Ireland, I'm not your bridge to an ancient past that never existed outside of some fireside tales,, and I'm certainly not your girlfriend!" Her breath hissed between clenched teeth. "I'm your cousin's fiancée, that's all I am, and that's plenty, thank you very much."

"You're a whore" he croaked, and knew even in that moment that he would torment himself with his own words on the rack of a thousand empty nights to come.

"A whore?" she spat at him. "Well, maybe I am, but I'd rather be that than whatever the fuck it is you want me to be! I'm not your girlfriend, Dermot, and I never will be! I'm a woman, and sometimes I want to be a whore. Sometimes I want a man to smack my arse or, or pull my hair, or slap my face. I love it when a man comes in my mouth,

---

[76] All too true. This, perhaps, is the genius of such a place as this hospital; the residents here are all wandering in a night of their own creation, the fog of the past, the thunderheads of unnamed fears. Yet it is precisely those people most oppressed by their own neuroses that reveal themselves most readily to the interested observer. Happiness hides our true essence; we are united in pain.

and I love getting fucked from behind, and that doesn't make me a whore, it makes me a real person."

"You used me."

"We used each other. We both wanted to fuck, and that was fine, until you decided that wasn't enough, and I wasn't enough, and I had to be some path to the stars for you. Well, that's it. God knows, Sean has his faults, but the things he wants from me, I can give him. And at least he knows what those things are."

I can't do this, not again, and again, and again. Let me just lie here, for a while, next to you, and if I can't go back, at least don't make me go forward, not yet. Let me lie here, and try to pretend that this is just a joke, or a tiff, something that couples do, regular, happy people. Let me stay in this moment, torn apart, shattered, but not quite beyond repair, not yet. Let me hover here, just for a while, forestalling oblivion, the moth in the halo of light that surrounds the naked flame.

"Dermot..."

Not now. Please, not now. Not with my enemies hovering just outside the doors, peering in at the windows, leering at me as I shiver naked at your feet. I'm not ready to face them, please don't make me. Without you they'll tear me apart.

"Dermot, don't..."

But I have to. I can't do it alone. You showed me the way into the underworld,[77] and you can't leave before you show me the way out

---

[77] The recurring theme of the underworld. It seems pertinent here to explain a little about the psychological and mythological background to Dermot's very personal tale.

Many researchers have drawn parallels in the past between the forms of mythological systems throughout human history and the imagery of the schizophrenic crisis. The basic argument is that the stories of ancient mythology, be it Celtic, as in this case, or Classical, Egyptian, Mayan, Navajo, Oriental or virtually any other culture on earth, may serve as a guide to understanding the human psyche. Certainly, even a casual reading of comparative beliefs serves to underline the fact that, beneath the trappings of local custom and ecology, most, if not all, mythic systems obey the same laws, describe the same problems befalling the same characters with different names throughout time and space. These are the

Jungian archetypes – the Mother-goddess, the warrior, the dragon or serpent, the virgin. The hero, born of a virgin, who is sacrificed for his people and is resurrected, becoming one with divinity – this is just one of the common threads running through the myths and folk tales, not to mention the great religions, of people the world over. And these exact same figures, according to the work of Dr. Pat Weir Perry, Joseph Campbell, Dr. Julian Silverman and many others, arise spontaneously in the alternately terrifying and euphoric hallucinations of the schizophrenic. These archetypes, in such a context, serve as energy-directing images, the universal keys to the collective unconscious. The schizophrenic, in such a case, is mining underground hollows that lie hidden within us all, searching for that person, that image, that god who will help him back to the surface of the daylight world. The function of mythology, therefore, besides the obvious purpose of explaining and reinforcing the scientific knowledge and social order of a given culture, is to provide the means by which the individual is reconciled to the world around him. When a mythology fails or is absent, then the individual is incompletely socialised, and the stage is set for a neurotic dislocation from the life around him, if not a full-blown psychosis.

As Joseph Campbell has argued, we live in a world largely without mythology. Science has chased away the sprites and imps of superstition, and shaken the foundations of the great religions, the socially-enshrined myths bequeathed us by our forefathers. In its place, we have only theories and dry 'facts' which seem to change with each new study or piece of research that emerges. Where once there was canonical authority, order, and certainty, now we have only speculation, a thousand competing voices telling us different things.

Dermot, in his own way, provides the model of such a societal schizophrenia. Cut off from the world he was born into, for whatever reason, he is drawn by the mythic forms of an older world again. If you leave me here, I'll never come back. The wave will close over my head, and the light will fade, and I'll be lost forever.

"Please, Dermot, don't..."

Take it. Take my pride, take everything, only don't leave me here. I'll give you anything, everything. I'll pull your hair and come in your mouth; I'll grovel at your feet and beg for scraps. I'll worship you until my lips bleed from your heels. Use me, spurn me, only don't leave me. Just let me look at you, once in a while, from whatever freezing corner you banish me to, and you can do whatever you want to me.

Her smooth skin was salty, and he wondered whether it was her sweat he was tasting or his own tears.

---

into an arena of struggle unlike any his modern, rational upbringing prepared him for. But it is by virtue of those same mythic forms, as revealed to him by Tim, the archetypal father figure and guide, and by Fiona, the perilous quarry our hero pursues to his undoing, that he is able to struggle through madness, back to the world above.

This is by necessity a somewhat incomplete survey of a large and fascinating subject, with which I will deal more fully further on.

27

I feel now like an end without a beginning, a winter without hope of spring. A body that refuses to rot, simply crumbling into useless ash. The shadows of bars[78] stripe the ceiling as I lie awake each night, thinking of old lost gods and the fading trails of stars. The end of life is the birth of the myth. From the bleak hills he wandered in his youth to the graveyard where he pupates until Armageddon, I followed his ghost like Finn's hunting hounds, chasing every hint and whisper my taut nerves could register. I followed him under the stars, under the earth, across bog and over mountain, along the twisted scar of the sea. Nothing. I escaped him, here and there, when I needed to, in foreign beds I knew he'd never find me in; but that could only last so long. I'm in no hurry now to get back to that rack, to trim the twigs of stunted love that grow in the shadow of a dark and great passion.

The halls here are full of shadows, the hunched shapes of nightmare scuttling by at the edges of vision, no matter what drugs they pump into me. Faces leer in at the windows, long howls shatter the night, my name hisses between the walls in every room, every hallway, demons come to claim one of their own. No one survives a season in hell; at least, no one survives unscarred.

---

[78] Hyperbole. Our windows are not barred, nor ever were during Dermot's stay here. See previous notes regarding the descriptions of the hospital; Dermot was not much of an ambassador for our facility. But we do our best to make it comfortable for those who have nowhere else to go.

28

The wind was hushed, the sun low in the sky, climbing in power over the mists of the world as Finn walked the golden courtyard of Almu. Shadows clung to the palisade walls, lurking in cold corners, hiding from the rising sun. Finn breathed the cool air.

He heard the clink of metal behind him, the heavy footfalls of warriors. Two men. Entering the courtyard with the sun in their faces. Oisin and Diorruing.

"Finn? Why are you walking the courtyard so early?" asked Oisin.

Finn turned. Oisin stood before him, squinting in the sun; Diorruing hung back a little, hiding his eyes in Oisin's shadow.

"I can't sleep" Finn replied.

"Why not?" Oisin asked. "Something troubling you?"

Finn smiled, paler than the young sun.

"It's hard to sleep without a wife" he answered.

Oisin smiled uncertainly.

"Well, that's easily fixed" he said. "You're the captain of the Fianna, the most renowned warlord in all Ireland. There's not a king has a daughter in all the land that wouldn't be happy to make an alliance with you."

"He's right there, Finn" said Diorruing, stepping forward. "In fact, I know a good match for you myself."

130

"Really?" asked Finn. "Who is she?"

"The daughter of the High King, Cormac son of Art son of Conn of the Hundred Battles."

Finn thought for a moment, his eyes reflecting the blueing sky in the bright opening of the day.

"Alliance with Cormac? If we could manage that… What's she like, this daughter of his?"

"Ah, she's a rare beauty" Diorruing grinned. "Tall, young, skin like milk, hair like honey – she's the envy of every maiden in the land. There'd not be a man in all Ireland that wouldn't be happy to be wed to such a beauty, even if she were the daughter of a nameless beggar instead of the King."

Finn scratched his cheek. Outside the fort, the grass sprang to green life under the golden eye of the sun. The sky shook with the song of the birds. It is not good to be long alone.

"Who can I send to talk to Cormac?" he asked aloud.

"We will take this on ourselves" said Oisin, stepping towards his leader, "and bring you back the answer of the king as soon as we may."

Finn considered his warriors.

"Ride quickly" he said finally, "and tell no one of your errand until all is accomplished." Oisin bowed quickly, then turned, his swinging shoulders quickly lost to the shadows of the doorway.

Catching movement at the edge of his vision, Finn turned his head. A hawk swooped low over the walls, left to right, and was gone.

Argent day hounded dewy-winged night across the barren lands. Breathlessly Finn waited, his horse unharnessed, his dogs restless in their kennels, for a day he alone looked for. Until in the hollow of a dreary afternoon a single rider came rushing with the wind across the plain, clattering up the stone steps to the gate of Finn's stronghold, demanding to speak with the lord of the Fianna.

"Oisin" said Finn, rising from his seat as the guards led the warrior to their leader, "I have long awaited your return. Where is Diorruing?"

"He feasts in the halls of Cormac as a welcome guest, and awaits your arrival, Finn" Oisin smiled, clasping Finn's shoulder. "Cormac gives his blessing, and asks that you ride with a complement of warriors to his palace at Tara to take the hand of his daughter Grainne."

It does not befit a man, nor a leader of men, to show excesses either of joy or sorrow; this Finn knew. His face remained as still and set as the stern cliffs that loom over the steel-grey sea; but a spark of hope caught the dry kindling of his solitude, and he allowed himself a single smile.

29

The sun blinked in the watery sky, wavering as though the rough winds from the sea could reach it in its cold sphere of space, as Dermot and Fiona wandered along the ridge. Seamus ran on ahead, head down, following the traces of nocturnal animals he could still pick up in the fields. The short grass yielded beneath their feet, sprang up again as soon as they had passed, eliminating their footprints in a wide green Sahara that would hold no trace that they were ever there.[79]

"Anything more in your dad's notes?" she raised her voice against the wind. Dermot walked ahead of her, shoulders hunched against the high cold air, and she had to struggle against the gale that swept her words away like music to twist and spiral out over the valley behind them.

Dermot half turned his head towards her.

"No," he said without stopping, "just the same old story. Diarmuid and Finn. Nothing more about my mother."

"Well," Fiona tried, "maybe that was his way of...processing it all. Expressing himself through the old stories he heard all his life."

"Do you think?" asked Dermot.

---

[79] It seems strange, given their previous exchange, that Dermot and Fiona should be together once again, talking as though nothing had happened between them. Perhaps I have erred in my ordering of the notes, but the subject matter seems most appropriate here. Perhaps their mutual boredom and isolation hold them in place, inertia overcoming their quarrels. Or perhaps Fiona simply fears the damage she might do to Dermot if she leaves him now.

"Well, why not?" she answered, and almost tripped over a mossy grey stone hidden in a tussock of grass. "He'd hardly be the first person to try it. Sort of reminds me of monks perfecting calligraphy in cold stone towers while Europe darkens around them."

She couldn't see his smile.

"It kind of makes sense, I suppose" he considered. "The story seems to be headed that way. But it doesn't really tell me anything. Even if Finn ends up bringing up Donn's bastard child, that doesn't necessarily mean that that's what happened with me. If he never goes back to being a bit more personal, then I'm always going to wonder."

"But you still think there's a good chance he wasn't really your father?" She was being strangely persistent. Dermot was struck by the feeling that she was working on something, that every word she said was another step on an upwards climb to something he couldn't see.

"There's always the chance" he growled. "I don't know. I'm really having a hard time keeping anything straight right now. I can't trust my eyes, I can't trust my ears. I can't trust my own mind." The ground levelled out beneath his feet, the sea heaving like a drunk out beyond the land's greenbrown edge. Beneath the flaking branches of a stunted tree, he stopped, turned, waited for her to catch up. Up ahead, Seamus chewed experimentally on a tall clump of grass.

"The thing is, I can't trust myself to know what's real and what isn't. I could read a signed confession by my mother, with the pope and Finn McCool himself as witnesses, stating clearly that I am not my father's son, but what would that really mean to me now? I can distinguish between my visions and what's really there, for now; but how long will that hold? Or maybe I've already slipped over that line. I really have no way of knowing. For all I know, maybe you don't exist, and I dreamed you up out of my madness. It would explain a few things, actually." His smile was weaker than the sun, and her own was a dim echo of it.

"So what's the plan?" she asked, and flopped down on the grass, hugging her knees.

"What do you mean?" he frowned.

"Well, what are you going to do? You have to do something, no matter whose son you are. I mean, life goes on."

"Not for me. Not until I've finished this book. And when I've done that...I don't know." He squatted beside her, balancing himself with one hand on the soft ground. "It all depends. If it was all some crazy story, and I am really his son, then I guess I just go on with my

134

life. Except I can't, really. Not the way it was. This place has gotten to me now, and I won't be the same, no matter where I end up. This is where I'm from, spiritually. I might have been born in England, but every corpuscle in my blood tells me that I belong here[80]. And this is exactly where I should be, at least until I finish Dad's book. After that...we'll see. There's no point planning anything too far ahead, the way my head is now, because I could be a completely different person tomorrow. I'll stay here until I finish the book, and then we'll see."

"But that could take a long time" Fiona said, quieter now that they were face to face. "What about your job?"

"I've already lost it, as far as I know" Dermot grinned. "I was supposed to go back weeks ago. It doesn't matter, anyway. Even if I had gone back on the return ticket, I couldn't work like this, seeing things, hearing things, not knowing what's real. I don't care. It paid the bills, but that's all.[81]"

"But how are you going to live?"

"Well, Tim hasn't complained about giving me room and board, and right now, that's all I need. I help him out around the farm, as much as I can. I'm getting better at it, I think."

"So that's your plan? Stay here and become a farmer?"

"Why not?" he grinned at her. "There are worse ways to make a living."

"If you can call it that" she snorted. "I don't know what pastoral fantasies you've cooked up for yourself, but the simple life isn't as simple as you seem to think. You think Tim could maintain himself from the farm alone, without his pension? It's only stubbornness that keeps him at it. That and not knowing what to do with himself otherwise. He'd be better off if he sold that land to the government and let them plant trees on it, like most of the other old farmers have already done. There's no money in it to support a young man."

---

[80] Sadly, Dermot is hardly alone in feeling that the place he spent his formative years is not his true home. Perhaps we all need the bittersweet myth that we have some place to go.

[81] Dermot worked for a company that rented equipment to the many films and TV shows filming in Vancouver. Haven't I mentioned that before?

"Well, I'm not looking to inherit the farm" Dermot replied. "I told you, I can't think that far ahead. It's all I can do right now to get through the day without running off into the hills or leaping off a cliff. The arrangement I have works for now, and when it stops, I'll find something else. Or not."

His words hung between them for a while, stubbornly refusing to be blown away by the wind.

"What about Grace?" Fiona asked, almost tenderly now. "Don't you miss her?" Dermot frowned at the distant sea.

"Yeah, I do" he said. "I miss her a lot. But ….well, we broke up, actually."

"What?" Fiona gasped. "When?"

"Last week. I called her, and…well, since I don't know when I'm going back, or if I ever am, we decided it would be best just to call it a day. Go on with life, like you say."

"I never said to do that!" she snapped.

"No, of course not" Dermot struggled, rocking back on his heels. "It was a mutual thing, really."

"But you can't just do that, Dermot! What did she do to you?"

"Nothing" he replied, on the defensive now. "It's not about what she did, it's about me, and my problems…"

"Oh, it's always about you! You can't do that to people, you can't treat them like that!"

"What's wrong with you?" Dermot asked. "Why are you getting so worked up about it?"

"I'm not. I just think you made the wrong decision."
"Duly noted."

They both looked out to sea. He watched the black specks of gulls whirling on the air above the lightless waves. The wind moaned in the space between them.

"So what, you got bored of her, is that it?"

"Jesus, Fiona. It's not like that at all."

"Then what is it like?"

"What do you care?"

"I don't."

"Then can we fucking drop it, please?"

The shore was hidden from where they sat, the waves unbroken, rolling in ponderous grey battalions until the cliffs abruptly cut them off. All that purposeless power.

"Fiona, I'm sorry. I just don't see why you're getting so irate about me splitting up with a woman you'll never meet. We didn't break up because of you, if that's what's bothering you."

"Why would that be bothering me? Why would I even think that?"

why would I think that

"Fuck's sake, I don't know. You wouldn't, you would, I don't know. I just thought there was a remote possibility that maybe your mind might turn that way, so I thought I'd relieve you of that train of thought before it even left the station. If I've wildly misunderstood you, I apologise."

She stared at the ground.

He looked out to sea.

He could feel her looking at him.

He looked out to sea.

"Still, gorgeous up here, isn't it?" She hugged herself, eyes squinting into the wind as she turned to face the horizon. The wind lifted a strand of sunbright hair from her pale forehead. "Romantic."

Oh, fuck you. Fuck you and your fucking romance. You don't know love, you only know romance. Love is a chasm, a shrieking void that will swallow everything you have and give nothing back. I'll read your future in the guts of a pig: a farmhouse in the ass end of nowhere, a dozen squealing brats rolling on the floor with the dogs, your hips spreading as your bank balance plummets and a new black eye to explain to the neighbours every Sunday. Marry this man, and that's all your life will be. And one day, you'll hear it, that howl of regret coming on the wind from all the frontiers you'll never cross, and it will be too late. So here's to you and your dreams. Here's to your grand romance. Take your violins and your kisses in the rain and choke on it. You have love, right here; this is love, adult and raw, soaked in blood and pain. You can only love what you can't have; anything else is masturbation. If you'd let me, I'd kiss you the way the axe kisses the block, the way the sea kisses the rocks into powder. Come with me, and we'll warm ourselves by the flames of burning bridges. Everything you say you want is right here, waiting for you, but you won't take it.[82]

vile

regret

Static, static, static,

White noise, black noise,

Ghosts of fearful things

---

[82] Dark and light, good and evil are all conflated here. Love becomes utter consumption, tenderness is indistinguishable from violence. There is wisdom here, too; back to the Buddhist idea of non-discrimination – but Dermot is far from wisdom at this point,

He stared at her as though there was some lost path to glory mapped in the bones of her face. The wind sang through the grass, singing of love: love lost, love vanquished, love triumphant; love scattered like bones and smashed into dust.

"Yeah," he said, smiling tightly, "romantic."

---

his madness becoming increasingly obvious, and terrifying for those around him.

30

This is where fear drives us. In some sheltered bank, behind some pile of drifted snow, we seek that moment in which there is no time, with what limited resources we have at our disposal. The artist's brush does not create a flower, it merely describes it; and yet we walk past a thousand plants on our way to the gallery.

There is no time. For the lover, eternity is immediate. There is no self in this heavy darkness; no me, no her. Who we are means nothing. Our past means less than our future. There is only the moment, and we are shadows, wraiths, automatons, immediate expressions of a universal scene. We live fully in this moment, like animals, forgetting ourselves, ignoring our lives, free for a few sweet moments from the burden of time and the bitter knowledge of mortality; Eden is reclaimed, and lost again, ten thousand times an hour.

A thousand suns shone just below the surface of the water, the light rippling along the underside of her jaw as they walked, hand in hand, along the seawall. Yachts bobbed in the slight swell, steel and brass rails all gleaming, light bounced back and forth from sun to sea to ship; he could see a version of himself, distorted and bulging, in the curve of Grace's sunglasses.

On a sunny Sunday, the park is overrun. The seawall bucks and sways in the heat, recoiling from the footfalls of disappointed tourists and antagonistic locals. Spandex-sheathed joggers thud by joylessly, their jaws clenching back curses they'd like to hurl at those walking in their path. Bikes whizz by on the left, then stop without looking in the middle of the pavement, causing others to swerve and yell; they'll never win that race now.

He watched, overshadowed by ancient trees and the frowning mountains rising straight out of the water, as a cyclist muttered something in passing to a jogger in the wrong lane, crouching to re-tie her shoe in a spot guaranteed to cause maximum disruption to everyone around her.

"God, I hate people" Dermot growled, then contemplated himself in her shades, the park looming all round him, the sky utterly blue, her hair utterly black, still, unlike his already-greying mop. "With some exceptions."

She smiled her long, slow smile, her lips widening into a slight, very slight curve, because all her smiles are like this, always qualified, always shadowed, never free of the taste of sorrow, and this is why his heart breaks for her, still, because their sorrow is the same in a different key.

"That's the trouble" Grace said, and squeezed his fingers as she spoke. "Everyone is someone's exception."

Our breath boils, our flesh burns; we glow in the mutual darkness, desire leading our hands, our mouths, our boiling blood. Your hot breath coils around me, your skin burns me, your limbs draw me in as we coil around each other, lost in the pursuit of pleasure, feeding on each other's bliss. Rarely in life is selfishness so perfect; in chasing our desire, we bring each other joy.

I want you like this, forever; always the pursuit, always the edge of victory. I want you spread like this before me, the howling in my brain at last driven out by the deep growl of my blood. I want you like this, forever, while the world decays around us; your hair flaying the pillow in gales of gold, your fingers carving channels in whatever they touch – the sheets, the mattress, my back – the muscles of your body bulging, pleasure aping pain, nails broken and scarred, time breaking down around us as the cries are torn from your throat. I will have you, Fiona, forever, like this; I will chase the fire's golden glint through the waystations of your body: I will drive nails through your flesh as you drive them through mine, and we will scream together and lose ourselves in one another, our bodies erupting together, forever, beyond sex, beyond time, beyond ourselves: I will bury my hate in you, and you will love me.

The world is too much with us. Following the curve of the path around the park, surrounded by cyclists and tourists and stone-faced runners, she left the pavement without a word, his hand still in hers. They ducked under the bridge where a stream merges itself with the

140

ocean, the smell of fresh water intoxicating under the low stone roof
of the underpass. The other side is lit with green light, fresh young
leaves bursting from the ancient trees, and the gravel trail that leads
further into the forest is utterly empty.

"Better?" she smiled at him.

"Better" he nodded, and said no more, because nothing
needed to be said. She knows how he feels in a crowd; she knows
when he needs silence.

They walked alongside the river as it rushed past them, eager
to lose itself in the vastness where all the world's water begins and
ends, the endless ocean, a poem of the eternal.

"It's good to get out" she sighed, inhaling the damp pine-
scented air like a drug, the green smell infecting her lungs like smoke.
"Just a shame about all the people."

"I was just getting a bit...frazzled" Dermot said ruefully. "All
those voices...Still gets me, sometimes. Maybe I should change my
meds again. You don't want me going crazy and chopping you up or
something."

He hadn't heard the bikes coming down the path, and with
outrageous timing, a middle-aged couple rolled slowly by as he spoke,
their heads turning in perfect synchronization to stare at him. Dermot
stared back, at a loss for anything to say, when he felt Grace's hands
on his cheeks, turning him to her, to her, to her open mouth that fixed
itself on his. He still had one eye on the cyclists as they stared back,
frankly amazed, and Grace kissed him slowly, hungrily, pressing herself
against him, moaning theatrically in her throat. Dermot smiled through
the kiss, and forgot about the audience, and kissed her back.

I need you because of him. I need you because I can't have
you. I need you like this because this is not who I am. I don't do this;
she does. You do. I am the guy who stays at home and hopes one day
she'll stop; but she never will, and this is why. You carve hieroglyphs
into my back, not because of who I am, but because of who I'm not.
You fingernails will be rusted with my blood for days; but it doesn't
have to be mine, so long as it's not his. You use me, and I use you, to
show me how it feels to be some other, any other, anyone who's not
me. This is what it's like: I move through you, driving myself against
you, hissing between my teeth, growling deep down in my throat – and
you embrace me, draw yourself against me, shower my shoulders with
kisses when you're about to come. You love me in this moment, not in

spite of my hate, but because of it; you draw my hate into yourself, impale yourself upon it, your love feeding on it the way the flower feeds on the rot of the tree; the more I hate, the more you love. But not me.

    The hunger is always there, that unreachable sexual itch, the taut wires in her blood – she could still feel Dermot's body pressed against her. [83]She could still taste him, could see only the dark patches under the trees where shadows would hide them from passers-by – but sometimes a kiss must stay a kiss. This one, definitely. This afternoon, Grace will be chaste.

    The trees thinned, the short trail throwing its arms around a sad, dark lake, and the sky branched above them, her sister, smiling down on her as she smiled up at it. The kiss; the sky; her body throbbed invisibly as she felt herself as a part of some alien perfection. Wonder can descend from a cloudless sky, when everything aligns just right – she knows this, and is prepared, and so she is not as surprised as Dermot is when they follow the path along the lakeshore, and a cloud of birds bursts from a bush and swirls around them. Sparrows. The air is filled with them; she can feel the air currents stirred up by their wings, her long hair twisting blackly in the stream of their flight.

    "What the –" Dermot mutters, and reaches out uncertainly. A sparrow lands on his outstretched finger, its jet-black eye considering first him, then her. It chirps, once, and flies away, the rest of the flock disappearing with it, back into the bushes, as abruptly as they came.

    Dermot laughs, puzzled, his finger still outstretched. The sun pours down around him like honey from a jar, the light transfiguring him as he stands still in the middle of forever, in a harsh and beautiful world, and he laughs. She can pinpoint the exact moment the image sears itself into her memories; she knows in that instant, as though this

---

[83] Now we see Dermot writing from Grace's perspective. This may be an extreme form of empathy with the woman he loves, or it may indicate his inability to relate to himself; Dermot is so much an outsider that he is, quite literally, outside himself at this point. The masks he wears, the masks we all wear, are not our real faces, and Dermot seems increasingly content to step away entirely and watch the mask he has created interact with those around him.

is all a memory, an old woman's dream of the past, that she will remember him like this, in her best moments, always.

We grind out the last throb of passion, and the sweet, sad silence hunches over us.

31

Fiona awoke with a start. Groaning, she rolled over onto her back. Dermot slid away across the sheets, making room.

"Mmm. What time is it?" she purred. He remembered the first time he heard that sound, the voice that spoke her first waking words. He had felt then like a legionnaire on the threshold of the temple sanctuary, a witness to something intimate and sacred that he had, perhaps, no right to see. But such is the nature of faith; the Holy of Holies is an empty room.

"I don't know. After one" he answered.

"Why did you let me sleep?" she whined, but the darkness couldn't hide the smile in her voice. "I have to go."

"Ok" he said. Fiona sighed deeply.

"But it's so comfy" she protested, and he experienced the now-familiar feeling that she was trying to nudge him into saying something particular, following a script she had concocted in her head. "You wore me out" and she turned, trailing blankets behind her across the narrow bed, her head nestling onto his chest.

"Are you alright?" and every trace of sleep vanished from her voice, as though she had never been the warm, tender creature he had just seen unfolding herself from the shelter of the night.

"Yeah, I'm fine" he replied. Because it didn't matter. Even now, when he realised the impossibility of his position, the ruthlessness of her motives, even in the full knowledge of just how little his agony meant to her, he knew he could never break loose from her. The best he could do was to pretend he didn't care.

"What is it, Dermot? What's wrong? Did I do something?"

Yes.

"No, not at all. It's not you. I was just thinking...you know, about my dad." He cleared his throat. "About my parents."

That which you idolise, you cannot understand; this we know. Jehovah never asked for the Hebrew's respect, only their obedience, and their suffering. My kingdom is not of this world. I love as God loves: He made you in the immemorial forge of the shrinking stars, and I formed you in the tomb of my own starlit mind. Editor, do not correct. Flesh calls to flesh like nails through the hands, ancient markings burned into the sand.

So what am I supposed to do? Lie here like a pillow and throw a cold arm around your naked back while my soul atrophies in my chest? She doesn't want a partner, she wants a crutch. It could be Sean, it could be me, it really doesn't matter either way. Just as long as there's someone for her to betray.

You cannot love what you worship, and vice versa; love is love only when it is accepting of faults, while worship presumes faultlessness. This is why God becomes man; perfection is just too fucking lonely.

Remembrance is dark and indulgent, musty rooms still smelling faintly of the last occupant, where you absorb the dried-out dreams of ghosts. They stood at the side of the long couch, their faces masked at the dark edge of the orange lamplight.

"That's me, on the right side of the couch. That's my mother."

"Who's next to her?" asked Fiona.

"That's Alex." Alex, nine years old, clutched onto his mother, sobbing quietly into her side. Thirteen-year-old Dermot sat with folded arms at the far end of the couch, glaring at them. Across the room, on a smaller sofa, Owen, a gloomy boy of twelve, sat next to his father.

"Oh my god" breathed Fiona. "Look at your father."

Dermot didn't have to. Every eidetic cell, every wretched scar of his body combined to conjure the image of his father in that moment of crystallizing pain as though waking from the dream his adult life had been to find himself still that child, still in that room, still locked with the rest of his family in that fearful silence in which they could hear a man's heart break.

His father sat on the edge of the sofa, his hands on his knees, trembling. His whole body seemed to vibrate like a figure seen through a heat haze or the dull distance of the stars; his pain tore him from them and made him something fierce, eternal, and yet remote. His eyes were rimmed with red, locked onto his wife across the room, as though she might burst into flame from the heat of his gaze. Hate and love and loss ran together there so viciously that Dermot wanted to cover his ears, look away, leave that room and its hopeless wrath to crumble once more into darkness. Those eyes. Burning holes through all the years between, burning holes in every lonely hope this brutish world could offer. Twin jets of flame ignited in his teenage soul that no long walks, no kisses in the rain, no holding hands beneath the stars would ever put out.

"That poor man" Fiona sighed. "He looks...*broken*."

"Yeah" said Dermot. "He does." He looked away, unable, like everyone else in the room, to meet those eyes for long. He hesitated to tell her; the words quivered on his lips, and were gone. What they were watching was the death of a man, and of a boy. Something left that room, years ago, that wore his clothes and his face; but the boy he had been died that night in fear and sorrow, and the man he was now had pupated in the shadow of that loss.

"God" Fiona sighed, her face sallow in the orange light, "it's so sad."

145

Dermot smiled sickly.

"This is nothing" he said. "This is just the start."

Inside the cafeteria, the voices of two hundred teenagers echoed under the high ceiling, the buzzing of a billion flies at a scene of apocalyptic carnage. Words and phrases ran together, sense merging into noise and back out again, so that in all the mangled hubbub, a metallic, disembodied voice kept calling his name. He ignored it. Fifteen years old, Dermot stood in line at the hole in the wall where disinterested women served flavourless slop to the ranks of children that jostled one another along the length of the lime green walls. He was alone, the warm weight of a single coin clutched in his fist. His stomach was screaming.

"Alright, Dermot." A short, tubby kid with a cluster of blood-red acne circling his mouth had recognised the classmate standing in front of him. Dermot turned.

"Alright."

"That little cunt there is Warren McLeod" Dermot explained to Fiona, leaning against the wall across the hall from his teenage self. "He went to my primary school. Grew up in the same neighbourhood. Same parish. So everyone knew what happened with my parents, and all those parents told their kids, and all those kids just couldn't wait to ask me about it. Little vultures. Look, he's practically drooling over it."[84]

There was a faint smile on Warren's flabby face. "Seen your mum recently?" he asked. Dermot scowled.

"No" he replied sullenly.

---

[84] Fascinating. Initially it seemed that Dermot was showing Fiona a photo of his past, but this passage makes it clear that this is not so. He is quite literally taking her back through his past, having her stand witness to his childhood traumas. This is of course a physical impossibility, but the desire to do so is something every therapist has seen in a patient. How many times have I felt as Fiona must here, a mute, ghostly witness at a scene that infects the psyche of a patient?

"Is it true that she was caught shagging Fr O'Brien in the sacristy[85] at St. Bartholemews?" The question rose above the din. A girl giggled. Fiona watched with a shock of recognition as both Dermots, fifteen and thirty, clenched their jaws and stood up straighter.

"Fuck off, Warren" the young Dermot spat.

"What?" McLeod smiled. "I was just asking."

Just asking, when he knew the answer. Everyone knew about the affair. As though nothing had ever happened in the last twenty years, the rumours of his family's disgrace had done the rounds of church and pub for the last two years, and still he had to hear about it from gobshites like this one. His parents told him nothing. Since that first night, when they had told the boys that their mother was leaving, there had been a black smoke of silence over the whole affair, as though by not talking about what was happening they could all pretend that it was no big deal. Everything he knew about his mother's infidelity, beyond his father's dark hints, he had learned from the kids at school. By now, he had learned enough. Wordlessly, he turned his back on Warren.

"What a little bastard" Fiona muttered.

"Just wait" said Dermot, gazing into the crowded hall. "It gets worse."

Timidly, Alex wound his way through the crowd towards his older brother. He had been at school with the 'big kids' only six months, and still had that hunted look that marked a first year student, constant victims of the cruelty of older children. His bag on both shoulders – an almost fatal faux-pas Dermot had warned him about before – he shuffled timidly towards the barely-moving line.

"Dermot" he said, tapping his brother on the shoulder. Dermot sighed; no teenager wants to be seen with his hopelessly geeky younger brother in front of half the school.

"Fuck's sake, Alex, stop wearing your bag like that. You look fucking gay."

---

[85] A room in a church where the ritual paraphernalia is kept when not being used in the Mass. We may dismiss the more salacious rumours concerning the personality of Dermot's mother, but the question remains: what exactly caused her to leave? It certainly casts the vague hints Dermot makes at Grace's infidelities in a new light.

Hastily, Alex slipped one arm free of the strap of his backpack, letting it hang from a single shoulder. "Have you got any money?" he whispered. Dermot sighed again.

"When my mother left, bless her," Dermot explained to Fiona, "she didn't just abandon us. She also cleaned out all the bank accounts to start her new life. Everything was half in her name, so there was nothing my dad could do. He was ruined; it was all he could do to keep the house. So he either couldn't afford to give us lunch money, or else he was so used to pinching every penny that he couldn't bring himself to do it. At the same time, he was too proud to apply for the free school meals program that half the kids here were on. So most days, we went without lunch."

"I've only got a quid[86]" Dermot said to his brother. "Chips cost 80p. 20p's not going to get you much."

Alex looked on the verge of tears. Dermot could feel the hunger scratching, rat-like, at the walls of his stomach. He had forged a sick note for Daniel Shaughnessy in exchange for two cigarettes, which he had sold to Patrick Doyle for the pound[87] he had now in his hand; a morning's work so he would have something to eat.

"You can share my chips[88]" he said to Alex.

"Is this your little brother, yeah?" Warren butted in. Dermot glared at him.

"Yeah," he said warily, "it's my little brother Alex."

"Yeah, I remember you from St. Bart's" Warren smiled. "You a first year now, yeah?"

"Yeah" Alex replied meekly, looking up at Dermot.

"So is it true that your mum was caught shagging Fr –"

Calmly, Dermot had transferred the pound in his hand to his pocket before stepping forward and hitting Warren in his fat face. Warren staggered against the wall, but bounced back, grabbing at Dermot's jacket. Dermot seized a fistful of greasy hair in his left hand, wrenched Warren's head back and punched him squarely in the nose. He felt a crunch; a jet of bright blood spurted onto Dermot's hand. He

---

[86] British slang for a pound; see below.

[87] Unit of currency in England; nothing to do with the more familiar measure of weight, lb.

[88] Presumably he means what we in North America would call fries.

felt Warren's grip weaken, but at the same time, something held him back from finishing the fat fuck off, something stronger than the rage boiling inside him.

"That's enough, Fallon" the teacher growled in his ear, holding Dermot's arms pinned behind his back.

"Let go of me, you f - Alex!" Alex stood immobile, wide eyes watching silently as Dermot was dragged backwards towards the door. "That's my little brother! I ain't given him his lunch money!"

"Should have thought about that before you started throwing punches" the invisible teacher said behind his back. "You can explain all this to the headmaster."

Fiona's head turned, following the wild-eyed boy as he was dragged out of the room. Another teacher followed, holding Warren McLeod by the elbow, a handkerchief pressed to his face.

"Quite the little gurrier, weren't you?" she said. Dermot snorted.

"Well, what was I supposed to do? To this day, I'm glad I sparked him. Vicious little prick."

He could hear her breathing invisibly in the pitch-black room

"Sorry" he said sheepishly. "I hate this, honestly, all this harping on childhood, as though all that matters in a person's life is the first twenty years or so. It's not like I had it that bad in the scheme of things. So my parents split up, so what? I could have been born infected with AIDS in some shithole in Africa, or sewing trainers in China for two dollars a month. Shit happens, you know? It just... still makes me mad, when I think about that hunger, all the time, and those fucking kids, and my dad...well, he did his best, I suppose. Just... well, forget it."

Fiona said nothing. He felt the blanket dragged across his body as she moved towards him, twisting in the bed to face him, and took his hand in hers.[89]

---

[89] Now, perhaps, we are approaching the crux of the matter: Dermot's unresolved trauma from the dissolution of his family. Although a common phenomena in this day and age, the psychic consequences of such break-ups, especially when the split is less than amicable, as in this case, can be devastating. Perhaps we should not wonder that Dermot pursues a relationship with Fiona that he must know can never go anywhere; he courts heartache as

32

More splendid was the feasting that night than Finn had yet seen, even in the hallowed halls of Angus, when Cormac presented his daughter to Ireland's greatest warlord before the foremost warriors of the King and of the Fianna. Finn looked into Grainne's pale eyes, a ringlet of greenspoked blue shining from within with a light purer and cooler than summer sun, and saw in them everything a renowned man had yet to accomplish: a wife to support him; a lover to witness the places within his heart he allowed no one else to see; a mother to the sons he would raise to carry on his name and work, the defence of the land against any who threatened it. Each barren widowed night of the dusty grey years withered like an autumn leaf and crumbled to nothing. Her hand was soft and warm as Cormac set it in his own, the young life flowing beneath the skin like the dawning of possibilities he had forgotten existed. In the presence of all, they spoke their vows of betrothal, and every word seemed carved in stone.

---

though daring it to destroy him. Of course, in so doing, he places himself in the role of the adulterer who split up his family, and his cousin, Sean, in the role of his own betrayed father – an irony I am sure was not lost on him.

The fires flared, the pipes blared, and the emissaries of Finn were received like visiting princes into the hall of Cormac, King of Erin. Three hundred men at arms stood to attention as Diarmuid, Oisin and Oscar walked towards the high table to be seated at the right hand of the king. The royal family rose, too; Cormac, the High King, raising his drinking horn to the men of the Fianna; his queen, proud and fair as one of the gods; and his daughter, Grainne, for whom they had come.

Her golden hair shone in the firelight; her eyes, large and pale, echoed the winter sea that pounds itself to foam on the indifferent cliffs. Her skin glowed, pale and pure, a beacon of beauty in a world of illness, infirmity and filth. Her lips, pale pink and softer than the first petals of a blooming rose that lifts its head to the gentle rain. She had her father's proud bearing, her mother's noble beauty, and something else: some hint in her of sadness, of regret, a lost heart hiding behind a beautiful mask, a sword-sharp melancholy in her granite-flecked eyes. No one ever looked so lonely in the midst of a crowd.

So Diarmuid, warrior of many battles, beloved of the women of Erin, beheld Grainne, daughter of Cormac King, betrothed of Finn McCool; and the blood pounded in his ears as though he were charging into the clamour of battle;

his breath caught in the vacuum of his ribs as though his enemy's spear had pierced his armour;

his knees trembled, as they had never trembled in all the battles of his young life;

and the warm blood blossomed in his breast, singing through his veins, bringing warmth and light to all his limbs until he lost himself in a golden glow so bright he never cared to return.

The night sang, wounded with stars and a hunter's moon.
Her hair shone like silver in the moonlight, the muted shadow of
daytime gold. Diarmuid paused on the grass, and she stood facing
him, daughter of kings, the mist of their breath twining together
beneath the stars. Behind them, the palisade of Finn's stronghold
loomed, pointed ramparts blackly piercing the sky. Torches blazed
within; the court slept.

"Grainne" Diarmuid whispered, the words billowing around
them, "we can't do this! Finn will find us, he will stop at nothing, he
will chase us the length and breadth of Erin to avenge himself if we do
this!"

"Diarmuid," Grainne replied, "why do you waste breath on
such ignoble trifles now? We have drugged the guards, leapt the
fence, fled as fugitives from the court of the Fianna; why do you pause
now, as though you had not scourged your heart many such nights of
agony and doubt? As though this were a choice we had made, you and
I; a choice to love as we love, to feel as we feel, when we both know it
will cost us everything we have. There is no choice for me, at least; I
love you, and will always love you. Do you love me?"

"I do" Diarmuid sighed.

"Then what choice is there?

"But – you are betrothed to Finn."

Grainne snorted, the contempt distorting her beautiful face in
the gentle moonlight.

"Betrothed" she sneered. "And what is that? A contract
between my father and Finn, the king and the warlord hammering out
a deal. I am betrothed to Finn because my father fears an uprising,
and hopes that with the most powerful leader of men in Erin as his
son-in-law, his kingdom will remain safe. For this am I expected to

give my life, my love, my heart to a man my father's age. But my heart is not a chess piece, and I will not be my father's pawn. I will be a beggar in the wilderness with you before I will be a captive queen in the court of Finn."

Her head held high, she strode into the night, her grey dress fading into the mingled moonlight and shadow, her hair dimming as she went. Diarmuid looked back at the fortress, looming black and impenetrable against the night. All the years he had spent here, all the feasts, the tournaments, the honour and glory that had been his within that serrated circular wall; all the camaraderie, all the love, a home for an orphan in the place of his father, a band of friends who would gladly die for him, for whom he would happily die – it loomed behind him now with the weight of years, blotting out the stars.

Grainne had not stopped, or turned back, as though her mind was made up, whether he was coming with her or not. He could barely see her now, out beyond the faint light of the sleeping stronghold, about to be lost forever in a night she would never admit she feared.

Diarmuid gripped his sword, and ran after her.

Grainne heard Diarmuid run towards her, his armour clanking softly as he sped through the gloom. Fear bloomed in the pit of her stomach, the awful falling feeling that they could not turn back now, that they were walking a road neither of them knew, on which everything they had ever been taught could be of no use, and their only guide was the tumbled roar of ecstasy and despair they felt in one another's presence. Ecstasy, because such perfection can still exist in a world where the gods no longer seem to visit; despair, because two people can never truly become one flesh; because no matter how great their love, they could never simply crawl into each other's arms, and rest. She felt the fear that all lovers must feel, because time is not on our side, Grainne, because death makes liars of us all, because forever is only a few short years, and no lifetime can last long enough for a love like this. Perhaps even then, a stunted shadow of disaster grew, the fear that happiness brings, the terror of losing what we have only just found. That which is born is doomed to die; the only safe love is the love that never truly lives.

But what use is that? Grainne felt a smile rise through her fear, the fear of the daughter of a feudal king, crushed by the hideous weight of duty into a thing, an object, to be traded for land or cattle or protection; a bubble of joy swelled within her as she listened to the breath of the warrior walking beside her, matching his long strides to her own, forgoing his own duties, his own obligations, everything he had ever known to accompany her into her great loneliness.

Grainne smiled, and the moonlight caught her smile, a bright cry of joy in a land of darkness and peril, throwing it back out into the darkness, shattering fear in a glowing arc of brilliance, turning night into day, day into eternity. She looked at Diarmuid; Diarmuid looked at her. The smile grew within her, searing itself into the muscles of her heart, spreading through her face, the glory of her eyes, until Diarmuid's stern warrior mask cracked, and fell away, and a boyish grin broke like daylight across his features, transforming the knight into a smiling child in a long-gone summer.

"What're you smiling at?" he asked her as they wound their way across the moors.

"Nothing" she grinned. "What are you smiling at?"

"Nothing" he smiled.

Their breath misted behind them, forming drifting crystalline clouds that slowly rolled skyward, becoming one with the stars, the cold home of the absolute. The fortress loomed behind, its walls lit from within now by swaying torches, the voices of dogs and men; it seemed the refugees had been discovered. The Fianna were awake. The hunt was about to start.

Up ahead, the pale moors abruptly ended in a wall of blackness, the tall trees of the forest leaping skyward to cut off the horizon in a shroud of featureless black, the abode of wild things. Danger lurked there, stalking along the edge of stories told to children to teach them that the world is a dangerous place, especially when you ignore the rules. There are bears; there are wolves; there are monstrous things that have no names, lurking in the shadows that existed before the fathers of men were born, thirsting for the blood of the lost, the vulnerable, the disobedient. Love lies in ruins among the wreckage of the world.

"Oh, Diarmuid" she sighed, the words forming a halo of fog around her head, crystals of light blooming where the slanted rays of the moon caught them as they danced skyward on the black twisting air, "I'm so happy you came." And she put her warm hand in his.[90]

---

[90] Written differently, on different paper (see introductory note), this is presumably from Dermot's father's notebook. If so, then this is truly remarkable: a man torn apart by betrayal presenting the abduction of another man's bride as something, if not positive, then at least excusable. Or perhaps Dermot has become a little loose with his transcriptions from his father's notes. Is this really from the notebook, or is Dermot trying to gain some kind of forgiveness from his dead father for his own adulterous transgressions?

33

"Yer quiet tonight."

Dermot smiled. Not a phrase he had ever expected to hear from Tim.

"Yeah" he said. "Just got things on my mind, you know?"

Tim nodded his great head. "Woman, is it?"

Dermot started in his chair.

"What makes you say that?" he asked guardedly. The old man chuckled like a tractor backfiring.

"Ye've a look about ye," he said, "a look a fella gets when he's taken with a woman. Tis no helpin him then; he'll be no use to man nor beast once he gets that look. Worse than the touch of the amadan[91], 'tis."

"It's just...well, it's complicated" Dermot sighed. Tim smiled.

"Always is, where a woman's involved" he said. "Every time's the first time."

"I don't know what she wants" Dermot said, his eyes gazing blindly into the fire's writhing heart. "It's a cliché, I know, but I don't get it. Sometimes I think she really likes me, loves me, maybe – but then sometimes, she can be...well, cruel, to be honest with you."

"There's nothing crueller in nature than a woman in love" Tim rumbled.

"But why do they have to be so difficult? I mean, if she wants to be with me, then why not say it? She knows how I feel about it. And if she doesn't want to be with me, then I'd rather she just said it, you know? It might hurt, but I'd rather know."

"Perhaps she doesn't know herself. She's not made her mind up about ye."

---

[91] The Amadan is *leath*, wide; he brings death.

"Well, I wish she would" Dermot said gloomily. "It's like waiting to be executed; I just want it over with."

"Doesn't she miss ye?" Tim asked.

"Who?"

"This woman ye have."

"Miss me? Oh. Yeah. I dunno."

"Good lookin girl?"

"Oh, yeah. Beautiful, Tim, beautiful. The kind of girl who you can hardly talk to when she looks you in the eye, she's so beautiful."

"Then what are ye waitin for? If she's waitin for ye back in Canada, she won't be lonely for long. If she's as good lookin as ye say, yer lucky she gives ye the time of day."

Dermot smiled again. "I am" he said. "I am. But...there's other things to it, too, other... problems. Nothing's ever simple."

The fire whined, a tiny explosion of blue flame.

"I think she's scared" he went on. "I think she wants to be with me, but she's too scared to give up what she has now. It pisses me off – she could be so happy, with me. I know she could. When we're together, it's like there's no one else, anywhere, like we've known each other forever. But then, at the end of the day, she goes back to the mediocrity she's used to. She's so much better than that, but she doesn't believe me when I tell her that."

"And she knows how ye feel about it?"

"Oh, yeah. Without a doubt."

"Then maybe she's made her choice. She might just be afraid to tell ye that."

Dermot grimaced. "Maybe."

"But ye don't want to believe that, do ye?"

"No," said Dermot, looking at his uncle across the firelit room, "no, I don't. I admit that. But if she would tell me that straight up, then I'd have to accept it, wouldn't I? But she doesn't. It's like an addiction. I know it's not good for me, that I should just let it go, and in the past, that's always what I've done. I've never got that close, because I didn't want to get hurt, the way my mother hurt my father. But it turns out, it doesn't matter how careful you try to be. You meet a person with that certain gleam in her smile, that particular curve in her body, and suddenly you have no choice. You turn into everything you never wanted to be. Is that really how it goes?"

Tim nodded slowly. "Ye have the gist of it, yeah" he said.

The halo of light on the hearth danced in the silence. Dermot breathed in its sweet smell.

"So how come you never married, Tim?"

"Me?" The old man grinned. "Never got to it, I spose. Tis not for me, really."

"But was there never a girl you liked? No one you thought you might settle down with?"

"There was the one" he said, his breathing heavy in the dark cottage. "Long time ago, now."

"What happened? If you don't mind me asking" Dermot quickly added.

"Well, she was a nice girl, and we went courtin for a little while, but – tis an old story. We were engaged to be married, but she met another fella she must have liked more, and the two of them took off abroad. That was the end of that."

"Oh. I'm sorry to hear that."

"Ancient history. As I say, tis an old story – the oldest one there is, almost. Same story yer father was writing about, you know – Diarmuid, Finn and Grainne. Old stories. They just keep going."

"And there's been no one since?"

"No one. You know, after a thing like that, ye lose what appetite ye had for the whole enterprise. Anyway, she was quite a girl. Quite a girl. A tough act to follow, as they say. Still, ye never know. I'll be down the pub at the weekend, and ye never know yer luck."

34

We do not wish to be as we are. We do not choose to be where we are, scratching around on the concrete floor of an asylum, imprisoned like some rabid dog by the stroke of a bureaucrat's pen. If there is an answer, something to make sense of the visions and the horrors we see and hear, nightly, then it is not in here. How can I get better when they keep me in this place? My dreams make no sense in here; my thoughts are sucked out of me before they are formed, leaving my mind empty[92], hollow, a ransacked womb robbed of its progeny.

I know what you're thinking. I do. I know what I thought, briefly. Who was that girl of Tim's, who eloped with another man? Where did she go? England, perhaps? Was my father the 'other man'? I remember, vaguely, the relationship between Tim and my mother, on our perennial family holidays to Ireland. Even at the time, I thought it odd; Tim was never a talker, but there was a certain heavy quality in the silence between them that I never understood at the time. As though words between them might be dangerous. I will not say that the thought did not cross my mind.

But it's too easy, isn't it? Tim being my real father – come on. I almost wish it were true; I would lose nothing from that revelation. My blood would still be the same, my heritage still my own; one bare strand of DNA to separate me from the man who raised me. It's not true. It's not. For all that Tim came to be like a father to me, for a while, he was not my father. This much, I know[93].

---

92 This sensation is extremely common among schizophrenics.

93 But how? Dermot displays a remarkable level of self-awareness in this passage, but stops short of answering the questions his commentary raises: how does he know his uncle did not have an

35

"Pick up these clothes now, for fuck's sake!"

Their father never said anything anymore; he just barked at them, like a rabid dog. As though he had been conducting a perfectly reasonable conversation in his head, imagining the part his sons would say, giving them sullen, defiant voices that they would never dare use in real life, until he was justified in snapping at them like this. Owen and Alex jumped to their feet, anxious to avoid another night of wrath. The two boys collected armfuls of ironed clothes from the armchair in the dining room where their father had piled them, and chased each other upstairs to their rooms. Dermot sighed inwardly. They would not come back, now; and he didn't blame them. There was no talking to the old man when he was like this, which was most of the time; they would hide in their room and mark the time, as they did, every night, doing whatever they had to do to avoid their father and his unpredictable rages. Dermot didn't blame them; he did the same himself, most nights. But they didn't know the half of it.

"Well? Are you going to pick up your fucking clothes, or what?" Dermot sighed again as he stood to face his father. He knew he shouldn't do this. He knew he should do as his brothers did, keep his head down, get out of this awful situation for another night. But the unquiet spirit within him railed against this domestic tyranny and compelled him to stand though he knew it was futile.

"You know, Dad, you don't have to talk to us like that."

"What?" His father's eyes grew wide and wild, staring in disbelief at an offence that could not be tolerated. Dermot's fifteen-year-old spirit shrank within him, but pride lifted his chin, threw back

---

affair with his mother? It would hardly be the first time such a thing occurred.

his shoulders, clenched his small hands into fists against the fear that tore along the canal of his spine.

"You could just ask. You could just say, 'pick up your clothes'. You don't have to talk to us like you hate us."

His father's mouth opened, unable to form words powerful enough to express the outrage he felt. Dermot could almost see the thin hair rise on his head like the mane of some ferocious animal preparing to attack.

"I'll talk to you any way I want in my fucking house, you fucking turd!" The dishes in the drying rack rattled as his father stomped across the floor, his shadow forming weird and terrifying shapes in the dim orange light as he flew towards the trembling boy, who stood firm despite the terror in his guts.

His father's left hand shot out, grabbing hold of Dermot's shirt front and lifting the boy to his toes. Instinctively, he grabbed his father's hairy wrist, pathetically trying to free himself.

The lamplight blazed, and dimmed, silver sprites of dizziness slinking around the borders of Dermot's vision as his legs abruptly forgot how to stand. He hung limply from his father's grip, a dull web of pain crawling slowly across his face from the red corner of his ruined mouth. The ceiling spun above him, his eyes rolling in his skull, gravity become suddenly oppressive, forcing his body downwards. His father was saying something, but the words came from too far away to be understood. A blackness crept into Dermot's vision from the outer edges, shrinking the world to a small circle in the midst of darkness, like dim light at the end of a narrow tunnel. He struggled to stay conscious, to stay afloat in the rising waves that threatened to swamp him, drown him in darkness and forgetting.

He felt his body fall, but he barely registered the pain. The light faded; the darkness was complete.

"Jesus, Dermot. I don't know what to say. That's... that's awful."

Their footsteps echoed one another as they picked their way along the black road, the stars rejoicing overhead in a sky torn by pink blooms of algaic cloud. There was no light in the valley; everyone slept. Even Seamus, in the still-warm kitchen of Patrick and Bridgid's house, twitching and whining from time to time in the restless dreams of animals. Fiona and Dermot walked the lonely road in the cooling nights, when the risk of discovery kept them from sharing a bed, when all they could have of each other was a disembodied voice in a darkness the stars barely pierced.

"It wasn't that bad. I mean, it's not as though he hit me often. It was pretty rare, honestly. He had a temper, and I guess I was a master at pushing his buttons."

"You were a child."

"Fifteen is a man in most cultures. Besides, what does it matter, really? It was a long time ago."

"What, the nineties? Jesus, Dermot – I don't want to talk against your father, but – fucking hell! It's outrageous, it is, for a grown man to do that to a boy – his own son, at that."

"He was under a lot of stress" Dermot muttered.

"What, because of your mother? Jesus Christ, Dermot – come on! Lots of people get divorced, but they don't feel the need to beat seven shades of shite out of their kids."

"He didn't beat me" Dermot said uneasily. "He hit me, once. It's not like he put the boot in."

"He knocked you out! What kind of man punches a fifteen year old boy in the face?"

There was a pause. Their footsteps rang on the cold asphalt, invisible in the thick darkness that almost sundered them from each other, only her hand in mine[94] to remind me she was even there.

"You know what bothered me most? It wasn't so much that he hit me, it was that he only hit me. As far as I know, he never laid a finger on Owen or Alex. Don't get me wrong, I'm glad. I'd never wish that on my little brothers; in fact, protective as I was, I probably would have fucking lost it if he'd ever hurt them. But the point remains: he never hit them, only me."

The silence drifted between them, invisible smoke in the impenetrable night. They each walked alone in their thoughts, afraid to voice what was kept inside.

"I was older than them, to be fair. And I was mouthier than them – that's a fact. Neither of them could stand up to him they way I

---

94 Perhaps the most abrupt narrative shift yet; Dermot goes from third to first person in a single sentence. It is interesting to note where this happens; as though while recounting his past, he distances himself from it, and only comes back to himself at Fiona's touch.

did. That's the way I always was; I just can't leave things alone. Especially shit like that. I always had to challenge him. Part of growing up, I suppose."

"And this is the man you're here for?" Fiona asked softly, as though half-hoping the question wouldn't be heard.

"He's still my father" Dermot scowled.

"Is he?" Fiona replied. "Isn't that the whole reason you're here, because you think he might not be? And frankly, Dermot – well, don't take this the wrong way, but why would you want him to be? If I were you, I'd pray to God that he wasn't my real father. Why would you want a share in that bloodline?"

"That man raised me" Dermot snapped, bristling.

"He doesn't deserve a son like you" she said, and sighed. "It's none of my business, really. Your relationship with your father is your own business, and it's not for me or anyone else to get involved." He heard her breathe in, as though preparing for something special.

"But?"

"But nothing. Like I say, none of my business."

The silence mounted.

"Alright. Here's the thing." She breathed in again, loud in the silence. "If this man wasn't your father, then good. That's some nasty, backwards genes you can do without. And, not to put ideas in your head, but did you ever wonder why he only hit you? Challenging authority is part of being fifteen, and I'm sure your brothers did the same when they were that age. But he only hit you.

"Anyway. You defend him when I say you should hope he's not your father, because he's the man who raised you. And yet you're on this mission to discover if he was your biological father like it's the most important thing in the world. Well, make up your mind, Dermot. Either the man who raised you is your father, regardless of whose cells you grew from, or else he was some tyrant whose care you were left in, and the sooner you stop defending him, the better, for your own psychological wellbeing."

"Wow" Dermot whispered.

"I'm sorry" said Fiona after a pause. "I don't know why I spoke to you like that."

I do. In the darkness, when we can't see each other's faces, we feel almost anonymous, free to say whatever we feel without repercussions, our souls naked, our words pure. When I can't see your face, I feel I can tell you anything, as though you're not even there, as though I'm talking to myself. This is the black magic of the confessional, the wisdom of millennia; secrets come out in the dark.

"I'll just say one more thing on the subject. I hope you won't think I'm interfering, but I have to say something." Dermot let the silence answer her, torn between anger and sorrow, and joy, a wild, unexpected joy, a sheer thrill in the knowledge that finally, for once, someone cared enough to take his side and say the things he wouldn't let himself say.

"If you, now, as you are, saw a grown man hit a fifteen year old in the face and knock him unconscious, for whatever reason – what would you think of that man?"

36

The morning changed everything. He rose with the sun, ten feet tall and growing, his shadow trailing behind like dark wings in the bright light. Stepping out of the door of the cottage, he turned his face to the sky like a relative, his immortal brother, the gold-pierced throne of stars and gods. The blood sang in his limbs; he could feel it. He could feel everything; the wind in the grass rippling through his hair, the river thundering in his veins, the trees swaying along his spine, and the sea washing the shore of his lungs clean of the filth of thirty years. The sun's fire boiled within him, a rising feeling like every song he had ever heard, life and light and majesty glowing like coals in his hands as the earth trembled before him. No ghosts, no ghouls, no phantoms of bog or tomb could stand before him now. He could see himself as though through their eyes, too vast and bright to look upon, a coruscating beacon of fire in the flat grey world they haunted, gnawing themselves thin in the shadows on scraps of mortal fear. He smiled. Today, there is nothing I can't do. Today, the world is mine; everyone else is just visiting.[95]

---

[95] This is the voice of mania. We might pity Dermot in his moments of hatred, fear, and sorrow; but this is the other side of the schizophrenic coin, the other edge of the sword. And while Dermot's state of mind, as described in this passage, might almost seem enviable, it is important to remember that even the upswings of his condition are not without a dark side: decreased sleeping patterns, irritability, inability to focus, the mind seeming to race through a thousand things at once. That Dermot was technically 'happy' in these moments should not detract from the fact that this, too, is a symptom of disease.

He heard panting behind him, the skitter of paws on the small stones of the yard in front of the cottage. He turned, and Seamus leapt up to greet him, pawing at his stomach and whining with the uninhibited joy of animals.

"Seamus, Seamus," he growled, playing with the mutt's ears, his own joy barely less than the dog's on this sun-shot day.

"Someone's happy to see you" Fiona said as she came around the corner of the cottage.

"Yeah. Seamus seems quite pleased, too" Dermot replied.

"Cheeky gobshite. You're full of yourself today."

"Play your cards right, and you could be too."

It took her a second.

"Oh, you dirty fecker! Where's Tim?"

"Don't know. Out bringing the cows in, or letting them out, or something. I have yet to wake up before he goes out."

He watched her come closer, his eyes half in the next world. He watched the light follow the curve of her limbs, as though she were a prism for all the world, breaking and remaking everything around her, bringing beauty and danger wherever she alighted. The monstrous geometry of her body, the daemonic machinery of eyes, lips, legs, hips; blurring the world she moved through until in a waste of meaningless light, there was only her, solid, real and whole.

She stopped, close enough to touch, though they both knew the rules. He leaned forward.

"What're you *doing*?" she giggled, leaning away, turning her face from his searching mouth. "Someone might see..."

"No one's gonna see" he snorted. "And so what if they do? If this is impure, then they can all sit on their fucking purity." Fiona laughed.

"Are you alright?" she asked, smiling, peering up into his eyes as though the rules had changed, and something she had known, measured, sized up and accounted for had suddenly revealed hidden depths, and she was struggling to keep up. Sunsets over the sea, the blazing star turning the water into beaten gold; the fury of springtime streams singing down the mountains as winter loosens its hold; the wild roar of life in the throat of every animal that ever lived – barely anything in his life compared to the beauty of her eyes in that moment, the cerulean blue shot through with veins of green and gold, sea and sky and sun meeting there at an impossible depth, all swirling around a well of absolute black, night piercing day, day circling night, world without end.

"I'm better than that" he said. "I'm alive. More alive than most people ever get. Angels are circling my head, flaming swords in all directions. I feel how God must feel on his birthday." One day in ten, or fifty, or a hundred, I don't feel down. I feel like a hero, like a god, like nothing can stop me, like I'm above everything. And that one percent almost makes the miserable ninety-nine worth it.

She laughed again, whirling giddily in the eddies of his own intoxication.

"Well, you've a way with words on you today, anyway. Shall we go for a walk?"

The stream burbled at their feet, tinkling against the round stones of the river bed, catching the sun like a channel of light charging out to join itself with the cosmos. Seamus ran ahead, following the trails of mysterious smells through the bracken and ferns that sprouted all along the high clay banks of the river. Fiona walked beside Dermot, their shoulders and elbows brushing against one another, their bodies striking the fierce sparks of illicit attraction wherever they touched. He could feel her breath in his blood. The fibrous nerves of his vertebrae reached towards her like tentacles. His heart missed a beat, trying to synchronise itself with hers.

"So what's brought all this on, then?"

"I don't know" he replied. "Depends on how you look at it, I guess. I know what a psychiatrist would say. This is a symptom of my disease, the highs and the lows.[96] But follow that to its logical conclusion: every extremity of emotion, every deep feeling is a symptom of insanity. So where does that leave passion? Where does that leave inspiration? What space is left for God?"

---

[96] See last note, and introduction re: Dermot's understanding of the processes of psychiatry. Unfortunately, his knowledge hindered rather than helped his treatment. Because he knew some of the basics, he was apt to not listen to his therapist, or to twist their words to give them a meaning the therapist did not intend. He would feed us made-up dreams and false neuroses. His intelligence became a shield against effective treatment which was incredibly difficult to break down.

"Jesus. Quite the philosopher today, aren't we?"

"Sorry if I'm boring you. It's just - I think this is something quite rare. It must be. I feel – everything. You know what I mean? It must be rare, because if everyone felt this way, even just once, they could never live the way they do. There'd be no room for hate, or anger, or small-mindedness, ever. I feel like part of the world, it in me, me in it – I know, I sound fucking crazy. Maybe I am. But if this is crazy, you'd have to be crazy to want to be sane, because this is a thousand times better. You could wake up every morning in the same bed, go to work, secretly hate everyone along the way, punch the clock, sit there for ten hours, then go home and find nothing that was worth the wait. Or, you could sit in a meadow for eight hours and watch the sunlight bring beauty to every living thing, and come to understand the infinitely complex, infinitely beautiful system of biology and physics and natural law that underpins the whole universe, and realise that you yourself are one tiny part of that magnificent harmony, one tiny fraction. But not insignificant. When you see the universe with those eyes, the only response is laughter. Maybe that's why the Buddha is so happy."

He watched her eyebrows climb the cliff of her forehead, watched a smile break like the racing dawn across her face, watched her slender fingers rake her hair back from her eyes like the wind in a field of yellow grain.

"Wow. I honestly don't know what to say to that."

Seamus bounded towards them, his paws wet, tail beating against his flanks. Dermot broke the branch off a tree, quickly stripped it of twigs and leaves, leaned back and hurled it downstream as hard as he could; watched it land with a long silver splash in the water and be swept downstream with the current. Seamus gave a bark of excitement and launched himself after it.

"I do" he said, watching the dog's haunches vanish behind a fern brake. "See that bush over there? How about I take you over there, rip off those jeans and show you three and a half minutes of heaven?" [97]

Maybe on some distant glorious otherworld, where people may die in peace together, we might watch these lovers, no longer

---

[97] Increase in sexual desire is another common symptom of a manic episode, often leading to some particularly poor decisions on the part of the sufferer.

young, vanish hand in hand into the watery distance; but here on this pellet of muck, we await only their destruction.

37

Winter awakes. Black puddles blackly reflect black crows, black clouds, charcoal-drawn trees on the black walls of a cave. *SPTIYKCOXI*[98]; not always, Grace, but forever. When I thought I couldn't be further from you, I was already on my way back.

VRTKITTE, Grace; patience. Only a madman could piece it together. *JFCVSXKOCHY* eyes are upon us always; discretion is the key here[99]. I will *IFMGFGTKHSXPOW*, Grace, *OGRQQOJE*; but I'm here for a reason. There are no accidents in a story, every seemingly random event serving to advance the plot to a conclusion long known to those not swept up in the narrative; and that's all this is, Grace. A story. The story. We all know how the story ends, but we keep on reading just to see how we'll get there.

We make our own myths; my boss is an ogre, my mother-in-law is a witch. Life is simpler when we can believe that people are one thing, either good or bad, but never as they really are: hovering somewhere on the infinite scale between the two. Hitler had many friends. To his faithful dog, the child molester is a benevolent deity. Who wants to admit that? There are no monsters, just heroes gone astray. *GCL QJ EFUT HKDOPW GIE ISJJ IP HOWFGVKET NMMYT.*

It's the same old story, and no one wants to see it. This hero's journey, wrapped up in fantasy and invention and symbolism, is the story of everyone's life. This is how it goes. This is the business of

---

[98] Presumably, this is the Vigenere cipher at work, as previously mentioned. However, the keyword here is not MIOTAS; that much, we know. No translation is available; I have neither the time nor the interest to play such games with my patients.

[99] No it's not.

living, while the stars ignore us and the gods grow old. Instead of dragons and giants, we battle bills and mortgage payments and the twisted shadows of our own battered psyches; but we struggle all the same. This is the story: we are born, and none of us knows from where. We face challenges. We die. The role of the mythic hero is simply to amplify.

So follow it further. This is a bridge, or a thread to follow in the labyrinth – see how the metaphor births the story, and not the other way around? – that shows us something simple and eternally forgotten: the commonality of our existence. We are, fundamentally, all the same, and not in some hand-holding, lighter-waving, commercially-sponsored politically-correct-feelgoodery kind of way. This is what myth is for, to remind us of who we are, our true, eternal, universal nature; to free us from the prisons of crumbling flesh we are trapped inside, our hot breath further clouding the narrow view from the too-small eyeslits, and to answer the old question, the important one – how should I live?

38

"Well in the merry month of May I started,
Left the girls in Tuam nearly broken-hearted,
Saluted father dear. Kissed me darlin' mother..."[100]
The bright stars wheeled in the merry sky, and his singing
breath frosted in the night air as Dermot walked the long road home
from Malone's pub. He had been tilting pints all night in the town.
Taking his leave of Sean, the evening's co-intoxicant, at the gate in
front of Bridgid's house, Dermot made his way now over the bridge
and into the thick darkness between the high hedges. The blood
gambolled in his veins, his heart singing in the careless joy and false
certainty of a rare drunk. He was young, still, a young man in his
father's land, still time to make the fatal choice of his life, still strength
and energy enough, if he wanted it, to carve a future out of this rocky
windswept earth, or else to disappear on the winds of the world, and
land wherever he fell.

The darkness was thick under the stars. Tim had headed for
home long ago, leaving the two cousins in the pub to swap stories of

---

[100] From "The Rocky Road to Dublin", previously heard at Dermot's
father's wake. cf. note 8. This is the kind of music every Irishman
hears as he dies, the pipes wailing the loneliness their intemperate
race is heir to, the cry of abandonment from every wasted ghost of
an unhappy land. This is the sound that drove the ancient Celts to
war, the drums pounding in their blood, the flutes doubled by their
wild cries, that intoxicating mix of rage, joy and despair that made
them charge naked into the well-ordered, well-armed ranks of the
oppressors, ancient and modern. Statistically speaking, Ireland is a
nation of schizophrenics.

love and conquest, to drink and sing along with the band that had got up in the corner, to follow every inclination of the intemperate hearts they were heir to, surrounded by their own people. Their own people; the thick-fingered, blue-eyed, round-shouldered old farmers of the parishes round about, the Morriseys and Mahoneys, the Callaghans and Kellys, the Farrels and Fitzpatricks that had been neighbours here through the centuries, facing down time like the cliffs that frown over the Atlantic, ancient and implacable. The cousins, mere boys in the presence of Tim's dogged generation, had behaved accordingly, roaring along with the songs they knew, beating time on the bar, overflowing into exaggerated displays of affection and camaraderie.

"God, though, Dermot, we're glad ye came back to us, after all" Sean had slurred, pulling his cousin close and almost sliding off his stool in the process.

"I'm glad I came" Dermot had hazily replied. "Where else – you know? Where else should I be? We're family, and that means more, than…than… *anything.*"

The cool air was sobering, though. The silence was absolute. Only the voice of the river, the low wind in the few trees, and his own footsteps on the cracked road, outrageously loud. The road rose near Tim's house, and the hedges shrank; there was no light in the small windows of the old cottage. Dermot stopped. The thick white walls seemed to glow grimly in the inky darkness of the fields all around. He thought of his father, as a young man, his life, his family, his betrayals still far ahead of him, coming home to this house, from that pub, on just such a night as this. Everything changes, and nothing does. His father's father, too, the grandfather he never met, must have come home by this road, just like this; and so on back into the dwindling past, like a reflection's reflection in the curved line of infinity.

He froze. The fields rolled on, black and silent, lightless slopes rising almost invisibly to a ridge that could be seen only where the stars abruptly disappeared behind it. But he had seen something. Out across the nearest field, back towards the river between the two houses, his eyes had tracked some shadowy movement.

He watched. There was no mistake. Something was moving in the darkness, over by the wall between fields; he could see it as a greater blackness against the murky grey of the stones. Fear chased the last shreds of drunkenness from his veins, and the past receded. He was himself again, small and alone. And different; a lifetime spent in cities had given him a wariness that Tim, or Sean, or even his father,

173

at home in this utterly known and knowable environment, would never possess. It was no bird, no trick of the wind or the darkness; something large was moving through the night.

His eyes fixed on the creeping shape, Dermot followed the road up, around the cottage, and into the fields.

His heart pounded in his ears. Keeping the dim grey line of the wall on his left, barely conscious of what he was doing, he moved towards where he had last seen movement. Something stronger than fear drove him onwards, into the teeth of his own terror; the demons can harry him all they want, but they won't make him run. Nothing moved now but the wind in the grass and the stars like jewels clutched in the branches of the trees, and Dermot, advancing through fear and darkness in the hidden field. He could hear the river again. The wind hissed. And then he knew, by some vestigial sense of prehistory more than any sight, that the thing, whatever it was, was in front of him, maybe twenty feet away.

It was big. He could see its hulking black shape against the dark trees behind. Maybe a cow had somehow gotten out from the cattle shed? Dermot inched closer.

"Hello?" he tried. It moved, a little. Dermot saw it rise higher, as though it had been sitting before, or crawling, and now it stood at its full height. Too tall for a dog, or any cow that Tim owned. And broad, too.[101] For a moment, Dermot thought it might be the old farmer himself.

"Tim?" he said hoarsely.

There was a noise, as of tentative movement. He could see nothing. Everything was still beneath the frozen stars. Then he knew; it moved. It was coming towards him. Like a cloud that speeds westwards, swallowing the stars, it came on, and blackness came with it. Dermot stood as though turned to stone, unable to move, to confront or to fly from this horror that approached like the long fall into madness, the black heart of lightless night.

"Who are you?" The creature advanced, wordlessly. Terror turned his shrinking blood to ice while his desperate mind scrabbled at the walls of his skull like a rat in a maze.

"This is Fallon land. You're trespassing" His voice was thin and cracked, squeaking out of a throat dry as dust. But the dark shape

---

[101] Didn't I fucking tell you?

stopped. He could see it, still silent, a great black figure now motionless, less than ten feet away. There was a flash of sudden movement, and he would have cried out if his voice had not deserted him.

But the stars shone out brighter, laced among the reappearing trees. The thing, whatever it was, was gone.

39

Seven winters scoured the green hills. Seven springs pushed fingers of new growth through the soil; seven summers blasted the forests with hot air from the south. Seven autumns rolled in from the sea, shrouded in mist and the shadow of death. The once-proud host of Finn McCool, most powerful warlord in all of Erin, dwindled year upon year, and still the traitor O'Duibhne walked freely with Finn's stolen bride. By witchcraft and the slow, steady sorcery of age, Finn himself had become an old man, his hair grey, his face cragged; but his eyes still burned with the fire of his obsession. His hand still held his sword steady, the blade unrusted in its sheath.

Blasted by the wind and by long years of fruitless wandering, eighteen men struggled down the hill.

"Just up ahead, my lord" said the peasant at Finn's side. "In the shelter of those trees, in an old crofter's hut, the man you are looking for is sleeping."

"You are sure he is still there? For years he has flown from us, or else fought his way free; why does he remain here even as we approach?"

"He is sick, my lord" cringed the peasant. "Some say he is dying. The lady comes down to the village, to buy food and such medicines as we have to offer; she has even paid, in gold, for the healer to go back with her and see what may be done for him. But nothing seems to help, and so they remain. She was seen gathering firewood this morning; they are surely still there now."

"This sits uneasy with me, Finn." Conan, fat and bald and wheezing from the downhill climb, lumbered up to his leader. Of the ragtag group of so-called warriors Finn had left under his command, Conan had become the leader, due mainly to the fact he was older than the rest. Neither the strongest in arms nor the swiftest in thought of the men of the Fianna, Conan had stuck around when all others left, even Finn's own kin, simply because he lacked the wit to know where else to go. Oisin, and Diorruing, and Oscar, and Cailte, and all the other leaders of the Fianna had abandoned Finn, one by one, to his own vengeful quest. He was left now with only a handful of warriors, mostly young and unproved and eager to earn the favour of their leader by whatever method it took. These were men who had never met Diarmuid, who had never stood beside him in battle and known him as a man of honour, and courage, and strength. This was all Finn had, and now it seemed he might lose even that.

"What?" Finn demanded sharply. Conan ran a hand across his bald, sweating forehead.

"Well, to take O'Duibhne this way, in his sick bed. I mean, it's not really.... fair, is it?"

"Fair?" Finn bristled. "Fair? For seven years we have chased him for his crimes against me and against the law, and now you question what is fair? It is my will that he be slain, and my stolen bride be returned to me; what has fairness to do with anything?"

"But...if he were not sick, at least he would have the chance...to defend himself...."

177

"Believe me, Conan, if Diarmuid were not sick, he would cut off your fat head in a heartbeat, and the beardless heads of this gang of urchins, too. Would that be fair enough for your delicate sensibilities?"

Conan muttered to himself, his eyes on the ground. The other soldiers had gathered around the two, stung by Finn's angry words.

"What is it? Speak, man!" Finn demanded. Conan lifted his head uncertainly, struggling to meet Finn's gaze.

"This is not warrior's work, Finn. To break into a hut where a woman tends to a sick man, and to slay that man and drag that woman off against her will – these are the actions of a bandit, not an honourable man."

"If it were warrior's work, I should have brought warriors, instead of the rogues and trembling boys I see here" Finn sneered. The men cowered before him, terrified of his wrath. "Go then!" he roared. "All of you, leave! Men of the Fianna, who desert your lord at will. You were all there for the feasting and the sporting, and not one of you will stand by me now. Go then! Back to your stinking hovels, or wherever you came from, fit for nothing but drinking and wenching. Go!"

"Come on, lads" said Conan, warily. "Let's head home." The young warriors trailed after him, looking back over their shoulders at the raging warlord.

"Come" said Finn to the peasant who guided him, "show me where he lies." And he drew his sword.

"There, my lord" whispered the peasant, pointing through the trees. "You can see the hut from here."

The walls were rough and unfinished, built of grey stone. The roof sloped, and seemed to have collapsed at one end. Ferns grew from cracks in the walls, and moss furred what roof remained. But a thin spire of grey smoke twisted from the unruined chimney.

"Well done" said Finn quietly to the peasant, and slipped a heavy purse into his outstretched hand. "You may go now." Nodding, the peasant shuffled back the way they had come, through the trees, breaking into a run once he was out of Finn's sight. It is not good for common folk to become embroiled in the affairs of the great and the powerful, though they do pay in gold.

Finn stalked silently toward the cottage, the greatest hunter in Erin moving on the forest floor without breaking a single twig. He pressed his body against the rough wall next to the rotten wood door, and listened. There was no sound from inside except the occasional crackling of the fire.

His sword in his fist, Finn burst through the door with a cry. A blonde woman in a dishevelled dress crouched on the floor – Grainne. At her feet lay a warrior, still in his battle armour, but no longer young and handsome. The long years of pursuit that had aged Finn had also taken their toll on Diarmuid; his face was pale and sweating, his breathing shallow. He looked indeed like a man on the verge of death.

But his eyes flashed open at Finn's cry and Grainne's scream; he leapt to his feet instantly, as though he had been merely resting, his warrior's instincts as sharp as they had ever been in Finn's service. Snatching up a branch from the woodpile beside the fire, he stood unsteadily in front of Grainne.

"Finn," he gasped, the wood shaking in his hands, "so you have found me here, as I feared. Where are your men?"

"I need no troop of warriors to take my vengeance on thee, Diarmuid" Finn growled. "By my own hand will I rid myself of the shame you have brought upon me."

179

"Shame?" spat Grainne. "How will the murder of a sick man lessen your shame, Finn? All Erin will know what you have done, and your name will be cursed the length and breadth of the land."

"Silence, whore" Finn croaked. "I'll deal with you once your – " and Diarmuid swung his branch at Finn's head, the old warlord stepping backwards as he raised his sword to protect himself. A foot of wood was sheared off by the iron sword, but Diarmuid came on, jabbing at his former leader with the branch as though it were a sword. Finn lunged forward, and Diarmuid lost the rest of the branch keeping the blade from his chest. But the hut was small, and Finn's sword was long; Diarmuid stepped in close, grabbing at Finn's wrist, almost falling into the warlord's arms. Diarmuid's fingers struggled to prise Finn's sword loose from his grip, and his other hand clawed at his neck, but Finn seized Diarmuid and flung him to the ground. Diarmuid crawled backwards frantically, scrabbling on the floor for some kind of weapon as Finn advanced, raising his sword. Then Finn stumbled from a blow to the head that made sickly lights bloom in his vision, his knees buckling as he battled the darkness that swarmed up to meet him. He crashed against the wall, but kept his feet, and turned to see Grainne holding the hatchet she used for chopping firewood, her fair face contorted with rage and fear. Finn growled, and pushed himself upright, his head clearing. He would kill them both. Grainne backed away, terrified, but even as Finn moved towards her, Diarmuid leapt at Finn, reaching again for his sword-arm, dragging himself up by the warlord's clothes. Finn bashed the hilt of his sword against Diarmuid's skull, but the weakened warrior held on desperately. Finn struck again, but Diarmuid caught his wrist as it came down, and pulled Finn down with him. Finn, struggling to keep his feet under the weight of Diarmuid, sank to one knee. As he fought, he felt a hand seize his hair, pull his head sharply back, and a cold steel edge pressed into his throat.

"Stop it" Grainne hissed. As the men struggled, she had come up behind Finn as he sank to the floor, and now she had him. A bead of bright blood sprang from the tortured skin under the notched blade of the hatchet. Panting, Diarmuid struggled to stand.

"Grainne," he wheezed, "don't."

"Drop your sword, Finn" Grainne said. Finn's eyes were locked on Diarmuid's. His sword clattered to the floor, and Diarmuid snatched it up, levelling the point at Finn's heart.

"Don't kill him, Grainne" Diarmuid panted.

"Why not?" she demanded, the hatchet in her white-knuckled hand digging in a little deeper. "He would have killed us! For seven years, this old snake has been trying to kill us. Why shouldn't I cut his throat like a pig and rid us of this evil for good?" Finn's breathing was shallow; he stared Diarmuid down with all the coolness he could muster, but he said nothing.

"We can't kill him" Diarmuid struggled. "If we do, then all the Fianna are oath-bound to avenge him. The hunt will be back on, like it was in the beginning, and this time the Fenians won't give up, whatever they think of me. They will avenge their leader, as they must, and Finn will have won."

"He doesn't win if he's dead" Grainne spat.

"He'll die a hero, or at least a leader – something he isn't while he's alive" said Diarmuid. "If we let him live, then he'll live in infamy forever, because he was never able to beat us. He's already lost the respect of his mean for hunting us the way that he has, and now he's proven unable to murder a woman and a sick man. That's enough."

"If we let him live, he'll come after us again" said Grainne.

"What about it, Finn?" asked Diarmuid. "If we let you live, you will swear a blood-oath that you will not pursue us any more, that you will not harm us yourself nor order anyone else to harm us, that you will let us live out our lives in a place of our choosing and will not harass us any further."

"Or?" asked Finn, his eyes blazing.

"Or you bleed out your life onto this dirt floor" Diarmuid shrugged. "Those are your options. You swear or you die. There is no third choice."

"If I die, you die" Finn growled.

"Perhaps" said Diarmuid. "Perhaps not. But you'll be just as dead, either way."

Finn stared angrily into Diarmuid's blue eyes. Seven years of pursuit, for this. Infamy. Disgrace. The steel was cold against his neck. His blood crusted on the blade. Grainne's hand was steady.

"I swear" said Finn levelly. "I will hunt the two of you no more. You may live out your lives with no harassment from me, provided you do not take up arms against me or my household."

Diarmuid nodded slowly.

"Let him go, Grainne" he said.

The hatchet pressed a little harder against Finn's throat. The hand that held it trembled. And it was gone.

Finn stood up, rubbing the sticky patch of blood on his throat. Diarmuid regarded him coolly.

"I will never forget the harm you have caused me, O'Duibhne" he said.

"Likewise" Diarmuid replied.

"You will never regain your place among my men."

"I wouldn't take it if it lay in a ditch by the roadside."

"You will never be my queen" Finn said to Grainne. She snorted. Diarmuid laughed.

"You're no king, Finn McCoul" he smiled. "And even if you were, some things royalty cannot buy."

"My sword?" said Finn, holding out his hand. Grainne gasped as Diarmuid slowly stepped towards Finn and handed the weapon over. Finn took the sword, and stood for a moment, holding it, looking at Diarmuid. Diarmuid stared back.

With a shrug, Finn sheathed his sword, and wordlessly strode out of the hut.

The wind whipped across the bare back of the ridge.

40

The ghostly cries of gulls haunted the salty air, their white bodies circling and dipping under the dark brows of the cliffs. Far below, the sea churned against the rocky shore, trailing circular white veins across the grey-blue skin of the water. Congregations of cormorants huddled along shelves in the black rock, bowing their heads as they stared out to sea, the dark beginning of eternity.

The grass flailed in the rough wind at the rocky edge above the cliffs. A thin fence of barbed wire was tangled there, nailed to rotting wooden posts that rose drunkenly against the sky. Beyond, there was the great void the cliffs surrounded, the roofless hall of air founded on the echoing deep. Dermot could hear it calling, the hulking silence between the shrieks of birds and the hissing of waves ruined on the wet stones. The fatal drop spoke to him, the seductive voice of the crumbling edge, the sea opening its arms to take him in, the rocks straining towards his tiny body, lost in the vastness of nature as he fell into oblivion. He saw himself, as he often did now, from behind, standing frail and vulnerable mere inches from the edge. Slowly, as though creeping up on himself, his figure grew larger, the viewpoint getting steadily closer, that final plunge growing nearer with every silent step –

"What's wrong?" Fiona asked, following his gaze as he turned.

"Nothing" he said hurriedly. Fiona tilted her head and looked up at him questioningly.

"Seeing things again?" she asked.

Dermot nodded. When you spend your life hiding something from everyone, it's not easy to get used to the idea of someone knowing about it, much less discussing it with you.

She reached towards him, briefly taking his hand in her own. Her soft skin was warm, despite the bitter wind from the Atlantic. She gave his fingers a squeeze, and let go. Secrecy is a hard habit to break.

His soul trailing behind, always,

Unable to survive in a body so torn, so toxic,

His corrosive heart, the lactic poison of a muscle eating itself

"I remember coming here on holiday, with my dad" Dermot changed the subject as thin nervous wires tightened his veins. "I remember the wind. The view, you don't really forget; anyway, there's a million pictures out there to remind you. But you forget about the wind." The hair was pushed flat on his head, his sunburnt nose stinging as he faced out to sea. A fat tear broke from the corner of his eye, pushed sideways along his cheek by the wind that rippled its crawling surface as it rippled the surface of the sea, three hundred feet below; the universe in a nutshell, atoms and solar systems, the wing of the bumblebee. The eternity of everyday things.

"Oh, you're crying" Fiona smiled, wiping the wind-worried droplet from his stubbled cheek with her thumb.

"Thanks" he grinned sheepishly.

"There's a picture of me, here, actually, back at my dad's house" Dermot went on. "I must be about three; barely standing up in the wind, this big kid's grin on my face. Right in front of the tower over there." Dermot nodded across the cliffs to the stone tower that peeked over a distant ridge.

"Aww. Sounds cute. Whatever happened?" Dermot echoed Fiona's smile.

"Those holidays. Every year we used to come here, I think. The family holiday to Ireland. Owen used to dread them. Sitting by the fire in Tim's cottage, no TV, no other kids, nothing for miles around. I used to like them, I think. We could slide down the haystacks in the barn, or chase cows around the fields. Not for everyone, I suppose."

'Come to think of it, after my mum left, that was the end of them. We never took a trip to Ireland again. I think the last time my father was here was when I was about eleven; right before mum left. He never came back, until – you know. I wonder why."

"Too many memories, maybe?" Fiona said uncomfortably.

"Maybe." They walked on a while, not speaking, listening to the noise of the sea and the mad wind that tore inland, back towards Cloonashee.

"He liked the countryside, though, my dad. You could tell he missed it. When we were a bit older, he used to go for long drives in the country. He'd be gone all day. Took me with him, too, sometimes. We'd park the car somewhere and just take off across the fields, walking for miles. He never seemed to get tired. I must have been about fourteen; you'd think the last thing I'd want to do is spend a Saturday walking with my father; but I really enjoyed it. It felt – special, like there was something he was trying to tell me without actually saying anything; trying to show me a little corner of his world, maybe."

"Was it only you he took? Not your brothers?" Fiona asked.

"Yeah, just me. Again, Owen would have been bored to tears by the whole thing. And if Alex got jealous, he never said anything. Maybe that's why I liked it; it was just him and me out there. We got on pretty well, sometimes. Other times – well, not so much."

"Maybe that's why he only took you. He only hit you, too."

"I don't know" Dermot sighed. "But it was – nice. For hours, we wouldn't even say anything – just walking, in silence. But it wasn't the same silence there was at home, that horrible, sullen, brooding silence, like a weapon, or a threat. This was nice; peaceful. He was calm, on those trips; at peace. So was I. Maybe it made him feel young again. Reminded him of a time before he even met my mother, when he used to walk these fields, these cliffs, before life hurt so much. Maybe that's why he took me, too; I reminded him of himself in some way. He said to me once, 'You and I are alike. Owen, and Alex, they're very different to each other, and to us. But yourself, you're like me, I think.' He never explained what he meant by that, but it made me happy at the time."

"Well, that's nice" Fiona said softly.

"Yeah. He was a quiet man, generally – same as Tim[102]. But when the two of us were out on those walks, he'd open up a lot. He'd talk about Ireland, his childhood, all the places he'd been – he even talked about mum once or twice. He didn't say much about her – nothing about the affair. Just a couple of times, he'd mention her as part of some other story, without any bitterness, and I used to hope that maybe he was over it, that maybe he finally didn't hurt anymore from what she did. Wasn't the case, unfortunately. But when we were out in the country, I think it didn't hurt him the way it did at home. He remembered who he was out there, in the silence, and I think he wanted me to see that.

'He taught me to read a map. He'd drive, and I'd navigate, and I'd take the map when we went out walking, though half the time we weren't going anywhere in particular. He'd always follow my directions, even though I think he probably knew his way around all along, and knew when I steered us wrong. But he'd never comment on it. Sometimes we'd find something – some old tomb, a castle, a standing stone or a hillfort. The hillforts were the best. They were

---

[102] Ha!

always empty, because there's not usually much to see – just a few ancient ditches and a good view. We'd be there alone, and he'd imagine what it must have been like, living in one of these fortresses back in the Iron Age. We'd wander around, trying to find where the entrance would have been, where the chieftain's hall might have stood. Then we'd go outside and try to imagine how we would attack the place, if we had to. We'd try and find the best way up the hill, the lowest part of the ditch – stuff like that. I think it was those trips that made me want to study archaeology. I wonder now how much I was interested in the ancient past, and how much I was chasing that feeling of being with him, seeing his eyes light up as he let his imagination sweep him to some other place and time."

"That's very sweet, Dermot Fallon" Fiona said, her blue eyes fixed on his.

"Yeah, well" Dermot shrugged. "That was all... before. A long time ago. As I got older, our relationship really deteriorated. We stopped taking those trips together. We stopped talking. But – I miss him, when I think of him like that, smiling, with the wind making him even balder than he was. Maybe he was right, and we are more alike than I realise. I don't know."

"That's the thing, Dermot" Fiona said, uncertainly. "He was your father then, in those moments, if he ever was. I mean, whoever your biological father was, this is the man who raised you. It sounds like he did love you, for all his faults. And I know you loved him. What else matters?"

"It matters" Dermot muttered. "Yes, he raised me. And I did love him – I do. I always will. He'll always be my father, in that sense. But it does matter who my real father – I mean my biological father – was. I have to know what sort of person my mother was – would she really have a child by one man and marry another? I have to know what sort of man my father was – would he raise another man's child, even after the mother abandoned him? Is that why there was so much tension between us when I got older? Is any of this mine? Ireland, my inheritance, my race, my family – is it all just a lie? Do I have any right to call this place home? That's why I need to know."

"Fair enough" Fiona sighed, turning her face to the sea.

They walked on, the grass whispering around their feet, its message lost on the streaming wind.

"He used to play these tapes," Dermot chuckled, "on our trips, in the car. The Dubliners, Christy Moore, The Fureys, The Chieftains.

The Clancy Brothers. All the old Irish folk tunes, you know. 'Peggy Gordon', 'Fields Of Athenry', 'Whiskey in the Jar', 'Rocky Road to Dublin', 'The Foggy Dew'. We learned those songs before we could speak, almost. Music's funny that way. In Canada, or England, wherever I've travelled, you can tell someone with Irish family, because they know and love those songs. They become like a badge that you wear, wherever you go, that proclaims who you are and where you're from, so that your own kind can pick you out, in the Irish theme pub, singing along with the band. Wonder why that is. It seems like it's the last thing to leave, as a family gets further and further from the Old Country, as time goes by. The Italians have their food, the Spanish have their language, the English have – well, I don't know what the English have that gets passed down. Their sense of humour, maybe. But this is what we have, the bastard sons of Erin flung haphazardly across the globe – we have our music."

Fiona sniffed.

"Funny, because I know a lot of Irish people who don't listen to that kind of stuff."

"I'm not surprised" Dermot replied. "People born in Ireland have no need to remind themselves of their Irishness – it's all around them. Every time you open your mouth, everybody can tell where you're from. But people like me, born and raised in a foreign country, we need something to set us apart, to identify us as Irish no matter what our accents or our birth certificates might say."

"That's one way of looking at it, I suppose" Fiona said. Dermot glanced at her out of the corner of her eye.

"You don't agree?" he asked.

"It's not that" she said hurriedly. "I'm sure you're right. It just seems to me that there's a lot of people who want to be Irish who maybe have one Irish ancestor who left during the Famine. And I don't mean you; I know your pedigree. I'm practically a member of your family."

Dermot winced.

"Jesus, don't say that" he muttered.

"Why not?" Fiona smiled broadly. "Once I marry Sean, you and me'll be second cousins, once removed."

"You can be really mean sometimes, you know that?" He smiled as though it was a joke. She seemed to believe it.

"What? I'm just saying. I don't make the rules."

But you do Fiona; you do.

"It's disgusting."

"Why?"

"Because it makes what I was planning to do to you in the car incest."

"Oooo, kinky. Do I get to know what it is beforehand?"

"Well, not now."

"Not even a hint?"

Dermot scanned the bare fields with slitted eyes. The rocky green waste was empty of human life; a bend in the path hid them from the more heavily touristed parts of the cliffs. His hand grazed the warm pit of denim between her thighs; she smiled as she lifted her face to him, and his lips found the hot pulse in her neck. She exhaled deeply, her breath by his ear outshouting the wind as he kissed her smooth skin, and pressed his hand hard against her; she gasped and rose to her toes as he drew his hand slowly back, feeling her hips follow as it went.

Dermot stepped back, hands at his side. The angry look on her face quickly melted into a greedy smile.

"Let's go" she said in a single breath.

"Well, I don't know. What's the big hurry? We haven't even – " Fiona took his hand, turned, and pulled him after her, towards the car park.

"No talking" she said sternly. "You're coming with me."

41

A dark speck in a waste of green, Dermot cut the hill towards the ridge.[103] The wind flattened the grass as it tumbled down the soft slopes, a singing child of the sea. Towers of cloud stood unmoving in the sky, rank upon rank of mottled grey shapes, the vaporous castles of a kingdom he could only see, could never touch.

He walked in the shadow of a stone wall where it burst from the grass like the spine of an ancient beast, following a rising wrinkle of land that rose like a great root from the valley to the windswept crest of the hills. This was the south-west limit of his uncle's fields; the other side of the wall was a wilderness where the grass grew thick as years uncounted. All around, the emptiness; more profound than any desolation, the silence of abandonment haunted these barren fields.

Quartz crystals sparkled in the tear-sharp stones that ran like a crest along the top of the wall. Dermot felt the rocks, held together

---

[103] There has been some confusion over Dermot's writing which has rendered it difficult for me to complete my work of annotation. It seems that some others of the hospital staff were aware that Dermot was keeping this journal, and wished to determine its whereabouts for reasons not entirely clear to me. Of course, I might have told them that the notes were safe in my possession; but all large institutions, even places of healing such as this, have their politics. I deemed it expedient instead to conceal my knowledge of the notes, and so we have endured a tedious search of offices and patient's rooms before certain parties were satisfied that the journal was not hidden somewhere on the premises, perhaps sewn page by rolled page into the seam on the mattress of a bed. In any case, the excitement has passed. Let us press on.

only by gravity and the skill of a vanishing trade, shift below his hand as he climbed over into an alien field. The grass sank under his weight. He was now outside his family's land, following the stars of a waking dream into unknown lands. The wind whistled through the loose stones of the wall, a child playing in the beached ribcage of a whale. Dermot pressed on.

As though the silence of this land had sunk in through his skin, trickled down his listening vertebrae and made its home in his blood, he had become used to these long walks alone in trackless fields, devoid of life other than the slow dreams of trees and cows. He had almost forgotten the traffic, the sirens, the cellphones and music and millions of voices of the city he had known so long. Out here, there was time, and peace, and a stony silence that held within it the losses of a blood-drenched history that he finally felt was his, just as it seemed it might be taken away.

Threaded through the constant moan of the wind, he could hear water. Slanting northwards across a shoulder of the hill, he could see a crease of land that must hide a river. The sound grew louder. Before long, he found himself standing on the undercut bank of a bright, clear creek that chattered merrily in a channel walled with damp clay. Following the course of the rushing stream southwards, he heard its voice change, its notes fluctuating in their constant song. The banks dipped slowly, until he found the water rushing right at his feet through a shallow course of smooth round pebbles.

"Hello" he said, his own voice loud and unlovely against that of the river. On the far side of the narrow water, an old woman was hunched, her gnarled hands washing rags in a small pool that collected before the water rushed away over the shallows of the ford. The wind lifted her thin hair in a white mist around her scalp, but she gave no sign that she had heard him.

"Is this your land?" he tried. "Do you live near here?" The river answered; the woman didn't.

Senile old crone. Dermot watched the water swirling around the dull stones, his mind already tracing the steps he should take across the shallow ford –

"Nil se ansin."

"Excuse me?"

The old woman turned her face towards him. Her papery skin was a pale mass of wrinkles and furrows, almost as though the flesh had started to melt, or else her face was like glass, slowly thinning above and thickening below with year upon year of glacial settling. The bones of her face stood out like boulders on the mountain slopes, trying to burst through the thin skin and erupt from her wasted body, her long chin jutting out from beneath her downturned mouth like a weapon. A tracery of cold blue veins spread across her crumpled cheeks, the blood frozen in the slow drip of years. She seemed a vision of a past long unmourned, a phantom of the Famine still clinging to creaking life on the blasted slopes of the empty hills.

"He's not there." Her accent turned English into a corrupted form of Gaelic. He had become accustomed even to Tim's thick Clare[104] brogue, but it took him a moment to decode her words.

"Who's not there?" he asked. Her eyes fixed on him, twin rings of washed-out blue, the tiny black dots of pupils almost lost in a pale and cloudy sky. There was no warmth in her gaze; no hate either. Just cold, dead space. Reptilian. He blinked.

"The fella ye're lookin fer" she answered. "Ye'll not find him up there. No one up there anymore. Just the wind and the stones."

"Sorry, I – you must be mistaken. I'm not looking for anyone." The hag stared at him.

"Is – is this your land?" he asked. She waited a long while before answering.

"Not mine" she said. "Not anyone's. Not anymore. People there were, once, but not anymore. All gone away now, over the water." She bent again over her washing.

"What are you working on there?" he asked, forcing a smile. This time she didn't look up.

"Few ould rags. Nothin for the likes of ye. So young ye are, so young and strong. Nothin here for ye." Her knobbed hands went on scrubbing.

Unsettled, Dermot crossed the ford. The old woman seemed to have said all she was going to say; once again, it was as though he wasn't there.

Dermot climbed on towards the top of the hill.

Up on the ridge, the barrow waited.

Dermot crested the ridge, and the sea wind swept around him, no longer sheltered by the jagged bulk of the hill. He hunched his

---

[104] Strangely enough, this is the first reference to the county that Cloonashee is in.

shoulders and pressed on through a wall of air that seemed intent on blocking his path. The hair whipped about on his head, tossed by the same gusts of air that threw the waves to the shore and dashed the sea into sparkling spray against the dark cliffs. A lone gull cried in the upper air; the noise reminded him of Vancouver, the grimy alleys down by the port where the hopeless bleed for crumbs.[105]

His breath caught, and not because of the wind.

On the very peak of the hill, a lesser hill rose, steep-sided and grass-grown. He had seen it before, but not like this. There was no way he could have known this place was really here and not simply dreamed up out of his dislocated madness; but here it was, low and dark against the seething sky.

The wind whipped across the ridge.

The barrow waited.

Dermot approached slowly, as though creeping up to a slumbering beast. On one side, huge grey boulders jutted out of the ground like broken teeth in rotting gums. He drew closer. Pale round lichens studded the flat rocks like dull stars in a dull grey sky. He circled the barrow like a hunter. Between the massive stone walls, below a low stone roof, the entrance to the barrow gaped, empty and absolutely black like night in winter and the void between indifferent stars.

The visions. The old woman. The impenetrable blackness. It stood before him like a wall.

He felt the wind blow through him, as though he was dwindling to a spectre in this land of ghosts.

For a moment longer, Dermot stood before the open tomb. The wind tore at his clothes. The gull wailed again.

His hair about his face, Dermot let the wind push him back down the hill, towards the valley.

Forlorn and forsaken again, the barrow waited.

The wind whipped across the bare back of the ridge.

---

[105] A shadow of the path Dermot's night-sea journey would take. Vague whispers of hell.

42

The night peered in at the windows, bottomless and utterly black. Inside, the fire cast a wavering glow around the hearth. Shadows moved fitfully across the floor. Tim's face was lit dully from below, where he sat, as usual, by the fireside. Dermot hunched in his seat at the edge of the dim semi-circle of light.

"So you've seen it yourself?" he asked.

"Of course I've seen it. Haven't I been facing the wind of the world in this spot these last seventy-odd years?"

"Well, what is it? A cave, or a tomb, or what?"

"'Tis a sidhe."

"A shee? What's that?"

"Jaysus. Yer father knew more of such things than any man in six counties, and he never told ye about the sidhe?"

"Not that I remember. What is it?"

Tim sighed, a noise like the gust of the wind going out of him. The fire flickered in the hearth, the bricks of turf glowing as they slowly gave up the heat of long years of decay.

"Many years ago, before Ireland was Ireland, there was a race of people living in the land. Like us, they were, but not like us. They had strange powers; they could change their shape, and cast spells, and all manner of other abilities they had. But they weren't the first people in Ireland; they had come with war and stolen the country from another race who were there before them. Likewise, in their turn, they were invaded and conquered by the Gaels, who sailed here from Spain, they say. When that happened, the Tuatha[106], the people I'm telling ye

---

[106] The Tuatha de Danaan, the prehistoric gods of Ireland. In time, under the millstone of Christianity and the machinery of the industrial age, they dwindled to fairies and folk-heroes, and finally

about, they fled to the sidhe, the ancient mounds that can be found out in the wild places all around the countryside. That's the origin of the fairie-folk, the displaced Tuatha who live now in the Otherworld, but still at times can be seen in this one. The sidhe are their palaces, and the entrances to the Otherworld, where mortal men rarely go. That's the stories they told us as children, anyway."

"Entrances to the Otherworld?"

"So tis said. Very dangerous places they are, especially at night. The people of the sidhe are generally friendly, but they don't like to be meddled with, and they can make a man lose himself in fields he's known since birth. Some of them are downright deadly, like the amadan.[107] A touch from him is as good as death, they say."

The writhing light made strange patterns on the flagstones, prophecies of doom in an alien language, lost in the shadows. Dermot felt suddenly cold.

"She said there was no one up there anymore" he muttered to himself.

"What's that?" said Tim.

"Oh, nothing" said Dermot. "On the way up there, I ran into an old woman – maybe you know her – and she told me I wouldn't find anyone up there."

"An ould woman? Sure what was an ould woman doing up on the side of a mountain?"

"She was just washing something, some clothes or something, in a stream up there, and –"

"She was washing clothes in the river? And ye spoke to her?" Tim leaned forward, the old chair creaking under his weight.

"Well, yeah" Dermot replied slowly. "I mean, she wasn't very talkative; we just exchanged a few words."

"What did she look like?"

"I don't know – old, white hair, wrinkles – you know, an old woman."

"Ugly, was she? A rare ould hag?"

---

to old tales only academics care to remember. Though I know at least one Irish construction worker who refuses to so much as swing a spade in a field where a rowan tree grows.

[107] The Fool, whose touch brings madness. The literature here is scarce and murky.

"Well, yeah. I mean, her eyes were the only thing that really struck me. Hardly any pupil in them, you know, just this tiny dot in the middle."

"God almighty, Dermot, if ye see her again, don't say anything, will ye? Walk the other way. Don't go near the ould witch again, d'ye hear?"

"Why? Who is she?"[108]

"No one" Tim said, leaning back in the chair, suddenly guarded. "It doesn't matter who she is. Just, whatever she does or says to ye, stay away from her. Will ye do that?"

"Yeah, I guess. Though I don't see what harm she could do anyway; she looked barely able to stand."

"Never mind about that." Tim tugged at the brim of his cap. "Anyway, these ould fireside tales; tis all nonsense. Comical, really."

But neither of them laughed.

---

[108] The Washer at the Ford, an ancient harbinger of death. One can almost feel the mythic world closing around Dermot, mounting like a wave above his head while he fails to see it. The Washer is associated with the Morrigan, the prehistoric war goddess of the ancient Celts. If Dermot ever realised the source of his uncle's fears, or if there ever was any such woman, we will never know. Certainly he never mentioned the Washer to me, or gave any hint that he understood the symbolic significance of this apparition. So much of his story remains shrouded in mystery and guesswork.

43

Dermot looked back down the hill the way he had come, down into the valley. Near at hand, the grass on the hilltop was coarse; green and brown and almost flat in the relentless wind. The valley below was a deeper, richer green, a patchwork of fields parcelled into irregular shapes by the stone walls and the twisted lines of trees that stood unmoving in the shelter of the hills. Here and there, a low grey building in the midst of empty fields, the only sign of human habitation. He could see the line of trees that marked the river, running its course between Tim's house and Bridgid's; could dimly see the squat shape of the bridge, and the hedges that lined the dull grey road as it climbed towards the old cottage. Across the road, looking east over the bog, more hills rose; lower and rounder than the wind-scoured ridge he stood on now. Beyond them, more fields, numberless green rectangles stretching low and flat to the very edge of sight, where the hazy rim of the sky lifted its pale margin above the edge of the world.

"Yes, I knew it was here" Fiona said behind him. "The name of the place says it all: Cloonashee, the valley of the sidhe.[109] Tim told me about it, years ago, when I first came down here."

"How come neither of you ever mentioned it to me?" he asked.

"Why would we? Tim only told me because he thought I might be interested, since I was studying this sort of thing back then. And really what's to tell? It's just a few old rocks on a windy hill."

Dermot turned to her. The mound rose again behind her, the highest point on the whole plateau between here and the sea. He could see over her shoulder, far enough away that the waves looked motionless, a pattern of ridges on the steely water like the fingerprint

---

[109] This seems etymologically viable.

of the gods. The cliffs curved inwards in a great bight, the ocean bulging into the land, the shoreline hidden from view.

"Hardly. This is it."

He walked towards the mound, his eyes fixed on the uneven trapezoid of night that yawned at one end. Like the corpse of a whale it looked now, its mouth gaping open, thrown far inland by a furious convulsion of the sea.

"This is what?" Fiona asked as Dermot grabbed the flashlight she had brought and advanced on the barrow.

"This is my way in" he said, not looking at her. "Things like this, these little clues, these are the closest I can get to evidence of the truth of my father's story. Remember the tomb, the barrow on the hills that the book starts with? And the lovers, my mother and this... other man – the same barrow. And here it is."

"What?" Fiona turned to follow him as he headed towards the darkness. "You think this is the same place your father was talking about?"

"Don't you?" he asked, clicking the torch. It cast a pale double ring of light on the outer edge of the roof stone, only just visible where the inner darkness mingled with the grey outside world.

"No, quite frankly, I don't."

Slowly, Dermot turned to her.

"You sound very sure."

"I am."

"But here it is, so close to his old home, up on the ridge just like in the stories – how can it not be the same place?"

"Dermot, it's not. I really don't think – well, you'll see for yourself. Go on inside, and you'll see."

Dermot grinned. Sometimes she was so sure of herself. She was never combative, but you could smash yourself into pieces against her sometimes.

He sat on the grass at the entrance, one hand above his head on the edge of the low roof-stone, and swung his legs inside.

"If I don't come back, remember me as a hero" he said. Fiona snorted. Still grinning, he slid into darkness.

It was cold, and the ground felt wet beneath his hands. The walls were damp near the level of the ground. At the entrance, a few ferns curled from under the stones, stretching their heavy heads towards the light; but the floor of the tomb was a shallow gravelly pit, devoid of any life. Sheltered from the wind, the air was close and still.

The chamber was smaller than it had looked from outside. It was sunk a little below the level of the ground, the creeping soil of the centuries rising up against the ancient stone walls, but there wasn't room to stand inside, even at a stoop. Dermot shone the torch beam around the walls. The tomb was hardly twice his own length, stretched out on the floor; the roof less than an arm's length above him, sloping down slightly towards its further end. Twisting around onto his hands and knees, he felt his shoulders brush the rock above. It was a tight squeeze, but he was just able to turn himself around to face the rear wall. Torch in hand, he crawled towards the back of the stone chamber. It ended in a wall, seemingly formed of a single large boulder; but in the torchlight he could see that it had cracked and split towards the bottom. There was a chunk of rock missing, a black hole opening onto a nothingness that the light of his feeble torch could find no feature in.

"Everything alright in here?" Fiona's head and shoulders appeared in the entrance, haloed by a light that seemed painfully bright to his subterranean eyes as he peered back at her through the tangled architecture of his limbs.

"Have you ever been in here?" he asked.

"Not all the way" she answered. "I peered in from the entrance, crawled a little way in, then left; a long time ago, now. I always meant to come back, but I sort of forgot, I suppose." Leaving the bag she had brought outside in the grass, she crawled headfirst down the passage towards him. "See what I mean?" Coming up behind him, she playfully smacked his backside. "This is nothing like the tomb in your father's story. That was a big place, big enough to stand in, with different rooms leading off the main passage. This is just the one chamber, and a small one at that."

"What's through here?" Dermot asked, tapping the plastic edge of the torch on the back wall, above the dark hole.

"I dunno. Nothing. Dirt. It's just a crack in the stone. Want to see something cool, though?"

"What is it?" he asked.

"You have to turn around" she replied. This proved to be no easy task. With two of them in there, it took a combined feat of clumsy choreography for him to turn on all fours and face the entrance of the tomb. Fiona lay on her side now, her back against the wall, her head propped on one arm, just below Dermot's.

"You see in the middle of the roof, at the entrance, how there's that big notch in the stone?" and she pointed with her free arm, back over her feet towards the daylight outside. "Right in the middle there? That's deliberate. I've never tried it out, but given the way most of these tombs are built, I'm sure that if you came here on a certain day of the year, at just the right time, you'd see the sun appear through that notch and hit this back wall here like a laser beam. In fact," she flicked her hair back from her face, "and I'm just guessing here now – but this tomb would once have had a stone closing it. God knows where it is now, probably propping up a three-hundred year old stone wall somewhere, if it wasn't smashed to pieces – but I bet it would have had a notch in it too, matching up with that one so there was a round hole for the beam of light from the sun to come through. Isn't that amazing, that they could calculate it like that?"

"Yeah" Dermot agreed.

"And the best part is, no one ever saw it. It wouldn't happen, at least not properly, unless the tomb was sealed, and only the dead would be inside. All that trouble, just so that the rising sun would shine into the underworld once a year for no one to see.[110] Isn't that beautiful?"

"Yeah" he replied, "it is. Do you have the camera? I want to take a picture." Fumbling in her pocket, Fiona passed him a small silver camera.

"Of course, according to the old stories, it's bad luck to be here. The sidhe are the underground palaces of the gods – like in your father's story. This is where the fairies live. That hole there, at the back of the tomb, that would be the entrance to the otherworld."

Dermot fiddled with the camera, only half listening to her.

"Yeah, Tim was telling me about that. The Tuatha, and the fairies, and everything."

"You can see why, though. I mean, back in the old days, when people had no idea who built these things, or why. And they're always out in these desolate, godforsaken places, where the imagination is more than willing to run off on you anyway."

---

[110] Gods of death are often also gods of sex. Death and rebirth, the dual nature of opposites. One thinks of the king with a sword through his head.

"Yeah" Dermot said, scrolling through byzantine menus, looking for something he had found by accident and now couldn't relocate.

"Though this little place is nothing on somewhere like Newgrange, where your man Diarmuid came from."

The camera's LCD screen went momentarily black, and then an image appeared. Dermot gazed at it a moment, wondering whether he should say anything about the picture he had just seen.

"Wait – what was that about Diarmuid?" he asked, her words seeping into his consciousness like rainwater through the purifying soil.

"Newgrange – have you heard of it? It's this huge tomb – well, a complex of them, really – away in the North. According to the legends, that's where the god Angus had his sidhe, and raised Diarmuid as a boy – you remember reading about it?"

"His shee? How is that spelled?"

"S-I-D-H-E. Why?"

"That was the word! In my father's story, he uses that word. But when I asked Tim about this place, and he told me it was a shee, I didn't realise it was the same word."

"Well, how did you read it?"

"I don't know. I kind of skimmed over it. I just figured it was some Gaelic word. I would never have guessed that that was how it was pronounced."

"Jesus, Dermot. We're going to have to teach you some Irish[111], if you're going to go on investigating these kind of things; at

---

[111] Irish and Gaelic; Dermot seems to use the two terms interchangeably. Though my understanding is that there are many forms of Gaelic - including Scottish, Welsh, and even Cornish - in the context of this story, it is clear which form of Gaelic is meant. English remains the first language of the population of Ireland, but Irish has made a resounding comeback in the last thirty years or so. Indeed, in Tim and Fiona, we may see two examples of the modern Irish speaker: the old farmer from the west, the Gaeltacht, who probably learned English as a second language alongside his native Irish; and the modern academic with a passion for the past, who studies the language of old farmers like Tim to reclaim her nation's heritage. Clearly, Dermot never learned the language.

least enough so that you don't look such an eejit." She smiled, but Dermot's face was serious.

"So Diarmuid was raised in a tomb" he said slowly, almost to himself. "What does that mean? Is that why he named me after him, because we both come from tombs, from the underworld? Does that mean the story is true?"

"Seems a bit tenuous to me" said Fiona, blithely.

"Diarmuid O – what is it? Duibhne?"

Fiona rolled her eyes.

"It's pronounced Dyna" she said.

"Ok. Diarmuid O'*Dyna* comes from a tomb, a *sidhe*, and is raised by a man who is not his father. Dermot Fallon comes from a tomb – or at least that's the implication. You see? That was my conception that my father wrote about!"

"I think this is what they call circumstantial evidence" Fiona tried.

"But that's the only thing I have" Dermot replied. "I know it doesn't prove anything, but it's reasonable doubt, no? Besides that couple of random lines my father wrote, now I have other hints that I might not be his son."

"It's almost like you don't want to be" Fiona muttered.

"It's not that" Dermot replied, too excited to feel angry. "It's just that, whatever the truth is, I'd rather know. Even if my father is some other man, I just want to know."

"But you'll only know if it's bad, right? You can't prove that the man who raised you was your father, not now. They only way you'll ever know for certain is if he's not, and even then, maybe not. You'll either know your father *is* this other man, or you'll always wonder, because nothing will ever prove you are the son of the man you thought you were."

Dermot sighed.

"Yeah, I see your point" he conceded. "Maybe that's true. But come on, can you honestly say that nothing in his stories seems eerily familiar to my own situation?"

Fiona said nothing, gazing out at the bright light through the crooked entrance.

"Besides," Dermot said, "weird as it may sound, I honestly think I'm supposed to know. Look at the whole code thing. I don't want to go so far as to say my father wants me to find out the truth, but there is this feeling, that this is the path I'm meant to tread."

"We should probably be heading back" she said. The cold, measured withdrawal. He wondered if she ever used that tone with Sean. She must do. Probably all the time. Poor guy.

"Here, look at this" Dermot said, and shuffled over slightly so Fiona could see the camera's screen. "This photo of the entrance you took, when we were outside, I just put a red filter over it. Look."

She raised her head.

"Doesn't it look like −"

She extended one hand towards the camera to steady it, her attention caught.

"Oh my god, it does!" she exclaimed.

The walls and the roof stone of the tomb crowded the photo, dark and red, only a thin strip of orange sky visible at the top of the photo. The outer lips of the rocks that formed the walls rose on either edge of the picture, filling the screen from side to side. The inside, dark as it was, appeared sullen and blood red, a stray shaft of sunlight cutting across the picture from the left, fractured by the lens into a diagonal string of glowing pentagraphs, like houses in a child's drawing. Details of the tomb's interior rose out of the red murk, bumps and bulges in the rock appearing organic, as though it were the heart of some ancient animal, or else the ridges and troughs were the quivering tendons and soft hollows of -

"God, that's amazing" Fiona sighed. "I mean, there's always those theories, you know? The shaft of sunlight, obviously, is male, penetrating the womb of the earth... I always thought, can't it be purer than that? But when you look at a photo like that, it sort of makes sense. And you know, the people who built these tombs five thousand years ago, they used to bury their dead in the foetal position, as though they were awaiting rebirth."

"Really?" said Dermot, switching the camera off and setting it aside. He crawled forward a little on his elbows while she spoke.

"Oh yeah. It's strange to think how modern technology can bring out something like that, you know? I mean, maybe it's just coincidence, but − hey!"

The jeans she wore that day had a button fly. They were tight, and after some initial resistance, Dermot deftly slipped each brass stud from its denim prison as though they had been waiting for this all day.

"What are you doing?" she said coquettishly.

"Nothing" said Dermot, and slipped a thumb beneath the elastic of her underwear. He shifted his weight, and she shifted with him, sliding away from the wall so he could place a knee either side of her head and balance himself properly.

"So teach me something" he said slowly. "What's the Irish for this?" and he pressed down, softly but firmly, with his thumb. In the tombal silence, he heard her breathing.

"Faighin" she said, and her hips wriggled adorably.

"Really? Well, that's an easy one to remember. How about this?" he asked, flicking something with his finger.

"Oh, God" she shuddered. "Uh....brillin...oh..." He could feel her tugging at the fly of his trousers, her breathing heavy, erratic.

"Interesting. So what do you call this?"

"ohhh... ag li...ag pog... ag ithe... Oh, Diarmuid, tá mé chomh mór sin i ngrá leat ..."[112]

"Jesus, is that really the time?"

Outside the tomb, Fiona stood on the windy heights, the orange rays of the sun blunting their edges against her slender form. While they were in the tomb, the sea winds had driven the high roof of cloud eastwards, and the light of the setting sun was able to peek underneath, turning the sea into mirrored glass and the grass into a million golden swordlets. The wind had dropped, but it felt colder now than it had before.

"How long were we in there?" Time ceases in the underworld, while above the surface, it flows on unhindered. Just one of its dangers.[113] "I've got to get home; they'll think we've been swallowed up in the bog. Come on, Dermot!"

---

[112] Unknown.

[113] There are indeed many stories of this nature; the traveller who spends a night feasting with the fairies, and returns to find a hundred mortal years have passed. Indeed, the tales of Finn, according to some sources, come from the mouth of his nephew Ossian, who, after the dissolution of the Fianna, entered the underworld and lived there many years, returning as an old man to a world where a thousand years had passed. Fortunately for Dermot, the disparity in this case could not have amounted to more than a few minutes.

He followed her down from the ridge, their long shadows going before them into the darkening valley. The brow of the hill soon cut off the failing light, and they wandered through twilight fields in a deep blue dusk. Night came on as the clouds fled eastward; above their trailing fingers, a lone star appeared, low and bright in the purple firmament. They heard the sound of running water. Fiona went on ahead, following the banks of the stream.

"Wait," Dermot called after her, "this isn't the way we came, is it? I thought the ford was further upstream than this."

"I'm taking a quicker route" Fiona said without stopping. "That way curves to the south, behind Tim's house, and then I have to go back north again. I'm trying to take a more direct way across the fields. If we follow the stream, it should join up with the bigger river in the valley, and then we can follow that all the way back to Bridgid's."

Dermot hurried after her. Even in the dark, the noisy stream made an easy trail to follow, tumbling down the slopes of the hill, but Dermot wondered. Whatever else happened, they would have to cross either this stream, or the bigger one it joined in the valley, if not both. Neither of them knew the land around here well enough to be sure they would find a place to do that safely.

Night came on. Fiona led the way through the gloomy fields, keeping the stream on their right, over stone walls and wire fences that loomed up suddenly out of the dark. He heard her curse softly.

"What's wrong?" he asked.

"Oh, nothing" she said. "Just slipped in a big pile of cow muck, that's all. Here, do you still have that torch?"

Dermot retrieved the forgotten flashlight from his pocket and held it out towards her. As she took it from him, he felt something sticky on his hand.

"What's..." she clicked the torch on, the beam dazzling at first in the murk. "Oh, Dermot, you're bleeding..."

"I am?"

"Yes, look! Jesus, that's quite a gash you have there. Doesn't it hurt?"

"No, not at all" he said, peering at his illuminated left hand. A wide fissure was torn across the skin, and his whole hand was smeared red, spreading along the lines of his palm like lichen on the rocks, drowning his future in blood. Below the jagged edges of skin, he could see small clusters of pale white fatty tissue floating in a scarlet haze.

"Oh, that's deep" Fiona tutted.

"Must have done it on that barbed wire fence back there" he said, puzzled. "I didn't feel a thing."[114]

"I don't know if I have anything to put on it – half a second" she said, rummaging in her bag. "Aha. This'll have to do until we get home." She held out a woollen hat. "Just hold it against the wound to stop the bleeding. I'll clean it up at Bridgid's."

"I don't want to ruin it" Dermot said.

"Don't be ridiculous. Won't look much good if I come home alone and they find you out in the fields, bled to death."

With a new sense of urgency, she led him through the grass, picking her way in the yellow light of the torch. More stars shivered in the sky overhead as the golden light died behind the high western ridges. The ground levelled out, the stream quieter now, rolling lazily over the flats. A dark line of rushes appeared ahead.

"There we are!" Fiona said triumphantly. "There's the river. We just have to cross over, and then a couple more fields and we'll be home."

She peered through the undergrowth that hung over the bank.

"It's not too deep" she said, "but we might have to get our toes a bit wet." Carefully she stepped down onto the wet rocks of the stream bed. Shining the torch behind her to light his way, she talked Dermot across. "Now just put your foot there, on that little gravel bank; then we go to this rock here," she grunted and shifted her weight, "and then – " and she leapt over the last rill of water, "we're across!" Dermot followed as best he could, still clutching his injured hand.

Fiona climbed a low place in the bank and extended a hand to Dermot. Out across the fields that lay before them, not too distant, they could see the squat white block and lit windows of Bridgid's house. Like ghosts, they slipped silently into the night, and vanished among the liquid shadows.

---

[114] Changes in the ability to feel pain, either lessening or increasing the sensation, are another fairly common symptom of schizophrenia. This often results in sufferers burning or otherwise harming themselves without realising it.

44

Had a nice long chat with the Toad today. I woke up, for whatever reason, in a grand mood, as though I had become a foot taller overnight. I could blame the drugs, but I'm not new at this; only the woefully uninformed think antidepressants make people happy. They take off the peaks of joy and the valleys of despair, bulldozing emotion into a flat, rocky field, like some state-sponsored massive civil engineering project requiring the relocation of thirty thousand peasants in the kind of Soviet republic that doesn't exist anymore. But I digress.

The Toad accosted me outside my room. I wasn't going anywhere, really – where is there to go? The staring window? The rocking-back-and-forth-and-muttering-to-yourself ward? But the sun was shining from my every pore that day; I thought I'd just walk the halls, see who I could grace with my presence.

It was like he'd been waiting for me, as though he stands outside my room all night in his dressing gown in the hope that I'll come out. And then when I do, he doesn't really have anything to say. Or maybe he does, and I just don't see it – everything is in parentheses around here, a consequence of everyone living in their own world, under its own obscure rules.

"Hello" says the Toad.

"Hi" I reply.

"Did you sleep well? Last night?" The toad is twitchy, forcing his words out in a rush as though he doesn't want to give you time to really hear them.

"Like a baby in a fountain of gin" I say. The toad grins hesitantly.

"Because you know, schizophrenics often suffer from bad dreams. Nightmares. Very vivid, sometimes. Very frightening. Do you ever have nightmares?"

"I may be having one right now" I say breezily, the way I imagine Oscar Wilde dispensing quips at dinner parties.

"It's quite a fascinating illness. Quite fascinating. The disease of the modern world, that's how I see it." It's always a mistake to bait a bore; but when institutionalized, you have to make your own fun.

"Really? How so?" The Toad is transformed when he tricks someone into giving him an opportunity to pontificate; he stands up straighter, arms firmly at his sides like a palace guard, his eyes finally leaving the face and mouth of the person he's speaking to and focussing on the middle distance, as though straining to read cue cards held up at the back of a lecture hall.

"Schizophrenia was not truly described until the Industrial Revolution. Pat Haslam in 1798, in his *Observations on Insanity*, described patients clearly experiencing delusions, hallucinations, and thought disorders. Philipe Pinel documented similar cases in France. As the nineteenth century progressed, more and more cases were reported and documented, leading Pat Hawkes to comment, in 1857, "I doubt if ever the history of the world, or the experience of past ages, could show a larger amount of insanity than that of the present day." Many modern studies conclude that the per capita rate of schizophrenia is far greater in cities than in rural areas. From being a rare and novel disease in the nineteenth century, schizophrenia has become the modern psychological disease, the disease of the city, a great ep – "

"So what are you in for?" If left unchecked, the Toad will go on all day. There is no known limit to his endurance when he gets to talk about one of his pet subjects; even the most catatonic listener will leave before he runs out of steam.

"What?" asks the Toad, struggling to come down off his soapbox.

"What are you in for?" And then he surprises me with a flash of humour, as though we were normal men, going about normal business, instead of being shut away in here because our brains have gone bad.

"Five to ten" he smiles.[115]

---

[115] There's that patient again, Dermot's confidant and foil, a constant presence of scorn or fear throughout his stay here. Ladies

45

"It'll be good to get out of the house today" Fiona muttered as the door closed behind her, Seamus squeezing past her legs and bounding towards Dermot.

"Really? Why?" asked Dermot, patting the exuberant dog absent-mindedly. Side by side, they crunched up the gravel drive to the road.

"Oh, nothing" Fiona replied. "You know how it is. Bridgid can be so nosy sometimes. 'Where are ye goin'? What are ye doin'?' I'm getting sick of that house, and having nothing to do all the time. I swear, if you weren't here, I'd have lost my mind by now. Maybe I should start looking for a job."

"I need to go back up to Tim's; I left my camera there" Dermot said. "Shall we drive, or walk?" Fiona shrugged.

"Let's walk there and back, then drive down to the sea" she said. They turned and headed up the road.

"What kind of job were you thinking of?" Dermot asked, keeping his voice agonisingly neutral.

---

and gentlemen of the jury, one last time, just to be clear: the Toad does not exist. Never did, never will.

Of course, the creation of an alter ego is not uncommon in cases of insanity. Many patients here feel pursued, watched, manipulated by fictional characters, or else real people who they have never met, and who therefore might as well be fictional. There have been not a few patients who thought they were me, that they were the doctor, utilizing some radical method of undercover psychiatry to treat me, the poor patient suffering from delusions of being a doctor. The paths of madness are indeed strange.

"I don't know" she breathed, smiling palely. "That's the trouble, isn't it? There's a surprising lack of demand for a Celtic Studies graduate in the modern workforce."

"So why did you study it?" he asked. They passed Seamus, leg cocked at the side of the road, a yellow stream bouncing off the nodding leaf of a ditch-born nettle.

"Oh, I don't know" she sighed. "It interested me. The language; the past. Like this hidden world just on the edge of the one we know, but so much more mysterious and inviting."

The road rose beneath their feet. Dermot could hear the stream singing under the stone bridge as they crossed, harmonising with its own echo.

"You hear these stories, growing up," she went on as the hedgerows rose around her, "you know, Diarmuid and Finn, Cuchulainn, King Arthur – and you think, are these stories true? Then you look into it, and find that they're not. Then you look a little further, and you find that they are, in a way, but the truth is so remote and inaccessible that no one will ever be able to say, this happened, and this didn't. So then you apply it to everything else you've been told, looking for that grain of truth in the stories of the Bible, or history, or even the things people tell you about themselves, and you realise that it's all myths. It's all in-between truth and fiction, and it always seems that the answer is just around the corner, but it's always ahead of you and you can never quite catch up to it. Or else, you find the truth, and it's a huge letdown. Jesus wasn't the saviour, he was just some rabid Jewish mystic who never said half the things they teach at Mass. King Arthur was a Welsh bandit who never set foot inside a castle. It gets to the point when you don't want the truth anymore; the story is far better."[116]

---

[116] It is indeed tempting to let the matter rest here. Perhaps Fiona never existed. The nurses tell me that they cannot locate the reports I filed concerning Dermot's case; without a paper trail, he may as well not have existed. That which cannot be verified is consigned to the dull glamour of the mythic, shining briefly here and there in the shadow of an empire of facts. Is it possible that none of these mythic heroes have any basis in truth? The stories we have inherited, of Finn, of King Arthur, of Gilgamesh, of Buddha, Moses, Mohammed and Jesus – can they all simply be just stories? I must

They walked on. Birds warbled in the hedgerows; Dermot blinked, shook himself. The light had suddenly changed, or else his eyes had; the unaccountable darkening that sometimes precluded a spate of visions.[117]

"How's the hand?" Fiona asked.

"Oh, it's fine" he replied mechanically.

"Let me see" she said, reaching across for his left arm. "Is it healing alright?"

"Oh, don't look" Dermot tried as she began probing the loose bandage wrapped around his palm. "It's really disgusting."

"Oh, please" Fiona snorted. "Let me see. Stop struggling, will you?"

Dermot stopped in the middle of the road as Fiona unravelled the bandage. White clouds whipped across the sky, the sun peeking out through great rents torn in their pillowy shapes by the western gales.

"Oh my God. Dermot...it's gone."

He watched the sun duck behind a bulbous pillar of vapour, its slanted rays burning the cloud's edges in a brief golden storm before the wind tore them apart again and the light fell cool upon the land.

"The cut, Dermot. It's completely healed."

"I know" he said, and lowered his eyes. Fiona held his left hand in both of her own, gazing disbelievingly at his palm. Only a slight pinkish trail of new skin showed where he had cut himself.

---

disagree with Fiona here, if she really said this; as seductive as it may be to abandon the path of reason and cling on to whichever lie suits us best, we have a duty as human beings to sort the real from the unreal, by whatever admittedly faulty measures we may have at our disposal. Dragons were a fact to the cartographers of the mediaeval world, just as atoms are a fact to us now, which may or may not be found in some unglimpsed future to be wildly false. But if we allow the enormity of what we don't know to prevent us from peering into the unguessable, then all progress and all human endeavour ceases. Despite the scorn of our peers, we press on.

[117] Another brief glimpse into the tortured inner world of the schizophrenic. If only Dermot had made this the focus of his journals, rather than the selection of holiday stories he left us.

"But it's only been three days! I've had cuts half as deep as the one you had take twice as long to heal. How can it be gone already?"

"I heal quick, I guess."

The wound throbbed, a hot ache, as though he held a burning branch across his palm. The skin had peeled back, the flesh underneath still wet and red, rivulets of blood forming like tears at the corners of the cut.

Dermot sat on the edge of his bed and stared into that lidless red eye. His fingers trembled. He imagined the blood cells at work, the hundreds of tiny blood vessels sliced in half now closing themselves up again. He imagined the blood hardening as it dried, turning into a scab stretching across the open face of the wound like a shield while the new skin formed slowly underneath. He imagined the skin cells splitting and multiplying, each one tiny beyond imagining, but together forming a line that advanced steadily across his open palm from the corners to the center, closing the wound for good, as though it had never been.

"I'll say you do. You ought to be in a lab somewhere. They should be taking samples from you to cure cancer. I've never seen a cut heal that fast."

Dermot shook his hand free of hers. What was he supposed to say? That he had healed himself? That by concentrating on the wound, by feeling the mechanisms of growth in his body and joining the force of his will to those mechanisms, he had accelerated the healing process? He was not so mad as to not care about seeming mad to others. [119]

---

[118] That strange writing again, the type Dermot used to delineate his 'visions' from the more realistic aspects of his tale. Whether he knows them to be delusions or believes in them as miracles, it is at least clear that he understands them as somehow extraordinary.

[119] As far-fetched as this account may be, we should perhaps not dismiss it out of hand. This is the basis of all faith healing and the miracles of the great religions; the notion that belief can alter the nature of the physical world. The fact that Dermot is clearly delusional does not necessarily mean that everything he reports is a delusion.

They walked on. Seamus paused up ahead, impatiently waiting for them to catch up before bounding away from them again.

"Maybe I could teach" Fiona said idly.

"Teach what?" asked Dermot.

"I don't know. Irish, maybe. Or mythology."

"I could never teach. The kids would drive me crazy."

"Oh, I couldn't teach kids. Maybe I could teach at a university. But I'd need more than a Master's for that. I could be an academic." Dermot smiled.

"You would make one sexy professor, that's for sure" he said. "Maybe if I'd had teachers like you, I wouldn't have dropped out of university."[120]

As they approached the cottage under the watery sun, Dermot saw Tim leaving through the open door.

"How do, Tim?" Fiona called. The old farmer smiled gently.

"Ah, yer lookin well, *cainteoir*"[121] he said. "Haven't seen ye around in a while." He headed towards a dark door at the side of the house; Dermot had never seen it open before.

"Will ye come look at something, Dermot?" Tim called without breaking stride.

"Just a sec" he said to Fiona, and followed after the lumbering bulk of his uncle. Seamus stared after him, padding towards Fiona.

Inside a small, windowless room, Dermot found Tim rummaging in the dark. Tools and ancient farming implements loomed abruptly into the light from the doorway like bones scattered in cold tombs, casting strange shadows on the floor. The air smelled damp.

"Here we are" Tim said, standing up in the shadows, "take a look at this now." He held something out towards Dermot.

The wood was old, worn smooth and yellow with the passage of years, but it was still sound. He could feel the strength of it in his hand, the balance weighted towards the flat end, pulling it edge-first towards the ground. He held it up to the light, watching the sun pick out dark rivers in the grain.

---

[120] Another glimpse of Dermot's past. Like the heroes of old, Dermot throws up not a few challenges to the would-be biographer. Vague hints of stories lost with the final closing of the mouths that told them.

[121] Unknown.

"'Tis yer father's ould hurl" Tim explained, moving carefully towards the door. "Thought ye might like to have it."

"Dad played hurley?"[122] Dermot asked. He could recall no instance from his own life when his father had ever expressed an interest in sports.

"Oh yeah" Tim said. "A grand hurler he was, when he was young, one of the best in the parish. Not so good as yer uncle Joe, though." The old man sighed. "Now he was a rare sportsman. Could run like a racehorse, and there was not a man in the province could catch up to him. He could have played for the county, but he emigrated before he got the chance. Come to think of it, that ould schtick might just as well be his. Anyway, tis his or yer father's, and neither one of them needs it now, so ye can keep it, if ye want."

"Really?" asked Dermot.

"Ah, sure why not? I was never much of a player, and I think I might be a bit long in the tooth to be getting the use of it now."

"Thanks, Tim. This means a lot to me."

"It has kept well, hasn't it? Might have rotted away to nothing in this mouldy old shed all these years, but it looks sound enough. Twas wrapped well against the water; that would be yer father's work. He was never a man to throw anything away."

Dermot stepped out into the sun, testing the weight of the stick in his hand. He slashed at the air in front of him, the thin edge

---

[122] Hurling, a game of ancient and obscure origin, is still played professionally in Ireland today. As I understand it, the highly physical game is played on grass between two teams, with each player wielding a stick, or hurley, or hurl, which is used to control the small, hard ball. The winner is the team who scores the highest by hitting the ball into the opponent's goal, rather like in hockey. The rules of the game are obscure and almost impenetrable to an outsider, and in any case have no relevance here. The hurley itself is made of wood, 22-24 inches long, with a broad, flat head that tapers to a thin edge, used for scooping up the ball. Many players reinforce the head of the hurley with a band of steel. Obviously, if used for such purposes, a hurley would make a formidable weapon.

humming in the emptiness. Seamus watched attentively, his legs bent, ready to chase the stick down, if that was the game.

"What's that?" asked Fiona, squinting in the light. "Is that a hurley?"

"That's right" Dermot grinned, trotting towards her. "It belonged to my dad, Tim says."

"But you don't even play" she laughed.

"No" Dermot replied, "but it's…emblematic." He slashed at the grass. The dog's head followed the movement hopefully.

"Really? How so?" Fiona persisted.

"I never knew my dad played, but he did, apparently. It's like a symbol of all the things I never knew about him."

"Sometimes a stick is just a stick" she goaded.

"And sometimes it's not. Meaning is in the eye of the beholder" he replied, squinting down the length of the wooden shaft.

"Quite the philosopher today. Are you taking that thing to the beach with us?"

"No" Dermot replied. "I'll go put it in my room, and then we'll go."

Dermot leaned his head against the window as the car swept between low stone walls, the broadening sky ahead reflecting the sea, still hidden behind the buildings of the town. Fiona was humming along with the radio, some repetitive tune he didn't recognise. In the back seat, Seamus paced from one window to the other, snapping his jaws at the world that flashed by on either side.

"This is all new" he said. Out of the grey-green fields, the sharp corners of pale cuboid buildings were rising from a patch of shining asphalt, growing as they sped towards them.

"What, the business park?" Fiona asked, glancing in his direction. "Yeah, they threw that place up a couple of years ago only."

"Pretty" Dermot snorted.

"Isn't it?" she smiled. "And really in keeping with the town, too. All the old streets, the little shops, the pubs – and then these great ugly warehouses right on the road as you come in. But that's the way of it. The Celtic tiger, you know[123]."

---

[123] A term used to describe the rapid growth of the Irish economy between 1995 and approximately 2007; a time in which Ireland

"It's weird" Dermot said. "Last time I was here, it must have been – well, early nineties. Not all that long ago. But even then, Ireland was – "

"What?" asked Fiona. "A dump?"

"No, not at all. But it wasn't like this. The business parks, these mansions up on the hills...."

"Monstrosities, most of them are" Fiona muttered.

"Oh, yeah. They look ridiculous. Totally out of place."

"But you know what that is? Partly, anyway. It's people like yourself."

"Like me how?"

"Well, not exactly like you. But a lot of it is people coming from abroad with tons of money, buying up the land their parents or grandparents emigrated from and building these huge houses."

"Americans, then" Dermot said. "No one's coming back from England with tons of money, I'll tell you that. And they're not moving to Ireland anyway."

"Why not?"

"Cos we're not welcome here, are we? Even as a kid, I remember what it was like here. Ten years old and they wouldn't serve me in the fucking chip shop because I had an English accent."

"Really? Maybe that's changed. We're part of the EU now. You watch when we get into town. You'll see girls in hijabs, Indians, Africans – even out in the sticks, you'd be surprised how multicultural it all is. The old English – Irish thing doesn't matter the way it used to. Who cares anymore?"

"Yeah. We'll see" said Dermot.

There was a new song on the radio now, another one he didn't know.

"You're not far wrong about the Americans, though, at least at first" Fiona started. "A lot of cottages on the seaside are full of Yanks."

"Well, there's no one as Irish as someone born in America" said Dermot. Fiona laughed.

"Right and all. I've this cousin – he came to visit a few years back. Jesus, it was Ireland this, Ireland that. Going to see the hurling, going on and on about 'the craic' – it was embarrassing. And fuck me if

___

went from being one of the poorest countries in Europe to one of the wealthiest.

he didn't have an accent by the time the two weeks was over!" She laughed, loud. Dermot grinned tightly.

"That's how you see me, is it?" he asked quietly.

"What? No, Dermot, not at all. Jesus, but you're awful prickly today. What's the matter with you?"

"Nothing" he replied. "Nothing."

The car bumped over a pothole in the road. On the seaward side of the business park, the old houses lined the street, narrow brick buildings covered in brightly painted plaster, each a different colour from its neighbours. Small businesses occupied the lower floors, their doors opening right onto the narrow pavement: Byrne's Restaurant, Hogan's Pub. This was the Ireland he remembered, the bright buildings, the family names above the doors in gold. Whatever Fiona said, he had yet to see a chain he recognised.

"The beach'll be a zoo, sure" she said, to be saying something.

Narrow streets and dour faces. He thought of England, trips to the sea with his father. Brightly coloured buildings there, too, in the resort towns; Brighton, Mablethorpe. Overpriced ice cream and gulls shitting everywhere. The oppressive smallness of everything. He experienced a sensation he had known before, on trips to England, a feeling like something draining out of him as he realised that Canada had made a profounder mark on him than he realised.

"Australians, that's the latest thing" Fiona said. "The beach'll be rammed with Australians."

"Why?"

"They come here for the surfing. Best surfing in Europe is right here."

"Yeah, but the best surfing in Europe is probably half as good as the worst they have in Australia."

She shrugged her bare shoulders. "Maybe" she said, "but there's no sharks here."

Gulls climbed banks of air above the cliffs like avenging ghosts rising from the sea. The ocean was steel-grey, a metal tide scouring the coarse sand and pebbles at the water's edge. The sun shone among clouds, but the wind was cold; in it he could feel the breath of autumn from the darkening parts of the world.

"Have you talked to Sean about this? Your teaching, or whatever?"

Fiona sighed, her breath audible above the waves and the cry of the gulls.

217

"No" she smiled. "I don't know that I'm really ready for that conversation yet."

"Because he wants to stay in Cloonashee?"

She nodded. "And a fine mess of things you've made, too" she added.

"Me? What did I do?" Her eyes reflected something of the sea's dull gleam.

"Do you really not know? You know, Dermot, sometimes you have this total ex-pat, second-generation cluelessness about you. I know it seems it sometimes at Tim's house, with the turf smoke and the firelight all around, but Ireland isn't a museum."

"I know that" Dermot scowled.

"Do you? I'm not so sure." She looked out to sea again, and he followed her gaze to where the white heads of foam appeared at the tops of the undulating waves.

"You coming here has muddied the waters," she said levelly, not meeting his eyes, "because here you are, this immigrant, this Englishman, living with Tim, learning how to farm, and you won't say how long you're staying, and maybe you plan to stay altogether. God forbid, but Tim's not a young man, and he's not getting any younger. So when he goes, who gets the farm? The easiest way, the way everyone imagined it would go, is that he would leave the land to Patrick. But Bridgid and Patrick have no interest in farming, so they would pass it on to Sean. He's never said it in so many words, but there have been hints. I think that's his plan for the future, to settle down on the family farm and raise cattle."

"But you said there's no money in it" Dermot questioned.

"Not much in Tim's farm, no" Fiona went on. "Definitely not enough to support a family. But Sean has money of his own, you know. If he sold the landscaping business, he'd have enough to buy a lot more land, maybe double the size of the farm, or more. There's too few farmers for the land these days, so it's going for a song. And there's all these government and European grants you can get, to encourage young people to work the land instead of letting it go to waste."

"And this involves me how?"

"You're a rival. You're a young man, and you're more closely related. Tim's your uncle, but he's Sean's great-uncle.[124] That gives you more claim on the land than Sean."

"That's ridiculous, though. Sean grew up on this land. Tim's not going to turn it over to me just because I'm a generation closer to him!"

"Isn't he? Maybe not. But even if he does intend Sean to have the farm, he can't figure without you now. You and your brothers were sort of forgotten all this time – I don't mean it in a bad way. But you lived in England, and you rarely visited, and no one really thought you would show up like this. But here you are, and you have a legal claim on that land, so even if Sean does get it, he might only get part of it. He might have to buy out you and your brothers' share, and if he has to do that, then he won't be able to add much to the farm, and it won't be profitable for him."

"So that's what everyone thinks? That I'm here for the land?"

"I wouldn't put it like that. They know you came over to bury your father, and that's grand. But I think they're beginning to wonder why you're still here three months later,[125] and why you moved in with Tim instead of staying at Bridgid's, and what your plans for the future are."

"But you know why I'm still here, don't you?" he asked. Fiona looked at him.

---

[124] Dermot seems to be approximately the same age as his cousin Sean, but Sean's father Patrick is the son of Owen, older brother to Dermot's father. I seem to recall Dermot mentioning that his father was the youngest boy of his ten siblings, with Tim being somewhere in the middle, and Patrick's father Owen presumably one of the oldest. In fact, Dermot's father was a seventh son; Dermot, however, has only two brothers, and in any case, he is the oldest of the three.

[125] Finally, some chronology! That would place this exchange in late September or perhaps early October 2007. In which case, I may be in error in my sorting of Dermot's notes, placing a passage set in winter much too early in the text – but editing is weary work, and I am plagued by headaches that will not cease. The nights are long, the days are cold. There is no grace for the eternal observer.

"Sometimes I wonder myself" she said blankly. "I mean, I know, the notebook and all that. But how is decoding it here any more helpful than taking it back to Canada with you, or England? So maybe there's some other reason you're staying, and that worries me."

"Why?" Dermot bristled. "Worried I might be staying for you?"

"I don't know" she said quietly. "Are you?"

The land, though rocky, was rich and green, fed by the river as it surged out to sea. The tombs hulked on the heights where the gulls soared, and the western wind brought sweet rain inland to fall like mist on the heads of the hills. The seasons turned, as they always have done. Friendly ghosts walked the fields, swirling around the timeless cottage as it sang once more with the age-old music of new life. A Fallon man farming Fallon land, as it had been these past four centuries, a constant light burning in the grand halls of Time. There was meaning there, and more than that; a kind of immortality, a losing of the self in the greater scheme of blood and place and time, so that there is only one man, only one family, these past four hundred years and more, tending the land they are as much a part of as the trees and the rocks and the river and the tombs their ancestors smile down from..

"Jesus, Dermot," she sighed, her eyes downcast now. "I'm not a farmer's wife. You and your cousin, you're so different, but so similar in some things. I love Sean, alright? I mean, God, I – if I don't want to live out his dreams with him, why would I want to live them with you?"

"I know. I know. Didn't I promise you, I'll never make things hard for you? I'll never ask you to choose. I'll never ask more from you than you're willing to give me."

"But you have made things hard for me, Dermot" she sighed, taking his hand gently, as though he might snatch it away. "You have."

The gull's voices no longer wailed. The sea roared in triumph.

"We met at university" she said, smiling in glassy-eyed reminiscence. "I was studying, he was landscaping. A big contract for him. I was sitting out on the lawn, reading something, and Sean and another feller were raking mulch into a flowerbed. It was May, and a hot day, and they were both stripped to the waist. He was sweaty, and the dirt clung to his skin on his arms and his chest, but – there was this *power*, this energy in him as he worked, and – well, anyway. He saw me looking, and I looked down quickly – it was embarrassing, you know? But he just smiled and went on working.

220

"Well, I saw him a few more times, working around the campus, you know. And one day I was sat at an outside table in a café they have there, with two friends of mine, and he came walking over, smiling at me. And he says to me, 'Hi. My name's Sean Fallon. I've noticed you around the place, and I wanted to talk to you, but I never got up the nerve. But our contract is up tomorrow, and we won't be working here anymore, so if I don't say something now, I'll never get another chance. I'd love to take you out some time.' He gave me a business card with his number on the back of it, and walked off without waiting for any kind of answer. I was just so shocked. I mean, it's a big university, and like universities everywhere, full of really beautiful girls, you know? I was flattered. And he had this – swagger about him, this confidence, like he didn't need to wait for an answer of any kind, like he knew I would call. So I did. And here we are, four years later."

Dermot smiled politely. "Love at first sight?" he asked, and couldn't entirely keep the bitterness from his voice. If she noticed it, she chose not to respond.

"I wouldn't say that" she replied thoughtfully. "He was attractive, of course – still is. And he was – interesting. He's kind of sweet, and old fashioned, and gentle – not many like him in Dublin, I can tell you that. He's so earnest, you know? He means what he says, always."

Cute. And how did we meet, Fiona? In the rain beneath a bleeding sky on the day of my father's funeral, as dry-eyed mourners shuffled into the church and distant cousins apologised for my troubles. You on my cousin's arm, blond hair in a sea of black like the sun inexplicably rising in a lightless arctic night. Your brief warm hand in my hot paw, and then we entered the church and a piece of my heart cracked off and disappeared below the waves.

46

"The grace of our Lord Jesus Christ and the love of God and the fellowship of the Holy Spirit be with you all."

It is the feast day of Saint Moninne,[126] born AD 432, died AD 518; converted, they say, by St Patrick himself. The watery sun ripples on the church's white roof. If you looked at this scene objectively, like some celestial being descended from the cold reaches of space with no points of reference to tell you what was going on here, you wouldn't think these people were grieving. You'd think they were embarrassed, or maybe waiting for something, like a bus or a line to move.

St Moninne retired at the end of her life to Killeavy and established a convent. She was buried there, beneath a granite slab. On the slopes of Slieve Gullion there is a well that bears her name, said to cure eye trouble.

"For this reason we never become discouraged. Even though our physical being is gradually decaying, yet our spiritual being is renewed day after day."

The priest sleepwalks through the too-familiar words, a letter from a maniac to a bunch of confused Jews no one remembers

---

[126] July 6ᵗʰ. Moninne is a typical early Irish saint, in that it is impossible to establish the fact of her existence. According to hagiographers, she worked closely with St Bridgid, a well-known pagan deity masquerading as a saint, which might indicate that Moninne is also a euhemerisation of some prehistoric god. The truth, however, is lost in the myth.

anymore[127]. You can trace it, even in Acts, the eclipsing of the man Jesus with the deity Christ. It's all there, in the letters, the names of people we can now only theorize about, the rival churches scattered across the Mediterranean, each clinging on to a different prophet, a different Messiah, a different Law.

The sun setting on Slieve Gullion, shading the church built on top of the saint's grave, sparkling briefly in the water of the holy well.[128] The same water – help me, Fiona, you know this so much better than me – that fooled the hero Finn McCool and reduced him to a wizened old man, his famed golden hair dwindling to a shadowy grey. The same mountain, we must believe, where the witch Milucra hid in a fairy mound and the warriors of the Fianna laboured for three days to dig her out and avenge their enchanted leader.

"For we fix our attention, not on things that are seen, but on things that are unseen. What can be seen lasts only for a time, but what cannot be seen lasts forever."

But there's something here, a door to another life, just as the mounds, the *sidhe*, are the entrance to the Otherworld. I can feel the wind on the mountain, the mist gathering on the lower slopes as the

---

[127] St Paul, 2Corinthians4. It would seem appropriate at this point to observe that this passage must relate to Dermot's father's funeral, and so, if the text is arranged in chronological order, this should be near the start. However, I have chosen instead to locate it here. It was written rather later than many of Dermot's notes, and in it we may see him finally attempting to confront his grief at the loss of his father by writing about something he previously could not; the funeral itself. Thematically, therefore, it is of a piece with the later chapters, and so I have chosen to let it remain in its current position.

[128] The universal mythological symbol of the well keeps cropping up. This may be coincidence, deliberate foreshadowing, or something more profound: the recurring archetypes of humanity's collective unconscious manifesting themselves, as they do continually throughout this story.

rain sweeps in from the West, the ancient tombs casting vast shadows across the grass. The mounds were not graves, repositories for moulding bones; they were gateways to another world; a perilous one, to be sure, but a place of rebirth, where the creative force of all the worlds issues from.

Be with me now, Father, when I feel so close to something so ancient and vast and true. Something catches in my throat as the walls of the tiny church fall away on all sides and I stand naked in the wind. Take me back, back into the mist, back into the sea, back into the unknowing, unconscious state of being we knew before we ever knew this terrible world. Fall together with me, flesh and spirit, back into the womb of the earth, back to the beginning, the very beginning, and leave this illusion behind.

There's a taste like bleeding metal in my mouth. My teeth are on edge. You must understand. You must understand. There is something here beyond any of this, something that will explain me and my father and my country, and more than that, more than my madness, more than my life, more than my death or my father's or the death of a nation at the hands of a machine; you must understand. This thing, out there – no, in here, in here with us, massive and unseen, eternal, Paul's wild claim realized, but far older than that – this thing that words break against like waves, a force here, in my chest, a bubble swelling up to burst behind a tangle of knotted language, so strange and so familiar. Do you understand?

There's no time, I'm on the edge of it, I know, but the priest is bringing the mass to a close, the coffin is being lifted up by strangers, they are carrying my father away, and I am frozen to the spot, because to move I have to turn away from this thing I need and can't understand, and if I look away even for an instant I may never see it again, and everything depends on me chasing this feeling back to the beginning. Stay with me, Father, just a little longer, because I think you saw this thing too, this monstrous beauty just around the next corner, disappearing into the mist. Stay with me, Dad; you must understand. Your death, and my life, and this land that echoes behind my eyes in a way I can't explain, are all somehow tied up in this one thing, the way there'd be no rain without the sea. Stay with me, Dad, I can almost touch it –

"Go, the Mass is ended."

47

At night the air vibrates to the cries of diabolical things[129].

---

[129] That's it.

48

Every time I hear the gulls, I think of Cloonashee. The woods on the grounds of the hospital are haunted by crows, teeming up in gangs and shrieking at us poor inmates. Snakes reaching to swallow the sun. Every kind of animal, circling the mouth of the cave. The shadows here are puppets; I put on a play for the nurses and they love me because they think I'm sick. Sick of the flashing lights and sirens, lightning in the hallways, everyone pretending they don't see. They see, but they pretend not to so that I'll think it's not real, and when you stop believing, you stop seeing. The lunatic next door might be pulling the strings, my strings, everyone's strings, like spaghetti. The hospital is a big tent. The guy next door tells me he is in charge, that he really runs the hospital, and soon he'll fire the nurses because they won't do what he says. Fire doesn't do what anyone says. I see it in the hallways where I'm not supposed to. All kinds of hallways, reaching up, like roads, into the hills with light behind.[130]

---

[130] I include this rather nonsensical passage to illustrate a certain point. When reading Dermot's notes, one begins to form a rather inaccurate impression of his illness. In his writing, he is generally lucid and coherent, and it would be possible for the reader to wonder why this thoughtful, intelligent, certainly rather eccentric yet on the whole sane young man should be kept against his will in a facility such as ours, and what kind of danger his release could possibly pose. It is important to remember that Dermot wrote almost exclusively in his more lucid moments, when the medication was able to subdue the disordered thoughts and random associations on display here. The sad fact is that, much of the time, Dermot's actual speech was much like the gibberish

49

Moonlight picked out Dermot's hunched form, low to the ground and running hard across the grey yard in front of the cottage.

Up ahead, the metal flanks of the cowshed loomed out of darkness. The walls echoed with the sound of the animals, the deep cries rising to a high pitch that tore the night. He held the hurley just behind its broad head as he ran, the long shaft held out behind him balancing the weight. It was back. Whatever it was he had encountered in the fields that night, it was back.

He cleared the gate separating the yard from the barn and the cow shed in a leap and landed on the other side still running, hurtling to the door like sudden fire.

---

written here, the schizoid mind roaming between poles of euphoria and grief, following conversational tangents in a manner no sane mind could hope to keep up with. I have given only a sample here; this passage went on for several pages, but I will spare my readers the tedium of sifting through the scribbling of a maniac for some crumb of insight: there is none. I have pored over hundreds of such pages, and they illuminate nothing. It reminds one of those apes that have been taught to type, in English, so that they may converse on an equal footing with humans around the world; though the idea of such cross-species dialogue is fascinating, in practice the whole affair is banal and rather depressing. The mad may in fact have something to teach the rest of us; but there are troughs of insanity into which it is futile to venture. Truth lies on the edge of human experience; Dermot here, like others with his condition, has slipped off that edge into the void of unreason.

Inside the barn, all was dark. The lowing of the cows rang from the metal walls. Dermot slipped on the floor, covered with shit and strands of hay. The air was warm and heavy with the sweetish stink of beasts and their filth.

The blood raced in his ears, and his breath came in ragged gasps. Slowly, now, he picked his way between the stalls, careful of the slick floor. Over at the far end, judging by the noise, the herd seemed most disturbed. Dermot held the hurley in both hands now; its wooden weight lay across his shoulder, ready to strike.

He advanced. The cows shuffled in their stalls, their breath steaming. Over at the end of the barn, he saw something move; a dark shape, big enough for a cow, but outside of the stalls. None of the barred gates were open.

"Hello?" he called. There was movement in the undistinguished gloom. And he knew for certain; the wide, squat patch of moving shade – it was back.

"Get out of here!" he yelled at it. There was no answer. But he heard it move. The shadows of deeper night on the barely visible bars of the pens told him that the thing was moving towards him. Panic took him then, and a violence born of fear, and with a yell like the wild cry of a warrior from the dark dawn of history, he launched himself at his enemy, the flat edge of the stick screaming through the air as he swung at the night with all the power his body could muster.

The hurley met no resistance, and the force of the blow threw him forward as the weapon cut the innocent air. Off balance, he slid again in the muck and fell. Scrabbling in the dirt, he twisted around to see the darkness closing over him like a cloud, as though he had gone right through the creature without harming it, and now it loomed over him, shutting out what little light there was. Terrified, he cried out.

"Dermot! Where are ye?"

The darkness halted, and was gone. There at the far end of the shed, a familiar shape loomed in the open doorway, a torch slashing the blackness into orange ribbons.

"Tim" Dermot panted, struggling to his feet. "There was – there was something...in here...with the cows..."

"Jaysus, lad, come on out of there with ye" Tim said. "There's nothing in here now but yerself. Go and get cleaned up, will ye?" [131]

---

[131] Fanciful, perhaps. But this is schizophrenia. There is no reason to doubt that Dermot experienced these sensations in every bit as

50

The Toad is a pitiful creature, with his skeletal limbs, his clammy grey skin, his watery bug eyes peering at the world in fear and condemnation. The Toad is pathetic, scratching around the margins of other people's madness, scraping up what crumbs of company he can from the criminally unhinged. The Toad is miserable, standing alone at the window, watching the rain, in those moments when it seems he is sane enough to realise that he will never leave this place. Even worse in the rare, very rare moments when he seems to catch some dark whisper, among the saw-toothed trip-wires of his jumbled brain, of who and what he is.

The Toad is not the only one with a library card and internet access. The Toad is not the only one whose madness still allows him to do a little research. The Toad is not the only one who can feign abject catatonia in the presence of gossiping hospital staff who talk as though we are not here. Lest we forget; this is the Toad.

---

real and meaningful a way as you feel the paper in your hands right now. We might snipe from behind a parapet of empiricism, and argue that there was no monster or demon in the barn that night, nothing in the fields before either. We might be right. But what if we're not? What if the hallucinations of the 'mad' are in fact sacred visions of a deeper truth, as Dermot hints at? Being among the mentally disturbed, seeing how real and absolute these worlds of pain and ecstasy are to those trapped inside them, one may well question where exactly we draw the line between madness and sanity, the real and the unreal. Perhaps we all –

Damn these headaches.

The Toad was some kind of therapist, ironically[132]; the old cliché of the psychiatrist who loses his mind, collapsing under the weight of other people's neuroses. Is there such a thing as evil in the world, real evil, I mean? An absolute blackness of the heart that can swallow a person's humanity, make them into something worse than an animal, worse than a machine? I wonder. We'd like to think that no one is beyond redemption, that there is no one who, in time, we could not come to understand, in some small way; but maybe that's bullshit. Maybe some people are just plain evil, and that's it. And I wonder, as I look at this wreck of a man, if evil is somehow contagious, if close contact with absolute darkness can blacken the soul of an average man until he finds himself in the jaws of some horrendous act, the blood in his mouth, the knife in his hand, the world he thought he knew reforming around him until the monster he slew becomes the love of his life and the glory of heaven becomes the shadow of the lights from the police car that pulls up outside.

This is the Toad, ladies and gentlemen. Pity him, but do not trust him.

---

[132] Highly unlikely. As elsewhere, Dermot dips here into fiction; rather unsuccessfully, I might add.

51

The wind harried the hill, the grass bent flat to the ground, whipping and twisting in the sea-born gales that brought tears to his eyes. His hands felt numb, his feet were numb; his whole body was numb and hollow, like a bell waiting to be struck. Still he didn't move.

Fiona was breathless as she reached the top of the hill, from the climb and the jealous wind; she paused a moment behind Dermot to catch her breath.

"Dermot" she said finally. He closed his eyes. The wind whispered now. The sky closed around him. Wrapped in cold lead and bitter air, he turned to her.

"You're leaving me, aren't you?"

She almost choked on the answer to that question; he could see her stumble over the words that pooled in her mouth like poison. Her eyes flashed, that mercurial spark of anger he loved, now that he knew he was about to lose it forever.

Then she nodded.

"I'm going back to Dublin" she said, making a determined effort to get the conversation back on the tracks she had imagined for it. "I might get a job. It's time I got on with my life, and I think maybe you should do the same."

He nodded.

"Dermot," she sighed, and seemed to collapse in on herself, the inner resolution that had driven her uphill against the wind and into the jaws of an abandonment they had both long foreseen suddenly snapping, "will you go home? This is no place for you. There's no life here for you. Go back to England, to your family. Or go back to Canada, back to Grace. Can't you do that?"

He nodded. "Maybe" he said.

"I'm serious, Dermot. You can't stay here, living in the past, or your own head. If you don't know who you are, then do what everyone else does; just make it up."

He smiled, the sickly grin of suppressed pain she had been learning to hate all summer. "I might" he said, unconvincingly. "I might."

"You won't though, will you?" Ignoring the cold, she sat down on the grass, facing him. "This is doing you no good, can't you see that? This – obsession with the past, with your father, with this place, it's pointless. You don't belong here."

"This is my past" he replied. "My family's past. My family's land. Where do I belong if not here, in my father's house?"

"Your father moved out of this house fifty years ago and never came back" Fiona snapped. "That's what people do, Dermot. That's how life moves forward. You and Sean both, you're obsessed with this place! The past is gone, Dermot. Who your father was – whoever he was – that's not who you are."

She stood then, brushing imaginary specks of grass from her hands. He stared at her feet.

"How – just then, when you said I was leaving," not leaving *you*, you arrogant prick, "how did you know?" He smiled again, the blood draining from his colourless lips.

"My father told me" he spoke into a rush of wind. From four feet away he could feel the tension of her body, the exasperation, the confusion, the disappointment; he felt he should be acquitting himself better than this. There ought to be something he could say to make her miss him; because nothing now was going to make her stay, he knew that. The only way he could reach her now was to leave a splinter in her, something that would stick and stay and come howling back to her every time the wind blew from the sea to tell her: here was a man, and you left him. The victim's revenge. But he couldn't do it. For a lopsided heartbeat, she stood solid in the streaming gale, looking down at him; then she turned and let the wind push her down the hill. He watched her go, the synapses of his retinas burning her image like a photograph onto his brain, every cell of his body remembering her in the moment of her departure like the shadows seared into white walls in an instant of atomic destruction.

Her figure dwindled in the expanse of green, beauty shrinking in a widening world. He watched her go, drunk on the sweet agony of loss.

52

Dermot awoke.

The room was dark, and cold. Morning was still far away.

He listened. Silence. What had woken him up? Then he realised. The silence. There was no noise of snoring coming from Tim's room.

Dermot slid out of bed and padded across the cold flagstones. The door to his uncle's tiny room was open. The covers of the bed were thrown back. The old man was gone.

A cold fear rose up from his frozen toes, weakening his knees, churning his bowels, settling low down in his stomach. Crossing quickly to his own room, he threw on whatever clothes were near to hand, grabbed his father's hurley from the corner by the door, and went outside.

The stars wheeled overhead, white ribbons of light over the sea, fading in the east where a red light brooded that was not morning. The air was thick with grey smoke, and flakes of ash like hot snow danced in the murky air. Tim was nowhere to be seen. Hurrying around the cottage, Dermot ran out into the road. The air was full of the sweet smell of burning turf, but it was overwhelming now, like being in the tortured center of Tim's homely fire. East of the road, the world was burning.

On the other side of the hedge, the river ran through a low-lying fen where it deposited the sediment from its inland tributaries before racing out to sea. A large bog rotted there, grown over with soil and bracken and heather, except where generations of farmers had cut a sheer face into the dark peat. For as long as people had lived in the valley, this was where they got fuel for the bitter winter nights, old men huddling in damp cottages, burning the earth to keep warm. It was a quiet place at this time of year, usually; the turf cutting had been done early in the summer, and now it was the haunt of birds and little else. But not tonight.

The soft ground hissed beneath Dermot's feet as he walked out into the bog. Some way back from the road, a huge plume of smoke rose from a thick base in the heather. Fiery red glowed through the smoke, and spurts of flame leapt from the damp ground at intervals, twisting and writhing in thin columns in the hazy air.

Dermot picked his way over to the hulking shape of his uncle. "What's going on?" he asked.

"The bog's burning" his uncle replied.

"Shouldn't we call the fire station or something?" Dermot asked.

"I have, yeah" Tim replied without moving.

"Well – is it safe to be here?"

His uncle said nothing. Dermot suddenly felt very foolish, half-dressed with an ancient wooden stick in his hand. What was he going to do with that?

"This happens, sometimes" Tim said suddenly. "All it takes is the one spark. A spot of lightning, maybe, or some eejit dropping a fag[133] in the wrong place. The fires burn mostly underground, where the turf is drier. Can take days to put it out. Tis a shame, though; all the good turf going to waste. Did the cainteoir ever tell ye about the bogs?"

"No" replied Dermot, "I don't think so. What about them?"

"The ould people. They used to think bodies of water were sacred. Lakes. Rivers. Wells. They were paths to the underworld.[134] Like the sidhe. There was a whole other world down there, below the water's surface. And when someone died, a warrior or something like that, they'd take his weapons and throw them into the water, so that he'd have them on the other side. But in the bogs, there's no air, so a lot of things don't rust or rot away. They just get covered up, year after year, as the bog grows. Sometimes, you'd be cutting turf, and you'd come across some ould coin, or spearhead, or god knows what. Even wood, bog-oak they call it; it all gets preserved."

---

[133] Strange as it sounds to North American ears, Tim is using the British/Irish slang for a cigarette.

[134] Again, again, that crystallizing whisper in the freezing night. Shadows become more real than the walls we cower behind; horror lurks under every word. Every story we heard as children comes back to shatter sleep with nameless fear.

Dermot gazed out at the twisting smoke and spurts of spiralling fire, a dull red landscape from a mediaeval vision of hell. His uncle's eyes glinted beneath the brim of his cap.

"Sort of like a cake, ye know, with the layers? It's all history, down there, the things left behind by all the people who lived here, sinking deeper and deeper each year."

And now it's all burning, fires raging without air or light below the sodden surface. The past burns.

"Still, not much to be done 'til the fire trucks get here. And that might not be for a while" Tim said.

"If you want to go back to bed, I'll stay here until they come" Dermot offered.

"Ah, no, I'm fine" the old farmer replied.

There was no sound other than the faint crackling of heather as it ignited in the heat and the rush of air as the fire breathed through the soil. Neither of the men moved, standing silhouetted as dark shapes against the blaze while the towering smoke choked the stars above them.

"Gates to the underworld?" Dermot asked.

"So tis said" Tim replied tonelessly. Dermot thought of the skeletons sinking beneath them, and the weapons of forgotten warriors whose ghosts now carried the ghosts of swords in the next world.

Choosing his path through stagnant pools by the dim light of the fire, Dermot walked towards the smoke. He could feel the heat of it on his face and hands as he splashed through the mire. The smoke tickled his throat. Covering his nose and mouth with the sleeve of his shirt, he walked on until his skin started to prickle and the heat became a wall in front of him. He swung the hurley sideways towards the fire, heard the slap of it striking shallow water up ahead, watched the black shape of its handle slowly, slowly sink beneath the water and the top layer of soil.

Carefully, he made his way back towards Tim. The night felt cool now, away from the warmth of the blaze.

Together, they watched the smoke rising above Cloonashee.

53

The wind whipped across the bare crown of the hill.

Blades of grass rippled and tossed in the stream of pure cold air, flattening themselves against the earth. Finn slitted his eyes against the wind, grey hair flying around his head like the wrack of clouds. Rising on the mounted shoulders of the wind, a noise climbed the hill towards him, the baying of hounds, the shouts of men, a clash of weapons. The moans of the dying. He could smell the stench of the great beast, tearing through his warriors in relentless animal fury.

There was a metallic noise behind him, the measured breathing of someone whom the long climb uphill into the wind did not discomfit. He did not turn.

"I heard the noise of a hound in my sleep" said Diarmuid. "What hunt is this?"

"This is no hunt for you, Diarmuid O'Duibhne" Finn spoke into the wind. There was a pause.

"You well know, Finn" replied Diarmuid slowly, "that not a man of the Fianna, even unto Finn McCool himself, has dared do more in the hunt than Diarmuid son of Donn." Finn smiled at the rancourous pride in the warrior's voice.

"That may be," he said, still facing the valley below, "but this hunt will be the death of you. It is certain. Have you not been forbidden the hunting of pigs?"

"I have" Diarmuid replied uneasily. "Is that what you are hunting?"

Finally Finn turned to face Diarmuid. For a while they stood, facing one another, a lifetime of mistrust and fear etched on each of their faces. Diarmuid looked into Finn's cold eyes, and saw there, as clearly as though it had been told to him, that though he might have officially pardoned the fugitives, though he might have found himself another wife long ago, though all might now be well between Diarmuid's household and the ranks of the Fianna, Finn would never forgive his old friend his elopement with Grainne. There was a hatred in Finn's face that would outlast the span of a man's life, and bring them both down into ruin, along with the world they had known.

"Not a pig" said Finn, a slight smile on his lips that did not reach his eyes. "A demon. A ghost in the form of a great boar, possessed by the spirit of a murdered innocent. A boy your father murdered, Diarmuid son of Donn. The son of the steward, Roc Diocain, slain in the hall of Angus mac Oc on the very first night you and I met, when you were a mere boy. It was said then, by the father, wild with grief, that this spirit would be your destruction. There is no curse like that of a parent bereaved. It has travelled the wide world with that purpose before it. And now here you stand, and it comes, and your death comes with it. Do you hear it?"

Finn cocked his head towards the valley, and Diarmuid heard it; like the din of battle he knew so well, the shouts of men and the clash of arms, carried on the wind and growing louder.

"Thirty of my men have fallen to the beast, and countless hounds," Finn went on, "and it is coming this way. I can smell its stink. I can smell the blood of my men on its tusks. You should leave, Diarmuid. Your death is here."

Diarmuid growled. Finn's joy at his approaching doom was clear now, the old chieftain not bothering to hide it. There is no lying to the dead.

"You are known as the greatest huntsman in Erin, Finn" he muttered. "Can it be by chance that this thing came upon you? How long have you sought it, tracking its movements, luring it on to compass my ruin? That which you could not achieve by arms, not even with all the battalions of the Fianna at your disposal, you hope now to get by plotting and treachery."

Finn's jaw clenched.

"Treachery?" he spoke, and his eyes glittered. "If of treachery we speak, what of yours, Diarmuid O'Duibhne? Is it not treachery to rebel against one's lord, to kidnap his betrothed, to defy him in battle seven years up and down the length and breadth of the land? For such treachery, I might have had your head hollowed out for a drinking bowl, and your beloved harlot given to my slaves for sport, were it not for the love my warriors still have for you. You have defied me, you have mocked me, you have cuckolded me in the face of my warriors and my court. Did you think I would forget?"

"Treachery you may call it, Finn" Diarmuid replied proudly, "and treachery it may be, for I swore obedience to you the day I took my father's place in the ranks of your host. But what amends I might make, I have made. For seven years, I was hunted like a wolf across the land, and my beloved with me, and in all that time, I never spoke a word against you. You know I have the love of your men; is it not true that many of them refused to harm me, rebelling themselves against your orders? And yet I never abused their loyalty or tried to usurp your position, easy as it might have been to do so. You yourself would be dead, had I not allowed you to live. I fell in love, and remain in love, and will die in love, this day or some other. But I will not take the name of traitor from a warlord who has not the respect of his own men, who has not the courage to face his enemies, but plots their destruction in darkness, who spins webs that bring no joy to himself, but only ruin to all around him."

Another moment they stood, facing one another, the rough wind circling them. Their eyes held one another, as though duelling, though neither man moved a muscle.

Finally, Finn spoke.

"Your words are useless" he said dismissively. "Begone from this hill, if you wish to spend another day with my stolen bride. For myself, I will not stand foolishly and seek death at the hands of a ghost. I hear it approaching us still. It won't be long now."

His head held high, Finn passed by Diarmuid, their shoulders brushing together. As Finn began to head downhill, Diarmuid called out:

"Finn! Wait!"

Finn turned.

"I cannot run from this thing, as you well know," said Diarmuid, "for when, in your service or otherwise, did I ever fly from danger? But if I must stay, and your malice must work itself out to whatever ending it may, I ask in the name of our old friendship, and in the memory of many years of faithful service to you, that you lend me your hound, Bran. No other dog on earth would stand by me as I face this thing."

Finn smiled that cold smile again.

"No" he said, and turned away.

"Finn!" Diarmuid called, but the chieftain was already starting down the hill, and a new sound was filling Diarmuid's ears,

239

the harsh breath of some great beast charging towards him. He could smell it now, too; the rank stench of animal sweat and blood and fury, the ground shaking as it came. Diarmuid took his spear in his hand and stepped forward.

On it came. A great black shape thundering up the hill, huge and unstoppable. Bigger than a bear it seemed, its broad head lowered, cruel tusks curving from its snout like the scimitars of heathen warriors. Spittle flew from its mouth, trailing in the wind of its speed, its legs a blur as it came on, faster than the racing horses of the king of Erin.

On it came. His guts alive with fear, Diarmuid stepped forward, facing the horror, his spear raised behind him. He stepped into the cast, his body following the long shaft of the spear as it whistled through the air towards the charging monster, arcing gracefully over the intervening distance as the boar came on. The spear struck. Diarmuid watched the heavy iron point glance off the thick skull of the pig as though he had thrown a twig. The shaft splintered on impact; the boar hardly broke stride.

On it came. Diarmuid saw the red rage in its tiny eyes, and something else: an eerie intelligence, a malice he had never seen in any animal, whether attacking or fleeing. He barely had time to sweep out his sword before it was on him.

The boar thundered to the top of the hill, sweeping its head upwards like a great shovel, trying to skewer him on its tusks. Diarmuid sprang over its snout, seizing a clump of bristly hair in one hand and bringing the sword of the sea-god down on the nape of the animal's huge neck.

The blade rang, and snapped.

The pig roared in bestial fury, twisting about as it tried to get the warrior in front of it again. Its hooves tore up the grass of the hilltop, churning the turf into a morass of mud. Diarmuid held onto the handful of hair, trying to avoid the flashing tusks and find some footing in the muck. The beast squealed and bucked, its feet flailing. An iron-hard hoof caught Diarmuid in the knee, and he staggered, pain lancing up his leg and bringing with it a fatal numbness. As though it sensed his weakness, the monster sprang away, tearing loose of his hold, and charged. Its searching tusk caught in the gauntlet of the hand he flung up to protect his face, and he found himself being dragged like a ragdoll around the hilltop as the beast writhed and twisted, trying to grind him into the earth.

Its weight pressed down on him, obliterating his senses. The breath left him in great ragged howls, and did not return. Dimly, he could feel the warm blood trickling down his arm; its tusk must have cut him as he wrestled the thing. Its breath was loud and hot on his face. Won't be long now.

But the warrior blood rose within him like the skirl of pipes, the blood fury that had carried him unscathed through a hundred battles against unconquerable odds. To die here, alone, at the mercy of some wretched animal, demonic or otherwise – what a fitting elegy that would be for the son of Donn!

Writhing in the mud, ignoring the sharp pain of his torn arm, he pushed the creature's snarling face away from him. His left arm still caught, he reached up with his right, and his hooked thumb found the pig's raw red eye.

Squealing in pain, it pulled away, its tusk torn free of his arm in a spray of blood. He fell on his face in the mud, but quickly struggled to stand, facing the boar. It pawed the ground, preparing itself to charge, battling its own rising fear – none of the Fianna, nor their fierce hounds, had withstood it like this one man, bleeding now, but standing still. Nothing in its wretched life had ever hurt it the

241

way this man had. But fear stoked the fires of its murderous rage. Hunching its shoulders, it rushed towards the man in one final, fatal lunge.

Hunched over with pain, Diarmuid had seen the indecision in its weirdly human eyes; but they both knew that this battle would end in death. The blood pouring freely now from the fingers of his left hand, his broken ribs flaring red pain with every breath, Diarmuid crouched, and snatched up the remains of his sword, the heavy hilt and seven inches of broken blade. Rising again, facing the animal, he set his feet, spread his arms, and faced its last charge.

He felt its snout crash into his already tortured ribs, and a new pain, both sharp and dull at the same time, erupting inside him. Dizzy with agony, he wrapped his arms around its broad head, holding it down, embracing the agony as it drove towards his heart, and brought the hilt of his sword with all the force of his warrior's arm down onto the boar's forehead.

It grunted, and pushed against him, the pain escaping from his lips as a cry. His feet slipped in the mud, but he would not fall. Screaming, he brought the sword hilt down again, and felt the boar step back, as though dizzy, or uncertain. Something moved in his guts, something like fire; he hit it again, and again; a spout of blood painted the air, and the animal sank to its knees. He struck again, and again, each time right in the middle of its broad forehead, and suddenly there was a new softness there. With a yell, he drove the hilt of his sword into the skull of the monster, spattering his face with its blood. The great bulk of the beast quivered, its hooves churning in the mud, driving pain like lightning up through Dermot's chest. He felt a tearing, and its razor tusk broke through his abdomen as it thrashed in its death throes, pulling free of the fallen warrior. Dermot sank to his knees in a pool of their mingled blood, and felt the life gushing out from the ragged hole in his stomach.

Panting, its great sides heaving, the boar lay still. Dermot could taste blood. He could hear it pouring out of him. The world dimmed, like a cloud passing over the sun. Slowly, pain raging in his arms, his chest, his legs, he lowered himself onto the wet red ground. Nothing to do now but wait. Grainne. He smiled, and the darkness took him.

54

The road rang. The river sang. It was warm for November. [135] Dermot marched uphill, the land rising against him, determined to keep him circumscribed in an orbit of loss. The sky was pale, blank, an indifferent veil too diaphanous to tear even if man or god could reach it. His guts were empty. His lungs were empty. Hope dissolved into dream, dream evaporated into regret; grey trails of grief threaded through his veins, tightening with each step away from her.

With a grunt, he squeezed the large bag into a space behind the driver's seat and stood back. They formed a ragged semicircle around the open car: Patrick, Bridgid, Michael, and himself. Seamus paced back and forth, stopping from time to time to bark at nothing, possessed by the excitement of a moment he didn't understand. Sean was loading up the car, the bags and cases already almost inside. Fiona fussed over her fiancé, a blur of pointless activity, directing something that needed no direction. Anything to keep busy; he envied her. He didn't know what to do with his hands. They hung stiffly by his sides like the pendula of a stopped clock. God, get me out of here.

All around was decay. He could see the brown stains of the shrivelled berries as they shrank back into their bed of thorns; could hear the dry leaves rattle in the cold wind from the sea that brought death and loss to the once-green valley. The river cackled as he approached, the bridge slumped wearily across it like a dead thing. No flowers now, no butterflies or bees flitting like transient love from one den of perfumed copulation to another. That which still was green grew in defiance of the seasons, the tangled knots of briar and nettle,

---

[135] Duly noted. Duly noted

feeding darkly on decay. Even in the sun, he could see the creeping hand of winter spread out through the fields and moors, a premonition of disintegration and loss.

"Right. We'll be off then." Sean had the driver's door open. Fiona, her arms crossed, stood beside Bridgid; as far from Dermot as possible. Michael idly stroked Seamus, who licked his lips and sat down in the driveway. Bridgid turned to Fiona.

"Come back soon, will ye?" she said. "Tis lovely to see ye."

"We will, Bridgid, yeah" Fiona mumbled into Bridgid's hair.

He watched her make the rounds; pressing her body against the entire family. She shared some muffled words with Patrick; knelt down on the floor and wrapped her arms around Michael, who, to his credit, looked completely embarrassed by the whole affair; even Seamus got a kiss on the top of his head. Sean had followed her lead; he could see him hugging his mother, a sideshow in the tragicomic theatrics he himself was about to be inveigled in. There was a noise in his head; he realised he was grinding his teeth. Sean shook hands with his father. Dermot wiped his own sweating hands on his trousers in preparation and hoped no one noticed. Fiona would. He knew she would. She must. How can two people know each other's bodies so intimately, and remain unresponsive to the shattered physicality of heartbreak?

She stood in front of him. Gazing sightlessly at the ground, he saw her feet first. Fashionable, cheaply-made trainers. The ubiquitous jeans. A silver ring on her left hand, hunters and kings! An olive green jacket. Her hair tarnished and brazen in the focusless light.

"Bye then" she said. He had never seen a smile worn less convincingly.

These were the rules, and he knew it. This was the twisted bargain he had made, hoping somehow that the day would never come. But here it was. He stood like a man cast in plaster, his insides rusting over unseen with hatred and pointless remorse.

No one can know. Her arms extended stiffly from her sides, her hands too far from her thighs. He could read the indecision in her body, the always-awkward decision waiting to be made: to hug or not to hug? He held out a hand.

"Bye" he mumbled, and she took it, but didn't shake. Her palm was warm. He looked at her chin, her lips. Not there. The top of her head; the wide bare fields, as grey as they were green today. Anything to avoid looking into her eyes.

Civilisations topple and bury themselves in their own filth; worlds burn and rot forever in tombs of ash for less than this. The iron rang in his mottled blood, sorrow condensing into cataclysmic rage and the mad lust for pain; his own, the world's – hers. The sky buzzed like a swarm of flies in the late heat and a black wave swelled beneath his heart as he called on God, his father, his family name, every dream and demon and wasted ghost of the pathetic bog of Irish history to come now and face him in his wrath. Nothing. The empty road, and a dim voice calling his name. The dull metallic flavour of hell.

From tragedy to comedy; from the sublime to the ridiculous. Sean lumbered over. Will this hateful farce never end?

"Well, see you later" he said. Dermot took the proffered hand like an insult.

"Yeah. Bye." His hand felt dwarfed in his cousin's warm paw, the utter indignity of losing to a man who didn't even know he had won twisting the tender cords of his spine into a Gordian knot of helpless rage. Go. Away. Get in the car and leave, in the crippled name of mercy.

"It was good to see ye again" Sean went on endlessly, his voice slug-crawling through vaults of infinity, spiralling helix-like across the dull void of Dermot's grief. "Will ye come back again soon?" To his endless bitter gratitude, he managed a Dostoevskian smile at that.

"Who said I was leaving?" he replied, finally meeting Sean's eyes. His cousin grinned back at him.

"Grand" he said. "Perhaps we'll see ye when we come back down, then?" Dermot's smile fell like snow. Pustules of guilt metastasizing in his stomach.

"Maybe" he mumbled, looking at the floor again. You won! Stop being the victim. Stop making me feel guilty for losing to you. You have everything else I want; can't you at least let me be the better man?

But the helpless, hopeless, remorseless show ground on. Waving like royalty, the two of them got into the car, he driving, she in the passenger seat. The car started and groaned forward, tires growling on the gravel as it swung towards the road. The back end bumped over the cattle grid at the top of the driveway, the brake lights glowing red briefly as Sean presumably scanned the permanently empty road through Cloonashee. Then they turned, and headed up the road, away from the house, the cottage, the valley, following the trails of second hand dreams into a faint and colourless horizon. He watched them go, the car's taillights blinking between the high hedges on either side like the raw red glow of her beauty, fading in graduating gradations of radial velocity as he toppled redshifting into empty space.

On the uphill side of the bridge, he stopped. There was nothing. His past was not his own, everything was a question without an answer – but with Fiona around, he could stand it. Now she was gone, and there was nothing. Only the long death of the land, and the empty wind from the sea.

The branches of the trees stretched like clouds over the road, twisting in the wind. He watched their tortured movements, the fury of a thousand miles away stripping the leaves from the plants, here in his family's valley. His heart, pawing at the cage of his ribs like an excitable dog, suddenly lurched, pulled back on its chain by some greater force. He felt it slow, each echoing beat rising higher in his chest. What's wrong? My heart hurts; that's what they do. This is my life, year upon year of hardened growth until the core dies away and the only the hide remains. I can feel, but I cannot touch.

Strange; a bitter composite of memories swirled like a forming galaxy in the dim basal layer of his brain. Her lips, red and flushed and liquor-hot, tugging at the lobe of his ear. Her pale brow furrowing, eyes slitted against the wind, as in a mania of cruelty he demanded details of antemarital copulation, and she stared out to sea, saying nothing, her lips twitching around words she refused to speak. Her long hand following the throb of boiling veins along the shipwreck of his body beneath a riot of stars.

Enjoy your prison cell, he thought, and instantly felt sorry. In a moment of frozen clarity, the waves hovering unbroken above the sharp-edged sand, he saw the melancholy truth: that the tragedy was not his abandonment by her, but the fact that he had systematically and callously attempted to rip her away from the happiness she might have found, with Sean, in the mad hope she might fall in love with him. His blood flushed red again, darkening with the recollection of each time he had hurt her, the hours he had wasted on a madman's dream, the monomaniacal pursuit of a future she had correctly seen as one of unending pain, for everyone tangled in the mesh of his fantasies.

How long since his heart last beat? It lurched again, a tiny drunkard in a vibrating cell; he breathed slowly. Goodbye, he thought, that fatal final handshake lancing through the moment in a corona of sun-bright shame. Be happy with him. But know, should he hurt you, as you knew I would have done, I swear by every dark god of vengeance and every blood-soaked idol of the twilight pagan world, neither the vaults of heaven nor the sick guts of hell will hide his shrinking soul from my claws -

- his heart stumbled again, tripping over itself, seeming to be racing and sluggish at once. Tiny silver-black gremlins of dizziness swarmed at the edges of his vision. He shed his past as the snake sheds its skin, as the moon sheds its shadow, leaving behind every stain, every scar; stepping forward clean and new, his wings, damp and dripping, folded behind him. [136]

---

[136] I found her!

Despite my limited resources, despite the burdensome weight of a huge caseload, despite the open obstruction of my own staff, I have succeeded in researching some of the basic facts of Dermot's story. I found Fiona.

She had returned to university, and it was only when it occurred to me to search the University of Dublin website that I found a link to a recently published paper on "Madness and Myth: The Theme of Insanity in Celtic Mythology" by Fiona Callaghan. Still not married, then.

Once I had that, it was not difficult to find an email address; the internet must be putting many private detectives out of work.

To: Fiona_callaghan@tcd.ei
From: drbuaf@gmail.com
Subject: A mutual friend

Hello Ms Callaghan

My name is Dr Thomas Kinsella, and I am the director of Riverview Psychiatric Hospital in Vancouver, British Columbia, Canada.

In treating a patient of mine, it has become necessary to establish some facts concerning the story he has given us regarding his actions and whereabouts in the fall of 2007. Does the name Dermot Fallon mean anything to you? If you did indeed know the man in question, any details you could give us about the nature of your relationship could be invaluable.

I appreciate your time, and assure you that any information you can give me will be held in the strictest confidence.

Dr Thomas Kinsella

To: drbuaf@gmail.com
From: Fiona_callaghan@tcd.ei
Subject: Re: A mutual friend

Dear Dr Kinsella

Dermot Fallon is the second cousin of my fiancé. We met in July of 2007; he was in Ireland to attend his father's funeral, which my fiancé and I had also travelled from Dublin to attend. We stayed with family for two weeks, returning to Dublin around the end of July.

Dermot mentioned to me that he was undergoing psychiatric treatment; I'm sad to hear he has been hospitalized. As far as I am aware, he stayed in Ireland right through until the end of the year, finally heading back to Canada in early December – but I'm sure you know all that already.

I'm not sure what else I can tell you; our acquaintance was brief. You might be better off talking to his cousins, Bridgid and Patrick Fallon; with your permission, I will forward your email address to them so they can speak to you directly. I'm sure they will be happy to help, as am I; Dermot is family, after all.

Please let me know if there's anything more I can do; perhaps it might be possible to pass along my regards to Dermot, or else to give him my email address? I don't know if your patients have internet access, of course; but I would love to hear from him personally. Of course, I leave it to your judgment.

Fiona Callaghan

To: Fiona_Callaghan@tcd.ei
From: drbuaf@gmail.com
Subject: A few more questions

Hello Ms Callaghan

Sorry to trouble you further, but it is really quite crucial that I verify the truth of Dermot's immediate past. According to Mr. Fallon, the two of you spent several months together on his uncle's farm, enjoying one another's company while your fiancé, Mr. Fallon's second cousin, conducted some business he had in the area. Clearly, the time spent together made a great impression on Dermot; many of the things he claims you said to him he has committed to memory, as though they were scraps of sacred verse.

I appreciate that the matter is delicate; proper appearances must be maintained when one has a promising academic career ahead of her and a new marriage to look forward to. Rest assured anything you tell me will go no further.

Dr Thomas Kinsella

To: drbuaf@gmail.com
From: Fiona_callaghan@tcd.ei
Subject: Re: A few more questions

I don't appreciate the tone of your last email. I have told you the truth, and given you all the information I can; your insinuations are way out of line.

Kindly do not attempt to contact me again; I have said everything I am willing to say on this matter. If Dermot wishes or is able to contact me himself, please pass on my email address, and I will correspond with him personally. I have nothing more to say to you, whoever you are. Why is the director of a hospital not using that hospital's website as his domain? On second thoughts, don't answer. I do not wish to hear from you again. Any further emails will be deleted without being read.

Fiona Callaghan

Some people are very touchy. But no matter; I have proved something valuable. Fiona, the fiancée of Dermot's cousin, is a real person; but the Fiona Dermot so clearly loves, Fiona in the fields, in the sun, under the stars, glorifying the world by the radiance of her presence – this Fiona is a myth, a total fabrication of a diseased mind. We can now read Dermot's story for what it is: a work of fantasy, utilizing the names and places he knew, perhaps, but based on nothing more solid than his own nebulous dreams.

55

"Bitch."

The ugliest word in any language. That one syllable, over and over, night after night. Sometimes shouted; more usually muttered so that they could barely hear it, could only make out the spat-out *B* and the bitten *ch*. 'Bch.' 'Bch.' Like a Pavlovian[137] response, the sound always sent a hot wire of hatred and fear racing up his spine, the hairs of his neck bristling. Sometimes, he'd not even realise what his father had said, hearing only a grunt. Once only, he made the mistake of asking his father to repeat himself. The old man just stared, with such wildness in his red-rimmed eyes that Dermot froze to the spot with fear and pity. The next day, he told the teachers who bothered to ask that his brother gave him the black eye.

He'd iron obsessively – clothes, sheets, towels, anything. The steam would rise in the dim rooms and stick to the black, blank windows, condensing and rolling slowly down the pane like borrowed tears. He couldn't be still, not from the moment he woke in a huge, barren bed to the bitter end of the day when he'd crawl back to that same nothingness. Even at night he couldn't rest. For hours he'd pray to a God he didn't know, begging Whatever might be out there to help him. Just bring her back. I don't care what she did, just bring her back to me.

The three boys watched him become a monster in their eyes, and he watched it too, and was powerless to stop it. He couldn't hide his pain, not from his children, a wound so huge and raw and ragged that it threatened to swallow them all. What do children know of adult desire and despair? All the child Dermot could see was that nothing, no joy on earth could ever be worth this kind of pain.

---

[137] Google it. I have a fucking headache.

"What's this?" His father sat at the table, bald patch shining in the overhead light, a piece of white paper held in both hands. Dermot looked up from the garish TV screen.

"What's what?" he asked, not wanting to know, not wanting to hear about it, but knowing that this game was going to play itself out, whatever he did.

"Says you've been suspended from school for fighting." His father stared at him, as though he couldn't possibly comprehend that his son might get in trouble, no matter how many times they had been through this before.

"Yeah" Dermot intoned blankly. "Got in a fight."

"With who?" his father barked.

"Some kid. No one you know."

"About what?"

Dermot shrugged.

"Dunno, really."

"You don't know? You get in a fight, and you don't know what it was about?"

Dermot said nothing; what was there to say? I got in a fight because he asked if Mum was a whore. I got in a fight because he asked Alex if Mum was a whore. I got in a fight because I'm lucky if I get one meal a day, because you're too fucking cheap and miserable to provide food for your children, because I'm raising your sons while you mope around the wreckage of your dreams. I got in a fight because that's what I know; that's how a man deals with his problems – by hitting someone. What the fuck else did you ever teach me? How to throw a punch; how to avoid one. How to explain constant black eyes and bruises to nosy adults.

I know you're hurting, Dad, I know. But is the loss of a wife to a middle aged man that much more painful than the loss of a mother to a thirteen, or ten, or nine year old boy? For two years we've been living in the shadow of your pain, tiptoeing around your moods, your rages, your black depressions, our own feelings always taking second place to yours, as though children can't feel pain as keenly as adults do, as though your misery is some great and tragic thing, and ours is some childish trifle to be ignored. How many nights of this, Dad? How many nights of you storming around the house, muttering under your breath, calling our mother a bitch to our faces? How many times have you held up her image to us, twisted and corrupted beyond all recognition, pouring out your sacred heart until the only concept of evil we have is the image of her face?

His father stood up.

"I asked you a question." But there's something he doesn't know; his son is beyond intimidation. You can only scare someone for so long before they get bored. Yesterday's fear becomes today's mundanity, even as guilt blurs to apathy. Dermot glanced idly at his father, his eyes blank.

"Some kid annoyed me, so I punched him" Dermot replied dully.

"That's it? That's all you have to say for yourself?" His father began pacing, short, swift strides; they'd seen it before. Silently, Owen slid from his chair in the corner of the room and crept upstairs.

"What else can I say?" Dermot replied. His father cut him off.

"Don't get surly with me!" he thundered.

"I'm not getting surly with you" Dermot replied.

"Don't get surly with me, you little shithead!" his father barked, lost now in a world of his own creation, where nothing his son said could reach him. "Don't even think about starting to treat me like shit!"

In the same corner as before, their faces hidden by the same lamplight, Dermot and Fiona watched. She could feel him tense as his father began shouting; feel him lean into the scene playing out before them as though there was something he could do to stop it.

"You know, there's an atmosphere of resentment in this house" his father went on. "There's a total lack of respect. I don't know what it is; maybe I was too soft with you. It was the same thing with your mother." And wrath blazed within Dermot at that; Fiona felt his arm tense under her hand. As though she could hear the feral blood coursing in both their veins, she felt no surprise when the boy sprang up from his seat.

"Don't start that" he cried, and his father exploded. Crossing the room in three strides, he seized his son by the front of his shirt and dragged him across the carpet.

"Don't you dare tell me what to do! This is my house! You little gobshite, you're just like her! Little bollocks! I'll break your fucking nose for you, you ungrateful prick!" Forcing the boy backwards, he pushed him towards the door. "I'll throw you through this fucking door, boy! This is my house!" Flinging open the door, he all but threw Dermot out into the dark garden. Stumbling, the boy regained his footing, to see his father advancing on him, his fists held high, ready to strike. All fear melted away. The boy Dermot stood up straight, hands by his sides. Hit me then, he thought to himself. Hit me, like you always do. Be an ogre, be a tyrant, if that's what you think you should be; but you will never again be a man.

Charging forward, his eyes wild and glaring, his father collided head-on with Dermot's cold stare. Dermot didn't move, standing still as a statue, his hands by his sides, saying nothing. You can hit me, little man, his eyes flashed. You can hit me, and I won't strike back. I won't even defend myself. What will you be then?

His father stopped, panting. His fists sank slowly to his sides. Dermot did not move. His father began pacing again, beating down a small path in the dark grass of the garden, haranguing his son in words that meant nothing; Dermot was no longer listening. Too many years of bowing to your misery and hiding my own. Too many years of pretending nothing is wrong, while hunger wracks my body, while grief wracks my mind, while voices shout my name and demons leap out of nowhere to shred my soul into quivering fragments. It's not enough that my mother abandons me, doesn't contact any of us for two years, steals the money that should have gone towards feeding her children and leaves us wondering what it was we did to make her hate us so much; now I have to listen to you compare me to her, as though nothing she did affected me, as though my grief means nothing, when in fact she destroyed every half-formed belief any of us had in beauty, justice or love. You fucking coward. Do what you want, I don't care. I'll never fear you again.

Dermot lay back on the grass, his insides racked with helpless pain. To hell with love, if this is it; a full-grown orphan shivering beneath indifferent stars. Red crystals of guilt bloomed in his tumbling blood; his father lay not half a mile from here. What do we, the living, owe to the dead? Our lies? Our silence? Memory grows into a moral imperative, and truth is the duty we pay on the soul, for virtue left untested quickly atrophies. She taught me that in the white-hot glare of her absence. Heroes are made, not born.

"It's a sad story, right enough" Fiona sighed, her face lit from within by a cold night sky. "Teenage years are rough at the best of times."

"Well, that's where my troubles began" Dermot said levelly. "I don't know if it was the pressure at home that set it off, or whether it was going to happen anyway, like some genetic time bomb ticking away in my DNA, but as far as I remember, it all started after my mum left. Panic attacks, then voices, then hallucinations. I thought I had it beat, for a long time. But it's all back now, like my life for the last ten years was just a holiday that eventually I would have to come back from. God – it just makes me mad, when I remember – being hungry all the time like that. And the rage, the black rage that swelled up sometimes out of nowhere, that I had to hide from everyone."

"So you never told anyone?"

"Alex, once. But he was just a kid – what was he supposed to do? He had the same shit to deal with himself – except for the hallucinations. He looked so scared when I told him about those that eventually I had to tell him it was all a joke, that I was making it all up."

"And you never told your father?"

Dermot snorted.

"How could I?" he replied. "He couldn't deal with life as it was, let alone having to worry about his son going crazy. A lamp getting broken was a major catastrophe with him – I'm not even exaggerating. That actually happened. He broke a lamp and didn't speak to any of us for two days. Thank God it wasn't one of us who did it."

"But you loved him, still" she persisted, beside him now, her vapourous voice threading itself down the glowing wires of his spine. "You came all the way here to bury him."

"Well, he's my dad" Dermot said quietly. "'Course I loved him. As hard as he was to be around at times – most of the time – at least he *was* around. He was pretty emotionally distant, but at least he was physically there, putting food on the table, and that's more than anyone else ever did for the three of us. He was hurt, I know, carrying that wound for the rest of his life, bleeding through the years. At least it's stopped now." His gaze travelled the fields as he spoke, tracking a lightless path over the hill, searching beyond the algebra of physics and light for a grass-grown hump in a field of stone crosses.

"But the past is the past" Fiona whispered, the wind tearing ragged holes in her words as she spoke. "You're not a child anymore. Can't people transcend their past?"

"They say we make our own traumas" Dermot spoke, fingers laced behind his head, tickled by the long grass. "They say children wait patiently for something to happen, something big that will make their life a serious matter. If nothing happens, they'll find something, anything, to be the line between childhood and the adult world. What do you think?"

Fiona said nothing, her pale smile barely visible in the starlight.

"I guess my mum leaving was my trauma" he went on. "I mean, it's a common story now, right? What's the divorce rate, fifty per cent? More? That's our generation, the product of what they used to call 'broken homes'. My mum left – so what? My dad went a little crazy – sometimes he got violent. Not all the time. Not even most of the time. I mean, he had a temper – what Irishman doesn't? But that was my trauma, right there; that's when I stopped being a kid, when my life became serious. The first crack that lets the light in. My own private mythology – my mother as the devil, my father a wounded king, and me, the hero, searching for the grail."

"How's that going?" she breathed. Her voice now could barely be heard over the faint wind and the distant roaring of the sea.

"Not great" he smirked. "Think I had it for a while there, but I couldn't keep it. That's what the stories don't tell you. You can't live happily ever after. You might slay the dragon, rescue the girl, get the treasure, but there's always another dragon to kill. It never ends."

She was fading back into the darkness now, only her eyes still shining as the cold seeped into his lungs. He sighed, watching his breath twist in grey columns, merging with the cosmic radiance. The past was gone, done, dead; those who meant the most to him had all deserted him, one by one; there was nothing now but the lonely howl of a helpless creature under a neutral sky, and the fantasy that she had been, briefly, what he had always madly hoped someday someone would be for him. He knew now what he had always suspected – the warm light glowing in a window at the world's cold edge, if it existed at all, was not meant for him.

Her words, her lies; those wild, red-rimmed eyes.[138]

---

[138] This is a lie.

We are not fooled. All this talk of mythology, the truth hidden in basal layers of history and memory, the lies we tell ourselves in order to glimpse a deeper truth. We are not fooled. Dermot is clearly deranged, the image of Fiona permeating his consciousness so that she may bear witness to scenes she could not possibly have been present at – we are not fooled. There is no

56

"God almighty, Dermot, why did ye not call for an ambulance?" Patrick thundered. Dermot hunched over in a wooden chair beside the stone-cold fireplace, his arms wrapped around his body.

Fiona; like the Amadan, the Washer at the Ford, like his father's notebook, like Cloonashee itself, Fiona is a product of Dermot's tortured mind, the guide through the underworld of dementia that he instinctively creates for himself – because this is what myth is, and this is what mythology does. It renders the epic, the majestic, the terrifying, in human terms, so that humans may use these stories, these lies, to guide them through the maze of existence in a world no one can explain. Fiona supports him, nurtures him, helps Dermot to heal the broken psyche she herself is a product of, and, ultimately, replaces the mother he so clearly feels rejected by, just as the myth of Ireland replaces the modern society he is unable to find his place in. There are moments in psychoanalysis when a patient's neuroses almost disappoint the therapist; "Is that it?" To have come so far through the underworld of madness, only to discover that Dermot has Mommy issues.

How much of this story has any basis in fact, and how much is a madman's dream? My resources are limited here, my academic efforts critically hindered by the actions of a staff virtually in open mutiny against me. Everything I do is watched, every movement reported to some higher authority. They think I don't know. They think they can fool me.

We'll see.

"I – I didn't know" he whispered, his breath misting in the freezing cottage.

"Ye didn't know? Jaysus, your man's sat there dead in the chair all day, and ye didn't notice?"

"Ah, hush now, Patrick" Bridgid said, her voice fat with tears, "can ye not see he's as upset as anyone? The doctor says he might be in shock."[139]

"Shock my arse" Patrick spat. "How do ye sit beside a dead man all night and not think to call a doctor?"

"I didn't know" Dermot whispered, his eyes on the flagstone floor. All night, tendrils of frost had crept in under the door, finding ruts and channels in the ancient stone, reaching like freezing fingers towards him. Fear had wrapped itself iron-hard around him, stopping his heart with cold, and he had huddled motionless beside the empty fireplace and his uncle the whole night through, trying to ignore the awful howling he could hear all around the cottage and the terrible faces that looked in at the windows as he spoke with a dead man. Bridgid had found him in the morning, coming up the hill to bring the two of them some groceries. Tim was stone cold, his skin grey and waxy. After phoning an ambulance, she had tried to get some details from Dermot, with no more luck than her husband was having. It was as though he too had died in the night, leaving behind this pale ghost of himself that couldn't relate to the daylight world. His face was blank, like that of an animal, his eyes wide but empty.

Dr Tubridy entered the cottage, black leather bag in hand. Outside, the ambulance doors slammed shut, the heavy body finally safely inside.

"Terrible business" said Tubridy, shaking his bald pink head. "I'm awful sorry for your troubles."

"When did it happen, Doctor?" Bridgid asked, her hand on Tubridy's tweed sleeve. "Was it during the night?"

"We can't say with any real certainty, Bridgid," Tubridy spoke with the familiarity of a man who had been present at the birth of all her children, "but it seems like he probably passed as much as twenty four

---

[139] If Dermot was truly in shock, or if he really were as disturbed as he seems to be in this scene, how could he have witnessed the details of his own and his cousin's behaviour? This, too, must be fiction, written long after the fact. More lies; more myths.

hours ago. His heart simply stopped. He was remarkably healthy for a man his age, but after all, he was pushing eighty. These things happen." Up on the road, the ambulance's engine growled, the wheels crunching on the fallen leaves at the side of the lane.

"What about this – gobshite?" Patrick snapped, waving an arm at Dermot.

"Patrick!" Bridgid protested.

"Now, now" said the doctor with practiced equanimity, "it's quite understandable. This is a singular case. May I talk to the two of you outside?" he added, glancing in Dermot's direction. Dermot had not moved, his head down, eyes fixed on the floor, as though no one was in the room but himself. Angrily, Patrick followed his wife and the doctor into the yard.

"Your cousin, is it?" he asked. Bridgid nodded fiercely, her hands clasped in front of her as though in prayer. "Your cousin has had an awful shock. Naturally, he ought to have called for an ambulance the minute he found Tim like that, but... sometimes these things take people rather strangely. In any case, if it helps at all, it wouldn't have done any good: Tim died instantly, with no pain. There was nothing anyone could have done."

"It's... indecent" Patrick muttered, staring angrily at the dark doorway of the cottage.

"We can never know how a death like that might take us" Tubridy responded. "Especially if we are contending with other troubles at the time. You mentioned the young man had been acting strangely even before this – incident?"

Bridgid nodded rapidly.

"He had, doctor, he had" she babbled. "This whole last month, he's been barely talking to anyone, wandering the fields by himself. Sometimes the things he said made not a lick of sense. It was getting so I was starting to worry about him." Tubridy nodded slowly, as though everything the distraught woman said fit in with some theory of his, rubbing his shiny forehead as she spoke.

"I wouldn't leave him alone if I were you" he said measuredly. "Take him down to your place, and try to look after him as best you can. There's no telling how long a thing like this might last, but he'll need people around him if he's to come through it at all. And, Patrick," Tubridy went on, "go easy on him. I know it's hard, but there's nothing he could have done. He wasn't here when Tim died, that's for sure. By the time he left your place – around eight, didn't you say, Bridgid? –

Tim was long gone. Besides, for him to be hit this hard, he must have loved Tim a great deal. It's your help he needs now, not harsh words." Patrick stood with his arms crossed, kicking at an innocent patch of gravel in front of the house. He said nothing.

"Well, I'll be off so" the Doctor said. "I'll try and drop in on you all tomorrow and let you know if I've any news on the cause of death and such like. In the meantime, I'll call the undertaker and have him give you a ring about the arrangements. We'll try not to keep him at the hospital too long."

"Oh, thank you, doctor, thank you" Bridgid said, following him halfway up the path towards his car and raining thanks and goodbyes at his retreating figure. Coming back down to the cottage, she found Patrick still standing in the yard, squinting out across the fields into the grey distance. She passed by her husband and went into the cottage.

Dermot had not moved. Bending over him, she reached out and touched his arm, as though approaching a wild animal.

"Dermot?" she said, peering into his face. Dermot looked up at her, but as though he didn't understand who or what she was; his blank eyes roamed her face as though lost, searching for some clue or a way of escape.

"Dermot, will ye come down with us? This cold cottage is no place for ye alone now. Patrick'll grab your bags. Just come on with us, now; there's a good lad." As though he were a child, she took his cold hand in hers and led him towards the door.

57

This body was warm once
This body was loved
Burned out from within
a dry husk around a column
of flame
A relic from scripture
The story hides behind
the title
Beware the quiet beauties,
the dancing space between
atoms
The paths through the woods
that keep changing
Her face a waste in the prism
I have become
She is forever leaving
Betraying herself in every
room, with any man
the final loss of all losses
Spending her life waiting
For something she can't imagine
the light curved around the
swell of breast and hip
the tracery of blue vein,
spreading branches
reflected in the lake's
pale surface
fine-boned hands,
slender arches, bridges
between her emptiness and his
paths of blood to follow

His spreading fingers
Eating earth, drinking
water
starlight pooling in
his empty eye
sockets
hunger, forever
Growth and decay
dance together
through time
Like rain
in trembling shadows,
beneath the wings of
warring angels
molding darkness
into a weapon
every day is
Christmas Eve, the
birth-pangs of
shoulder and rib push
through soiled earth
Subterranean cathedral
of vaulted bone
drowned in dark
waves of dirt
the open palm of
abnegation,

to a heart that shed
its scars
and left behind its nobler
half
 silent chambers torn
by time

all trace of work
of slow years
 ground out in dust

The rivers stopped,
 clotted with iron and filth
  filled now with refuse
  and muck

Vanished into the blue
horizon

vanished into the black
earth

And gone.

The wind rippled the grass in Cloonashee. Whispering over the ridges, muttering in the hollows, whipping the thin coating of snow on the bare branches of the trees into powdery eddies, it followed the tumbled lines of the valley from the sea-carved cliffs into the wild bare country.

It moaned low around the roof of Patrick and Bridgid's house, a barely-heard counterpoint to the confused vibrato of voices inside. Only Michael, alone at his computer, lifted his head at the sound, the breath of the sea in the eaves of the house. For a moment, he sat listening, his head to one side, ignoring the glowing screen and his parent's rising voices. Seamus whined briefly, curled at his feet. Idly, Michael patted his head. He turned back to the computer.

The wind pressed on. It shook the dry bushes that lined the river's edge, the trees tossing their arms in the wild air like a gaggle of widows, the water's grey surface rippling opaquely in the gale. A clump of snow fell from a branch onto the slate grey river, and immediately vanished. The noise of the wind echoed beneath the bridge like a wild boar at bay. A red notebook rotted beneath the water's scoured surface. The wind pressed on. It flattened the long grass of the fields, piled the thin snow up in haphazard drifts, flung drops of meltwater against the blank windows of the old cottage. Built four hundred years ago by Fallon men, and finally empty. The cold Atlantic air whistled through the keyhole, as though calling on an old friend; but no ear remained to hear it. The ashes were cold and barely stirred in the hearth.

The wind pressed on. The land was empty, barely a light to be seen in the grey country as the sun dimmed in a violet-streaked cage of cloud, as though the violent sea-borne storms had finally succeeded in driving all settlers from this hopeless rocky shore. It whispered in the branches of the stunted trees, howled in the gaps in the ancient stone walls, roared triumphantly on the high ridges that hemmed the valley in; but there was no one to hear it.

The wind wailed like a lost child in the empty valley left to it.

Up on the ridge, the barrow waited.

Dermot lay still in a cold pocket of earth, listening to the muted wind through the thick stone walls. Let it blow, vainglorious voice of an empty world. Let it blow, let it storm, let it drive great waves against the shore and smash this barren promontory into nothing; let it blow like the final trumpet blast, like the herald of Armageddon, and bring this hateful story to an end. Dermot lay on his back, heedless of the cold, damp earth, his hands folded on his chest like a statue on the tombs of kings. The wind was just the wind. There were no ghosts, no banshees. No demons to face. No one to save. Dermot breathed, and hated the mechanism within himself that still sought life, air, light, as though there were anything in these things that might help him now. There was death, only, in this place of death; all of his life and all of human history was one long tale of death, and the circuitous route we plot towards it. If I must die, then let it be now, when this world means nothing to me. Let me die now, broken and ashamed, crushed by the weight of this monstrous life, wherein we feed on death, glutted with it, until a world of death will no longer sustain us, and we export extinction to the stars. Let me die in this temple of death and pointless rebirth, let me fall into the hideous cycle and lose myself in the masterpiece, don't make me face another day with these eyes. Where are you now, father? I could feel you all around me, in the stone and in the breath of the wind, as though I needed only to turn that last corner, and there you would be, waiting for me, able to explain away every doubt and every demon in this haunted place. But I've followed this shadowy path to its end, and you're not here.

The ancients buried their dead in a foetal position, as though awaiting rebirth from the womb of the earth. Dermot swung over onto his side, drew his knees in towards his chest, the gravel floor cold beneath his cheek. Alright. Where is it? Where is this rebirth? Do I have to wait, like the tomb builders did, for time to strip my flesh away and make relics of my bones? Is it the songs, the stories, the ritual?

What are we lacking now that used to make life make sense? At the end of belonging is a loneliness so vast that galaxies cannot contain it. He felt it closing over him, a black void whose limit is nowhere, whose centre is everywhere. He kept breathing as the wind groaned, tired too of empty searching, of never being answered.

Abruptly he sat up, as far as he could beneath the low stone roof. Everyone was gone, and if Dermot had any chance of getting them back, it was not by lying here. Hadn't Tim shown Dermot himself, back in the too-bright dawn of this eternal midnight? Awkwardly, Dermot shuffled feet first towards the utterly black entrance of the tomb, and the waiting wind. There was one final gambit to try.

The clouds rose in great banks, whipped into towering masses by the same wind that harried Dermot as he stumbled blindly downhill. It tore at his back as he picked his way across the lightless fields, through massed ranks of phantoms and ghosts and those sickly voices calling out to him from the grey edges of nowhere. It followed him past the lightless cottage where he barely dared raise his head, the blank windows and dull white walls speaking endlessly of loss, always of loss. It mounted around his shoulders, pushing him towards the road, driving him uphill and back down the other side, following the trackless trail of memory towards dissolution.

The ancient iron gates reared up on his right. They were padlocked shut; Tim had the key, and who knew where it was now? Maybe only Dermot knew that it even existed. But there was more at work here then simple iron and steel. Seizing the cold bars in his hands, he leapt upwards, scaling the old gates like a squirrel. The ornate points along the top caught in his clothes as he dragged himself over; there was a tearing sound, and he was free. Dermot landed feet-first in the graveyard, his breath fast and loud in the silence of the dead. He could see columns of expelled air drifting from his lips out into the headstone-punctuated darkness, the only movement this place had seen in weeks.

Where was it now? With no guide, Dermot struggled to find his way around the cemetery. He knew it was downhill, obviously. But where in this dense growth of grass and hedge -

Stumbling, he caught his foot in a low stone wall, and knew. Here it was. Kneeling on the wet grass, blind in the now absolutely lightless night, his fingers crawled across the rough wood surface of the well's cover. He found a handle of knotted rope, and drew the board aside. Sheer blackness. He felt around. There was a frayed rope trailing down into the earth. He pulled on it, felt a hanging weight, pulled some more. The small metal bucket clinked against the side of the well, and he reached down, felt its wet chill in his hand, drew it out of the darkness, and drank. The water was freezing cold, and tasted like earth. He drained the bucket, the icy water running down his chin, and let down the rope until he heard a splash. Hauling the bucket up again, he drank like a man dying of thirst, waiting for visions beyond comprehension, a message from the Otherworld, some sign of continued existence beyond the veil of hateful time and wretched space. Nothing. He threw the bucket into the void, and hauled it dripping back into the world, and drank again. Again. He drank and drank, the water spilling from his mouth and soaking his clothes, chilling him to the bone, calling upon his father and his family name, hoping for a sign of something, of anything, no longer caring what. If there's a hell worse than this, then show it to me, but I have to know.

Nothing.

With a low howl of despair, Dermot flung the bucket clinking into the abyss. He leaned on the wall, panting. So that's it then, a part of his brain shrugged. After all this, it's back to the wasteland, and all my suffering is worth about as much as the squeals of a dying pig. That's it.

He stood, and stumbled a little. He shivered. The road shone in the black night, its dull surface the only thing he could see beyond the imposing gates. Alright. I've done this before. If I have to walk away from everything I ever loved, then so be it. It only gets easier with time.

266

58

Between crumbling brick buildings, the alleys run like dark arteries clotted with filth. Wasted people huddle in doorways, pace the streets in orange light, twitch and tremble under the assault of powerful drugs. They are oblivious, the people here; if you can call them people in the common sense of the word. They pace, they mutter, they stumble along the sidewalks with the airy, boneless walk of the damned, some shrieking at unseen tormentors, some slumped wherever they fall, abandoning the hopeless story of their lives, sucked down by fearsome gravity into the bowels of hell, these few blocks of horror down by Vancouver's port.

Grace drove slowly down the almost carless street. There was a police cruiser parked across the road, its lights flashing blindingly in her mirrors. The viral life of the street went on all around it, emaciated teenagers in hoodies smoking crack through plastic pipes at the entrances of alleys, their hollow faces lit by flickering orange flames. She drove slowly because you never knew around here; people were liable to leap out right in front of a speeding car, blind to the danger approaching as they battle the horrific visions in their heads, or else not caring to scrape out another day of survival in this nightmare that they must know, in their lucid moments, was going to kill them. This wasn't the only way she could come home from where she had been, and had been going regularly for weeks now; but a perverse taste for horror drew her here, every time. This is where the hopeless come to await destruction. Women in shiny boots stalked among the crowds; fat women with sallow faces, or horribly thin ones, walking skeletons in hot pants and heels. In this place, you fall back on whatever you have, whatever will get you that poison that makes another day in hell easier to bear, even as it keeps you locked in the holding pattern of ultimate extinction. These twitching, gaunt, fearful faces, wild eyes tracking the paths of invisible dangers; these are the many faces of addiction, the inevitable result of a dependency, a need to fill a void within that she, too, felt, the vast grey silence that nothing could eradicate.

Another hunched figure scuttled across the street and disappeared, rat-like, into the mouth of a damp alley, lit briefly by her headlights as she passed. A chill rippled down her spine. Something in that movement, barely glimpsed amongst so much pestiferous activity, resonated weirdly with a hollow in the pit of her stomach that she had thought buried forever. Reason threw up its defences; the place, the hour, the danger, the cruel mathematics of probability; there was no way. A torn pair of jeans, some battered shoes, moving quickly into the darkness; that was really all she had seen. But the hole in her insides only got bigger as she got further away, stretching out behind her in the coiling darkness.

She stopped the car. A few people looked on, standing idly in the street, absolutely nowhere to go. For a moment she sat, at war with herself, her judgement pitted against this wild feeling that had exploded inside her like a sudden fear when we know we are safe. The car engine rumbled. She switched it off. For a moment she paused, caught by her own eyes in the rear view mirror. This is madness.

She stepped out of the car.

The alley was ten feet behind her. Four men stood idly at its entrance, talking in low voices, their eyes on the street. She walked towards them, tall and erect. She was wearing heels that echoed on the pavement, her hair swept up behind her head, her makeup subtle, but carefully so; she always tried to look her best on these nights. Any lone woman was in danger here, she knew that; but a pretty woman in expensive clothes, wandering the wild street at this hour, was practically looking to get robbed, raped, or worse.

The alley yawned before her, reeking of corruption and stale piss. The men watched her, their eyes wide and black, the absolutely black and lightless eyes of those who have fallen completely into the underworld and have no way to get out. The murky shapes of dumpsters loomed inside the alley, their heavy lids thrown open, plundered for recyclable bottles, food, clothing, anything that could be got for free. The dark eyes followed her. Her guts crawled with fear. Drawing a deep breath, she entered the alley. She never did a braver thing in her life.

The floor was wet between the high brick walls, as it always was. The stench was overpowering. Garbage lay scattered from wall to wall, the rejected detritus of the desperate search through the dumpsters. Rats scuttled in the shadows, and Grace shuddered.

At the head of the alley, two of the men peeled off from the group and walked quickly after her.

It got darker as she went, the buildings shutting out the filthy orange streetlight. Her heels clicked as she walked. Her breath came fast. She knew if anything happened, it would be hard to run in these shoes; and no one would pay attention to one more scream in the kingdom of the damned. But she was almost more scared of what she thought she might find, the mad impulse that had drawn her here beyond her comprehension. Just that brief flash of movement, to base a decision which might end up being her last.

Some sense other than sight made her stop, the invisible electricity of another human in close proximity. There was barely any light here. She pulled her cellphone from her pocket, holding it in front of her and letting its dim light illuminate the filthy alley.

There was a figure huddled behind a dumpster. It could be anyone; some maniac crackhead ready to stick a syringe in her eye for the change in her pocket, or just a lonely tramp looking for a place out of the wind to spend the night. But she had already crossed the invisible boundary that separates the living from the dead. She was in the underworld now, subject to its laws and complexities; if she was ever to come out of this place, she had to follow this through to its end.

The greenish light lit up a shoulder, a mound of hair. This was madness. But then, what better place for madness than here?

"Dermot?"[140]

---

[140] The men who followed Grace into the alley were, it seems, the same the police arrested for brawling with Dermot.

dermot

dermot

Dermot

Grey.   Everything grey.

All feeling, all hope burned out of me, the life
sucked from my veins, the world a bloated vampire
fat with the suffering of billions.

This is the end of life, the end of hope, the
wretched lanes of madness and despair. This is where I
belong now, not some pastoral utopia at the edge of
the western seas.

The stars in my father's garden.

Fire asleep in the stones of the city

This is it, these stinking alleys, these addicts
and thieves and whores; this is the world. This is it.
This is where you end up when you lose yourself in
something dark and small. I am my father's hand.

The iron edge in his blood

Demons always guard the treasure. "Over our heads
the hollow seas closed."

Sorrow is the house of God.

"Here," she said, and she kissed him, "take this. You'll
need it, those nights the howls die on your lips."

Every moment is the threshold of eternity.

I stand firm on this rock among howling
seas while fate circles me like the wandering stars.

The path to Heaven is not outside of you,
   waiting to be found. Step back, and look up.
      The last drop of
      glory leaks out of
      my corrupted flesh.

Let them find me here in the spring, emaciated
and frozen, scraps of paper clutched in my icy fists.
I'd give it all now, my history, my heritage, my
birthright, the wild flashes of mania that light up
the stormy sky, all my love,
all my hate, all of it – I'd give everything I ever had
to give to be left alone, in silence, forever.

dermot

No chance.
     Words ripple through the alley, threaded
through the mutters and shrieks of the hopeless
dead, my brothers. Words full of hate, malice, evil,
whispering things I am powerless not to hear. At
least in this place, there is no hiding, no explaining,
no pretending;they know me here. They know
what I see when I jump at the sight of
 dark doorways or empty windows; they know
what I hear on the evil wind. They know the
demons
                    half of them are demons
and the rest are on their way.
     Forget the beauty, forget the awe, forget it all.

Forget I ever lived to draw my breath in pain.
     Forget me, orbiting a black hole on this squalid
shit-heap planet, and let me in turn forget her

and the mnemonic hell I circle each night.

Put out that pointless light; let me die in the dark.

"Dermot?"

59

Diarmuid opened his eyes.

He was standing upright, a flagstone floor firm beneath his feet. Indoors; the air was still. But everything was black, walls and ceiling hidden by banks of shadow that closed in around him. What dim light there was seemed to come from nowhere, falling softly about him, unable to pierce the darkness more than a few feet away. He turned his head. Nothing. Wherever he was, however he had got here, there was no immediate way out. The fine hairs of his neck bristled.

"Hello?" he called. His voice rang in the stillness, echoing off of unseen walls, scuttling around the seemingly vast space like some hunting creature in the primordial night. The echo faded. The silence returned.

His footsteps echoing as he went, Diarmuid began walking into the shadow. The blackness closed in behind him.

In this place there was no marker, no change to distinguish the endless miles of dull grey floor. The dim light still surrounded him, moving with him as he wandered. The ground seemed to move under his feet, as though he were walking the same four steps on a revolving stone sphere in the midst of a lightless void, each step serving only to allow him to take the next, for as long as he could keep himself going before despair and madness tipped him into the chasm that waited all around. He longed for a friend, an enemy, a crack in the smooth floor, anything to break the monstrous emptiness in which he

wandered, directionless and forlorn. He walked on, the pride of his
warrior spirit propelling him when all hope failed.

The darkness came on behind.

Finally, his legs burning with fatigue, Diarmuid stopped. At
the end of the dim light, at the fine edge where sight merged into
blindness, a figure dark as the night was waiting. As though it heard
him approach, it turned: a woman, her face disfigured with age, her
eyes cold and empty as a clear November sky. Thin trails of white
hair coiled around her wizened face, writhing like snakes beneath the
black hood she wore. Dermot felt cold, as though buried in damp
earth, his skin and flesh melting away like a corpse while the
indifferent stars wheeled unseen overhead.

"Greetings, mother" he said courteously. "Can you tell me
where I am? I've been walking many miles now, and I've yet to see
a living soul, save yourself. Tell me, what is this place?"

The old woman's face split into a morass of wrinkles and
crevasses, a few broken yellow teeth leering from her crooked mouth as
she smiled horribly at the young warrior.

"'Tis the hall of death" she sneered. "D'ye not remember what
happened to ye? 'Tis the place where all defeated heroes end up, to
wander away eternity in hopelessness."

An iron claw gripped the pit of Diarmuid's stomach.

"But I'm not defeated" he said. "I'm still here, aren't I?"

"And here ye'll stay" cackled the old crone, "like all the rest of
them, strength gone, hope gone, wandering empty halls where valour
counts for naught, until the world ends."

"Tell me how to get out of here" Diarmuid said, fear turning his
insides to steel, a feral rage building inside him like the desperate
charge of a cornered beast.

"No way out" the hag muttered, as though to herself, her voice flat, not echoing in this seemingly endless space, "no way out for the dead. No way back, not for ye. No way back for those who spend their lives shedding the blood of others."

"Then if you won't help me, I'll find my own way out, even if I do wander these halls forever." Diarmuid took a step forward, intending to pass the senile old hag and continue searching, trying to forget the despair her words had planted in his heart. But as he drew level with the old woman, his vision blurred, as though he were falling, everything passing before his eyes too fast to register — and she stood before him again.

"No way out, I tell ye" she hissed.

"Step aside, crone" Diarmuid said haughtily. "You are no mortal woman, I deem; yet still, I do not wish to harm you. But know this; I, Diarmuid son of Donn, mean to leave this place, whatever it is, and neither you nor legions of your impotent ghosts will stop me. Therefore step aside, or else these halls of death will earn their name with your blood." The old woman cackled again, a hideous sound like dry leaves crunching underfoot.

"Ye can't harm me; d'ye not know mightier men than ye have tried? Not a warrior has gone to his grave without battling me, and yet none have succeeded. Who are ye, that ye will succeed where so many have failed utterly?" And she laid a withered hand on Diarmuid's arm, coldness deeper than the depths of space leaching into his muscles as a howl of absolute loneliness and despair rose in his throat, the cry of every forsaken creature that faces its dismal end alone and far from home. The breath froze in his lungs; his heart hung still, suspended over a pit of ice. Strength drained from his muscles in the face of overpowering fear and hopelessness, the certain knowledge that nothing that anyone has ever said or done means anything in the face of inevitable extinction. The hag smiled as Diarmuid's vision dimmed, the blackness growing thicker, heavier, closing in on the tiny pool of pale light that flickered around him. He felt the power drain out of him, felt himself fading to a squeaking ghost, to hopelessly wander these endless halls, powerless and forgotten, even as the witch had said. Not long now. The letting go is easy.

His dying eyes caught a fading glow of gold at the edge of the light, like a beacon in this colourless world, and new life blazed with memory, flooding every muscle and sinew with the radiant paths of forgotten glory. Grainne. Hope and wrath blazed within him, spiralling together in a coruscating column of twin flame, and the blood ran red in his awakening veins. With a hand like steel, he tore the hag's claw from his arm, the coldness driven away by the red heat of his warrior blood, and stood to face the phantom with fists raised.

He thought he detected something like surprise amid the tumbled mess of her features, but the hag smiled again.

"Ye can't hurt me" she spat. "There's not a weapon in the world that could do me any harm. Ye think yer auld dead hands will do ye any good?"

Without bothering to answer, Diarmuid reached for her. Old woman or not, he would rip this demon apart with his fingers and teeth.

His outstretched fingers passed through her throat with no more resistance than they met in the black air. She laughed again.

"D'ye see? No warrior can defeat me."

Diarmuid felt despair choking him once again, a black wave rising beneath his heart, choking his breath, drowning his vision in blood. To be overmatched by this old crone, while his love slipped away, wandering in these hopeless black halls, vulnerable and alone —

His right hand felt heavy with a familiar weight. There was nothing there that he could see; but the sinews of memory knew that he held a weapon.

The old woman was no longer smiling. One withered hand raised in the air, she stood facing Diarmuid, as though calling for aid from the impenetrable shadows that hulked around them both, the light dying where she stood, as though she was summoning the darkness itself to defend her from this suddenly dangerous warrior.

Diarmuid stepped forward, the invisible weapon held above his head. Long years of violence guided his arms; he swung it whistling through the lightless air as he drove towards the hag, its unseen edge splitting her hand between the second and third fingers, shearing away the thumb, trailing an arc of blood towards her temple as it drove on through her paper-thin skull. Her pale, pupilless eyes bulged, and popped; her jaw shattered, the few remaining teeth exploding out of her ruined mouth to scatter across the grey floor. The weapon drove on, tearing her weathered skin, shattering her collarbone, divorcing her shoulder and arm from the rest of her ruined body as it continued its fatal, unstoppable arc.

Diarmuid didn't see her ruined body collapse into the black pool of her spread cloak, the darkness closing over her as the light faded: the old instincts of battle made the blood boil in his veins, and he sprinted towards the darkness, towards that faint vision of gold, before the old woman's corpse hit the ground. The flagstones flashed beneath him as he tore through the darkness, his lungs bursting with the sound of her name: Grainne! Grainne! All thought of an exit from this terrible place had disappeared, unless it came through her; Diarmuid had one purpose now, one goal – to find his lost love. Everything else could wait.

The miles flashed by. He felt no fatigue, no despair, nothing. Only desire was real, exploding within him like a furnace, driving his muscles beyond fatigue, beyond pain, pushing him through the darkness like a storm moving over the nighttime sea, his face wet with the old woman's blood. Up ahead, another flash of gold, shining out like the moon in the waste of a cloudy winter night, his guide, his salvation. He chased the flecks of sun through the underworld like the ghost of spring in winter, running backwards through the seasons, impatient of rebirth.

The first thing he felt was a hot pain in his side, as though something was burning him. Suddenly he felt weightless, directionless, spinning endlessly in a vacuum that has no up, no down, no borders — and then the breath was forced out of him as he crashed onto the floor. Ignoring the pain, he sprang to his feet; the rogue traces of memory told him what he was facing even before he saw it.

For a moment, there was silence; Diarmuid alone in the thin circle of light that surrounded him, struggling to his feet to face what he knew was coming. Then he heard it, a great squealing roar, full of hate and rage, despising what it could not destroy. On it came, charging through the darkness, the huge boar he had killed on the hill, and that had killed him, here again to destroy him utterly. It appeared at the edge of the light, and in a second it was upon him, bearing down on him with its tusks flashing, its wiry hair bristling, the dim light reflected in its human eyes, its hooves scratching on the stone floor as it came.

Diarmuid stood to face it, left foot and shoulder forward, weapon held behind him, almost touching the ground. Fight the fear. Face it. Hold still. He could smell its hot breath, a reek of blood and filth pouring out of it as it came on like judgement beyond the end of the world — and Diarmuid swung, the force of the blow lifting him off the ground, spiralling into the air as he sheared off the end of the boar's snout, almost lifting its massive body clear of the floor. A cruel tusk shone as it whipped through the dark and skittered along the stones behind Diarmuid, sliding into darkness. The boar screamed as it tumbled backwards, blood erupting from its ruined face – but on it came. With an agility he had never known in himself, Diarmuid spun to the ground, his weapon flashing a wicked semicircle in front of him, aimed at taking the monster's legs out from under it – but with uncanny speed it sprang over his thrust and was upon him, its weight crashing into his chest, hurling him backwards as it pressed on. It was on top of him now, pressing down on him, its one remaining tusk tearing at his side. He could feel the blood pouring out of him in great tides, each beat of his tired heart bringing death closer. Am I going to be fighting this creature forever? Is killing me not enough?

Summoning what strength remained to him, he seized the boar by the coarse hair of its head, pushing the vicious tusk away from him. Lifting his knees, he pushed with both legs, lifting the boar over his head to fall with a crash on the floor behind him. Man and pig sprang instantly to their feet, facing one another again.

Diarmuid raised his blood-soaked left hand, palm outwards, towards the creature. The boar snorted, but did not charge.

"Look" Diarmuid panted, his breath tearing ragged wounds in his ruined chest. "We've killed each other once already. If this goes on, we'll do it again, if anyone can die in this wretched place. Or else we'll be fighting each other for all eternity, bleeding pointless blood on the indifferent stones. And for what? My father murdered you. But I am not my father. He is long dead, and so is yours, who put this curse upon you. Nothing we can do can right their wrongs, or atone for their failings. We have already killed each other once, you and I; and what did it achieve? Here we are again, fighting a battle we inherited that neither of us can win. If the only purpose we have in life is to avenge the past, we will be murdering each other for the rest of time."

The boar grunted, pawing the ground with its hoof; but its eyes remained locked on Diarmuid's, big and brown and unmistakably intelligent.

"We were raised as brothers in Angus' house" said Diarmuid sadly. "Now, I'm going on. My love is in this hall, somewhere, and I need to find her. This has nothing to do with you, or your father, or mine. But if you need to, then try and stop me, and we'll destroy each other again. Because I swear that nothing will stop me from finding her. This is beyond history, beyond vengeance, beyond anything I know. And if we can't transcend our past, then we are stuck here, shedding each other's blood, forever. The only peace we can ever know is the one we make for ourselves, here and now. So make your choice. Either you let me go, to seek the only thing in my life that could make the past mean nothing, or else we kill each other here, again and again and again, dying endlessly from hate while the world turns cold."

The boar stood still, blood dripping from its mutilated face. Diarmuid stood firm, still holding whatever ghostly weapon he had been blessed with that was able to harm the creatures of this abyss.

With a soft grunt, the boar crouched, splaying out its front legs, lowering its broad head to the ground. Diarmuid looked into its brown eyes.

Cautiously he stepped forward. The boar grunted in approval, almost contentedly, as though this was exactly what it had been hoping for. Its horribly human eyes watched as he raised his weapon. Some mute impulse between them told him what to do.

Diarmuid swung downwards, towards the creature's bared neck, and flesh and bone split beneath his stroke. With one blow, he severed the boar's huge head from its prostrate body. Though he knew it was impossible, it seemed as though he heard a great gasp go up, spiralling among the unseen pillars of the great hall, reaching towards something beyond his sight.

But he had no time for sentimentality. Springing forward, he followed his last vision of Grainne, chasing a glimpse of gold into an eternity of darkness.

The miles rolled on. There was nothing beyond her. A thousand rain soaked nights that used to mean everything melted into nothingness; he shed his past as the moon sheds its shadow, leaving behind everything but his memory of her, hunting her ghost through a thousand miles of night, soaked in his enemies' blood. Neither fatigue, nor injury, nor phantoms from a past life could stop him now; the sticky blood ran from his tortured sides, but he ignored it. She was out there, and he would find her, and whatever happened then would not matter.

The miles flashed by. One grey flagstone after another disappeared beneath his feet. He ran as though in a dream, as though endless miles could not subdue him, as though each stride was worth a hundred, soaring over the face of the earth like a bird, the floor rushing beneath him.

And then he found her. In a pillar of light that smashed the dark into a million dancing atoms, he found her. In a dream of perfume and silver, he found her, golden hair shining like a thousand suns in the long dark winter of the soul, her body almost transparent, unable to hide the light that shone from within.

"Diarmuid" she smiled, "you came."

"Grainne," he replied, "nothing could have prevented me."

281

"Will you come with me now, Diarmuid?" she asked, smiling.

"Anywhere" he replied. Lost in a dream beyond hope, he followed her progress through pillars of gold. The distance was no chore; he could have followed her forever. There was no way to know how much time passed; the minutes melted in her presence, and all life dwindled to one long breath, as though there were no diminishment, only growth.

She stopped. The column of light that surrounded her illuminated an object in the featureless void. It loomed out of the darkness, seeming to grow as Grainne moved towards it and her light lit more of its tangled immensity. A tree grew there, a massive, ancient tree, its roots rising like hills out of the shattered flagstone floor. Diarmuid gazed upwards in wonder at the vast spread of branches, reaching off into unguessable darkness hundreds of feet above him. Even the limbs of this tree were bigger than any other tree Diarmuid had ever seen; its pitted grey trunk seemed endlessly thick, too big for the light that played around them to find its edges.

"This way" said Grainne softly, not looking at the tree, as though she had been here before. Filled with awe, Diarmuid followed her around the trunk, clambering over the high ridges of its mighty roots. Seventy seven steps he counted around the tree, and still they had not come back to where they started. Grainne stopped, and Diarmuid drew level with her.

In front of them, the ruined flagstone floor finally stopped. Huge roots twisted into nothingness, curling around the crumbling edge of the floor like fingers of a gnarled fist. Beyond that, there was nothing, a darkness deeper than the permanent night in the depths of the sea, emptiness greater than the vaults of infinite space between shivering stars. Diarmuid's mind recoiled from the impossibility of this place, even he who had been raised in the strange court of Angus, Son of the Young.

"Wha – what is this place?" he whispered, as though afraid speech might bring some new doom down upon them.

Grainne turned to him.

"This is the starting point" she said. "This is where everything starts from, and where everything returns to in the end, to start again. This is where we can start again, Diarmuid."

"But – what's holding up the floor? What's underneath us? That tree must weigh – it's impossible!" Grainne smiled.

"Don't trouble yourself about what's possible in this place" she laughed. "This is not the world we know. But we can get back there, Diarmuid, we can live again, together, you and I. All your wounds can be healed." Even as she spoke, Diarmuid remembered the pain in his side that the boar had ripped open, the sticky blood thickening on his hands, the immense tiredness in all his limbs. "Come with me now," she said, "and we'll live again, together."

"What's that?" Diarmuid asked, his eyes, turning away from the void, catching a faint glimmer of some other light in that lightless place, shining out fitfully from behind the vast bulk of the tree.

"Nothing. Diarmuid, this place is full of danger and distractions – well, you know that. But the way out is here. Take my hand, and we'll leave this place and see the sun again. Don't you want to see the sun again, Diarmuid? The grass, and the trees? The water running in the sun, the wind on the hills? Come back with me."

"I think it's – what is it? That light – do you see it?"

"Yes, I see it, but – Diarmuid, forget it. Please, Diarmuid. I'm offering you a chance to live again, to live and be happy, with me – why won't you take it?"

"I will, but – just a minute." With a grunt of pain, Diarmuid began picking his way back over the roots of the tree, circling the endless trunk, moving steadily towards the light.

"Diarmuid! Come back here! Diarmuid!" Grainne called after him, but he didn't turn.

What here could bring more light than she did? It called to him, this mysterious glow, pulling him towards it as though by some invisible string that began in his chest. Filaments of agony crawled along his ribs, but he pressed on through the pain, his heart pounding like the war drums of the Fianna in the mists of the past, his past, anybody's past. Seventy seven steps he counted back to where they had started, and seventy seven more around the other side of the ancient tree, the light growing, the tree's grey bark brightly illumined now, the tumbled roots casting shadows on the floor. Dermot scrambled over the last root, and found the edge of the floor, the same void Grainne had shown him – but there was the light, huge now, immense, a great blinking sun hanging in the emptiness, blinding him with its gentle radiance.

"Diarmuid" Grainne panted, coming up behind him, "come on now. Leave this thing and come with me."

"What is it?" Diarmuid asked. The light flashed once like a signal.

"I don't know" said Grainne, "but I don't like it. I don't like this place, and I want to go home."

"Do you think we can reach it?" said Diarmuid, his toes on the edge of nothingness. He stretched out a hand towards the light, but the terror of the abyss beneath was too great; he recoiled as his skin burned from the freezing void.

"Come on, Diarmuid, let's go" Grainne pleaded.

"Don't you feel it, Grainne? That light — I can feel it, within me. Do you understand? Don't you feel it?"

"I feel scared, Diarmuid. We have to go, now. Something bad will happen."

"Nothing bad could come from this light, Grainne, I swear it. There is no evil in it, no harm — no intent of any kind, as we would understand it. It simply is. I want to touch it."

"But you can't" said Grainne slowly. "You can't reach it. And I'm here, and you can touch me, you can reach me; I'm real, not some phantom in the darkness. Everything you ever wanted is here; everything you fought so hard for is here. Come on, Diarmuid!"

"Everything I ever wanted" Diarmuid said slowly. "Yes, Grainne; you are everything I ever wanted. I would have died a thousand times over to spare you the least harm; I fought all the legions of Finn to keep you by my side. I abandoned my lord, my comrades, my oaths, my family, because you asked me to, and because you meant more to me than any of that. I want to be with you, alive or dead, or anything in between — but there are things greater even than that."

"What do you mean?" Grainne's eyes narrowed as she spoke.

"I don't know — that light. It calls to me. I think —" and a sudden new pain flooded his ravaged body, high up on the left side now, near his heart. He turned, to see the handle of a knife protruding from his chest, dark blood pooling around it and dribbling down the front of his shirt. Grainne stood shaking in front of him, her hand still outstretched, frozen in the moment of stabbing him. The light flashed more strongly than ever behind him; he could see it blaze in her wide eyes. His war-hardened instincts flared at the first eruption of pain; the weapon was in his hand, held high, ready to strike with all the force he could muster at this new enemy before he had time to

285

think. The darkness thickened, the light withdrawing behind him. Grainne cowered from the blow, but it never fell. Slowly, Diarmuid's arm dropped to his side. His weapon fell silently away. Unsteadily, he stepped forward, his other hand covering his bleeding wound. Grainne trembled like a blade of grass in the wind from the sea. Diarmuid pulled the knife from his chest, an explosion of blood following the slim blade as he ripped it loose, a jolt of red pain lancing through his chest, cutting his breath short. His lungs were filling up with blood, he knew. He had seen this death before.

Grainne stood still before him, the statue of a beautiful traitor. Her eyes had changed, the pupils shrinking to a tiny point, her face disintegrating before his eyes, fine skin flaking away like ash to expose the slick surface of the monster that shone through her crumbling smile. The breath hissed between her teeth.

"There's no way out" the hag snarled through Grainne's corrupted lips. "Ye can never escape me."

Diarmuid turned his head. The light flashed supernovas, keeping time with his struggling heart as the life drained out of him. He turned back. Grainne had not moved.

"Fuck it" said Dermot. Placing the knife in Grainne's outstretched hand, he stepped forward and took her in his arms. He felt the knife go in again, glancing painfully off a rib; felt it withdrawn, felt it thrust forward again, ripping his tortured flesh apart. He held on to the shadow of his love as though it were really her, as though hate and steel were nothing to him. The blade pierced his side again. He felt suddenly light, his limbs remote and weightless. He watched the light grow in the branches of the tree above.

Light

Light

Light[141]

---

[141] There comes a point in the mystic's journey beyond words, when even images have been transcended, and the visions finally cease. He pauses at the last limit, contemplating the final image the mind hides; sheltering beneath the branches of a vast tree ζ hanging suspended in blackness, he pauses, one moment away from enlightenment and annihilation.

ζ The world tree; the Bodhi tree under which the Buddha achieved enlightenment; Yggdrasil, the ancient Norse tree binding together heaven and earth, from which the god Odin hung in torment; the tree of knowledge, tempting Adam and Eve with its forbidden fruits; the tree at Calvary on which Christ was crucified. Somewhere in the gloomy recesses of the human mind, this tree grows.

287

Here I stand, Grace, on the threshold of the great Mystery that men sought in caves when the world was young, that our species has chased forever through the spirits of slain animals, the ancestors, rocks and trees and sacred springs, princes and kings, rabbis, healers, shamans, sufis, Brahmans, philosophers, mystics, scientists – always searching for the same thing. The revelation that the source of all life is behind the world, but also of the world, active in every manifestation of the physical universe, ourselves included. God hides in the shadows of our minds, each image a doorway, each vision a clue. It takes a schizophrenic to see what the mystics have always taught; the forms of this world are illusory. No matter how real and concrete it seems, it is a phantom. My visions were no less real to me than these walls that close me in; I could hear them, see them, touch them – and yet they are a product of my imagination, the refuge of God. How do we accept one, and not the other? How can the monsters be fake, and these walls real? What they call my madness is a path – a dark, difficult, dangerous path through the forest, as the myths tell us it must be – to a personal experience of the divine, ecstatic true nature of existence.

I am one with all things, and they with me, world without end. To speak to me is to speak to God, just as I speak to the unknowable, eternal God when I speak to you. When we finally surrender our ego, stepping out of it like a shell that we have outgrown, realising our place as an infinitesimal part of the infinite symphony of being, then the physical melts away, and all is possible. These walls cannot hold me in, any more than they can hold God out. A man must die to himself to be reborn, as the rot of the seed-germ feeds the growing plant. When we die, the ego crumbles, all sense of self disappears, and paradise awaits.

But it does not end here.

This is not my story. This is not my life. This is simply one more in a million manifestations throughout human history of the one great Story, the same tale our ancestors told their children by the light of Palaeolithic fires, the same Story that has sprouted in the consciousness of our species since before the ice retreated. It goes back to the first man, or ape, the first shuffling creature in a long chain of stunted mutants to gaze up at the space between the stars and wonder. It goes back to that moment that we have all felt in the presence of beauty or awe, the mysterious sense of Otherness, the sudden consciousness that we are simply one part of a world infinitely vast, infinitely cruel, infinitely beautiful; that everything we care about is ultimately meaningless; that all is well.

And this is not how the story ends, a madman raving in an eggshell cell, a forgotten hero bleeding in the underworld, two lovers blasted by betrayal, a maniac picking through the bones of another man's life. It ends here, in the graveyard at Cloonashee, a white comb of cloud painted on the blue ceramic sky. It ends with the song of the sun on the grass. It ends in trails of green moss following the lines of carving on the slate- grey stones. It ends with me, here, my feet on my father's gravestone, lying back in the thick grass, my heart directly above his, facing the sky. It ends in my blood, in bubbles of warm air, in the endless dance of matter and form. It ends with this smile.

Afterword

And that, as they say, is that.

Throughout the course of his treatment, Dermot showed next to no improvement, no matter what quantity of pharmaceuticals I had the nurses administer. I have no reason to believe that he attempted not to comply with these treatments; he took his medication dutifully, but unenthusiastically, as though going through a ritual for the benefit of the staff that he knew was ultimately futile.

Likewise, therapy was of very limited use. As previously mentioned, Dermot was well versed in the therapeutic process, and here his non-compliance was more evident. He was an expert at diverting a direct question, discoursing on the theory of relativity or Buddhist belief systems rather than discussing how he slept the night before. Once, in frustration, I suggested he consider a career in politics, so adept was he at side-stepping questions he didn't want to answer. He smiled knowingly, but the dance went on.

However, in the final week of his stay, Dermot was transformed. He could be seen in the TV room, mixing with the other residents, laughing and joking, expressing himself clearly and coherently and dealing admirably with the often disquieting non-sequiturs of his fellow patients. On several occasions, I witnessed him helping the nurses in their treatment of other patients, as though he had finally stepped out of the morbid self-obsession of the neurotic and embraced the active life of service to others. His hallucinations ceased; or at least, he stopped reacting to them. No longer would we see him in the hallways, paused as though listening to sounds only he could hear, his face drawn and full of fear; now he became the hero of the hospital, beloved of nurses and patients alike. It was gratifying, as well as astounding, to see such an abrupt and dramatic recovery; though it was somewhat bittersweet for me personally, since I knew that any improvement there was could hardly be attributed to my care. Hard as I and my staff worked on this singular case, we made no headway; it seemed as though Dermot was locked into a peculiar hell that he himself had the key to, and from which he would emerge when he judged the time was right. Nothing anyone else did seemed to make any difference.

In one area only do I allow myself some token of professional satisfaction: it was my decision to give Dermot writing materials, and encourage him to write about his experience. We may never know to what degree this helped with his treatment; but if nothing else, his story makes for compelling reading. He has left us with a penetrating account of a man's struggle from the depths of despair back towards the light, and in doing so, confounded not a few scientific minds.

As previously stated, this is the very model of a purposive psychosis. By fantasizing so comprehensively, by creating a fictional world around his trip to Ireland, Dermot created a kind of chrysalis in which his psyche could molt and change, shedding the burden of the past, with all its trauma and neuroses, until he was ready to step forth into the light of the world once more, a wholly new creature. It does not matter, ultimately, that Fiona knew him only briefly, as I have proved. It does not matter that their affair was the product of a fevered imagination. It does not matter who the historical Jesus was, or whether King Arthur really existed, or what exact route the Israelites took out of Egypt. What matters is the story that has grown up around these things, the stories that point towards a truth greater and deeper than a dry assembly of facts, the fictions and falsehoods that lead us, stumbling, into the presence of ultimate Truth.

One more dry fact, for those at the back whose attention may have wandered. For those still chained to the old lie of narrative, for those men of science who demand that everything be reduced to the empirical, forgetting Truth in the quest for truths, let me say this: a week after his sudden, miraculous recovery, Dermot was gone.

I passed by his room early in the morning, to see how he was doing. We doctors have learned to be wary of miracles; they have a nasty habit of evaporating as quickly as they materialize. I was half expecting to find him sunken in black despair, as though the whole recovery had simply been one more manic episode, one more symptom of his condition – but he was not there. Instead, I found a young nurse changing the bed clothes, her gaze calm and insipid as the bland stare of a cow. Every trace of the former occupant was gone, all personal possessions vanished, as though he had never existed.

"Where is Dermot?" I demanded, to be met by the same bored stare. "The patient who had this room, Fallon – where is he?" The useless nurse simply shrugged, as though the disappearance of a patient confined against their will to a psychiatric facility was of no moment to her at all. Bristling with rage, I marched to the office of the head nurse.

"We don't know where he is" she replied insolently to my frantic questioning. Nor could she show me any discharge paperwork, as I feared would be the case; as previously mentioned, my staff were always adept at mislaying any files concerning this particular patient. Somehow, I could not impress upon her the seriousness of 'losing' a patient. She simply went on filing, as though this sort of thing happened all the time.

For the uninitiated, let me explain: as the Director of this facility, it is my decision when to discharge a patient. Particularly in the case of a patient who is involuntarily admitted, like Dermot, I alone have the authority to release him. My decisions are overseen by the College of Physicians, naturally, and challenges may legally be made to any decision I might make; but no one is admitted to or discharged from this hospital without my signature. Patients do not simply walk out. But now one had, and only I seemed to care. The security guards and orderlies, whose job it is to prevent such an unauthorized absence, could tell me nothing. They did not know the patient I described, had never seen him. Once again, their indifference stunned me. Incensed, I demanded to see the security camera footage for the previous day and night, from the time I last saw Dermot right up to the moment. Grudgingly, they obliged, and I was forced to postpone my other duties in order to peruse hours of grainy footage, huddled over a flickering screen. There was nothing. I watched every tedious minute of those tapes at least twice, and there was no sign of Dermot in any of them. Every door and ground floor window is monitored, as are the grounds and gates of the facility; it is inconceivable that a patient could leave this place without being recorded on several cameras; and yet Dermot had done so, simply vanishing into the air as though he had transcended the limits of the physical, the limited reach of the possible, and become one with the air around him.

So now I sit, and await judgment. The blame is squarely on the shoulders of my staff, whose incompetence and indifference are solely to blame for this disaster; but it is the Director who will bear the wrath of the powers-that-be. The good people of the city hear that a patient has disappeared from this facility, and their thoughts turn instantly to Hollywood horror, the hockey mask, the knife. They will bay for my blood in the courtyards of the prefect. So be it. This case study shall be my legacy, though it may have cost me everything. Here is a man weighed down by the modern condition, perhaps the most prevalent and most urgent of all psychiatric conditions; a man on whom no modern treatment seemed to have any effect, whose madness seemed beyond both drugs and therapy; a man who, in the end, found a centre within himself on which to base his life, a man who transcended first his madness, then his ego, and finally his physical being, melting into the ether like a ghost. There is hope here, and not just for schizophrenics. Dermot achieved a wisdom that many a modern philosopher might envy, for without years of study, without special teaching, with only the pain of his tortured mind, he achieved a revelation of the Absolute that many a holy man has sought in vain. Let this be my legacy, when I am cast down in shame; that I had some part, however small, in such a revelation.

Dr Thomas Kinsella
Riverview Hospital
December 2008

ACKNOWLEDGMENTS

I am grateful to my first readers, Becca Patterson, Jean-Paul Savoie and Amy Lancelotte, for their assistance and encouragement.

Front cover art by Michael Yakutis.

ABOUT THE AUTHOR

Ryan Frawley was born and raised in Coventry, England, and emigrated to Canada at the age of twenty. *Scar* is his first novel. He can be found on the internet at:
www.ryanfrawley.com

Made in the USA
Charleston, SC
29 November 2011